HAWKING'S HALLWAY

BOOK 3 OF THE ACCELERATI TRILOGY

THE ACCELERATI TRILOGY
Tesla's Attic
Edison's Alley
Hawking's Hallway

HAWKING'S HALLWAY

BOOK 3 OF THE ACCELERATI TRILOGY

NEAL SHUSTERMAN
AND ERIC ELFMAN

Disney · HYPERION

LOS ANGELES   NEW YORK

In memory of Mari Lou Laso Elders,
a good friend and great writer.
We'll miss you, Mari Lou.
—N.S.

For all the writers I've met and read and worked with and learned from,
and for my mom, for Robby, and always for Jan
—E.E.

Text copyright © 2016 by Neal Shusterman and Eric Elfman

All rights reserved. Published by Disney • Hyperion, an imprint of
Disney Book Group. No part of this book may be reproduced or transmitted
in any form or by any means, electronic or mechanical, including photocopying,
recording, or by any information storage and retrieval system, without written
permission from the publisher. For information address Disney • Hyperion,
125 West End Avenue, New York, New York 10023.

First Edition, February 2016

Printed in the United States of America
10 9 8 7 6 5 4 3 2 1
FAC-020093-15319

Library of Congress Cataloging-in-Publication Data
Names: Shusterman, Neal, author. | Elfman, Eric, author.
Title: Hawking's hallway / Neal Shusterman and Eric Elfman.
Description: First edition. | Los Angeles : Disney-Hyperion, 2016. | Series:
    The Accelerati trilogy ; book 3 | Sequel to: Edison's alley.
Identifiers: LCCN 2015032648 | ISBN 9781423148050 (hardback)
Subjects: LCSH: Tesla, Nikola, 1856-1943—Fiction. | CYAC:
    Inventions—Fiction. | Colorado Springs (Colo.)—Fiction. | Science
    fiction. | BISAC: JUVENILE FICTION / Action & Adventure / General. |
    JUVENILE FICTION / Science & Technology. | JUVENILE FICTION /
Mysteries & Detective Stories.
Classification: LCC PZ7.S55987 Haw 2016 | DDC [Fic]—dc23
LC record available at http://lccn.loc.gov/2015032648

Chapter opening illustrations by Owen Richardson

Reinforced binding

Visit www.DisneyBooks.com

Life would be tragic if it weren't funny.
— Stephen Hawking

1 A HOUSE DROWNS IN SCOTLAND

The woman realized she was in trouble the moment she saw the boy at her front door. It was the kid from the garage sale. She screamed and slammed the door in his face.

She had never heard of Nikola Tesla, and had no idea who this boy was. All she knew was that he had sold her something that allowed her to travel in ways she never dreamed possible.

She'd found out quite by accident how the strange globe worked. On the silver arc that held the globe in place, there was a movable arrow. She had rotated the globe and lined up the arrow with Turkey—one of the many exotic places she wished she could visit, but never had. Then she pressed a button on the base that she thought was a light.

She found herself instantly transported to the Istanbul Grand Bazaar. Beside her was the table holding the globe, and beneath her a perfectly circular section of her parquet floor, about four feet in diameter, which had been shorn away by the teleportation field.

A Turkish salesman, unfazed by her sudden appearance, offered to sell her a teapot.

She screamed, hit a second button marked only with an exclamation point, and found herself back home where she'd started . . . except she, and the table, and the section of floor fell through a perfectly circular hole into her basement.

Rattled but unbroken, she quickly surmised what the globe could do. And her first order of business had been to go back for that teapot.

Since then, she had made jaunts to Spain, Switzerland, China, and even Antarctica, just so she could say she'd been.

She had been contemplating a long-overdue return to her native Scotland when the boy from the garage sale appeared.

Whether he was an angel, a demon, or just some laddie with a magic globe didn't matter. All that mattered was not letting him take it back.

In her panic, she hit the globe's button to escape his incessant knocking. She didn't realize the teleportation field was set to its widest diameter.

For an instant, she didn't think anything had happened. She was still standing in her house. Then water—very cold water— began to gush in from every window and doorway.

It didn't take long for her to realize that she had transported her entire house to Scotland, and it had materialized on the surface of one of Scotland's many infamous lochs.

The lochs of Scotland are known for being unusually deep, unusually murky, and unusual in general. And, as luck would have it, this particular loch was rumored to be home to a monster affectionately known to the locals as "Nessie."

Unlike ships, which may take hours to sink, a randomly teleported house sinks with remarkable speed and single-minded determination. The house desired nothing more than to be at the bottom of the lake at its earliest possible convenience.

With her transplanted home foundering, the woman forgot anything unrelated to survival. She was not a strong swimmer, but adrenaline can turn even an elderly widow into Wonder Woman.

Fighting the surge of icy water, she climbed upon her floating sofa. There was no way to get out of the first-floor windows, because the lake was pouring in. Not even a salmon could fight that current.

Instead she paddled her way to the staircase, which was leaning at a fun-house angle. Then she made her way to the second floor, and hurled herself out of her bedroom window into the lake.

It was only when she surfaced and looked back that the terror of it all struck her. Her little suburban house, where she had spent the past twenty-some-odd years of her life, was bubbling out its last breath. In a moment, only the roof remained above water, then just the chimney, and finally that was gone in a churning of bubbling white.

And then she remembered. "The globe!"

She could bear the loss of everything else, but not that.

Just then she heard—or more accurately *felt*—something behind her, moving across the surface of the water. Struggling to stay afloat, she turned, fully expecting to see the dark, inscrutable eyes of a hungry plesiosaurus. Instead, she saw a small fishing boat.

"Hoy! What's all this, then? You all right there, ma'am?" called an old fisherman.

She tried to answer, but with all her adrenaline spent, she felt herself going down. The fisherman reached out, and with strong arms, pulled her up and into his boat. He gave her his flannel jacket and offered her his thermos of tea.

"So what brings ye to Loch Ness?" the fisherman asked. "And in a house?"

Since the tale was a little tall for the moment, she let her chattering teeth be her only answer.

He put his arm around her to stop her shivering. "There, there," said the aging fisherman. "My cottage is right there on the shore. You'll be safe and warm in no time."

And it occurred to her that this was, in fact, her dream. Not the teleporting-in-a-house-and-almost-drowning part, but the being-in-the-arms-of-a-fisherman-in-the-wilds-of-Scotland part.

She was unaware that life on Earth was about to be threatened by an asteroid, followed by a massive electrical disaster.

All she knew was that she was where she wanted to be, and that the globe, whatever it was, now rested at the bottom of one of the world's deepest lakes, lost forever.

Or not.

2 THE WICKED STEPMOTHER OF INVENTION

"Welcome to Loyal Order of the Accelerati," Thomas Edison told Nick Slate. He extended a 170-year-old hand for Nick to shake.

Nick grimaced as his hand clutched Edison's. It wasn't just Nick's burn wounds that made him wince. Even through Nick's bandage, shaking hands with the man was like holding moist papier-mâché an hour short of drying.

Edison seemed amused by Nick's response but said nothing of it. He grabbed a little bell from the antique rosewood end table in his antique Victorian home and rang for his housekeeper. She appeared quickly, as if she'd been waiting just outside the door, always at the old man's beck and call, which, in fact, she was.

"Mrs. Higgenbotham, show Master Slate to his accommodations."

"More than 'appy to," she said in her thick cockney accent. "It's been a long time since we've 'ad anyone in the guest room."

Nick followed her up the stairs, relieved to be, at least for the moment, out of the ancient inventor's presence.

The woman led him to a small bedroom filled with furniture that his grandmother's grandmother might have liked, and wallpaper that seemed straight out of an old ice-cream parlor.

"'Ere we are," said Mrs. Higgenbotham, and then she just

stood there smiling at him, happy to let the moment become awkward.

"So," said Nick, "how does it feel to be a robot working for an evil genius?"

"First of all," said Mrs. Higgenbotham, "Mr. Edison isn't evil, 'e's morally ambiguous. All the greats in 'istory were. Charlemagne. Queen Elizabeth. Michael Jackson. And second, I don't fancy being called a robot. It's an oversimplification. I am an anthropomorphic servo-automaton. Although that is a bit of a mouthful, isn't it? I'd call myself an android, but I don't want to be confused with a phone. Although I am a phone. But you really don't want to access that function, dearie. It's not a pretty sight."

She clasped her hands and smiled warmly. "Will there be anything else? Some tea, perhaps, or a raspberry scone?"

"No, thank you," said Nick.

"'Ow about a nice, tall sarsaparilla?"

Since Nick had no idea what that was, he said, "Another time."

"As you wish, dearie. As you wish. I'll be back in about an hour to change the dressings on your poor hands." And she left Nick to ponder his situation.

A secret society of scientists was blackmailing him into reconstructing Tesla's greatest invention. If he succeeded, it would harness the limitless energy being generated by a copper asteroid that was now a natural satellite, orbiting the earth like the moon. But all that power would be in the hands of the Accelerati, to do with as they pleased.

Nick removed the little pin from his lapel and looked at the golden *A* crossed by a figure eight. He was Accelerati now. He'd had no choice but to join the organization in order to save his father and brother—Edison had made that clear. But that didn't mean Nick had to like it. Yet his deepest fear, too deep perhaps for him to even be aware of, was that he would.

It is said that necessity is the mother of invention, but, sadly, she is often a mother who dies in childbirth. Instead, invention is usually raised by its wicked stepmother: greed.

Nick Slate was no more immune to greed than anyone else. He would take the last jelly bean in the jar before his brother could, for instance, and he would scoop out the last spoonful of Ben & Jerry's while nobody was looking.

On the other hand, he was just as likely to offer half his sandwich to some random kid who'd left his lunch at home that day, or give his skateboard to a kid whose family, he happened to know, was living in a garage.

Human nature is a dance between self-interest and generosity of spirit. Now that Nick was in the bosom of the Accelerati, he was doing that dance on hot coals.

Bright and early the next morning, Nick was summoned to join Edison at the lab.

The fact that Edison was kept alive by a six-foot-tall wet-cell battery of Nikola Tesla's design by no means meant that he was housebound. He had a travel coach, perhaps built by Henry Ford himself, that accommodated the huge battery and the wheelchair, allowing the "Wizard of Menlo Park" to ride in style.

He didn't have to ride far, though, because his lab was just a few hundred yards away from his home. And just like his home, his workshop was a perfect replica of his original laboratory.

"Today begins a future brighter than you can possibly imagine," Edison told Nick as they entered the building. "Hold your head high. You are Accelerati now. There is no pursuit in this world more noble than ours."

Nick found that harder to swallow than Mrs. Higgenbotham's raspberry scones, which were dry, crusty, and seemed to contain only virtual raspberries.

"And what pursuit is that?" Nick asked, not even trying to hide his bitterness.

"Excellence for the sake of excellence," Edison answered. "And innovation for the benefit of all mankind."

"Did they put that on your tombstone?" Nick asked.

Edison chuckled, not at all put off by Nick's derision. "They might have. I've never visited. Call me superstitious."

Edison's wheelchair/wet-cell contraption rolled slowly down the wide hall of the building, with Nick by its side.

"Our outpost beneath the bowling alley in Colorado Springs is only our secondary facility. This is where our most important work is done."

And as he spoke, Edison gestured his bony hand toward the various labs they passed. "In here, we're developing glass that's as strong as steel but will still shatter when we want it to."

"Why would you want it to?" Nick asked.

"You never know when you'll need your own technology to fail," Edison said. He gestured toward another lab. "And here, in this room, we're working on a membrane that will allow divers to breathe underwater."

"When you want them to," Nick added.

Edison looked up at Nick. "The wise inventor knows the importance of controlling his inventions. Even your beloved Mr. Tesla knew that, or he wouldn't have gone to so much trouble to hide his greatest creation."

Finally, they turned into a large laboratory in which objects from Nick's attic were spread out. It gave Nick a sudden sense of déjà vu, because it looked eerily like the fateful day of his garage sale, when he had sold the antiques before knowing that they were parts of a bigger machine.

"The device you had constructed fell apart when your attic came crashing down," Edison said. "We have all of the individual objects here, plus other pieces that you didn't have."

Nick walked among the items. It was true: they were all there. The reel-to-reel tape recorder that spoke your feelings. The cosmic-string harp. The brain-expanding hair dryer. The miniaturizing clothes dryer.

But as Edison said, there were also other things that Nick hadn't seen since the day he had sold them. The rusted bicycle was there, and the object that looked like a chest of drawers but probably wasn't, and the blender-ish thing.

Nick counted twenty-nine objects in all. He knew which three were still missing: the glass prism that he hadn't been able to get from the old man's strange family back home; the battery that kept Vince alive; and the globe, which, as far as Nick knew, could be anywhere on the planet. Or off, for that matter.

"The asteroid will build up a dangerous charge again in a few weeks, but between now and then we hope to reverse-engineer many of these individual objects."

"Right," said Nick. "Reverse-engineer. . . ." He picked up the blender. It was heavy; the pitcher was made of copper instead of glass. "Where's the lid?"

"Was there one?" Edison responded.

Clearly there were grooves for screwing on a lid. Had there been one when he sold the blender at the garage sale? He couldn't quite remember. Either way, its absence troubled him.

"Maybe you should ask whoever found it for you," Nick suggested.

"Well, in any event, we hope to figure out what each individual object does, and then adapt the technology. It is my wish that you help us." Edison paused, studying Nick. "And ultimately, when the time comes, you will take these pieces and rebuild the larger machine."

"It's still missing some pretty important parts," Nick said.

Edison rolled closer to him. "But *can* you put it together? Do you remember how?"

Nick was not a liar by nature, but he knew that if he told the truth, the Accelerati would own him completely. So he said, "There was something about my attic that made it easy. A kind of gravity in the center that made things clear."

Edison furrowed his brow. "Jorgenson spoke of that. I told him it was his imagination."

Nick shook his head. "No. It was real. I'm not sure if I can still put it together. You might have most of the pieces, but you left behind its soul."

Edison waved his frail hand. "Poppycock. A machine is a machine. And we made a deal. I will protect your father and brother in exchange for your efforts here. Are you a man of honor, Master Slate?"

Nick shrugged. "I like to think so."

"Then do me the honor of keeping your end of the bargain."

Nick held up his hands, still covered in bandages. "Not much I can do with my hands like this," he said.

"You'll heal," Edison told him. "We can't heal you instantly, of course, but we've developed some microorganic salves that will speed up the process. Until then, you'll have plenty of other hands to help you."

Then he called in two engineers to assist: a man and a woman in lab coats who had all the eagerness that Nick lacked.

"I'll leave you to it," Edison said, and rolled out.

The engineers introduced themselves as Doctors Bickel and Dortch, but since that sounded more like a law firm than a pair of engineers, they told Nick to call them Mark and Cathy.

"So you're the one who started this whole thing," Cathy said with a rueful smile.

Nick didn't answer.

"We've already captured the technology from the atmospheric kinesis stimulator," Mark said, pointing at the tornado bellows.

"We thought we'd work on the toaster next," said Cathy.

"Fine," said Nick, resigned. "Just keep it away from my head."

In truth, Nick wasn't the one who had started all of this, as Cathy had suggested. It had been started by Tesla long before Nick was born.

But for Nick it had begun on what was, by far, the worst moment of his life: the fire at his home in Tampa that took his mother's life. He had suppressed the raw pain of it for as long as he could, but was unable to do so anymore. Now it was never far from his mind. Every flame he saw reminded him; every time he flexed his fingers, the sting of his more recent electrical burns reminded him. Those burns were beginning to heal, but the scar from the fire that took his mother several months before never would.

Yet now there was a new twist to his recollection of that awful night. Something he had only realized the moment he shoved his hands into Tesla's malfunctioning machine. The shock of the electrical jolt had sparked something in his mind—a single stray memory had leaped to a lonely synapse in his brain.

Someone else was there that night.

His father and brother had been just ahead of Nick, scrambling to the front door to escape the burning house—Mr. Slate had thought he was leading his family to safety. Nick remembered glancing back at his mom, his eyes stinging, barely able to see. She was there, urging him forward—then, for an instant in the billows of black acrid smoke, he thought he saw someone else, someone behind her.

Then he was out on the lawn and she wasn't. She never made it out, and the porch exploded from the heat and the roof came crashing down, further feeding the flames, and his world had ended, and nothing else mattered.

Whatever he had seen must have been a false memory—or maybe a reflection off a picture frame. There was no one else in the house, so what else could it have been? And, in that desperate moment, how could he blame himself for seeing things that weren't there?

Still, the image sat in his brain like a rusty old fishhook, waiting for Nick to reel it in.

For him, this breathless misadventure had begun on the night of the fire. As it would turn out, it would end on the night of a fire too.

❸ CHICKEN OR FISH?

Caitlin Westfield felt like smashing something, and not for her usual artistic purposes. This time she was just plain mad.

"Miss Westfield, this conversation is getting us nowhere," Principal Watt said, leaning back in his comfortable chair.

Caitlin wondered how hard she would have to push before he would topple over, but knew she couldn't do that, no matter how much she wanted to.

She took a deep breath and said, very slowly, her words evenly spaced to get through to him, "Nick. Slate. Goes. To. This. School!"

Principal Watt shrugged. "So many people left Colorado Springs after the last disaster, I'm having a hard enough time finding the students whose existence we can prove, much less the ones we can't."

"How could you not remember him?" Caitlin shouted.

"Whether I remember him or not is irrelevant. In fact, if I didn't remember him, this would be much easier. But the fact is, there's no record of him ever having existed, and since he never existed, he couldn't have disappeared."

"Well, obviously the records are wrong," insisted Caitlin.

Principal Watt sighed. "I have learned in my many years as a school administrator, Miss Westfield, that it is pointless to stand against the crushing force of public record. Down that path madness lies."

"But—"

Principal Watt put up his hand to stop her. "We're done here. I have students to discipline and teachers to reprimand. Your friend's lack of being is not the problem of Rocky Point Middle School."

Caitlin knew that Principal Watt's attitude was less about his devotion to paperwork and more about the fact that he didn't like Nick. Yes, weird things had begun happening as soon as Nick arrived at his school, but it was shortsighted of the man to assume that those things would stop now that Nick was gone. Pandora's box could not be closed by merely pretending it had never been opened in the first place.

The truth was, Nick had disappeared in the blink of an eye. Caitlin had been talking to him in his hospital room after the disaster that had destroyed his house. She'd gone out to a vending machine, and when she'd returned the room was empty, all evidence of him gone. It had to be the work of the Accelerati.

That was about two weeks ago.

Colorado Springs was still licking its wounds from the massive electromagnetic pulse that had blown out everything for miles, frying computer hard drives, exploding streetlamps, and melting electrical towers.

The wreckage of Nick's house was now surrounded by police tape, a tall fence, and TRESPASSERS WILL BE SHOT signs. The site was supposedly under investigation by government agencies, but Caitlin knew it was really the Accelerati. She could see them behind the fence, in their miserable pastel suits, sifting through the rubble. They had taken all the parts of Tesla's machine, the F.R.E.E., which she and Nick had so painstakingly put together. They were also excavating the underground metallic ring that encircled the house, clearly another part of Tesla's great invention.

In school, people had already stopped talking about the electric surge from the asteroid, which would have wiped out practically all life on Earth had not Tesla's machine grounded all that electricity.

The massive chunk of celestial copper was still generating power with each orbit. The next deadly electrical discharge was only two weeks away, yet people acted as if nothing were going on, just like they had the first time.

"People never learn," Mitch said to Caitlin as they waited in line for lunch in the cafeteria.

"Now that the Accelerati have Tesla's machine," Caitlin said, "it will be up to them to save the world next month. Somehow I don't put much faith in that."

"Oh, they'll save the world, all right. And then take credit for it. And then make the world pay for having been saved." Ever since the incident, Mitch hadn't been himself. He'd been gloomy and fatalistic, as if he were channeling Vince.

Like Nick, Vince was also AWOL—although at least they knew where Vince was, off in Scotland with his mother. He had told them he was going there to get himself and his life-giving battery away from the Accelerati, but Caitlin suspected there was more to it than that.

Around them, students complained about the length and slowness of the food line. "New staff," someone commented. Caitlin didn't think anything of it at first.

"The Accelerati have Nick," Caitlin told Mitch, "and we're just sitting here, taking pop quizzes and doing homework. We should be out there finding him."

"The only way to free him," said Mitch, "is to bring down the Accelerati, once and for all."

"And how do you propose we do that?"

"Grinthon," Mitch said. "Brandon Gunther's alligator."

"You keep saying that," Caitlin said, throwing up her hands. "What does it even mean?"

"I don't know," said Mitch. "But when I do, it'll be the key to everything."

Mitch had told her how he'd extracted that puzzling piece of information from a terrified Acceleratus by threatening to pump him up with the windstorm bellows.

Apparently, even under threat of death, the Accelerati still spoke in riddles.

With the line barely moving, and scores of hungry kids getting more and more disgruntled, Mitch abandoned his spot. "I'm not hungry anyway," he said, and left, allowing Caitlin plenty of space to stew and simmer on her own.

The snaking lunch line finally reached the steam trays, filled with earth-toned glop that someone had convinced the Board of Education was nutritious.

And as she looked up above the trays, Caitlin stopped short.

"Hey!" the kid in front of her said to the new server. "What happened to our regular lunch lady?"

"Ms. Planck no longer works here. I'm the new lunchroom attendant," said Dr. Alan Jorgenson.

Back in the Middle Ages, before science was even a thing, some very educated men sought to discover how the universe was put together. These men were alchemists, and they began with the flawed premise that there were only four basic elements in nature: earth, air, water, and fire. This threw them profoundly off track.

They believed that by combining these four elements in the proper proportions they could achieve three goals: the distillation of the Elixir of Life; the production of the Philosopher's Stone; and the transmutation of lead into gold. Many alchemists, including such early scientists as Sir Isaac Newton, spent decades of their lives fruitlessly trying to turn lead into gold. Of course, the alchemists never bothered with turning gold into lead. What would be the point?

But in this instance, it would appear that is exactly what had happened.

The gold that had been Dr. Alan Jorgenson, Grand Acceleratus, was now Rocky Point Middle School's second assistant lunch server. Instead of a vanilla spider-silk suit, he wore a white cotton apron. And in place of his vanilla fedora was a black hairnet.

Caitlin's glare could have liquefied steel. "What are *you* doing here?"

To which Jorgenson replied, with the flatness of a man condemned, "Chicken or fish?"

"Where's Nick?" Caitlin demanded. "What have you done with him?"

From the line behind her, another kid shouted, "Will you shut up and pick one?"

But Caitlin would not be bullied while she was bullying the grand bully. "Answer me or I will scream so loud they'll hear me in that stinking bowling alley of yours!"

Jorgenson still showed no sign of emotion beyond abject resignation. "I don't know what you're talking about." He handed her a plate with chicken, string beans, and Jell-O. "And even if I did, I'd have nothing to say to you."

Caitlin banged her tray down on the counter, making the Jell-O bounce. "What did you do with Ms. Planck?"

"She is in a better place," said Jorgenson. "And as you can see, I am not." Then he called to the next kid in line. "Chicken or fish?"

• • •

By skipping lunch, Mitch Murló had missed out on the fact that Dr. Alan Jorgenson had been demoted to being a sleeper agent at their middle school.

It might have given Mitch a small amount of satisfaction to see what goes around coming back around, but the humbling of Jorgenson was only a drop in the deep well of retribution he wanted to exact from the Accelerati.

My father is one of them.

He had known the truth from the moment he had tamed the tornado. When those winds had stopped spinning both in front of and inside of him, he'd been filled with a rare clarity of thought.

His father was Accelerati. Petula was Accelerati.

Everything he thought he knew about his life had funneled its way down the toilet, leaving him with the burning desire to make the Accelerati pay the ultimate price. For over a hundred years they had worked behind the scenes, manipulating science. They'd used his father to steal $750 million, one penny from every bank account in the world. And yet, even though his father was one of them and had known what he was doing, Mitch still believed they had used him and then let him take the fall.

Mitch might not have been a computer genius like his father, but he was smart enough to know that the stolen $750 million was a direct path to the jugular of the sinister organization. No one, not even his father, knew where that money was. If Mitch could find it and take it from them, he could bring the Accelerati to their knees.

And then what? thought Mitch. He decided he would cross that bridge when he came to it. But to see the Accelerati on their knees . . . what a fine bridge that would be.

. . .

Caitlin walked home alone that day, politely refusing invitations from her friends to hang out at the local coffeehouse. While most everyone else in school was gearing themselves up for finals, the prom, and the annual field trip to Washington, D.C., school was the furthest thing from her mind.

Since the day she'd met Nick at his life-changing garage sale, she had found that the mundane social niceties of Rocky Point Middle School interested her less and less. She now felt disconnected from the life she had grown so comfortable in.

"It's like you're becoming, I don't know, a hermit or whatever," her friend Hayley had commented, and her other friends were quick to agree.

"It's like, you're so, kind of, you know, out there, or something," said her friend Brittany.

Caitlin was fluent in this dialect; she knew exactly what to say to get them to leave her alone. "I know, right?" she began. Then, rather than telling them that she was involved in something larger than they could possibly imagine, she said she was "still stressed out, you know, about the world almost ending and everything," hoping to leave it at that.

"Really? That's so last month," said Hayley.

Caitlin fought the urge to tell them that it was going to be next month too, and the month after that. People assumed that the discharge from the Felicity Bonk asteroid had solved the problem—and that whenever the electrical charge built up again, it would just spend itself in another massive lightning strike somewhere on the globe, blow out some lights in a place they didn't care about, and life would return to normal.

Only a few people knew the truth: that the only reason the discharge happened at all was because of Tesla's F.R.E.E. device. Without it, the charge would continue to build until the planet became a massive bug zapper—one that would zap a whole lot more than just bugs. Without the F.R.E.E., life on Earth would come to an electrifying end.

But she didn't tell them that. What would be the point? By her calculations, there were fourteen days, more or less, until the charge reached lethal proportions again. Fourteen days for the F.R.E.E. to be reassembled by the Accelerati. And if they didn't . . . well, all the worrying in the world wouldn't amount to anything.

As she walked home, she took note of Colorado Springs' recovery. The EMP had burst every light bulb and blown out every electrical device in a three-mile radius of Nick's house—even the ones that weren't plugged in. Stoplights were still all out, but that was less of a problem than one might expect, because more than half of the cars in town were still nonoperational due to fried electrical systems, despite auto mechanics working 24/7. Utility-company cranes could be seen on dozens of corners, replacing transformers and streetlights. The mayor had assured the public that the city's electrical infrastructure would be up and running at full speed by July.

The confused despair that had followed the electrical surge marked what newspapers called Colorado Springs' "Dark Time." But that despair was now giving way to a dizzy sort of hope. The kind that usually follows a war. There were still lunatics prophesying doom on downtown street corners, of course. Sadly, the lunatics were closer to the truth than they knew.

The appearance of Jorgenson behind the lunch counter was an unexpected left hook for Caitlin. Once she recovered from the shock, she realized it could work in her favor.

Because now she had someone to question. And even though he would continually give her non-answers, the nature of those non-answers would provide her with plenty of information.

For instance, she already knew he was here against his wishes. And if her incessant and insensitive badgering made him lose his temper, she was bound to learn a whole lot more.

My God, Caitlin realized, *I sound just like Petula.*

The thought of Petula made her jaw clamp so tightly it hurt. That two-faced, pigtailed, poor excuse for a human being had been working against them all along! Caitlin had always known she couldn't be trusted. And although Petula had never openly confessed to being part of the Accelerati, it was clear she'd been working for Jorgenson.

Caitlin had confronted Petula when Nick disappeared from the hospital. Petula was also there, being treated for the arm she had broken during the disaster at Nick's house.

When Caitlin got to her hospital room, she thought Petula was waving hello, until she realized that the wrist-to-shoulder cast and accompanying brace kept her arm in a perpetual hand raise.

The moment she'd seen Caitlin, Petula had begun frantically hitting the nurse call button.

"If you don't tell me what they've done with Nick," Caitlin had threatened, "I will break your other arm and both of your legs."

Threatening Petula had been a mistake. Petula had managed to make a case to hospital administration that Caitlin was a mentally unstable stalker. Caitlin's parents were called, anger management therapy was suggested, and Petula took out a restraining order that prohibited Caitlin from being anywhere near her.

It would have made going to school very difficult for Caitlin, but so far Petula hadn't turned up there again. Caitlin had no idea what Petula was up to. She only knew that she had to be a hundred yards away from whatever it was.

But now, with Jorgenson slinging slop, and no sign of Nick for two weeks, Caitlin decided it was time to throw caution to the wind and pay a visit to her least favorite citizen of Colorado Springs—even if it landed her in jail.

Petula Grabowski-Jones had already lost three pen caps down her cast trying to scratch beneath it.

The doctors had warned her that if she inserted any foreign object beneath the cast, it could fuse with her skin. But what did doctors know? And even if they were right, she could claim it was an intentional body modification.

As for why her arm had multiple fractures, she blamed Nikola Tesla, who seemed able to predict everything that would happen around his diabolical machine years before it happened.

During school hours, she now went to the Accelerati's underground headquarters for her education. Theirs was an eclectic and unusual curriculum to be sure, but it was far more practical than anything she could learn in a regular classroom.

She was training at the right hand of the new Grand Acceleratus, watching as world-changing decisions were made right before her eyes. It sure beat math work sheets.

After school she went home, just like always. Her parents didn't have a clue about what was going on.

"Honey, I have your dinner," her mother said, coming into her room with a tray.

While Petula was perfectly capable of walking into the dining room to eat dinner, she insisted that her meals be served to her in bed, because the trauma of spending time with her family was just too much after the trauma of the fall.

Her mother seemed to take great joy in the fact that she had to cut Petula's meat again. Indeed, she got so absorbed in the nostalgia that she began serving her daughter's meals on the little plastic baby plates she had saved from Petula's early childhood.

Petula was now subjected to Care Bears and Disney princesses gazing up at her from beneath her precut food. She took pleasure in spreading ketchup all over them to make it look like they were bleeding.

Shortly after the doorbell rang, she heard her mother threatening to call the police, so Petula knew the visitor must be for her.

"I'll handle it, Mom," Petula said from the hall when she saw Caitlin on the porch.

Reluctantly, her mother stepped inside, and Petula, in her bulky cast and brace, awkwardly brushed past her to go out.

Petula maintained a safe distance from the intruder. "You're violating the restraining order," she pointed out. "I could have you arrested, and you'd spend the rest of the school year in juvie."

Caitlin held up her hands in a gesture of surrender. "I just want to talk."

"Fine," Petula said. "As long as you start with an apology."

Caitlin shook her head incredulously. "For what?"

Petula shrugged as best she could in a shoulder cast. "It doesn't matter. Hearing you apologize for anything is reward enough in itself."

Caitlin sighed. "I'm sorry, Petula."

And although it sounded like a poor imitation of sincerity, Petula accepted it. "You may proceed."

"I just want to know if Nick's okay."

"He's better off without *you*, if that's what you mean." She watched as Caitlin balled her hands into fists, then released them.

Caitlin took another deep, slow breath. "The Accelerati wanted to kill him. I just want to make sure they haven't."

"You don't have a clue what the Accelerati want or don't want."

"Well, Jorgenson wanted him dead."

Petula looked down her nose at Caitlin. "Jorgenson isn't running things anymore."

Caitlin gasped. "Then it's true. You *are* one of the Accelerati."

Now Petula got a little cagey. "I didn't say that. What makes you think I said that?"

"You didn't have to. It's obvious."

"Maybe I should call the police after all."

"Don't bother, I'm leaving. But just tell me. Please. Is Nick okay?"

"No," Petula told her. "He's not okay. He's dead."

Then she slammed the door heavily in Caitlin's face, and returned grumpily to her room to eat precut meat off of smiling princesses.

Caitlin's miserable little exchange with Petula could have left her full of grief and despair, except for the fact that it was Petula.

Petula saying that Nick was dead was definitive proof that he was alive. And now Caitlin was even more determined to find him. She could only imagine the horrors the Accelerati had been inflicting on him.

4 RECIPES FOR DISASTER

I'd offer you a glass of Dom Pérignon," Edison called from the far end of the table, pouring himself a glass of the champagne, "but you're underage."

Nick was dining in style. He sat at the opposite end of the long table, which was set with fine china and sterling silverware. They were having lobster (which he liked) and escargots (which he did not). His hands had mostly healed, making eating a whole lot easier than it had been.

"Coke is fine," Nick said, taking a sip from the crystal goblet in front of him.

"Thank you for all your hard work these past two weeks," Edison said, raising his glass toward Nick.

Nick's instinct was to say, "You're welcome," but he didn't, because he didn't feel Edison was really welcome to anything Nick had done. The fact was, Nick's helpful nature was sabotaging all his attempts to sabotage the Accelerati.

First of all, the engineers working with Nick were nothing like the pompous, smug thugs Jorgenson had employed. Mark was all about his kids, and Cathy reminded Nick a little bit of his mother. As much as he tried, it was hard not to like them.

They seemed pretty smart, but they were often bewildered by things that were obvious to Nick. In the first few days, Nick had offered them as little help as was humanly possible. They failed to crack the mystery of the toaster, and Nick watched as they struggled to figure out what Tesla's "clothes dryer" did. They measured its dimensions, and the electrical field it generated when it was turned on. Then they put various objects inside it and were stymied when nothing happened.

Finally, after observing half a day's worth of failed experiments, Nick couldn't stop himself from telling them what he knew. "It's got to be wet," he said. "It's a dryer, remember? Whatever you put in has to be wet."

So Mark and Cathy put in a wet towel, and in less than a minute, it shrank to the size of a dollar bill.

Their excitement was contagious. Nick began to forget they were working for the Accelerati.

Edison, of course, was thrilled with the discovery, which left Nick disgusted with himself.

"Once we figure out how the thing works," Edison told him when he first saw the shrunken towel, "it will have a thousand applications. Imagine, we'll be able to shrink tumors."

"And armies and bombs," Nick added, knowing that was the more likely Accelerati use for it.

Edison was unfazed. "We can't choose the way the world will use the things we invent."

"We didn't invent it," Nick reminded him. "Tesla did."

And yet, in spite of himself, Nick couldn't help but look forward to working with Mark and Cathy each day, solving problems, figuring out the objects that the Accelerati had snagged from Nick's neighborhood before he could find them: the pump vacuum that sucked all the oxygen out of a room, the old chain saw that cut holes in the fabric of space-time, and the sewing machine that mended those holes.

Mrs. Higgenbotham entered the dining room, removed Nick's

lobster shells and untouched snails, then set in front of him a large silver bowl containing a hot fudge sundae.

"'Ere you are," she said. "Everything a young Acceleratus could need."

Suddenly Nick's lap of luxury felt as icy as the silver bowl. Is that all he was now? A young Acceleratus?

In a burst of frustration, Nick swiped his arm across the table, flinging the bowl of ice cream to the floor.

Mrs. Higgenbotham was not at all perturbed. "My, aren't you the irascible child today!"

"What I need," Nick said to Edison at the other end, "is to see my father and my brother."

Edison laid his hand gently on the table. "I have given you every assurance that they're fine."

"But I don't believe your assurances. I've done everything you've asked me to do. I want to see them for myself."

Edison reached into his jacket and pulled out an after-dinner cigar. He put it to his lips, and Mrs. Higgenbotham scurried to the far end of the table to light it.

"It wouldn't be in your, or their, best interests," the old man said between puffs.

"That's not for you to decide," Nick said.

"That's where you're wrong, boy. *Everything* about you is for me to decide. It would be fitting for you to show some gratitude for all I've done, and all I *will* do, for you. I'll hear no more about it."

Mrs. Higgenbotham moved toward the ice cream on the floor, but Edison held up a hand.

"No!" he said sternly. "Let the boy clean his own mess. It's time for my bath."

Mrs. Higgenbotham wheeled the old man out of the room.

Alone, Nick stared down at the overturned silver bowl and the creamy rivulets that were already seeping into the antique Persian carpet. Finally, he grabbed a napkin, stooped down, and began to mop it up.

Tesla knew as well as anyone the consequences of experiments gone awry—because for every grand success, there was at least one miserable failure. Take his resonant oscillator—better known as his "earthquake machine." When he turned it on, it nearly shook down his laboratory and an entire city block in New York before he smashed the thing to pieces with a sledgehammer. Then there was the power surge from his Colorado Springs lab that knocked out all power in the city for days.

Any scientist will tell you that great achievement can only come through trial and error—something about which both Edison and Tesla were in perfect agreement. The cost of that error, however, can be devastating.

Nick was in the break room of Edison's workshop complex when the alarms went off. Emergency in Laboratory Four.

That was the lab Cathy and Mark were in.

Currently they were attempting to reverse-engineer the weight machine. On this Nick had offered them little assistance, other than suggesting that all sharp objects be removed from the room, because screwdrivers and such become a real problem when weightless. And even more so when gravity suddenly returns.

The day before, Mark had proposed that the range of the antigravity field might increase if they could get the piston on the weight machine to pump faster.

"I don't think that's a good idea," Nick had told him. Tesla's objects all did exactly what they were meant to do, at the exact pace they were meant to do it. Nick instinctively knew that messing with things was a recipe for disaster. But then, what were they here for, if not to mess with things? That was what the Accelerati did. If they managed to blow themselves up, Nick would usually say that it served them right. Except this was Mark and Cathy.

When the alarm began to blare, the room went into lockdown. Now Nick could only peer in from the hallway, through the small window in the door.

"Turn it off! Turn it off!" Nick heard Cathy scream from somewhere above. He craned his neck and saw that she was plastered to the ceiling, along with everything else that had been in the room. Her face was stretching farther than seemed possible.

"I can't reach it!" Mark shouted. He was pressed against the far back wall, his own body enduring wave after wave of gravitational deformation, unable to move.

When Nick and Caitlin retrieved the weight machine from the obese man who had bought it at Nick's garage sale, they'd merely had to deal with an *absence* of gravity. If they didn't move, they floated in place.

What Cathy and Mark were facing now was worse: true antigravity; a repulsive force many times more powerful than the relatively weak pull of Earth. In the middle of the room stood the weight machine, connected to a hydraulic pump that forced it to piston at ten times its normal speed—and with each pump a surge of spatial distortion expanded outward, warping space with muscular gravitational waves. Chairs were pressed against the walls, their frames bending and breaking. The desk—which had been bolted to the floor as a precaution, had torn loose from its moorings and was in pieces against the ceiling—along with everything that had been inside the drawers. Wrenches, pliers, hammers, and, yes, screwdrivers. All the things that Nick had warned them to put away before turning on the antigravity machine. They would be deadly if and when the machine was turned off.

As for Mark and Cathy, the two engineers were pressed to the ceiling and far wall with what must have been the equivalent of ten G's. They were barely able to breathe, much less move.

Around Nick, other Accelerati scientists, engineers, and techies had begun to gather, but none of them took any action. They seemed content to gawk through the window and share worried glances.

"We have to help them! We've got to get in there!" Nick yelled.

"That's a lead-lined lab," one of the scientists pointed out. "Those walls are the only thing protecting the rest of the building. If we open that door . . ."

Nick knew he was right, but also knew he couldn't leave Mark and Cathy to die—and they would. The human heart could only withstand ten G's for a few minutes before it would collapse from its own weight.

Nick watched the gravity waves in the room expand in spherical pulses, one pulse every second.

And then he remembered something.

He turned to highest-ranking Accelerati scientist there: a Kenyan woman known to everyone as "Z."

"The Accelerati have a time-slower-downer-thingy, right?" Nick asked. "Is there one here?"

She looked at him, confused.

"You know—the thing you use to build a Starbucks overnight."

"Ah, yes," said Z. "The Selective Time Dilator."

"Do you have one?"

Another scientist stepped forward. "There's one in my office!" And he hurried to retrieve it.

Inside the lab, Mark and Cathy continued to struggle against punishing waves of artificial antigravity. In between waves they were able to breathe, but trying to do anything more than that was futile.

The scientist quickly returned with a device that looked something like a flashlight and handed it to Nick.

Clearly no members of the Loyal Order of the Accelerati were going to volunteer to enter the lab. It was all up to him.

"Set it for wide beam, and aim it at the area where you want time to slow down," instructed the scientist. "It can only stay on for three seconds before it needs to be recharged."

"Three seconds?"

"In objective time," Z explained in her musical Swahili accent. "But for you, and all things in the field, those three seconds will be closer to three minutes."

Z had security clearance to override the lockout. As she prepared to swipe her ID card and open the door, she said, "I have to warn you: this may not work. You could very well end up as they are."

Tell me something I don't know, thought Nick, but he only said, "Got it."

"Stand back, everyone," ordered Z, then she said to Nick, "I will have to shut this again immediately, or we will all fall victim to the gravity field."

Nick nodded, and held the time-thingy tightly. Z swiped her card, and the door swung open violently under the force of its own weight. One overcurious Acceleratus, who had been leaning in to get a look, was caught by the antigravity waves and thrown backward against a wall.

The effect on him was horrifying. On each wave, the man's

wrinkled skin stretched back on his face and his eyes sank in, making his head look like a skull shrouded in thin, cloudy cellophane. He groaned with the pain of it.

Nick took a deep breath and started counting the pulses, realizing this was like leaping into a moving jump rope. Then he aimed the time device toward the machine and hit the button.

Suddenly everything seemed to stop—but not entirely. The Accelerati struggling to close the door behind him were still moving, but in extreme slow motion. And inside the lab, the next gravity pulse had just formed in the machine and was expanding slowly outward like a balloon.

Nick ran toward the middle of the room and promptly fell over sideways. The antigravitational force dipped between waves but didn't go away entirely.

It took him a moment to get his bearings; when he did, he cautiously put his hands flat out on the floor like a lizard and began inching his way toward the machine.

The gravity shift seemed to be about forty-five degrees, so crawling across the floor was more like climbing up the slope of a pyramid while weighing three hundred pounds. Not impossible, but not as easy as just walking up to the machine and pulling out the pin.

Nick spent most of that first minute pulling his way toward the machine, but as he neared it, the expanding balloon of the next gravity wave caught him.

He couldn't avoid it, and as it slowly hit him, he was lifted up. He felt his skin stretch back across his face, just like Mark and Cathy and the man outside. But worse, he felt pain in every cell of his body, now swelled by its own immense weight. He felt like the stretched skin of a drum that had been sliced by razor blades.

Nick spent that entire second minute suspended in midair,

caught by the expanding wave, until he was slammed against the wall behind him. He knew he didn't have time to recover from the pain or the disorientation. He had to be faster. And so he began to climb the floor again, this time as quickly as he could possibly move.

He reached the weight machine just as it began to generate the next gravity wave. The time-thingy was beeping and blinking red, about to run out of power. This would be his only chance. He thrust his hand forward, grabbed the pin, and allowed the gravity wave to push his hand back—but this time, his fingers held the thin metal rod.

The instant the pin was pulled out, the time dilator failed, and his world was brought back to full speed. Without the pin, the weights crashed down, and the machine stopped.

Mark crumpled to the floor; Cathy fell from the ceiling—and so did everything else that was stuck there. Nick dodged knives and pens and hammers, but a piece of the broken desk hit his shoulder, cutting a gash two inches wide.

Immediately Accelerati flooded into the room to tend to Mark and Cathy, who were too weak to move. Z took off her lab coat and pressed it against Nick's shoulder.

"It is not deep," she said, "but you may have a broken clavicle."

Nick shook his head. "I don't think so. It doesn't hurt that much."

Just then, Edison rolled into the room.

"Brief me," he said.

Z explained what had happened. All the while Edison kept his eyes on Nick, his expression inscrutable. Then he gestured toward Mark and Cathy, who had not yet been able to catch their breath. "Take them to the infirmary," he said, "and call in our best physicians. We may need some special equipment."

"And Nick?" asked Z.

Edison considered him again. "You'll have a fine battle scar, Master Slate. A medal to remind you of your heroism today." He smiled widely and shook his head in bemused admiration. "You continue to impress me. Had it been our friend Dr. Jorgenson, he would have no doubt watched as they died and taken copious notes."

"And if it had been you?" Nick dared to ask. "What would you have done?"

"I," said Edison, "would never have allowed it to happen."

Edison instructed Z to take Nick to the infirmary as well, for stitches. But before they left, Edison took a moment to ponder, though his pondering always seemed more like scheming to Nick.

"Acts of bravery are often their own reward," Edison said. "But this calls for something more."

Everyone in the room waited for his decree of generosity.

"Rest up tomorrow," he finally told Nick, "and Sunday I'll take you to see your father and brother."

5 OH, THE HUMANITY

Like any inventor, Thomas Edison despised the bureaucracy of large organizations. But as a businessman, he knew it was a necessary evil. So, when the administrative work involved in running the Accelerati ultimately became too much of a burden for him, he had invented the position of Grand Acceleratus. The person in this role was tasked with handling all the details of the Accelerati's day-to-day operations, leaving Edison free to do as he pleased.

The first Grand Acceleratus, appointed in the 1930s, had experimented with nuclear fusion. Unfortunately, he'd experimented in the vicinity of Lakehurst, New Jersey, a few miles from Edison's lab, causing the *Hindenburg* to blow up, and incinerating himself in the process.

The second Grand Acceleratus was responsible for the Great Northeast Blackout of 1965, which knocked out power from Ontario to Pennsylvania. Few people died as a result of the blackout, except for the second Grand Acceleratus and his inner circle. They made the mistake of taking refuge in their airtight safe room inside the Empire State Building. Unfortunately, the lock was electrical, and they suffocated.

The third Grand Acceleratus died in 1980, in the terrible but secret tragedy at Mount St. Helens, which most people thought was a natural volcanic eruption. Since he had gathered almost all of the Accelerati to witness the event, the secret society was decimated. The only ones who remained were those who happened to have the flu that day.

It took years to rebuild their ranks under the next Grand Acceleratus, Dr. Alan Jorgenson, a man whose scientific brilliance could only be outdone by his bloated ego. While Jorgenson was the only Grand Acceleratus to survive his particular catastrophe, Edison had lost all faith in the man, and demoted him.

Now a fifth Grand Acceleratus had been installed, and Edison hoped that with new leadership, the Accelerati would be ushered into a kinder, gentler age.

On the same morning as the antigravity accident, Petula Grabowski-Jones had a meeting with the new Grand Acceleratus.

With her own personally monogrammed bowling ball—one designed by the Accelerati to knock down only the pins that the bowler required—Petula bowled a precise series of frames to unlock the secret entryway to the underground Colorado Springs headquarters. It was difficult to do with a cast on her other arm—but thanks to Accelerati sonic healing therapy, and a very gentle blast of a deep-tissue calcifier, her cast now only went up to her elbow.

As she walked through the great hall of the Accelerati headquarters, she glanced at the windows, and the scene beyond. This month's holographic projection was of an imperial coronation in ancient Rome, filled with pomp and ceremony, to honor the appointment of the new Grand Acceleratus.

When Petula reached the impressive door to their new leader's underground residence, she took a deep breath.

Everything will be different now, she thought as the door opened and she stepped inside.

There, behind an ornate, antique desk, sat the new leader.

"Petula, how good to see you," said Evangeline Planck.

"I want a raise," Petula demanded.

Ms. Planck chuckled. "How can we give you a raise when we don't pay you?"

"Then I want to get paid, and *then* I want a raise."

Ms. Planck came out from behind her desk. "The Accelerati don't deal with things as mundane as salaries, Petula. All of us work on a volunteer basis. You know that."

"Oh? What about the seven hundred and fifty million that Mitch's father stole for you?"

"That money will be used to further our causes throughout the world. Do you think the Accelerati paid me all those years when I was working undercover as a cafeteria worker?"

"You got 'paid' by being made Grand Acceleratus," said Petula.

"Exactly," said Ms. Planck. "Good things come to those who wait. And," she added with just a hint of menace, "to those who do what they're told." Then she clapped her hands and got down to business. "So, what do you have to report to me today, Petula?"

"Mitch has figured out that his father is Accelerati."

"We know that."

"Vince LaRue and his mother have vanished, with the battery."

"We know that too."

"There are only two other items that are unaccounted for. The globe, and some sort of glass prism."

Ms. Planck sighed. "We're aware of all of those things, Petula. Don't you have anything new for me today?"

Petula smiled. "I overheard Nick talking with Caitlin before his house went kablooey." She paused, making Ms. Planck wait for it. "Nick knows exactly where that prism is. He just couldn't get his hands on it."

That caught Ms. Planck's attention.

"I'll have to let Mr. Edison know that," she said.

"Nick will never tell him." Then she smiled. "But I can get it out of him."

"Petula," said Ms. Planck, "from what I've been able to observe, Nick doesn't like you very much."

Petula shifted uncomfortably. "So? I can change that. Remember, he never found out I'm Accelerati. I can go to Edison's lab undercover and charm it out of him."

"That," said Ms. Planck, "would require some charm."

Petula shrugged. "I can fake it."

Ms. Planck considered it and said, "Come, there's something I'd like to show you."

She led Petula to the research and development wing. There, a large window looked upon a soundproofed lab—the same one where Jorgenson had tested the explosive capability of the cosmic-string harp. Today, four members of the Accelerati were shackled to the wall, screaming, although no screams could be heard through the glass.

"What's happening in there?" Petula asked, as curious as she was horrified.

"A test in sonic dissonance," Ms. Planck told her. "We recorded a solo performed on the clarinet you provided for us, and are now playing it to them on an endless loop."

Petula watched as their faces contorted in the absolute agony of the damned.

Ms. Planck went on. "We're testing to see how much sonic dissonance it takes to crack the human mind—and if it's possible to build up a resistance against it." She put a hand on Petula's shoulder. "Do you recognize them?"

Petula looked closer. Yes, she did. These four had been Jorgenson's personal entourage. Three men, and the woman who had been temporarily frozen.

"Their loyalty to Jorgenson made them impossible to work with," Ms. Planck said. "So I asked them to volunteer as experimental subjects."

"Asked them?"

"No one refuses the request of a Grand Acceleratus," Ms. Planck told her.

Beyond the glass, the four Accelerati continued to writhe in torment to awful music that no one outside of that room could hear.

"Why are you showing me this?" Petula asked, trying to sound less troubled than she was.

Ms. Planck smiled. "As always, I just want to give you some perspective, dear. There are all sorts of rewards among the Accelerati. I have a shining new vision for our organization. Serve that vision well, and your rewards will be spectacular. Serve poorly, and your reward will be . . . well . . . something else."

Petula was quick to get the message.

6 YOUR MORBID PREOCCUPATION WITH NESSIE

Moss grows on many things in Scotland. Vince found this out very quickly when it started to grow on him.

For years he had looked forward to being old enough to shave. He never dreamed that instead of facial hair, he would be shaving moss from his neck.

"Honeybun," his mother called from the hallway of the quaint Scottish inn where they were staying. "Hurry on down or you'll miss breakfast."

"That was the idea," Vince muttered.

The beginning of this journey had been fairly simple. It had started the day after the EMP knocked out all electricity in Colorado Springs.

Vince had put it forth to his mother as simply as he could. "I want to go to Scotland," he'd said as they ate breakfast in their home by candlelight.

His mother had swallowed three measured spoonfuls of oatmeal before she responded. "You know, there is no proof that the Loch Ness monster exists," she'd said, knowing the way his mind worked.

And although his interest in that particular lake had nothing to do with the so-called monster, he'd said, "They haven't proven that it doesn't either."

She still wasn't convinced, so he'd added, "And then maybe we can go to Paris to tour the famous sewers, and to Italy to see the catacombs."

She'd quietly eaten another few spoonfuls of her oatmeal.

Vince knew that his mother loved to travel. In fact, she'd been trying to get him excited about visiting faraway places for as long as he could remember. But the very idea of going anywhere with his mother, all perky and full of liquid sunshine instead of blood, had made his flesh crawl even before it had become undead. But now he was not only open to travel, he was suggesting it.

Therefore, it was no surprise to Vince when, after her fourth spoonful of oatmeal, his mother had asked, "When shall we leave?"

By far the hardest part of their journey had been getting Vince on an airplane. His first thought had been to go as a corpse. But rules governing the international transport of human remains were very strict, requiring either embalming or cremation prior to being loaded as cargo, neither of which Vince had found very appealing.

In the end, his mother had come up with a plan. Somehow she'd managed to get his battery registered as a medically approved life-support device. Which was true, except for the medically approved part.

While he was onboard, however, a truculent flight attendant had insisted that his backpack go in the overhead bin during takeoff and landing, which had left him temporarily dead twice. What made it worse was that after takeoff his mother had left him that way for a few hours.

"So you wouldn't get jet lag," she'd told him, still not understanding that he didn't get tired like regular people. He suspected that those hours of being dead had made him susceptible to moss infestation, and the spore-ridden climate of Scotland in May had just made it worse.

They had been in Scotland for almost two weeks now, staying in a quaint stone-walled inn. They still ate oatmeal for breakfast, but on this particular morning it was served in the boiled stomach of a sheep.

"Vegan haggis," the innkeeper said proudly. "Just as ye requested. We like to be sensitive to our American guests and their peculiar eating habits." Of course the sheep's stomach wasn't vegan, but the innkeeper was only willing to go so far. "If y' find it offensive to your meatless sensibilities, eat around it," he told Vince, then turned to Vince's mother. "Although if ye ask me, y' need to get some good solid food into this boy. He looks a wee bit green around the gills."

The inn, which consisted of twelve bedrooms and far fewer guests, had had several brushes with fame—though those brushes were of the long-handled feather-duster variety. Winston Churchill's mother had spent time here before the war, and at the far end of the first-floor hallway was a room labeled the HAWKING SUITE.

"Did Stephen Hawking really stay there?" Vince's mother asked the innkeeper.

"That's the rumor, ma'am," the man said a bit flirtatiously.

But after he left the room, one of the other guests said, "Don't believe him. It's because someone once complained that the baseboards were full of little black holes."

As they ate their breakfast, Vince's mother studied brochures, occasionally trying to make eye contact with him. Vince made it a rule never to meet his mother's eye, because that was always a prelude to conversation. Yet it was hard not to look at his mother once in a while; whenever he did, she smiled.

"Are you enjoying your time here?" she asked. "You haven't

come on any tours with me. I'm beginning to worry that your morbid preoccupation with Nessie has you missing all the beauty and culture that Scotland has to offer." Since they'd arrived, Vince's mother had been all about exploring castles and appraising Scottish realty.

Vince shrugged. "Beauty and culture is your thing. I don't mind hanging out here and watching the lake." It was fine with him if she never discovered his real purpose.

So, that day, while his mother took her tour, Vince once again walked the shoreline paths of Loch Ness, searching for clues to the missing globe.

"Why, we had a monster sighting just the other day," said a one-eared guy who was selling plastic Loch Ness monsters made in China. "Rumor has it that if you buy one of these charms, Nessie is sure to come to the surface." Then he proceeded to spin the tale of how he'd lost his ear to Nessie.

Vince knew he'd get no information from the local vendors. Their only interest was in telling tourists what they wanted to hear. He knew his best information would come from people who *didn't* want to talk to him.

On the water's edge, he found a cottage with a garden just coming into bloom, and a rusted wrought-iron fence to keep visitors out. Despite the weight of his backpack containing the battery, he handily hopped the fence, and with a rusty iron knocker, pounded on the door until a person emerged.

It was either a woman in a skirt or a man in a kilt, Vince couldn't quite be sure.

"What ye be wantin'?" the man or woman said. "This is private land."

"I'm sorry to bother ye," Vince said. He tried to put on a Scottish accent to be more endearing, but it was so bad he realized it was only insulting, so he stopped. "About two months ago, something strange happened on the loch. And it had nothing to do with Nessie."

The dowager/geezer looked away. "Cain't say I know what yer talking about, laddie." But his/her nervous body language said otherwise.

"There was this house," Vince continued. "It came out of nowhere and sank to the bottom of the lake."

The codger/biddy said, "If ye know all about it, then why are ye asking me?"

Peering through the door, Vince could see knickknacks and "charming" memorabilia of all sorts on the shelves. "Well, you see," he said, "it was my grandmother's house. It fell victim to a secret military experiment, and her things, the knickknacks, well, they're of great sentimental value."

That seemed to touch a warm spot in her/his breast/pecs. "Then it's my nephew ye'll be wanting to speak to. He runs the dive outfit that found it."

7 FRIES WITH THAT?

Mitch had never been the most popular kid in school. Spending time with Caitlin Westfield, who *was* one of the popular kids, raised his cool quotient several notches.

And the fact that he had beaten up Stephen Gray for throwing pennies at him didn't hurt either. After that, nobody teased Mitch about his father stealing billions of virtual pennies.

Mitch had confronted his father in prison a few days after Nick disappeared.

"How?" Mitch had said to him. "How could you be one of them? One of the Accelerati?"

His father went pale at the mention of the word, and looked around the visitors' room, as if the Accelerati were listening to them. Perhaps they were.

"How did you find out?" his father asked, his head hanging in shame.

"Maybe I'm smarter than everybody thinks," Mitch said. "Maybe I figured it out myself."

His father smiled with pride. "You *are* smart, son. Never let anyone tell you you're not."

Mitch waited for an answer to his question.

Finally, his father said, "They offered me membership in the most exclusive club of geniuses in the world. They told me I was the greatest computer programmer they had ever seen, that I was destined to change history. And then they put in my hands the power to do it. Who could say no to that?"

"I could," said Mitch. "You should have."

"No one was hurt by what I did, Mitch. It was a victimless crime. One penny from seventy-five billion bank accounts worldwide. Not even the poorest of the poor missed that cent."

Mitch shook his head in disbelief. "But just the *idea* of it is wrong! Billions of tiny victims add up to one big one. Especially when you think about how the Accelerati are going to use that money."

"I don't know how," his father said, and Mitch believed he honestly didn't. "Maybe we don't want to know."

"Oh, you'll know all right," Mitch said, anger and disappointment in his voice. "Every time you hear of something horrible they've done out there, you'll know that you're the one who made it possible."

His father got a little angry himself. "Don't you understand?" he said. "Once I became a full-fledged member, you, your mother, and your sister all became hostages. If I didn't follow Jorgenson's orders, *I* wouldn't be punished—*you* would. The only way I could keep you safe was to do exactly what they wanted me to do."

But then Mitch asked the important question. "Would you have done it anyway?"

His father considered this, and gave an honest answer. "I don't know. Knowing what I know now, I wouldn't have. But back then . . . the Accelerati can be very seductive."

Perhaps Mitch was just being naive, but he felt sure he could never be seduced by them. Petula, sure. Even when he was dating her, Mitch knew she had the moral fiber of a cobweb. Mitch had to believe he was made of something sturdier than her, and his own father.

"Leave the Accelerati alone," his father warned in a whisper. "They guaranteed your safety to me. And as long as you steer clear of them, they'll have no reason to break that promise."

It took a few weeks for that discussion to sink in. Mitch understood at least part of his father's dilemma now. If he fought the Accelerati, they could go after his mother, or his little sister.

But could he live with himself if he didn't act on what he knew?

Grinthon. Brandon Gunther's alligator.

The fact was, he wouldn't know anything until he figured out what those words meant.

Beef-O-Rama, Rocky Point Middle School's hangout of choice, was temporarily serving only vegetarian selections, while resolving a lawsuit that accused them of using rodent meat in their burgers.

In truth, it was just a misunderstanding based on a typo on the menu, which meant to claim that their burgers were full of *nutrients* but was printed to read: *Our burgers are full of nutrias!* While nutrias might indeed be nutritious, they are closely related to rats.

But that was neither here nor there, because Mitch and Caitlin were just having fries.

"I want to thank you," Mitch said to Caitlin. "Your willingness to be seen with me has made me a little less uncool."

Caitlin grabbed a fry and dipped it in ketchup. "That works both ways," she said. "Being with you has made me less cool." She shoved the fry into her mouth.

"Well, I promise not to sit next to you on Monday's flight," he said.

"I didn't know you were going on the field trip to Washington."

Mitch shrugged. "My mother thought it would broaden my

horizons, and be nice for me to go someplace less stressful."

"If Washington, D.C., is less stressful than Colorado Springs, something is wrong somewhere. And you know what? I don't care about 'cool' anymore. When we're older and coolness matters less, I'm sure we'll still be friends, and you'll be running the company that people like Theo work for."

"I'd never hire Theo," Mitch told her. "He's too much of an idiot." Then he had another thought. "Has anyone seen him since the EMP?"

"A lot of people just up and left when that happened," Caitlin suggested. "His family never struck me as the kind who could endure hard times very well."

"Funny," said Mitch. "Last week, I was hurrying through the hall to get to class, and I thought I saw a life-size picture of him on the wall. I figured it was a baseball recruitment poster or something. But when I looked back, it was gone."

Caitlin just shrugged. When Mitch had seen the "poster," he'd convinced himself it was just his imagination, even though he knew, deep down, that there might be more to it.

"The thing is," she said, "you and I are the only ones left in town who know what really happened. It's hard to connect with people who are totally clueless about it, you know?"

"There's always Petula," Mitch joked.

Caitlin went a little stiff. Mitch had been kidding, but she was suddenly acting serious. "I spoke to her," she told him. "She knows where Nick is, and she knows that he's alive."

"She told you that?"

"No, actually, she told me he was dead. But coming from Petula . . ."

Mitch nodded, accepting the logic. "You think he's still here? Maybe underneath the bowling alley, being held prisoner?"

Caitlin thought about that, and then said, "It's probably more complicated than that."

Before them, the basket of fries began to dwindle. Although Caitlin only ate one at a time, she ate them very quickly.

Mitch began to feel like it was a competition. He grabbed three fries, dragged them through the ketchup, and shoveled them into his mouth.

"If we just had some clue about what's going on," Caitlin said.

"Grinthon," Mitch said, his mouth full of food.

"Princeton?" Caitlin said. "What about Princeton?"

Mitch swallowed. "No, I said *Grinthon*."

Caitlin took a moment to do some mental calculation, then leaned forward. "Mitch," she said slowly, "what exactly was going on when that Acceleratus said that to you?"

"I was threatening to blow him up like a parade balloon."

"With the bellows?"

"Yeah," said Mitch. "I put the nozzle in his mouth and threatened to blow him up. That's when he said 'Grinthon,' and 'Brandon Gunther's alligator.'"

Caitlin looked down at the basket before them. "Mitch," she said, "why don't you eat some more fries?"

"I don't know," he told her. "I'm kind of full now."

"EAT them!" Caitlin said.

And so he did. He bit down on one fry.

"More," Caitlin said.

So he took another fry. And then, to his shock, she reached into the basket, grabbed half a dozen, and shoved them into his mouth. His cheeks looked like a chipmunk's.

"Now talk!"

"Ah cahn't! Mry marth if furl offood."

"Exactly! Now say the words the Accelerati gave you!"

He said, "Vrandon Gumberth alligator."

She pushed more fries into his mouth. "Again!"

He said, "Vrandum Gumber allgirater."

"Again!" she said, adding more fries.

"Randum Gumber algeratem." Then Mitch gagged. He coughed, spewing chewed potato all over Caitlin. But instead of being mad, she smiled with a gleam in her eyes that almost scared him.

"Random number!" shouted Caitlin. "The first two words are *random number*! But I couldn't quite get the third."

Mitch gasped. "*Algorithm!* Before my father was arrested, all he told us was that he was working on financial algorithms."

"Princeton," Caitlin said. "Random number algorithm."

"What does that have to do with Nick?" Mitch asked.

"I don't know," Caitlin said, "but it's the only clue we've got. The answer is in Princeton. We have to go to New Jersey."

And Mitch gagged again.

8 WEIRDLY WEIRD IN A WEIRD KIND OF WAY

If you looked up the expression *just shoot me now* in a dictionary of slang, it would not be surprising to find a picture of Dr. Alan Jorgenson in an apron and hairnet, serving food at Rocky Point Middle School. It was clearly the lowest point of his illustrious career.

After all he had accomplished, this is what he was reduced to.

"I can't have that," said the whiny snot-nosed child in front of him. "I'm allergic to green stuff."

"Good," Jorgenson snarled, giving him a double portion. "Enjoy your anaphylactic shock."

While he wanted to blame this entirely on Nick Slate, he knew it had been the Old Man's decision to demote him. But exactly how he was demoted had been left up to Evangeline Planck.

Dr. Jorgenson had room in his heart to hate many people, but currently she was at the very top of his list.

"There's something wrong with the pizza," said a zit-faced girl. "I think you left the plastic on it when you cooked it."

"A little bit of carbon disulfide never hurt anyone," Jorgenson said. Then he added, "Except for causing the occasional cancer, but you won't have to worry about that for years."

How could they have forgotten that *he* was the one who'd found the advertisement for Nick Slate's garage sale? That *he* was the one who'd had the foresight to realize that these were Tesla's lost inventions? That *he* was the one who'd turned on the F.R.E.E. at the crucial moment, thereby saving the world? And this was the thanks he got?

"Excuse me, Mr. Lunch Lady," said a kid with more hair on his skull than brain matter within, "this chicken tastes funny."

"That's because it's not chicken, it's *long pork*. Made from the last student who complained about the food."

"Yeah, whatever," said the kid, walking off, clearly not believing it was true in the least. Next week, if Jorgenson had anything to do with it, it *would* be true.

For obvious reasons, Jorgenson did not get along with the other cafeteria workers. In fact, one of them actually complained about him. The next day she mysteriously lost her voice, and it hadn't come back since. After that, nobody said a peep about Jorgenson.

Ralphy Sherman was spreading rumors that the lunch server was some kind of warlock who worshiped wallabies. Jorgenson never denied it, because it made the students somewhat afraid of him. In fact, his ability to instill fear in kids was the only perk of the job.

When the shift was done, Jorgenson lingered "to clean the trays," or so he told his coworkers.

After everyone was gone, he knocked on a steel cabinet. "You can come out now."

And from the half-inch gap behind the cabinet slipped Theo Blankenship, to stand very literally flat against the wall. Because he could do nothing else. It's hard to do anything but stand against the wall when you're only two-dimensional.

In the book *Flatland*, mathematician and author Edwin A. Abbott described his version of a two-dimensional world. It was a place populated by squares, triangles, and other geometrical figures one might draw on a board.

Few people knew that, in addition to being a brilliant mathematician, Abbott was also a member of the Accelerati. He had conceived of and ultimately designed a weapon that could rob anything or anyone of depth, leaving them nothing more than a living projection on a wall.

Such was the case with Theo, a fairly shallow boy who had become that much more shallow. He, like Alan Jorgenson, had Ms. Planck to blame for his current predicament, for she was the one who had fired the weapon that flattened him.

Theo's family lacked both the open-mindedness and the courage to deal with a dimensionally challenged teen. Whenever they saw him, his sisters would scream, his mother would sob, and his father would visit the liquor cabinet. When Theo told them he was leaving to seek out kinder, more tolerant surfaces, they gave him no argument.

Dr. Alan Jorgenson was the only one who had shown Theo some kindness.

"I will make you three-dimensional again," Jorgenson told him, when he found Theo lurking on a neighborhood billboard, "if you help me take Evangeline Planck down."

Theo was more than happy to agree.

Jorgenson, of course, had no idea how to return a person's third dimension, but he wasn't about to tell Theo that.

"So what have you found out?" Jorgenson asked Theo in the cafeteria kitchen.

"Besides that being two-dimensional is a pain in the butt?" Theo said.

"May I remind you that as a two-dimensional being, you no longer have a butt?"

"Sure I do, when I turn sideways," Theo said, demonstrating.

Jorgenson sighed. "I stand corrected. And I ask again: What have you found out?"

"Okay," Theo said, "so I was hanging out on a tree near Nick's house—and by the way, that's really kind of unpleasant, because of the bark. And don't get me started on stucco—"

"Stay on point," Jorgenson reminded.

"Yeah, right," Theo said. "They haven't done much with the ruins of his house. But they're digging in a circle around the outside. There's this giant metal ring they're trying to get out."

"Interesting," Jorgenson said. He sat down and crossed one leg over the other. "I wonder if it's somehow important to the device."

"Well, they must think it is, because they're digging like crazy."

"Here's what I want you to do," Jorgenson told him. "I want you to follow Petula Grabowski-Jones."

"Do I have to?" whined Theo. "She's weirdly weird in a weird kind of way."

"Your vocabulary is inspiring," Jorgenson said, but apparently sarcasm was lost on the two-dimensional. "Hide in some crevice somewhere, and shadow her when she leaves her house. Eventually she'll go to Accelerati headquarters. You'll follow her there, crawl down the lane of the bowling alley when it opens, and then spy on Evangeline Planck—until you know exactly what she's up to."

"And then what?" Theo asked.

"Then we find a way to reclaim my position as Grand Acceleratus," Jorgenson said, as if it were obvious.

"Cool," said Theo. "I can get behind that." But then, in his current state, Theo could get behind anything.

9 A WEEBEE CLOISTER-FEEBEE

Whether or not Stephen Hawking had ever traversed the dim hallway of a Scottish bed-and-breakfast toward the Hawking Suite, he did have a certain interest in corridors. Not the kind of corridors found in country inns, but those that cut through time and space. Corridors more commonly known as "wormholes."

According to a bit of quantum sleight of hand called the Casimir effect, space-time has been proven to warp, perhaps enough to allow for a tear in its fabric, through which otherwise impossible travel could be accomplished. Which means that wormholes could account for a great many mysteries in this universe: socks that vanish from dryers, purses that seem to hold more things than can possibly fit inside them, the impossible distance between your bedroom and the bathroom in the middle of the night, and the magic of David Copperfield. Even the Loch Ness monster's curious appearances and disappearances could be chalked up to wormholes.

In fact, the wormhole hypothesis was one of the less outlandish theories that attempted to account for the creature. Speculation abounded, little of it based in fact. But what does fact matter when lore is so much more entertaining? It was rumors and lore that kept Once-Upon-a-Loch Underwater Excursions in business.

· · ·

Once-Upon-a-Loch Underwater Excursions had a tiny office in a small village on the less populated side of Loch Ness.

"Aye, the house," said the bearded, rotund owner of the company. His name was MacHeath, but everyone called him "Mack the Fork," because he was so fond of eating. "We spotted it down there weeks ago, but no one believes us. They think we Photoshopped the picture."

"I believe you," Vince said. "In fact, I know it's true."

"Hmm. Got a call said you were comin' by."

"Yes," said Vince. "Your uncle." And, based on the man's baffled look, Vince said, "I mean, your aunt."

Mack the Fork stood up. "I'm tellin' ye right now, boy, I'm claiming full salvage rights. Anything I let ye take will be out of the goodness of me heart."

"I understand," Vince said. "The thing I want won't be worth anything to you anyway. Just an old globe. It goes back in our family for generations."

Mack the Fork nodded. "Of course, salvage commissions are expensive. If ye want to go get it, 'twill cost you a pretty penny."

Vince suspected that would be the case, but that's what his mother's stolen ATM card was for. "I can give you three hundred today, and three hundred tomorrow."

"Six hundred U.S.?" said Mack the Fork, stroking his beard. "Ye got ye'self a deal, laddie. When d'ye want to go down?"

At breakfast the next morning, Vince's mom tried to convince him to take a couple of days to explore Edinburgh with her.

"There are supposed to be lots of ghosts and dead things," said said enticingly.

"Nah," he told her. "I'm just going to take a boat out on the lake." Of course, he didn't tell her what *kind* of boat.

Mack the Fork owned two state-of-the-art submersibles:

Synchronicity I and *Synchronicity II*. The first was large enough for a crew of three. The second was much smaller—a remote-controlled robot, able to squeeze into tight places and retrieve objects with its claws.

Mack the Fork began to shimmy his way through the hatch of *Synchronicity I*, following his pilot, a sinewy man who spoke with such a strong Scottish brogue that Vince could only pretend to understand him.

"Ye'll have to leave that behind," Mack the Fork said, pointing to Vince's backpack. "Not enough room."

Vince didn't know what he could say except, "I'm kind of attached to it."

Mack the Fork shook his head. "Ye Americans and yer eccentricities." Then he sighed and handed Vince a bag. "Put my lunch in it, and I'll let ye bring it."

So Vince made room in his pack for a thermos and a sandwich.

"Ever been on a dive before?" Mack the Fork asked when they were all inside.

Vince shook his head no, and the two men laughed, as if they were in on a joke that only mariners knew.

"It's a weebee cloister-feebee," said the pilot. "But yeega yeastie."

Then the two men were all business. They knew what they were doing, and it made Vince a little less worried.

As they descended, the water got dark very quickly. The pilot turned on the lights, but they barely pierced the murk. For the most part the two men were quiet, the only sound the *ping* of sonar as they navigated deep into the lake's central trench.

Suddenly Mack the Fork grabbed the steering column and jerked it to the right, making the entire submersible jolt. "Watch out fer that fin!" he shouted.

Vince might have died of a heart attack if he could have.

Then the two men looked at his expression and burst into laughter. "Just havin' a wee joke on ye, laddie," Mack the Fork said. "All me years doing this, I only seen Nessie once. And even then I might be lying."

It took half an hour to reach the house. When the lights hit it, there was no mistaking what it was.

It lay there like the farmhouse in Oz, misplaced in a fundamentally surreal way. The door was wedged halfway open, many of the shingles had come off of the roof, and fish swam in and out of broken windows.

The submersible came to rest on the floor of the lake bed, just a few feet away from the housewreck.

"All right," said Mack the Fork. "Send in our little friend."

The pilot, with his hands deftly on the controls, sent the smaller robot submersible in through the front door. On a screen before them, they could see everything inside the house. The living room was in ruins—broken china, overturned sofa and chairs, a grandfather clock on its side, its face smashed.

"Don't ye love it, boy?" said Mack the Fork. "It's like the *Titanic*, but with a house."

The robot claws grabbed a fallen drawer, tossing it aside. But beneath it were only the remains of books, open and undulating in the turbulence like anemone.

"Are ye sure it was here?" asked Mack the Fork.

"Watusi we leekifer?" the pilot asked.

"We're looking for a globe," Vince reminded him. "A steel globe."

But it didn't seem to be anywhere.

"Could anyone else have been down here?" Vince asked. "Maybe people in pastel suits?"

Mack the Fork shook his head. "Anybody dives this loch, I know about it."

Vince closed his eyes, trying to recall the hole left in the ground when the house had disappeared. The field had extended only to the front door but all the way into the backyard, taking half of the garage. He opened his eyes.

"It's toward the back of the house," he said. "Maybe in the kitchen."

As the robot made its way down the hall it bumped into a display shelf, creating a hailstorm of collectible thimbles from various countries.

In the kitchen, the oven had fallen over, glassware had crashed to the floor, and there, just beside the overturned kitchen table, was a metallic sphere.

"Yarooga," the pilot said.

Mack the Fork nodded. "Eureka, indeed."

The robot gently grabbed the globe and slipped it into its catch net.

Vince released his breath, realizing he'd been holding it for at least five minutes. He hoped his companions hadn't noticed.

"Awright," said Mack the Fork with a satisfied grin. "Let's bring it home."

The lake was not so deep that they needed a decompression chamber to surface. A good thing too, considering what was waiting for them when they arrived.

No sooner had they opened the hatch than a shotgun was aimed right in Mack the Fork's face, turning him into Mack the Incontinent.

"Awrite, MacHeath," said the old man with the gun. "Fine afternoon for a dive, is it?"

"What in blazes is wrong with ye, Bertie? Point that thing somewhere else."

"Step on up to the dock," called Bertie. "It's not ye I'm after."

Vince heard all this and hoped beyond hope that someone had a vendetta against the pilot, but he was pretty sure that wasn't the case.

When Vince emerged, the old fisherman with the shotgun smiled. "Is he the one?" he said to a woman sitting in a motorboat behind him.

She squinted and shook her head. "No," she said, "he's not the one from the garage sale. This is someone else."

"Well, one American kid's as good as another." The fisherman gestured with the shotgun toward the globe caught in the submersible's net. "Bring that thingy and come with us."

Vince stood his ground. "And if I don't?"

"You don't want to follow that path, laddie. Scotsmen don't bluff."

"Ay, that's true," Mac the Fork said solemnly.

For a moment Vince wondered what would happen if the man did blow a hole in his chest and he just kept on living. That might scare them all off. But then he'd have a hole in his chest, and that couldn't be a good thing.

Ultimately he realized he could tweak this situation to his advantage, because here was the woman who had used the globe, and she was the only one who could tell him exactly how it worked.

So he gathered up the globe and stepped into the launch. The old fisherman left the others with a stern warning to speak nothing of this, then he guided the boat to the north end of the lake.

10 MEMORY OF A MEMORY

On Sunday morning, Nick dressed in his best clothes. And since all of his clothes were picked out by Edison, they looked like something a boy would wear to church in 1912. Corduroy slacks, suspenders, and a heavy tweed jacket, all mud brown.

"You look very dapper," Edison told Nick, whatever that meant.

It would be somewhat humiliating to be seen by his father and brother while dressed like this, but at least he was going to see them.

"Do they know I'm coming?" Nick asked as they rode in Edison's old-school travel coach, with windows dark enough to protect the ancient man's delicate skin from the sun.

"No," Edison said. "They were not informed."

"Oh," said Nick. "So it'll be a surprise."

Edison nodded. "In a manner of speaking."

"Where are we going?" Nick asked.

"Your father has a new job, not too far from here. He's working at Princeton."

They drove through a neighborhood at the edge of the university, just past the fraternity and sorority houses, and parked.

And there they were, out in front of a small, unassuming home. His father was throwing a baseball to Danny, and Danny was catching with a mitt that did not pull meteorites out of the sky.

Nick's heart missed a beat. Edison had been telling the truth. Here they were; they looked happy, they looked healthy.

That should have been Nick's first indication that something was wrong. Because they shouldn't have been happy. He was missing from their lives. The Wayne Slate that Nick knew would have left no stone unturned trying to find his son. But Nick was so glad to see them, he didn't consider that such normal behavior was not normal at all.

Edison put a hand on Nick's shoulder. "You see? There's nothing to worry about."

Nick tried to open the car door but couldn't. It was securely locked.

"Driver," Edison called out, "we're done here. It's time to go."

"What? No! Wait!" Nick pounded on the door.

"I promised you could see them, and you have. Now it's time to leave."

"No!" Nick wailed, and he climbed over Edison, opened the other door, and jumped out.

"Nick, you can't!" Edison said. "You don't understand."

But he had come this far; he wasn't going to let Edison stop him now.

He ran to the yard where they were playing, pushed his way through the picket gate, and threw his arms around his father.

"I'm so glad you're okay!" Nick said, tears springing to his eyes.

"Whoa," said Wayne Slate. "What's all this?"

And from ten yards away, Nick heard Danny say, "Dad, why is some kid hugging you?"

That was enough to make Nick let go. He looked up, and saw something in his father's eyes that he couldn't explain. Not love, not even surprise. Just . . . nothing.

"Dad?" said Nick.

"I'm sorry, kid, I think you're a little confused."

"He called you Dad," said Danny. "What's up with that?"

"I wish I knew," said Mr. Slate. Then he looked down at Nick, still baffled. "Is this some kind of joke?"

Nick backed away. "What are you talking about? How can you not remember?"

Danny stood there, glaring at Nick, offended by the intrusion. "Is he crazy?" asked Danny. "Should I call 911?"

"No," said Mr. Slate, and he looked kindly down at Nick. "I think you just made a mistake, didn't you, son?"

"That's right—*son*," Nick insisted. "I'm your son."

Then his father's attitude turned just the slightest bit chilly. "All right, enough of that. It's not funny anymore."

That's when Edison's driver came up behind Nick and grabbed him. "We have to go now."

Nick struggled, but only slightly, because his heart wasn't really in it. How could his heart be in anything when it was shattered?

"Well, that was weird," Nick heard Danny say as he was pulled away.

Then they continued throwing the ball as if it had never happened.

In a moment, Nick was back in the car with Edison, crying tears of betrayal and fury. He wanted to be angry at his father and brother, but he knew it wasn't their fault that they couldn't remember him.

"What did you do to them?" he demanded.

Edison sighed heavily. "Their memories of you weren't helping anybody," he told Nick. "If we didn't do something about it, they would have created a great deal of trouble for themselves. This way they can lead productive, happy lives, and never be the wiser. And you can be free to find *your* destiny, which lies on a very different path from theirs."

"How could you do that?" Nick said, forcing his tears to stop. "How could you rob me from my family?"

"Serving the greater good is not always easy," Edison told him.

"I hate you," Nick said, looking him square in the eye.

Edison accepted that with a nod. "I suppose I'll have to live with that." Then he signaled his driver to take them home.

Danny Slate and his father continued to toss the ball back and forth, but that thing with the strange kid had left them both a little distracted.

What struck Danny most about it was there had been something weirdly familiar about him. "What do you think that was all about?" he asked his dad after the ball had passed between them three or four times.

"Darned if I know."

That kid made Danny recall their short time in Colorado Springs. He tried to place him back there, but the fact was, he couldn't place anyone there.

He knew they had moved to Colorado Springs; he knew he had gone to school there for a month and a half; but although he vaguely remembered faces, he couldn't think of a single name. Not his teachers, not his friends. So if he had wanted to call them, he couldn't, because he couldn't remember who they were. Was that normal?

The more he considered it, the more anxious he became. He felt the same uneasiness every time he thought about the weird house he and his dad had lived in. Something had happened there. Something not too nice.

And that brought him back to the fire just a few months before that, the one that had taken his mom's life, leaving him and his dad alone. Something was missing from that memory too.

There was a moment, he remembered, just as they were about to leave Colorado, when Danny had a flash that made him gasp. But it was gone too quickly for him to hold on to it. All he had now was the memory of having had a memory. It happened just as he went through the metal detector at the airport. He'd never told his dad about it, because it was hard to put into words. But, for some reason, seeing that kid come out of nowhere and hug his father had made him think of it.

Now his father was just standing there, pondering the ball in his mitt, his eyebrows furrowed, clearly with the same unsettled feeling that Danny had. He looked up at Danny and sighed.

"Wanna go grab some lunch?"

"Yeah," Danny said, even though he had suddenly lost his appetite.

11 HAVE YOU SEEN THIS BOY?

Approximately seventy students had signed up for Rocky Point Middle School's Washington, D.C., trip; an opportunity to explore the nation's capital, visit museums, and, if the more politically minded students had their way, harass their congressperson. Mitch and Caitlin, however, had a very different agenda.

While a huge amount of documentation was required for children to fly in a group—permission letters, birth certificates, and the like—buying two train tickets from Washington, D.C.'s Union Station to Princeton, New Jersey, required nothing but cash and, as Caitlin observed from the other people in line, barely half a brain.

Their escape from the larger group had been simple: arrive in D.C. on Monday morning, check into the hotel and go to their rooms like everyone else; then leave their rooms and sneak out of the hotel while the others were still bleary-eyed from their overnight flight.

Madness, of course, would ensue when the teachers and parent chaperones noticed that two of the kids were missing. But luckily for Caitlin and Mitch, none of that madness would concern them until they returned and faced the music—music that would no doubt be about as pleasant as Tesla's clarinet.

There was a train nearly every half hour from D.C. to New York, and nearly every one of them stopped in Princeton. They arrived there early in the afternoon, right around the time their school group would realize they were gone.

"What if they file a missing persons report or something?" Mitch, always the worrier, asked.

"Mitch, you're a genius," said Caitlin. And then she scrolled through her phone and found a decent photo of Nick. "We'll use this picture and print up a missing persons flyer, and if anyone in Princeton has seen him, they'll call us."

"But what if the Accelerati see it and call us?" Mitch asked.

Caitlin looked grim. "That's a chance we'll have to take."

Math was not Caitlin's best subject, but she knew that when two equidistant objects approach the same point, the one moving faster will get there first.

There were two entrances to the Princeton copy shop. In one door stood an African American teenager holding what looked like a thousand-page thesis.

At the other door stood Caitlin, holding her flash drive containing the missing persons flyer she had designed on her tablet.

The clerk stood bored at the counter, not caring who got there first.

There were two copy machines behind him. One had been pulled apart, and a repairman had his head deep inside, as if being devoured by it. The second machine sat there, ready for a job.

Caitlin eyed the teen at the other door. He eyed her back. And the race to the counter began.

The teen was tall, his legs long, and all things being equal, he could have covered the distance faster, but he was hindered by the huge, clumsy manuscript in his arms, and he had to circle the laminating station directly in his path.

Caitlin darted forward, dodged an exiting UPS man, bumped

a woman trying to decide which color Post-its she wanted, and shouldered her way to the counter a split second before the kid with the thesis got there.

"Oh, man," said the teen. "You can't do that. I was here first."

"Well," said Caitlin, "as I'm in front of you, apparently not."

"But you came in after me."

"Your presence in the vicinity does not guarantee you the first place in line."

Caitlin held her flash drive out to the clerk, who didn't seem interested in helping either of them.

Then the teen said, "Hey, Bob, could you help me out here? My mom needs five copies of this treatise right away."

But Caitlin chimed in simultaneously with "I only have one digital page to copy. It'll go a lot faster."

Bob the copy clerk looked from one to the other with well-practiced indecisiveness.

"If you serve him first," Caitlin said, "it's blatant sexism."

"And if he serves *you* first, it's blatant racism!"

Caitlin backed off a bit. "Look," she reasoned with the teen, "I only need thirty copies of a single page. On a high-speed copier it will take less than a minute."

He plopped the large treatise on the counter and caved. "Fine."

So Bob the clerk plugged Caitlin's flash drive into the machine, it spat out nine copies, and then promptly broke down.

The teen with the treatise looked at the blinking red error message. "You gotta be kidding me!" he howled.

"Sorry, dude," the clerk said. "There's always the Office Depot in Plainsboro."

The teen grabbed the tome from the desk and glared at Caitlin. "This is all your fault," he said, and stormed out.

Mitch, who had been helping the Post-it woman pick up the

fallen display, finally reached the counter. "You got them?" he asked.

Bob the clerk handed Caitlin the nine copies.

"That's a dollar thirty-five," Bob said.

"These will have to do for now," Caitlin said to Mitch.

"Okay," Mitch said. "After we put them up, let's go to the math department. Someone there has to know something about that random number algorithm."

Mitch read the words on the flyer above the photo of Nick. "'Have you seen this boy?' That sounds so sad."

"It's supposed to," Caitlin told him. "It makes people sympathetic."

They turned to leave but never made it to the door, because when the repairman pulled out the crumpled copy that was still stuck on the drum, he shouted to them, "Hey, wait! I've seen this boy!"

Caitlin and Mitch turned to him, and for a moment they just stared in stunned silence.

The copy-machine repairman was Wayne Slate.

Stephen Hawking notes that the history of science has been the slow realization that things are not random or arbitrary; instead, they reflect a profound underlying order.

To even suggest, therefore, that Caitlin and Mitch's encounter with Wayne Slate was mere coincidence would foolishly contradict the wisdom of the greatest mind of our time. They knew he was a copy-machine repairman; they knew he was being closely monitored by the Accelerati; and they knew that the Accelerati were somehow connected to Princeton.

Add all that to the interconnected nature of the universe, and the question becomes: Why didn't they run into him sooner?

• • •

Slowly Caitlin and Mitch approached the counter, only half believing what they saw.

"Yeah," said Mr. Slate, holding the flyer, "he came to my house yesterday."

Caitlin had gathered enough of her wits to say, "Mr. Slate?"

"Do I know you?" he asked.

"Don't you remember us?" Caitlin said. "We're friends of your son."

"You're Danny's friends?"

Caitlin was about to say "Nick," but Mitch cut her off. "Yes," Mitch said, throwing warning eyes at her. "We're friends of Danny." Then he held up the picture of Nick. "Tell us everything you know about this kid."

Mr. Slate shrugged. "He came into my yard yesterday. He hugged me like he knew me. He was dressed in clothes my great-grandfather might have worn, and he left in a limousine— a really old limousine."

Caitlin began to stammer. "But . . . but . . ."

"Thank you for your help," Mitch said, then he grabbed Caitlin and dragged her out.

"What are you doing? Are you crazy?" Caitlin yelled at Mitch as they exited the shop.

"He's been tweaked by the Accelerati!" Mitch said intensely. "He doesn't remember us; he doesn't even remember Nick. He's like a sleepwalker, and you can't wake a sleepwalker or his head might explode."

"That's absolutely ridiculous."

"Is it? What if they planted a bomb in his brain that will detonate if he remembers Nick?"

And that shut Caitlin up, because she knew, as absurd as that sounded, the Accelerati were capable of such a thing.

"They might be watching him," Caitlin said. "Which means they might be watching us."

"Which is why we have to get away from him," Mitch said. "At least now we know we're on the right track." And he marched off.

"Wait, where are you going?"

"The math building is this way," Mitch said. "It's time to talk to someone about random number algorithms."

12 HAIKU TUB ZONE

At Princeton University, there were forty-four full professors of mathematics, but only one of them specialized in the nature of random numbers.

Her name was Zenobia Thuku, and she was from Kenya.

Caitlin and Mitch walked down the hallowed halls of the great Ivy League math building, the same halls where Einstein had lectured, Alan Turing had proposed the computer, and J. Robert Oppenheimer had hinted at the atomic bomb.

Caitlin, having long since done a search on her tablet, had isolated Dr. Thuku as their not-so-random objective. But finding the woman was proving to be more difficult than she and Mitch had anticipated, because the offices of the mathematics department had apparently been laid out according to chaos theory. There was no directory, and no rhyme or reason to who was where. A sign that said THIS WAY TO THE ELEVATOR led to a dead end with vending machines.

Finally, after forty-five minutes of weaving through the mazelike building, they came upon a door on the top floor with a small brass plaque that read: OFFICE OF DR. HAIKU TUB ZONE.

It was Mitch who figured it out. "It's an anagram, see? The letters of her first and last names are all in there, get it?"

"Must be how mathematicians get their kicks," Caitlin said.

Confidently, they pushed open the door, and inside sat a familiar teen, playing what appeared to be solitaire.

The student looked up when they entered, and his expression, which had been neutral, clouded toward a glare. He quickly gathered his cards protectively. "You? What are you doing here? What do you want?"

"Oh," said Caitlin, a bit flustered, "well, we're here to speak to Dr. Thuku."

"My mother isn't here," the teen snapped, standing and approaching them. "She went to get more time to deliver her treatise, which she couldn't get copied, thanks to you. Which means this office is currently closed."

He pushed Caitlin and Mitch out of the office and shut the door behind them.

"Random numbers," said Mitch. "What are the chances?"

Caitlin knocked, and knocked again, banking on the fact that the kid would enjoy tormenting them far more than he would enjoy just seeing them leave. She was right.

The kid opened the door. "Professor Thuku is far too busy for the likes of elementary school students like yourself."

"We're in middle school," Mitch said.

The kid shrugged. "Like there's a difference?"

Caitlin figured the kid couldn't be any more than a sopho-more in high school, so she struck back with "What are you doing here? Is it bring-your-kid-to-work day?"

"I'll have you know I graduated from high school at fourteen and I'm now a junior at Princeton University."

"Oh, I get it," Caitlin said. "Riding mommy's coattails."

For a moment he looked like he would go volcanic, but then he took a deep breath and said, "Who are you, anyway?"

Thus communication had begun, although they were still

trading insults across the threshold when Dr. Thuku arrived.

"Zakia, why are you making them stand outside the door?" Dr. Thuku said. "Invite them in."

And although it was clearly the last thing he wanted to do, his mother was a very commanding woman. He had to obey.

"Interesting name, Zakia," said Caitlin.

"It's Zak," he told them, "to everyone but my mother."

The mathematician sat behind her desk and gestured for Mitch and Caitlin to sit before her, while Zak stayed by the window, shuffling his deck of cards over and over, with a rhythmic *flick-whoosh* that was irritating and distracting. She offered them tea, but they both refused—although Caitlin slipped a couple of tea bags into her pocket when the professor was looking the other way.

"Now, what can I do for you?" asked Dr. Thuku.

"My name is Mitch Murló," he announced. "Does that name mean anything to you?"

Dr. Thuku seemed completely oblivious. "Why? Should it?"

Caitlin cut Mitch off before he could answer. "I've heard about your work in random number algorithms. We wanted to meet you personally for a project we're doing at school."

"A project on me?"

"Yes, on your work," Caitlin said. "If we could just spend a few minutes talking with you about the practical applications of random number algorithms . . ."

Dr. Thuku smiled warmly. "Applied mathematics is a completely different department. My realm is the theoretical, not the practical."

"How about practically stealing seven hundred and fifty million dollars?" Mitch practically shouted.

Taken aback, Dr. Thuku turned in her chair, regarded them for a moment more, and said, "I do not know what you're talking about, but it is making me very uncomfortable. If you need information on my work, it is all online. Now I am going to have to ask you to leave."

Through all of this, Zak sat shuffling his cards until his mother said, "Zakia, would you please escort them out?"

"With pleasure, Mom," he said.

He herded Mitch and Caitlin to the door, then leaned into the hallway. Caitlin was sure he'd deliver one more parting shot, but instead he whispered, "Meet me at the student center at six tonight."

Then he closed the door and locked it.

13 A IS NOT FOR ACHIEVEMENT

Princeton's student center, like most everything else at the university, was in a beautiful, landmark building several hundred years old, awkwardly retrofitted for twenty-first-century living.

Zak waited for the two obnoxious kids in an area that was loud enough to mask their conversation, and nondescript enough to avoid drawing anyone's attention to them. He resisted the urge to pull out the deck of cards that sat in his back pocket like a pack of cigarettes. Shuffling helped to calm him, and playing the hundreds of games he knew focused him. He was endlessly intrigued by the mathematical perfection of a simple, standard deck. But now was not the time for games—not when those two kids held all the cards.

He still had no idea who they were, and he remained somewhat aggravated that the girl had beat him to the copy-shop counter. Truth be told, she had won fair and square, and even if he had gotten there first, the machine still would have broken down on the tenth page.

At first he had believed her when she told his mother that they were doing a report on random number algorithms. So when the boy, Mitch, brought up the stolen money, it made him sit up and take notice. He hoped his mom hadn't seen his reaction.

He had been doing his own investigation, because the random number biz seemed to be shrouded in unnecessary secrecy.

He knew that academics often had petty squabbles and didn't like to share information about their works-in-progress. But somehow his mother's secrecy seemed different.

At six o'clock sharp he watched the two kids come into the student center, and he said nothing as they sat in front of him. Then Zak spoke in a hushed tone, making them lean forward to hear him. "What makes you think my mom stole seven hundred and fifty million dollars?" he asked.

"I don't think *she* stole it," Mitch, admitted. "I know who stole it—but I'm pretty sure she had a part in hiding it."

"Who stole it, then?" Zak asked.

With a look, the girl, whose name he still did not know, stopped Mitch from speaking. "That's not your business," she said.

Zak ignored her. "Who stole it?" he asked Mitch again.

"My father," Mitch told him.

The girl exhaled loudly through her nose, irritated at being overruled. Since irritation would get them nowhere, Zak decided to offer her an olive branch.

"What's your name?" he asked.

"Caitlin."

"Listen, Caitlin, I want your help, and you want mine. If this is going to work, we can't withhold information from one another."

"Why do you need our help?" Caitlin asked.

"Because," Zak said, "I think my mom is being blackmailed."

In her office, Dr. Thuku sat behind her desk in silence, trying to pull order out of the randomness in her head.

In mathematics, answers were precise. Proofs might be complicated, but they were always elegant. Her work with randomness, however, had proved otherwise. There were states in which even mathematics broke down, just as physics broke down in the unimaginable gravity of a black hole.

Try as she might to solve the problem before her, no elegant solution presented itself. And so she did what she knew she must.

She picked up the phone and dialed.

"Hello?" said a voice on the other end.

"This is Z," Dr. Thuku said. "I need to talk to Edison."

"Blackmailed how?" Caitlin asked.

"I know how," Mitch said, even before Zak could speak. "Do you have a father? Do you have brothers and sisters?"

"It's just me, my mom, and Dad," said Zak. "Why?"

"It doesn't take much to blackmail a good person," Mitch told him. "All you have to do is tell that person that their family will remain safe as long as they do everything the Accelerati asks."

"Technically that's extortion, not blackmail," said Caitlin.

Zak looked at them like they were more nuts than he already thought they were. "The Acceler-who?"

Then Caitlin produced the tea bags she had taken from Dr. Thuku's tea tray. "This is very special tea," she told him. "It's called Oolongevity. It makes people say things they might not want to say—and the only people who have it belong to a very secret organization." She looked Zak in the eye, unflinching. "Does your mom have a pin?" she asked. "A little gold pin in the shape of an *A*?"

"Yeah," said Zak. "It's an earring. She wears it backward, behind her earlobe. She told me the *A* stood for achievement, and she'd turn it forward once she won the Nobel Prize in mathematics."

Mitch and Caitlin looked at each other, and their looks unsettled Zak.

"The *A* stands for Accelerati," Mitch told him. "My dad's one of them. And your mom is too. Maybe they lured her in with promises of scientific freedom, and hanging out with other great minds. If your mother is the woman you say she is, the only reason she's still with them is to keep you and your dad safe."

Zak let out a shuddering breath. When he was in his darkest places he suspected the truth might be something like this. But he always told himself it was crazy, that he was being paranoid. He had a sudden urge to pull out his cards and shuffle himself calm, but resisted.

"I know it's a lot to get used to," Caitlin told him. "But the Accelerati aren't invincible. And you might have the key to taking them down."

"What is it?" Zak asked.

"If we can find where they've hidden the money, we can strike a blow that might just be deadly."

Zak considered it. Like his mother, he had a quick mind that could run variables and simplify the most complex equations. It took him only a few seconds to realize the answer. "Money is digital," he said. "My mom must have used a random number algorithm to hide that money deep in the Web."

"Can you find it?" Caitlin asked.

Zak ran a few more variables in his mind, and smiled.

"Oh, yeah," he said. "Easy as π."

14 THE SUPERVILLAIN SPECTRUM

Pi was not easy at all, as it had an infinite number of decimal places, and neither were Nick's emotions after his horrifying visit with his father and brother. He refused to respond to the dinner bell that night. It was the same at breakfast and lunch. He would not sit down to eat with Edison.

So the inventor went to him.

"It pains me," Edison told him, "that you're in such despair."

"Get out," Nick replied from his bed, feeling annoyingly like a pouting child who wouldn't come out of his room.

Edison said nothing for a moment, then finally spoke. "I believe, in my heart, I did the best of all possible things for you."

"Make it so my own family no longer knows who I am?"

"Tell me, Nick, what would you have done in my situation?"

Nick sat up. The answer was simple. "I would have left me alone."

"Really?" Edison asked. "After the electrical incident that destroyed your house, the Accelerati and I should have just backed away? Is that what you would have preferred?"

"It would have been better than this," Nick insisted.

Edison folded his hands. "How?" he asked. "Tell me exactly what would have happened. You're very smart, so I know that you'll probably get it right."

Nick thought about it, then thought about it some more. For

a moment he wished he wasn't so smart, because then he might have said something like *Everything would have gone back to the way things were before, and everyone would be happy with their lives.*

But the truth was far different. "The government would have seized all that stuff instead of you," Nick allowed.

"Yes," agreed Edison. "And?"

"And they would have done exactly what you're doing with it. Experimenting. Figuring out how to use it."

"Yes," said Edison again, pleased. "How successful would they have been?"

Nick shrugged. "I don't know. I mean, they've got the Army Corps of Engineers, right?"

Edison chuckled. "Nick, which engineers and scientists do you think they get?"

Nick knew the answer but hated to say it. "The ones you leave behind."

"So," said Edison, "as I asked, how successful do you think they would have been?"

Even though Nick wanted to turn away, he looked the man in his yellow, rheumy eyes. "Not very."

"In fact," Edison suggested, "they might have have created far greater disasters."

Nick had to admit he was probably right.

Edison wheeled himself over to look out the window. "I was faced with a choice. I could take all those objects myself, and put them in the hands of scientists who could figure out not only how they worked but also how to safely discharge that asteroid once every four weeks and save the world . . . or I could have given them to the government and let them blow up the planet. So I ask you again, what would you have done?"

Nick didn't answer him, because he knew he would have done exactly as the old man had.

"That doesn't excuse what you did to my father and brother."

"Okay, then," Edison said agreeably. "Let's say I let them keep their memories of you. Tell me what would have happened."

Nick stood up. "No."

"Are you afraid of the truth, Nick?"

"It's not about truth."

Edison shook his head. "It's always about truth."

"Get out," Nick told him, pointing to the door. "It might be your house, but this is my room. I want my privacy."

"Not until you answer the question."

Nick wanted to throw something at him, but he knew that if he did, the fragile man would break. As angry as he was at Edison, as much as he hated everything about the situation he was in, he couldn't break the man.

Nick found himself in tears, then he spoke, and told Edison the truth, which he well knew. "My father would have stopped at nothing to find me. And the government, and anyone else who wanted to know what happened to that house, would never have left him or my brother alone." Finally he looked at Edison again. "Jorgenson said my father would be arrested as a traitor, and my brother would be put into foster care. When he said it, I thought it was a threat from the Accelerati. But it wasn't, was it? That's really what would have happened."

Edison nodded. "If I, and the Accelerati, hadn't intervened, yes, that's what would have happened. But we did intervene."

Nick wiped away his tears. "And if my father and Danny didn't remember any of it, and were far, far away, then they'd be safe."

Edison rolled his chair a little closer to Nick and asked, "So if you were me, what would you have done?"

Nick closed his eyes tightly and said, "Exactly what you did."

. . .

Nick came out for dinner that night.

Instead of sitting at the far end of the long table, he forced himself to sit just a chair away from Edison. They took dinner together.

"Mr. Edison?" Nick asked, halfway through the meal. "You say you're not evil. Then why have the Accelerati been guilty of so many evil things?"

Edison pushed his fork through his mashed potatoes, contemplated the peas and carrots for a while, then finally said, "People have souls; organizations do not. But organizations have more power than any one person does. The best we can hope to do is apply our individual humanity to the wielding of an organization's power. When that fails, we end up with brilliant scientists who would destroy everything in their path to achieve their goal. Men like Alan Jorgenson."

"And," Nick added, "Thomas Edison."

Edison set down his fork, perhaps having lost his appetite, and looked to Nick. "Guilty as charged," he said. "But it is my undying wish that you won't make the same mistakes."

And for the first time in the weeks that he'd been there, Nick smiled at the man.

The next day, in the lab, Nick worked with two new scientists. Mark and Cathy had recovered from their ordeal but were taking temporary medical leaves. "With full benefits," Edison had reassured Nick.

With the countdown at T minus five days until the next surge, the reverse engineering being done in various workrooms was wrapping up, and all the objects were being brought back to the main lab.

The aurora was already visible again everywhere throughout the night sky, and carpet shocks were increasing in intensity.

Around the world, no one was as worried as they should have been. Neither were the Accelerati, because they had the device, and they had Nick.

The scientists were getting ahead of themselves, extrapolating how the device might fit together. They were getting it completely wrong, and although Nick should have kept his mouth shut, he couldn't help himself.

"No," said Nick to the scientists. "The hair dryer goes over the lamp. Like this."

"But then the fan won't fit," one of them said.

"That goes in the back, to cool the mini–Tesla coils."

"The toaster?"

"No," Nick said impatiently. "The hair curlers."

"Ah."

They did get one thing right, though.

"I assume," said one of them, peering into the dryer, "this is where the missing globe goes?"

Nick nodded. He had never seen it in place, but he instinctively knew. Just as he knew the prism would fit into a slot in the globe.

"If only we knew where the missing items were," one of the scientists lamented. "We could move to the next phase."

"And that would be . . . ?" Nick asked.

The scientists looked at one another. "We haven't been told," one of them said.

Nick wasn't surprised. When it came to information, Edison was extremely tight-lipped. Suddenly he heard Caitlin's voice in his head. *How could you be helping them?* she asked, with the kind of disapproval only she could generate. *They'll use it to control the world's power supply, which means they'll control the world.*

But, on the other hand, the Accelerati first had to *save* the world in order to control it. If he could help them do that first thing, he could deal with the second thing later.

In his mind, Caitlin only shook her head in disgust. But she wasn't here, was she? She couldn't see the way things were.

Nick grabbed the hand mixer from the perplexed scientist beside him and shoved its odd, flat paddles into the toaster, where they belonged.

Ten minutes later, Edison burst into the lab with such force that the liquid in the huge battery attached to his wheelchair sloshed dangerously from side to side.

"Nick, I have a surprise for you," he said. "A good one." He hesitated for effect, his nearly skeletal smile never changing. "I know you've been feeling melancholy. So we've arranged to have your girlfriend visit. In fact, she's here right now."

Nick was both stunned and overjoyed. Caitlin was here? Now he could have the conversations with her that he was already having in his head. The good ones *and* the bad ones.

Edison rolled aside, and into the room strode Petula.

"Nick!" she shouted, and ran to him, throwing her unbroken arm around him and kissing him all over.

Nick pushed her away, but she came back at him, clunking him in the head with her cast and holding him in a death grip with her other arm.

"I missed you so much!" she shouted, then whispered in his ear, "Play along. I told them I was your girlfriend."

"Why?" Nick whispered back.

"It's the only way to save my life."

"Why would I want to save your life?"

But she hugged him so tightly with her good arm he couldn't get another word out.

The other scientists looked on, smiling.

"We'll let you two have some time alone," they said, leaving the room.

"Wait!" Nick managed to call after them. "We don't need time alone!" But they were already gone.

Edison wheeled himself out as well. "I'll be waiting outside. I hope Miss Grabowski-Jones will be our guest at dinner."

"You betcha!" Petula said.

The door swung closed, and Nick finally succeeded at keeping her at arm's length.

"Have you totally lost any concept of your mind?" Nick asked.

"After I saved you from Jorgenson," Petula said, "and fought him so valiantly to stop him from taking control of that machine, I thought you'd be more grateful."

"Being grateful and being your boyfriend are two different things."

"Saying that was the only way I could infiltrate this place. I'll tell you what I found out."

"What is that?"

"Ms. Planck is Acclerati!"

"I know that," Nick said.

"Vince has flown the coop."

"I know that too."

"Caitlin went back to Theo."

"You're lying."

"Yeah, but it felt good to say it."

"Petula, I'm telling them the truth. I don't need or want you here."

She looked at him, aghast. "If they know I'm not you're girlfriend, they'll probably kill me."

"No they won't," Nick said.

Petula's eyes peeled in horror. "You're one of them, aren't

you?" She backed away and pointed at him. "You're wearing one of their pins!"

"Stop it. It's not what you think."

"Do you know what they'll do to me if you don't tell them what they want to know? They'll torture me."

Nick wondered if wanting to see Petula tortured, if only even a little, moved him further along the supervillain spectrum.

"What could they possibly want to know that I haven't already told them?" he asked.

"The prism. They think you know where it is."

Nick didn't respond right away, and he knew that was as good as an admission.

"It's the last bargaining chip I have."

"Great," said Petula. "You can use it to bargain for me."

Nick shook his head. "I was saving it for something *important*."

"You're just going to let them hurt me?"

"Well . . ." said Nick.

"Fine," said Petula, storming away. "I'll suffer for you, Nick. It's what I do."

Then she flung open the door. "Take me to your dungeon or whatever," she told Edison. And she was escorted away by security.

Petula did not join them that night for dinner.

"She's feeling under the weather," Edison told Nick, making him begin to wonder if what Petula had told him was true.

And then, when she began screaming that night in the room next to his, he really began to wonder.

"Stop! No! I can't take it!" he heard Petula scream. She spoke of chains, pokers, and branding irons. It was when she screamed, "Just kill me now! It'll be less painful!" that he couldn't stand any more. "No! Not the neck! I'm going to be sick!"

When he went into the hallway, Edison was already there.

"What's wrong with the poor girl?" Edison asked.

"You aren't, by any chance, having her tortured, are you?"

Edison shrugged. "Not that I know of."

Nick tried the door and it was locked. But the door was made out of very old wood. He threw his shoulder against it three times, and the third time it broke open.

Nick found Petula, on the bed, as comfortable as could be, screaming while reading *Twilight*.

"No! Make it stop!" she wailed.

"Good Lord," said Edison. "Stop that caterwauling! It'll wake the dead."

"And he should know," said Nick.

Petula, caught red-handed, stood up and backed away.

"Would you torture her a little if I asked you to?" Nick asked.

"Absolutely not," said Edison, indignant.

"I can explain," Petula said.

"Please do," said Edison, "before I quickly run out of patience."

But apparently Petula was not ready to explain, so Nick started. "First of all, she's not my girlfriend. Even calling her a *friend* is pushing it."

Petula scowled at him. "You want me to hit you with this cast again?"

"Then why are you here?" demanded Edison.

Petula looked at both of them and sighed. "All right. Fine. Ms. Planck sent me here to get information out of Nick. That's why I was pretending to be tortured." Then she flipped up her collar to show a little gold pin. "I'm Accelerati too."

Far from being surprised, Nick found himself relieved. "That explains a lot."

But Edison looked very disgruntled. "Why was I not informed?"

"Don't ask *me*," said Petula. "She's *your* Grand Acceleratus."

Edison harrumphed and wheeled out of the room.

"So," Petula said to Nick, once they were alone, "we're both Accelerati. Wanna make out?"

"Ew," Nick responded, then handed back the book. "Here, torture yourself some more," he said, and then he left.

Instead of going back to his room, he sought out Edison. He found him in the parlor, having a cigar lit by Mrs. Higgenbotham.

"She was sent," Nick said, "to pressure me to tell you where the prism is."

"You told me you don't know where it is."

"I lied," Nick said. "I do know."

"Are you going to tell me?" Edison asked.

"No. But I'll get it for you."

"Why are you willing to now, when you weren't before?"

Nick hesitated before he answered. And then he told Edison, "Because you wouldn't torture Petula, even if I asked."

Edison stubbed out his cigar before taking a puff. "I'll have the plane prepared for you first thing in the morning."

A few hours later, Nick was jetting west toward Colorado Springs, escorted by two fairly intimidating Accelerati guards and, of course, Petula.

"The worst part about being Accelerati," Nick told her as they took off, "is knowing I'm on the same side as you."

"Someday," said Petula, "we'll look back on this and laugh."

"Or more likely vomit," said Nick.

Petula thought about that. "Any physiological response is acceptable."

Once Nick was gone, Edison had Mrs. Higgenbotham bring him the phone. He made a long-distance call.

"Did it go well?" Ms. Planck asked.

"Yes," Edison told her. "Not as planned, but we achieved the desired result. He's on his way back to Colorado Springs to get the prism. You were right. He does know where it is."

"You realize," said Ms. Planck, "once you have all the items, you won't need him anymore."

Edison considered that. "That will be my decision to make when the time comes," he said a little curtly.

He could hear Ms. Planck's smirk over the phone. "Are you getting soft in your old age, Al?"

"I will admit the boy brings a certain . . . idealism to the Accelerati that's been missing for a very long time."

"We're not idealists, Al. We're pragmatists."

"Well, as Z often says, the idealism of theory must always come before practical application."

Ms. Planck scoffed again. "The boy certainly won't be your friend when he learns the part we're going to play in what happened."

Edison started to get frustrated. "*We* don't even know what part we played!" he thundered.

"That may well be," Ms. Planck said, "but I do have my theories. . . ."

15 SILVER LININGS

Dr. Alan Jorgenson, a low-level Accelerati sleeper agent recently of the food-service industry, strode through the halls of the underground headquarters. First, though, he had had to wait until some other agents entered, because Evangeline Planck, his "superior," had changed the pass code on the bowling balls and apparently told everyone but him.

He knew the woman had never cared for him, but the level of misery she put him through made it very clear how much she despised him.

That was fine. He was certain he despised her more. Just because she was the great-great-granddaughter of a famous scientist did not mean she had any of his greatness. Genes do fade over time, after all.

Freed from his apron and hairnet and uninspired civilian clothes, he wore his new Accelerati suit. Its pale pink color looked like a white suit had been washed with several red socks. Even his overcoat was pink. The vanilla-colored suit was reserved for the Grand Acceleratus, a rule that Jorgenson had once appreciated but now detested.

His fellow Accelerati averted their eyes when they saw him coming. He was a pariah among his own now, an outcast, untouchable. They didn't notice him pausing to look out of the windows of the great hall, where the grand Roman coronation continued. They paid no attention to him talking to the holographic projection, as eccentricities were more the rule than the exception among the Accelerati.

A few minutes later, he went to his appointment with Ms. Planck.

"Alan, come in," she said when she saw him on the threshold of her office, the office that just a short time ago had been his. Gone were the Picassos, Dalís, and Armans that had graced his walls, replaced by hideous Kincaid cottages and Goddard walking cocktail olives. Jorgenson couldn't hide his displeasure. Her artistic taste was one step above velvet Elvises.

She didn't rise to greet him. She didn't even offer to shake his hand.

"I requested an audience with you," Planck said, "but you're an hour late."

"Perhaps if you had told me that you rekeyed the entry, I could have properly programmed my bowling ball."

She grinned with the malice of a tiger. "I guess you didn't get the memo."

"I guess not."

"Your new assignment was to keep close watch on Mitch Murló and Caitlin Westfield and anyone else at Nick Slate's school that could pose a problem."

"And?"

"Are you aware that Mitch and Caitlin are no longer in Colorado?"

Actually, Jorgenson was well aware. He had the full list of students who would not be attending lunch. He had had a choice: either find a way to prevent them from taking the Washington trip, or simply let them go. He had realized that by failing to do his job he would be hurting himself—but when you're a world-renowned physicist forced to serve lunch at a public middle school, how much more could they punish you? Any failure in Colorado Springs might make him look bad, but it would make the new Grand Acceleratus look much worse.

"Well, how could I be expected to keep an eye on every student? Do you have any idea how hard it is to prepare and serve several hundred meals in under an hour? There are onions to be chopped, my dear Ms. Planck, potatoes to be mashed, and what good would my cover story be if I didn't do my job to the best of my ability?"

She wasn't smiling anymore. She was tapping her fingers rhythmically on the table. "You know, there are other functions you could be serving for us," she said, not even trying to hide the threat in her voice. "We've already reassigned your former allies here—as experimental subjects. I only need sign an executive order to add you to their number."

Jorgenson fumed. "You wouldn't dare. The Old Man might allow you to humiliate me, but he'd never let you go that far."

"The Old Man isn't here," Planck said. But she didn't push the threat. Instead, she said, "We will find Caitlin and Mitch, no thanks to you. But one more slipup, Alan, and you may find your fate worse than the experimental division. Right now the Old Man sees you as a disappointment. Once he sees you as a full failure, you'll go the way of all our failures."

Jorgenson felt the blood leave his face. His nose began to tingle and his lips felt numb. He had signed many a termination order in his time as Grand Acceleratus. Clearly, the tradition would continue if he didn't make himself valuable again.

"May I offer you a word of advice, Evangeline?" he asked. "It has to do with your little project in the desert."

She sat a little stiffer when he said it. "I have no idea what you're talking about."

"Of course you do. That massive hangar you're building out

there. Although I wouldn't call it a hangar, exactly. If you ask me, its dimensions are too boxy."

"You're not supposed to know about that," she told him.

Now it was his turn to grin. "I hear things. But be that as it may, here's my advice to you: in order to build it, you've stretched us very thin financially, taking out loans and such from questionable sources."

"You forget we have seven hundred and fifty million dollars to back us up."

"You haven't dipped into that, have you?" he asked.

"Of course not," she told him. "The money's safe. I've only borrowed against it."

"That money isn't there for you to gamble with—because there's always the possibility you might lose."

Although she tried to hide it, Jorgenson saw concern come over her face. Meaning deep down she must have known he was right. It made Jorgenson wonder how irresponsible she had been.

"I'll take your concerns under advisement," she said, and then dismissed him.

Theo Blankenship had quickly discovered that being a two-dimensional spy for Alan Jorgenson was a thankless job. There was no pay. There wasn't even food. And although Jorgenson had pointed out that Theo's flat metabolism no longer required that he eat, it didn't make him any less hungry.

To avoid being spotted, he'd had to spend most of his time lingering in the projected coronation of Julius Caesar. Despite the fact that the light-show figures were somewhat vapid, he was still out of place there, because even holograms are three-dimensional. But it had been adequate camouflage.

Theo missed baseball. He missed his dimensionally intoler-ant family. And even if he couldn't quite connect the dots, he knew that somehow Nick Slate was responsible for his current predicament.

Since Jorgenson also hated Nick, their partnership had a solid foundation. Theo trusted Jorgenson, not because the man gave him any real reason to, but because he had no choice.

When Jorgenson arrived at Accelerati headquarters, Theo, who had spent the week gathering information like a smashed fly on the wall, gave him the lowdown on all that he had seen. Then, a few minutes after Jorgenson's meeting, Theo was horrified to see the man striding toward the exit, having completely forgotten him.

Theo slid out of the hologram and followed him along the hallway wall. "Hey, Dr. J! You can't leave me here! I can't get out the way I came in without being spotted."

Jorgenson sighed. "Very well," he said. As it happened, Jorgenson did have a plan for extracting Theo. When the coast was clear, he unzipped the lining of his coat.

"I've added this false lining so you can slip in and I can get you out of here."

"No way," said Theo. "I don't want to hide in your clothes. That's awkward with a capital *Awk*."

"Come now. It's lined with titanium foil, so the scanner won't detect you as we leave," Jorgenson said, and added, "It's either that or stay here, hiding in a hologram."

Theo sighed. *I guess it's true what they say,* he thought as he slipped into the secret compartment of Jorgenson's coat. *Every clown has a silver lining.*

Jorgenson left the bowling alley and walked to his new residence, a modest town house overlooking Acacia Park. It was where Planck had lived before she was promoted to her current, undeserved position.

Along the way he stopped in the park to take a moment to compose himself and find at least a small bit of serenity. The sun was bright, and the spring day was warm, so he removed his jacket and sat down to take in some much-needed vitamin D.

To his left, children played in the dancing waters of Uncle Wilbur Fountain. To his right, vagrants slept on benches—even they seemed oblivious to the woes of these troubled times.

And in this calm space something highly pleasurable dawned on Dr. Alan Jorgenson, former Grand Acceleratus: bringing back his glory days would actually be a very simple matter. All he had to do was kill Evangeline Planck. Putting it in such plain terms made him feel so much better than he had just a moment ago.

He stood up and left the park with a renewed sense of purpose and an uncharacteristic optimism. But for some reason, and for the rest of the day, he couldn't help feeling that he had forgotten something.

That evening, in Acacia Park, a vagrant found an expensive-looking pink overcoat and slipped it on, certain it would keep him warm for the night.

16 A GAME OF JERSEY HOLD'EM

Mitch and Caitlin sat in Zak's dorm room, watching over his shoulder as he cracked firewall after firewall on his laptop with lightning speed.

"The best hackers can get in, get the information, and get out," Zak said, "without ever being noticed."

"Yeah, but what about you?" Mitch asked.

"I was talking about me."

Zak hit the keys with single-minded, maniacal clicking. "Okay, I'm in my mom's *virtuum*."

"Ew," said Caitlin. "What's that?"

"It's a multidimensional virtual universe she set up within the mainframe." On the screen were endless strings of numerals that seemed to flow out from an imaginary horizon. "It's a numerical construct that works in eight theoretical dimensions."

"Is that possible?" Caitlin asked.

"Not in the real world, but in math, anything's possible. An eight-dimensional algorithm can generate codes that are impossible to break in three dimensions. We can only break it with something like this."

"The money will be in a bank account somewhere," Mitch said. "With an account number generated by your mom's system."

"No it won't," Zak told them. "It's not designed to generate a static number. It generates numbers that are constantly changing."

"Maybe the money's divided between hundreds of different accounts," Caitlin suggested.

"Maybe . . ." Zak said slowly. "But I've got another thought." He quickly tapped some more keys, and out of the figures spewing at them, a twenty-one-digit number emerged and hovered on the screen. "There!" he said.

"Found it?" asked Mitch.

"Yes." Then he pounded the desk with his fist, aggravated. "But with a dimensional quotient that's twenty seconds in retrograde."

"English, please," Caitlin said.

Zak sighed. "I found the account where the money was twenty seconds ago. See, the money isn't physical anymore, it's all digital. The algorithm creates a new account number somewhere in the world every twenty seconds, then instantaneously redeposits all the money into the new account. That's why no one but the Accelerati can access it. Every twenty seconds it's hiding somewhere different."

"But you've got the algorithm," Caitlin said. "So you can find it."

Zak shook his head, clearly frustrated. "Having the algorithm isn't enough. All it can tell me is where the money's just been. What we need is a *nine*-dimensional algorithm, which can jump ahead of it in time and predict the next number it will generate."

"Can you do it?" asked Mitch.

"I don't know." Then Zak reached into his pocket, pulled out his deck of cards, and, of all things, began to shuffle it.

The others watched him, a bit baffled. "I don't think now's a good time for a game of rummy," Caitlin said.

"Just shut up, okay?" said Zak. "It helps me think."

It was then that Mitch looked out of the window. "Uh-oh."

There were three opalescent sedans at the curb. A dozen agents in pastel suits jumped out and headed straight for the dormitory.

Zak put away his cards. "Those guys aren't exactly stealth, are they?"

"When you can do what they can do, you don't need to be," said Mitch.

"We've got to get out of here," said Caitlin.

Mitch shook his head. "They'll be watching all the windows and doors."

Zak shoved his laptop into his backpack. "I know another way out."

He led them to a forgotten basement utility room where a rusty ladder that had to be a hundred years old led down into foul, web-infested darkness.

"There's an access tunnel down there," he said. "I don't know where it goes, but wherever it is, the creepy dudes in the funky clothes won't be there."

Caitlin looked into the univiting opening. "This might not be the smartest—"

Mitch cut her off. "I know! Make me mad!"

Zak looked at him like he was crazy. "What?"

"Hit me, yell at me, just make me mad!"

"Yes," said Caitlin. "Do it."

"Are you both totally out of your minds?"

"Just do it!" Mitch said.

Zak tapped him lightly on the shoulder.

"No! Harder! Make it hurt."

Zak hit him again, but still not hard enough.

"Here, let me," Caitlin said, and she pushed Mitch against the wall.

"Ow! That hurt," Mitch said. "But not enough."

Zak, clearly not ready to become a wholehearted part of this, stood back and watched as Caitlin dished out uncharacteristic nastiness.

"You stupid, half-wit loser," Caitlin said. "Sorry."

"No, that's good," Mitch said. "Don't apologize! Mean it!"

Caitlin realized what she had to do. They needed something cruel. Something hurtful. The kind of thing someone who really didn't like Mitch would say. It was hard to find it within herself, because now that she'd come to know him, she really did like him. And she realized she liked him enough to give him what he needed.

"Nobody likes you," she said, her voice hard. "You talk too much, you've got no common sense, and people just put up with you."

She could see tears spring to his eyes.

"Is that true?" Mitch asked, his mouth a grim line.

As hard as this was, she knew she was almost there. "You're clumsy, and insensitive, and loud, and oblivious to everyone's problems but your own."

Then Zak, thinking it was all about insults, said, "You're the worst—"

"—foosball player within twenty-three yards," blurted Mitch, blinking back angry tears.

"Huh?" said Zak.

"Bingo," said Caitlin. She grabbed Mitch's arms. "If we go down that tunnel—"

"—we'll all get bitten by rats and get rabies."

"Yuck," said Zak.

Caitlin continued. "We'll find the answers we need—"

"—back in Tesla's lab in Colorado Springs," Mitch said, surprised by his own words.

Zak caught on and said, "We can get away from the creepy dudes in funky clothes if we—"

"—do the opposite of what we think we should do," said Mitch.

"Okay," said Caitlin, and she looked at Zak. "What's the worst possible thing we can do right now?"

"Walk out that door and right into the hands of the Accelerati," Zak said.

So that's exactly what they did.

Six Accelerati brought the three of them to the math building, to the office of Dr. Zenobia Thuku.

"The Old Man told us to bring them to you, Z," said one of the agents. "There were only supposed to be two of them, but this third kid was with them."

"Leave them with me," Dr. Thuku said with authority. "Wait in the hallway until I'm done."

The Accelerati obeyed, and once the kids were alone with her, Dr. Thuku looked at her son. "Zakia," she said with disappointment, and a little bit of fear, "what have you done?"

"What have *you* done?" he countered. "I know about the money. I know what you're using your algorithm for."

"There are things you do not understand," she told him, "and there is no time to explain them now. All you need to know is that the three of you are in grave danger."

"Yeah, I already did the math on that one," said Zak.

"You must run," Dr. Thuku said. She reached into her desk drawer and handed Zak her wallet and key chain. "You know where my car is parked."

From another drawer Dr. Thuku pulled a small device that looked something like a flashlight. "I'm going to open the door. When I do, aim this into the hallway and push this button."

"What'll it do?" asked Zak.

"It will give you a three-minute lead."

Three minutes later, Dr. Thuku went out into the hallway and looked at the six Accelerati there. "Where are they?" she asked them.

"They were in there with you."

Dr. Thuku hit her palm against her forehead. "They must have a Selective Time Dilator! Didn't you have antidilation measures engaged?"

"Uh," said one of the men, looking at the others, "we didn't know we were supposed to."

"After them!" she shouted. "They must be heading to the new test site in New York! I'm sure of it." Then she gave them a cold stare. "I'm extremely disappointed in your performance here tonight."

"Sorry, Z," the man said, and they all hurried after the three fugitive kids.

As Dr. Thuku watched them go, she shook her head. For geniuses, the Accelerati could be incredibly dense.

"Do you have any idea how screwed I am?" Zak said as he drove them south to Washington. "I have finals next week. And a paper due tomorrow that I haven't even started yet!"

"You heard Mitch," Caitlin reminded him. "We have to get to Colorado Springs."

"I couldn't care less what Magic 8 Ball here said," Zak muttered. "An EMP nearly wiped that place out, didn't you hear? Why would we go there?"

"Because that's where we live," Mitch said from the backseat.

"I wasn't talking to you. In fact, I don't want to hear another word out of your mouth, prophetic or not."

"I'm sorry we dragged you into this," Caitlin said.

"I don't even know what *this* is all about," Zak said.

"Oh, good point." Caitlin looked at Mitch.

Mitch leaned back and put his hands up. "It's all yours."

So Caitlin nodded, gathered her wits, and began. "It all started with a garage sale. . . ."

As Zakia Thuku had discovered, a deck of playing cards is a fascinating thing. It arrives in perfect order, ace of spades through the king of hearts—but shuffle the deck even slightly and that perfect order is torn asunder. The laws of probability prove that if you shuffled a deck at the very beginning of time until now, the cards would *never* be in the same order twice.

And yet we do order our cards, time and time again. Into royal flushes, and full houses, and any number of desirable combinations. This is the greatest gift of life: the ability, for a brief moment in time, to defy the laws of chaos and entropy; to go all in, and win the pot in the universe's grand game of poker.

The events that had led to Mitch, Caitlin, and Zak's current circumstance were an odd shuffling indeed, and as Zak listened to Caitlin's tale, he realized that this was truly a high-stakes game.

And he'd just been dealt four jokers and the square root of two.

"So let me see if I've got this right," Zak said. "Your friend had a garage sale and sold off all of Nikola Tesla's potentially deadly inventions without realizing it, and then had to get them back before the Accelerati did."

"We did get most of them back," Caitlin said, "but then the Accelerati took them all—and took him."

"And they didn't kill him," Zak said, still trying to wrap his mind around it, "because Magic 8 Ball's girlfriend said they *did*."

"Exactly," said Mitch.

"And why are you a Magic 8 Ball again?"

Mitch sighed. "One of the objects was some kind of a quantum truth-telling device, and I sort of absorbed its power."

"Uh . . . okay. . . ." said Zak.

"Oh, and let's not forget Nick's father," Caitlin added.

"Wait, his father's Accelerati?" asked Zak.

"No," Mitch said, "that's *my* dad."

"Nick's father told us he saw Nick," Caitlin said, "so that proves he's still alive. But he doesn't remember him."

"Oh," said Zak. "So he's the kid on that flyer you made. The guy with big ears."

"His ears aren't that big," Caitlin said defensively.

"They are," said Mitch. "That's why he always wears that baseball cap."

"Can we try to stay focused here?" said Caitlin. "We still don't know exactly where Nick is, or how to get him back." She growled in frustration. "And we were so close to finding him."

"We also need to find where that algorithm leads," Zak said.

"And we have to be careful," Mitch added. "The Accelerati are everywhere, and they know we're back in the game."

"All they know is that we tried to find Nick and failed," Caitlin said. "They don't know we have the algorithm, unless your mom tells. And she won't, will she?"

Zak shook his head. "She won't."

. . .

Three hours later, they walked into the lobby of a Washington hotel filled with HAVE YOU SEEN THESE KIDS? posters, not unlike the one Caitlin had made for Nick, but with her and Mitch's faces on it instead.

They were recognized by the concierge immediately, and escorted to the teacher in charge.

"Do you have any idea how worried we were?" she asked. "We had the police scouring the city for you."

"We did exactly what you told us," Caitlin said, putting on her best ditz. "You told us to go to the mall, so we did."

The teacher threw up her arms. "Not that kind of mall. The National Mall! The park between the Lincoln Memorial and the Capitol Building."

"See?" said Mitch. "I *told* you we were in the wrong place."

"Oh," said Caitlin to the teacher. "You mean, like, with the really tall thing, right in the middle? You should have said so."

"That 'tall thing' is the Washington Monument," the teacher said. Then she looked over at Zak. "And who is this?"

"Uh," said Mitch, "this is, uh, Ace . . . Diamond."

Zak glared at him, but Caitlin went on. "We met him at the mall, y'know? And he brought us back. He lives, like, in Denver, so he'll be on our same flight tomorrow night."

"I will?" Zak said. "Oh, yeah, I will."

Zak got his own room. Mitch and Caitlin offered to hang with him for a while and play hearts, but he refused. "Nah, I need some time alone. You two scare me."

So Mitch went off with the boys he was rooming with, and Caitlin went with the girls sharing her room. But before they split up, Caitlin stopped Mitch.

"Hey," she said, "that stuff I said when I was trying to make you mad? You know that's not how I feel about you, right?"

He smiled at her. "Yeah, I know. But thanks for caring

enough to say it when I needed you to." He dropped the smile and added, "Anyway, that was the old Mitch you were talking about. I like the new one a whole lot better."

"Well, I like them both," Caitlin told him, and gave him a hug before she left.

17 MENTAL DETECTOR

Wayne Slate found that the business with the strange boy weighed heavily on him. So did the run-in with those two kids at the Princeton copy shop—who, for an instant, had looked familiar, and then not.

He had kept the flyer of the boy. He didn't know why, exactly. But when he thought back to their encounter, the oddest thing about it was a brief instant of recognition of the kid—not of who the kid was, but of who he looked like. He very distinctly reminded Wayne of himself at that age.

The past few months had been traumatic for him and Danny. But the haziness of his memories of Colorado Springs seemed more than just shock- and grief-related. He couldn't shake the feeling that there was something crucial he was missing.

To escape his thoughts, he decided to take Danny to the beach that weekend.

The Jersey Shore was not exactly like the beaches in Florida. And in May, even though the day was warm, the water was far too chilly for swimming.

"I don't like the sand," Danny said as he tried to build a sand castle. "It's too brown."

There weren't all that many people on the beach with them. Some couples, a few muscle-bound posers, an old man scouring the sand with a metal detector.

As the man moved closer with the device, Wayne Slate began to feel a sense of growing dread. There was a memory on the cusp of his mental horizon, trying to force its way through. An important and terrifying memory that seemed to peak every time the old man swung the metal detector toward their blanket.

It wasn't only him. Danny sensed it too.

"Dad," he said, looking up at him for some explanation, "I feel weird."

Wayne nodded, and glanced at the metal detector.

"Excuse me, sir," he said. "I seem to have dropped my keys in the sand. Do you think you could help me find them?"

The old man was happy to oblige, swinging the metal detector around them and over their blanket.

Now the sensation was even stronger. *The magnetic field,* thought Wayne. It was giving him the same feeling he'd had when they'd passed through the metal detector at the airport— a feeling he'd never said anything to Danny about.

He reached into his bag, grabbed a pen and a crumpled napkin he found on the bottom, and gave them to Danny.

"What do you want me to do with these?" Danny asked.

"In case you feel the urge to write something."

And though Danny didn't get it, he took the pen and napkin and stood at the ready anyway.

"No, over there," Wayne said to the man with the metal detector. "Over where my son is."

The man swung the metal detector closer to Danny, scanning the sand right near him.

Danny gasped, and began to write on the napkin.

Then he seemed to throw himself away from the magnetic field, as if it was just too much to bear.

Wayne reached into his pocket. "Will you look at that? My keys are right here. How silly of me."

The old man chuckled. "Happens to the best of us," he said, then continued along the beach in search of buried treasure.

As soon as the man was gone, all sense of lost memories vanished.

"Dad," Danny said, "I wrote something, but it's weird. It doesn't make any sense."

Wayne Slate took the napkin. In hastily scrawled block letters, Danny had written a simple sentence:

I HAVE A BROTHER AND HIS NAME IS NICK.

18 A SINGULARITY OF PURPOSE

Wayne Slate's older son—the son he didn't know he had—rode in a pale opalescent SUV that seemed to change color from moment to moment. Occasionally a passing driver would notice it and make a mental note to himself: *I want one like that.* Of course, the motorist would never be able to get it, at least not until the Accelerati licensed the electrostatic pigment technology to the automotive industry for a ridiculously high price.

While Nick was with Edison, he was stuck wearing Victorian fashions. For work out in the field he'd been offered his own Madagascan spider-silk suit, but he'd refused, insisting instead on a cotton polo shirt, jeans, and a light nylon jacket.

"You really should try it," Petula said, sitting next to him in the SUV. "Spider silk breathes when it's hot out and insulates in the cold." She wore an Accelerati blouse of seafoam green. "Wanna touch it?" she asked Nick.

The thought of touching anything that was touching Petula was beyond questionable. "I'll pass," he told her.

"Suit yourself," she said, and shrugged. "But if you're gonna be Accelerati, you're eventually going to have to buy the whole farm."

Nick looked out the window to avoid Petula's gaze. Originally he had agreed to wear the pin, and to be Accelerati in name only, in order to save his father and brother.

But here he was, actually working for them.

He could tell himself that Edison was the only one with the resources to make Tesla's machine work properly. He could also tell himself that the Accelerati represented more than the greedy desires of Alan Jorgenson. Still, none of that changed the fact that Nick was now doing the bidding of the very organization he had been trying to protect the world from.

He had never felt so divided.

"If I were you," Petula said, "I wouldn't try to get in touch with Mitch and Caitlin. Bringing them back into this would only hurt them."

"Really?" said Nick. "And who's going to hurt them? You, with your online theoretical jujitsu course?"

"Theoretical jujitsu is only used in self-defense," Petula said. "But there's an Accelerati enforcement division, and I wouldn't want to rub them the wrong way."

If only he could pick up a phone and call Caitlin just to talk to her, even if she told him he was an idiot for what he was doing, it would make him feel better.

But Edison was very strict about keeping Nick as isolated as possible. Even here in Colorado Springs, there was a whole team in a second SUV behind them to make sure he stuck to the plan.

"Why aren't you riding back there with them?" Nick asked Petula. "Why are you here with me?"

Petula looked away. "You won't always be this angry," she said. "Someday you'll realize I'm only trying to help you."

Nick wondered if Petula really believed that. It was hard to buy that she was trying to help anyone but herself. That's what made her a perfect Acceleratus. She was skilled at making herself believe that what was good for Petula was good for everyone else in the world.

But was Nick any better?

Things had been easier when the Accelerati were very clearly the enemy. Even if Nick didn't know *how* to fight them, he knew *whom* to fight. Now he didn't even know that. He couldn't even be sure there was an enemy at all.

No, that wasn't true. Time was everyone's enemy, because the copper asteroid was continuing to build up a deadly charge, and the machine was still the only way to discharge it.

When they arrived on the street where the man who'd bought the prism lived, there was a car in the driveway, indicating that someone was probably home.

As Nick, Petula, and the men in the second SUV piled out of their cars, Nick addressed them. "I'm going in alone."

The Accelerati seemed dubious.

So Nick made it very clear. "I'm going in alone, or we're not going in at all."

"We could go in without you," one of the Accelerati threatened.

"The Old Man left me in charge of this," Nick said as forcefully as he could. "And you don't even know what you're looking for. So you'll wait."

The Accelerati backed off, and Nick found it amazingly satisfying to be able to order them around.

"Well, I'm coming with you, right?" Petula said.

"I said I'm going in alone," Nick repeated. He turned and marched toward the front door.

The Accelerati, he knew, would tear the place up while looking for the prism, and bully the people inside, either physically or through subtle threats, until they got it. Nick had to believe he wasn't like them.

Edison had said he thought the Accelerati were capable of change. If that were true, Nick would be that change. He knocked on the door with confidence and a singularity of purpose.

The door was opened by a kid maybe six or seven years old. He took one look at Nick, said, "Get lost!" and slammed the door.

Considering Nick's previous run-in at this house, he concluded that this was an obnoxious family. He pounded again. Then a second time, and a third, making it clear they could ignore him all they wanted, but he wasn't going to go away.

Finally the man who had purchased the prism in the first place came to the door. He was perhaps sixty, bald on top, with a rim of gray hair.

Before he could speak, Nick barged past him into the house. If they wanted him out, they would have to physically throw him out.

"I don't know what you want," the man said, "but you can't come in here."

Nick ignored him. "We both know why I'm here," Nick said, "so don't play games. I sold you something that I need back."

"You can't have it," the man said, and he turned and stormed deeper into the house.

Nick pursued, only to be ambushed. A twenty-something guy grabbed him and held him while a kid his own age started punching him in the stomach.

Nick kicked high, breaking a lamp, but also connecting with the teen, bringing him down.

"Careful," said a guy in his thirties who was holding a baby.

The seven-year-old shouted, "Beat him up! Beat him up! It's all his fault!"

The teen, having hit his head on the table when he fell, was still rubbing his wound, giving Nick a moment to break free.

He had only an instant to take in the situation. There were

seven people in that living room. The man with the baby, the obnoxious seven-year-old, the kid his age, the twenty-something dude, the guy from his garage sale, and an extremely old man sitting on a rocking chair in the corner, mumbling to himself. They were obviously all related. It was a big family of all men. The house didn't seem large enough to accommodate so many people and so much clutter.

"Hear me out!" Nick said. They all hesitated. "The thing you got in my garage sale, the prism inside a vacuum tube, is part of a very important machine, and I need it back."

"What makes you think we want to give it to you?" asked the man holding the baby.

"That EMP that knocked out the power happened because you wouldn't give it to me the first time I came."

"That's not our problem," said the twenty-something guy.

"I'm willing to pay for it," Nick said, and he reached into his pocket. He had convinced Edison to allow him to bargain. His hand shook when he held out the bills, because they were all thousands. "What did you pay for it? Forty dollars? Here's twenty thousand to get it back. That's a pretty good deal, if you ask me."

The man with the baby looked toward the sixty-year-old, who must have been his father. "That would really help with expenses."

"The cost of food alone is killing us," grumbled Great-Grandpa, all the way in the corner.

"But we can't give it back," said the kid Nick's age. "If we do, we'll never—"

"Shut up," said the sixty-year-old, who seemed to be in charge.

"You know what? Just give it to him," said the twenty-something. "See if I care."

"Easy for you to say!" shouted Great-Grandpa, trying to rise from his chair but unable to. "You have your whole life in front of you!"

"Yeah! And I won't waste it like you did."

"Here we go again," said the seven-year-old. "Blah, blah, blah."

"Let's just take the money and then kick his butt out of here," said the kid Nick's age.

"Stop it!" insisted the man in charge, and he turned to Nick. "The answer is no. It will always be no. Now get out of here if you know what's good for you."

Nick put the money back in his pocket. "All right, then, if that's the way you want it." And he reached into his other pocket and pulled out something that looked distinctly like a weapon, because that's exactly what it was.

Edison had agreed to let Nick bargain for the prism, under one condition: that Nick also went in there armed with an Accelerati weapon to protect himself.

"What does it do?" Nick had asked.

"Let's just say it will remove the subject from the situation," Edison had told him.

The family froze when they saw the weapon.

"Don't you understand?" yelled Nick. "I need it to save the world!"

"Maybe the world shouldn't be saved," grumbled Great-Grandpa, shaking his cane from his seat.

Nick had never seen a more bitter collection of people. The man in charge looked at the weapon and shrugged.

"Then shoot us," he said. "We'll all be better off."

Nick leveled the weapon at him. "I'm not joking," he said.

Then the twenty-something guy lunged at him. Nick swung the weapon toward him, and out of reflex, fired.

The guy vanished. All that remained were his clothes and the earring he had been wearing, which fell to the floor.

"No!" yelled the seven-year-old.

"What did you do to him?" shouted the teen.

The baby started crying, and his father tried to comfort him.

Nick was as horrified as the rest of them. "I . . . I don't know," he stuttered. Then he cleared his throat and spoke more firmly. "But I'll do it again if you don't give me the prism."

Just a moment's more hesitation, and the guy in charge put his hand on his bald head. Then he reached into a cabinet, pulled out a little velvet bag, and handed it to Nick. Inside was the glass vacuum tube containing the prism.

"Just go," the man said. "Get out of here."

Nick dug in his pocket for the wad of cash. When he fished it out, the clip opened, and the bills fell to the floor. "Keep it," he said, but no one went to pick them up.

"Money can't save us," Great-Grandpa said.

Nick looked at the prism. Had these people been unhappy before it had come into their lives, or was misery the only gift it had brought?

"What does it do?" Nick asked the gray-haired man.

"You'll have to find that out for yourself," he said.

Nick backed out the door, holding the weapon on them with shaking hands, fearing that any one of them might leap on him and take it back. Once outside, he ran to the SUV.

"Did you get it?" Petula asked.

Nick held up the velvet sleeve. One of the Accelerati moved to grab it, but Nick put it back into his jacket pocket. *Mine*, he wanted to say. Instead he said, "Just leave it with me. I need to study it, so I can figure out how it works."

They got into their respective cars. Nick held his silence until he was alone with Petula.

"I think I killed somebody," he confessed, his face pale.

"With what?"

Nick pulled out the weapon and showed her.

Petula laughed. "No you didn't. You just gave him a spatial hiccup. In twenty minutes he'll appear back in the exact same spot, a little bit confused and a whole lot naked."

"Are you sure?"

"Yeah. We call it 'birthday-suiting.'"

Nick handed the weapon to her in disgust. He had told himself he wouldn't bully those people, that he would reason with them, and with reason he would get what he wanted.

But in the end, he was nothing more than another Accelerati thug, bending innocent people to his will.

19 HONK IF YOU LOVE TESLA

While Nick was bending innocent people to his will, Caitlin, Mitch, and Zak were a few miles away in Memorial Park, standing in front of Tesla's ruined historical marker. It had been run down a few weeks earlier when they were escaping from the Accelerati and the angry tornado filled with angrier felines.

"Don't ask," Caitlin told Zak when he wanted more information about that particular fiasco. There were parts of the story Caitlin chose not to share with him. As far as she was concerned, they were best forgotten by all.

"And we're here because . . . ?" Zak questioned.

"Because I said the answers were in Tesla's lab," Mitch told him. "And my predictions are always right when I'm angry."

Zak shook his head in what seemed to Caitlin a mixture of amazement and disbelief. "Someone ought to do a study of you. You definitely have pistons firing in alternate dimensions." And then he looked around. "You think it's safe to be out in the open like this?"

"The Accelerati are busy excavating the steel ring around Nick's house," Mitch said. "I'm sure they know we're back in Colorado Springs. If they really wanted to nab us, they'd have done it at the airport. I'd say right now they've got bigger fish to nuke."

"Good point," Caitlin said. "Let's hope they see us like ants at a picnic. Until we're in the potato salad, we're somebody else's problem." She looked around to get her bearings, then pointed north. "Nick once told me Tesla's old lab was up this street. There's just a house there now, at the corner of Foote and Kiowa."

They left the park, and as they approached the house they could see about a dozen people camped out on the sidewalk, to the chagrin of the guard dogs on the other side of the wrought-iron fence.

"Who are all these people?" asked Zak.

"I don't know," said Caitlin, a little bit worried. The crowd did not appear to be Accelerati. This was something else.

As they got closer, they noticed the people were wearing T-shirts with pictures of Tesla and Wardenclyffe Tower. One woman had weird Tesla-coil earrings. One guy held a sign that read HONK IF YOU LOVE TESLA. And people were indeed honking as they drove past.

"I think your secret is out," said Zak.

"This can't have anything to do with us," Mitch said.

A man wearing a tinfoil-covered baseball cap approached them and asked, "Are you part of Team Tesla?"

Caitlin remembered Nick telling her that the occasional Tesla fanatic showed up at this house. She supposed that the EMP had dragged out a fresh slew of them.

"Uh, kinda," Caitlin said.

"Tesla's cryonically frozen head is under Colorado Springs, you know," said the woman with the weird earrings.

"No," said Caitlin, "that's Walt Disney."

"Walt Disney is under Colorado Springs?" the woman asked, surprised.

"No, under Disneyland," Caitlin said.

"Actually, that's not true," Zak added. "I personally debunked that myth about Walt."

"We believe Tesla's coming back," said one of the fanatics, with eyes and a hairdo that made it look like he'd been struck by lightning. "The electromagnetic pulse proves it."

"Isn't that why you're here?" asked the man in the tinfoil hat.

And it occurred to Caitlin that *their* reason for being here wasn't all that different from the loonies'. *Who's crazier,* she thought, *those who believe in the outlandish, or those who live it?*

"We're determined to stay here until the dude who owns this house releases Tesla's frozen head to us."

"Ri-i-ight," said Caitlin. She wondered if it had occurred to these people that cryonic head freezing wasn't around when Tesla was alive.

She looked at the house, and from behind the curtains a man peered out nervously, probably wondering why his Realtor had never told him his house had been built on sacred ground.

Zak turned to Mitch. "Got any clue why we're here with the crazies, Magic 8 Ball? Do we gotta slap you around some more to get an answer?"

"I don't know," said Mitch. "It's the right place, but I'm not sure what we're supposed to do."

While Caitlin and Mitch were baffled, Zak had an inkling of what needed to be done. The crazies had such a limited point of view, it was as if they had blinders on. They couldn't see the forest for the trees, or the lamppost for the bulbs, as it were. What was required was an out-of-the-box thinker, and that was Zak's specialty. He looked beyond the crazies to all the homes down the street that they weren't bothering.

"What we need is a wider perspective," he said. Then he

moved away from the Tesla groupies, sat on the edge of the curb a dozen yards away, and pulled out his laptop.

Mitch and Caitlin sat beside him, trying to see what he was up to.

He accessed a satellite map of Colorado Springs, then zoomed in closer. "There's Memorial Park; here's where we are. Sometimes, you can see the remains of old buildings easier from up above—the outline of foundations, rows of trees that were planted years and years ago, marking boundaries that no longer exist." He shifted the angle of the view. "Look here." He pointed. "All these homes are built on a normal grid. But check out this old low wall running behind them. And this long hedge—it cuts at an odd angle and then continues across the street."

He pulled a stylus across his screen. It was like connect the dots. "And this pylon in this backyard." He drew another line. "All these things predate these homes." When he was done, they were looking at a seven-sided figure.

"Hmm," said Zak. "A heptagon."

Mitch gasped. "I've seen that before! It's one of the symbols that was on my Shut Up 'N Listen."

"These were the property fences around the lab. It was bigger than just this one house." Zak drew a dot right in the middle of the heptagon. "This is the center."

And that center wasn't the house that the Tesla groupies were harassing. It was a different house, three doors down.

So Zak, Caitlin, and Mitch knocked on that door instead.

The woman who opened the door was plump and friendly, and while not old, seemed somewhat well established, like the tree in her front yard that was pushing up the sidewalk. "Can I help you?" she asked.

"We're sorry to bother you," said Caitlin, in her nicest possible voice. "This might sound crazy, but . . ."

The woman looked at them warmly and said, "I'll bet you're looking for the secret tunnel!" She smiled and took a step back. "I'll show you. Wipe your feet on the way in."

The woman led them to a wardrobe in her basement. "I've always known it was there, of course," the woman said. "But no one ever came to ask about it. Instead they bother that poor man down the street."

"So you're telling me it's through the wardrobe?" Zak asked, incredulous. "Are we going to encounter a lion and a witch?"

"No, of course not. The tunnel's *behind* it."

"Have you ever gone down it?" Mitch asked.

"Heavens no. I wouldn't want to get bitten by rabid rats or something."

Caitlin and Zak both looked at Mitch, as if somehow all diseased rodents were suddenly his fault. Then, together, the three kids pushed the wardrobe aside to reveal a wooden door.

"I figured it was something left over from the mining days," the woman went on. "It gets a bit drafty here in the winter. But most of the time I just forget it's there."

They pulled open the door, and a gust of earthy air breathed out.

"Do you really want to do this?" asked Zak.

"I think we have to," said Caitlin.

Zak, because he was the oldest, chose to lead the way.

"Oh, this is so exciting!" the woman said. "Tell me if you find anything interesting in there. Like dead bodies." Then she closed the door behind them, leaving them in total darkness.

They turned on their flashlight apps and held their phones

in front of them. The tunnel was roughly hewn out of the earth but perfectly straight.

They slowly ventured forward.

"If we find Tesla's frozen head," said Zak, "I'm so outta here."

Nikola Tesla's head was not, in fact, frozen.

His ashes are in a golden sphere—Tesla's favorite geometrical shape—at the Nikola Tesla Museum in Belgrade, Serbia.

In 2014, the historic Church of St. Sava formally requested that the ashes be moved there to join the remains of other Serbian heroes—and to protect Tesla's remains from "suspected devil worshipers." The request caused great consternation among scientists, who insisted that his remains belonged in a museum. It sparked a heated "Leave Tesla Alone" Internet campaign.

Tesla himself remained silent on the matter.

Caitlin was not a fan of dark tunnels. In the movies, they usually heralded the untimely death of secondary characters. They were full of booby traps, or zombies, or booby-trapped zombies, and, of course, the aforementioned rabid rats.

If she had known what she was looking for, she would have felt a little bit better about pushing forward into the darkness. But Mitch's prophecies were always open-ended, and always led to more questions than solutions.

After about two hundred yards, Zak said, "There's something up ahead."

A dozen yards farther, the tunnel opened into a circular room with six other tunnel openings, all heading out like spokes on a wheel. There was no question that this was a structure Tesla had built, and it had lain hidden all these years.

"Mark which tunnel is ours," Caitlin told Mitch. "We need to remember the way we came in."

Mitch scratched a line in the dirt with his shoe, and they moved to the center. There, in a shaft of light, stood a dark lump that didn't look at all inviting.

Caitlin inched closer, shining her phone's flashlight at it. It was a badly rusted metal platform narrower at the top than at the bottom. And sitting on top of it was a black object with ancient cobwebs covering it like a shroud. Caitlin brushed them away to reveal—

"A telephone?" said Zak.

"No way!" said Mitch.

It was an odd-looking thing, not square or rectangular, but circular, with a thick, curly wire leading to a heavy handset attached to the side. Six large vents were cut into the sides, presumably to let out heat, and a crank stuck out of the back. On its face was a round dial with a single finger hole, and the dial was surrounded by a series of silver notched, concentric circles.

"I've seen something like this in the Princeton computer lab," said Zak. "It's one of the first telephones. But it didn't have all of those silver rings around the dial."

All the retro-phones Caitlin had seen had ten finger holes in the dial, not just one. There was something ominous about that single hole, as disturbing as the eye of a Cyclops.

"What's it doing here?" Mitch asked. "And where is *here*, anyway?"

"No idea, and no idea," said Caitlin. This was most certainly a Teslanoid object, yet not part of the machine. Her best judgment told her to leave it alone, but judgment was a weak force when pitted against curiosity. She began turning the hand crank, generating visible sparks through the vent holes.

"You probably shouldn't touch it until you know what it does," said Zak, always the sensible one.

"I know what it does," Caitlin said. "It's a phone."

After giving it a few more cranks, she lifted the receiver. Even though it didn't seem connected to anything, there was a dial tone loud enough for everyone to hear.

"Hmm," said Mitch. "Wireless."

"That can't be right," Zak said. "They didn't have wireless back then."

"Wrong," said Caitlin. "Tesla was experimenting with it decades before the rest of the world."

"But," Mitch said, "why would it be down here instead of—"

Caitlin realized the answer at the exact same moment as Mitch: they were directly beneath Nick's house.

She tried to peer up through the narrow shaft, which went up and up. This chamber was a part of the machine, she realized, even if the telephone wasn't.

Caitlin put the receiver to her ear and put her finger in the dial hole.

"Should I?" she asked.

"No!" said Zak.

"No," said Mitch.

But Caitlin did it anyway.

The dial spun around and clicked back. Then a very nasal woman's voice spoke through the receiver. "Please hold while I connect you with your party."

On the other end, the phone began to ring. Once . . . twice . . . three times.

Finally someone picked up, and a heavily accented voice said, "I'm very busy today. What do you want?"

"Who is this?" asked Caitlin.

And the voice said, "This is Nikola Tesla."

Time travel is an irritating endeavor. Paradoxes and advance knowledge of the future are only the minor headaches.

Which is why time tends to protect itself. As Petula noted with the box camera, you can only become part of the picture and not change it, lest our universe be destroyed, leaving behind cranky splinters of reality. The kind of places where your nightmares eat you.

Although the laws of physics might actually allow for time travel, it's improbable, and a real pain in the black hole.

Communication with another time, however, is an entirely different matter. If you're not convinced, ask yourself this: Have you ever spoken on your phone, only to hear your own voice echo back at you a split second later? And did you get the uncanny feeling that you were hearing what you said before you said it?

Perhaps there's a reason for that.

20 ANYTHING BUT WONDERLAND

Ten minutes before Caitlin made her phone call through time, Nick decided to visit his wrecked house.

It hadn't been his original intention to stop by the house. There was really nothing there for him now. But after retrieving the prism, when the SUV neared his old corner, he happened to glance at the ruins. He saw all the yellow excavation equipment—Caterpillars, backhoes, and the like—and he found himself tweaked by a morbid curiosity. More than that, he felt a longing for a simpler time before things got so complicated. He had to take a closer look, if only to say good-bye to the place that had been, for such a short time, his home.

"We have an appointment with Ms. Planck," Petula reminded him.

"Yeah," said Nick. "I bet she wants to take credit for getting the prism. I thought I knew her, but I guess I don't know anybody, do I?"

"She's better than Jorgenson," Petula said, but she couldn't look him in the eye as she did.

"Pull over," Nick ordered the driver with as much authority as he could muster. "As I'm the highest-ranking Accelerati here, you have to do as I say."

The driver couldn't argue with that, and neither could Petula.

All the homes in the immediate vicinity of the shattered

Victorian had been evacuated. Police crime-scene tape prevented access, and for those not held back by the tape, an electrified fence had been erected.

"Why don't you leave the prism with me," Petula said, reaching out her good hand.

"Forget it. Nobody touches it but me, until I give it to Edison."

"Have it your way," said Petula. "As always, I was just trying to be helpful."

When Nick stepped out of the SUV, the lone Acceleratus standing guard didn't quite know what to do.

"The Old Man told me to inspect the site and give him a progress report," Nick told him, and he let Nick through. Easy as that.

From this angle, it looked like all the heavy equipment was digging a massive moat around the house. But when he looked closer, he could see they had completely exposed the enormous metal ring that his father had found while planting a tree. The ditch encircled the entire property, even going beyond the boundaries a bit.

The ring was shiny, in spite of the fact that it was covered in mud and dirt. It was almost a foot thick, and at least ten feet tall. Nick assumed they would take it, like everything else, to Edison's lab in New Jersey, but how exactly they would transport such a huge thing was beyond him.

The house now looked like a broken-down castle on its own island. The attic listed sideways, having fully collapsed into the second floor, and half of the second floor had collapsed into the first.

There was a makeshift plank bridge over the ditch allowing access to the house. But no one seemed interested in the structural remains anymore. Nick imagined they would eventually bulldoze it, leaving no sign that it had ever been there.

Poor Great-Aunt Greta, he thought as he approached the threshold. All her fine things trampled by science.

"Hey, don't go in there!" one of the construction workers shouted. But Nick ignored him, pushed his way through the front door, which was off its hinges, and regarded what was left of his living room.

Much of the furniture had been removed by the Accelerati so it could be searched for other hidden artifacts. Rains over the past few weeks had ruined what was left.

Nick, filled with a sense of melancholy and loss, moved through the broken timbers and crumbling plaster. He didn't know why he should feel this way; he had lived here for less than two months. He guessed that being in the house reminded him of the much deeper disaster that had taken the life of his mother and ruined his lifelong home in Florida.

Two homes destroyed in the same year. Twice his life had been thrown into upheaval. He still didn't know where things would settle, but he knew he had to find a way to leave it behind him.

There was someone behind her. . . .

He forced the thought away. Reliving that horrible night, even with this new uncertain wrinkle, would bring him nothing but misery. There were more important things to be done right now. Moving forward was his only choice.

The door to the basement was in splinters, but Nick made his way down the staircase, which was still intact. What little they had salvaged from their house in Tampa was down there in boxes, still smelling like smoke.

He took one box off a shelf and began to sift through it. Singed pictures. A baseball trophy Nick had won, the plastic ballplayer on top half melted, yet still his father had chosen to save it. His father who could no longer remember him.

Who am I now? Nick wondered. *Not the person I was a year ago, not the person I was a month ago, not the person I'll be tomorrow.* Today, all Nick could feel was the void of transition between being one Nick and becoming another.

As he stood there in silence, pondering his place in the universe, he heard voices coming from somewhere beneath his feet. And as he listened, the voices became clearer. Was it his imagination, or was that Caitlin?

There was a grate in the concrete floor; its screws had long since rusted, so he was able to pull it out easily. As he leaned over the hole, he noticed that he cast a shadow. He looked up to see that light was streaming down on him from the grate in the floor above, and the grate above that one, leading all the way up to the ruins of the attic.

There was a vertical shaft under him that led to someplace beneath the basement. A sewer perhaps? No, because there was definitely someone speaking, and it definitely did sound like Caitlin. Nick leaned over farther, and farther still. Then, like Alice at the rabbit hole, he lost his balance and fell in.

What lay below was anything but Wonderland.

"Could you please repeat that?" Caitlin said, her heart pounding as she held the old phone. "I don't think I heard you right."

"I said this is Nikola Tesla."

Caitlin Westfield was not the kind of girl to freeze. Deer in the headlights was simply not a part she played. She was quick thinking, quick acting, and prided herself on her ability to keep her head while others panicked. But at that moment, Caitlin could do nothing but hold the phone to her ear, with an abiding inability to speak.

"Hello," said Tesla, "are you there? Who is this? As I said, I'm very busy. If you have business with me, then speak up."

Finally, she found her voice. "Hello, Mr. Tesla," she said very slowly.

Mitch and Zak gasped.

"My name is Caitlin Westfield, and I need your help."

Just then, a figure came crashing through the grate up above, landing on the phone and disconnecting the call.

Nick fell onto something hard that dug into his side. He yelped in pain, and suddenly Caitlin was there, helping him up, as amazed to see him as he was to see her.

"Nick!" she shouted, throwing her arms around him before he even knew where he was.

"No way!" said Mitch, who was also there, patting him on the back. "It *is* you!"

But then Caitlin looked at the object he had fallen on. "You disconnected the call!"

"What call?" said Nick.

"I was just talking to Tesla!"

Nick considered that this might not really be happening. It could be the result of a concussion. "Am I dreaming?" he pondered aloud. "Did I knock myself out?"

"We all did," said a tall black kid. "I'm still waiting to regain consciousness in my dorm room."

"Who are you?" Nick asked the stranger.

"Brandon Gunther's alligator," said Mitch, making Nick wonder once more if he had knocked himself out.

"We'll explain later," Caitlin said.

Nick remembered what was in his jacket pocket. He reached in, grabbed the velvet sheath, and slid out the vacuum tube with the prism at its center. Luckily, it hadn't broken. He didn't know what he would have done if it had.

"Is that what I think it is?" Caitlin asked.

"Yeah," Nick said, "I got the man who bought it to give it up." But he didn't tell her how.

"That's fantastic!" Caitlin said. "Now we can make sure the Accelerati never get it."

"Um," Nick said, "it's not that simple."

Mitch took a step closer to him. "Nick, is that a pin on your collar . . . ?"

"It's not what you think," said Nick, backing up slightly, but he didn't sound convincing even to himself.

Caitlin stepped forward and flipped up his collar, revealing the Accelerati pin hidden there. She gasped. "Nick, no!"

"So he's one of them too," said Zak.

"No!" Nick said. "It's not like that. Really, it's not."

"Then prove it," Caitlin said, and she held out her hand. "If you haven't switched sides, give me the prism and let's get out of here."

Part of him wanted to give it to her; part of him wanted to give it to Edison. Part of him just wanted to drop it and run, and yet another part wanted to keep it for himself. He needed time to think. He held the prism up, just out of Caitlin's reach . . .

. . . and up above, through the series of ducts leading to his attic, a shaft of sunlight poured down and hit the prism. In a flash of light, Nick found himself surging down a tunnel away from everyone.

But it wasn't just one tunnel; it was many tunnels at the same time. And Nick instinctively knew he was in trouble.

Caitlin shielded her eyes from the sudden surge from the prism. The room swam with a rainbow of colors for an instant, and when she looked again, the prism was lying on the ground, just outside the beam of sunlight. Nick had disappeared.

"Nick!" she called. "Where are you?" She craned her neck around, but he was nowhere to be seen.

"I think I saw him," Zak said, pointing. "He was running down that tunnel."

"No," Mitch said, pointing to a different tunnel, "it was that one!"

Then, up above, they heard angry voices.

"He went this way!"

"Look, there's a shaft!"

"He must have gone down that duct!"

"Nick!" Caitlin called again, but no answer came from any of the tunnels.

Up above, one of the Accelerati was already starting to shimmy through the narrow opening, blocking the sunlight.

"We've got to get out of here," said Zak, "or—"

And Mitch finished for him, "—or else."

Zak grabbed the phone, Caitlin scooped up the prism, slipping it back into its protective sleeve, and Mitch found the tunnel that he had marked when they entered.

"This way!" he said, and they hurried into the dark.

But when they got to the far end, they found the strangest thing: a baby sat before the old wooden door at the end of the tunnel, wrapped in a blanket and crying, as if he had been left there only seconds earlier.

Nick, dazed and disoriented, found himself wandering around the lowest level of a parking garage, wondering where he'd left his car. Then he realized he didn't have a car, although he should have one. He ran his fingers through his thin, graying hair, and knew that something was wrong, but he couldn't quite comprehend what it was.

Nick, uneasy and unstable, burst out of an abandoned barn, annoyed at whatever practical joker had left him in there. He stroked his trim goatee, adjusted his shades, and walked out into the bright light of day.

Nick, troubled and teetering, wandered through a secret passageway in the town dump. Wrecks and old appliances were piled up all around him. He was frightened to be alone in such a scary place, and he started to whimper, wishing his daddy would come get him.

Nick, bewildered and bemused, climbed the drainage tunnel beneath Uncle Wilbur Fountain in Acacia Park. He pulled himself up the metal ladder as best he could, but his aged arm muscles were weak, and his legs ached. He stroked his long gray beard with thin, wrinkled fingers and wondered how he had gotten here, and where he had left his teeth.

Nick, fearful and flabbergasted, emerged from a manhole. A car honked and swerved to avoid him as he stood up on the street and staggered away, feeling something like Rip Van Winkle, as if he had been asleep for twenty years.

Nick, stunned and shocked, stumbled out of a cave in the hills overlooking Colorado Springs, at least a mile away from where he'd been just a moment ago. He looked himself over. On the outside he was exactly the same, and yet he felt shredded in a way he could not define. Something dreadful had happened, and he was afraid to find out what it all meant.

And the baby just cried.

21 NICK, NICK, **NICK**, *NICK*, NICK, NICK & NICK

"All the world's a stage . . ." wrote Shakespeare, "and one man in his time plays many parts."

He then went on to enumerate seven deeply unflattering stages in a man's life: the puking infant; the whiny schoolboy; the lovesick teen; the angry young man; the harried businessman; the graying windbag; and finally, the toothless codger entering a second infancy before he dies.

Cheerful, Shakespeare was not.

But the bard did not invent the concept of these different stages. He was relaying in coded form a truth hailing back to ancient days, when Aristotle proposed this immutable law: every human being is composed of the braided strands of several distinct identities.

This perfectly balanced composition was what Nikola Tesla had apparently sought to shatter with his prism. But Nick Slate had no clue about that.

Not a single one of him.

22 PETULA, OFFENSIVE

Petula was not skilled at damage control. She was the one usually causing the damage that someone else had to control.

So when the Accelerati within the perimeter of Nick's ruined house started shouting to one another, panicking that they couldn't find him, she closed the door of the SUV and instructed the driver to put on loud music.

Fact: She was supposed to watch Nick.

Fact: Even though she had tried, the other Accelerati would not let her through the electrified fence into the restricted area.

Fact: She had specifically requested that Nick leave the tube-encased prism with her, but neither Ms. Planck nor Edison had given her the authority to command him to do so.

Probable fact: The Accelerati within the restricted zone were morons. Right now they were no doubt terrified of alerting the Grand Acceleratus that Nick had disappeared. Ms. Planck was not one to shoot the messenger, but she would aim wherever the messenger was pointing. Which meant that whoever notified her first and cast the blame elsewhere would be in the clear. So Petula phoned her and told her as clearly and succinctly as she could, "Nick went into his old house and your bozos lost him."

Certainly there would be more Accelerati to be "disciplined" for this. It was comforting to know she would not be among them.

Ms. Planck arrived on the scene with an entourage of pearlescent Bentleys instead of SUVs, because, with $750 million as collateral, she could.

Jorgenson's problem was that he thought too small. Soon all the Accelerati would be equipped with similar vehicles. And people everywhere, without even knowing who they were, would be aware that there was a group of individuals out there who were better than them.

Petula was waiting dutifully at the fence when Ms. Planck stormed forward, fury in her eyes.

Petula took the offensive. "They wouldn't let me in because I didn't have security clearance," she said. "If I had, Nick would still be here."

"And the prism?" Ms. Planck asked.

"He took it with him," Petula told her. "And I didn't rank high enough to stop him."

Ms. Planck ordered the guards to open the gate, and beckoned to Petula.

"Now you do," she said simply, and together they walked toward the disaster zone.

All around them, Accelerati were scrambling, looking under every bit of rubble, as if Nick might be playing hide-and-seek.

"Edison's going to be mad," Petula said, twisting the knife ever so slightly.

"It's his own fault for trusting the boy," Ms. Planck said.

Petula shrugged. "True. But you'll get blamed."

Ms. Planck threw her a dagger-gaze to deflect the twisting knife, but she couldn't deny that the girl was right.

A nervous Acceleratus approached them. "There are tunnels beneath the house," he said, out of breath, as if he'd just run a marathon. "We've sent teams down each one to find him."

"They won't," Planck said. "He's smarter than any of you. But we can't let this halt our operation. The helicopters are already on their way."

"Helicopters? Why?" asked Petula.

"You'll see soon enough," Ms. Planck answered.

And in the distance, they could hear the steady *thwap-thwap-thwap* of rotating blades. Four heavy-lifting Chinooks flew toward them, all of them pearlescent white.

It was an operation that could not be done stealthily. The best the Accelerati could do was coerce the media to look the other way, as they had when the meteorite had landed in Danny's glove.

Neighbors for miles around came to gawk as the four helicopters, with the help of four massive harnesses, rose in unison, lifting the shiny titanium ring, ten feet tall and one hundred feet in diameter. For a moment the ring hovered above the wreckage of Nick's old house like a silver halo, and then the helicopters spirited it away to the east.

In the desert twenty miles away stood a building large enough to hold the ring inside. From some angles the building looked like an overly tall airplane hangar. But from other angles it gave the distinct impression of being a giant clothes dryer.

23 YOUR PARTY IS NOT AVAILABLE

When Caitlin's mother opened the door to see her daughter holding a baby and standing next to a boy she didn't know, her response was the same as any mother's would be:

"Oh, dear."

"Mom," Caitlin said, "this is Zak."

The young man reached out to take her hand. "Pleased to meet you," he said.

"Oh, dear," said Mrs. Westfield once more.

Coming up the walk was a boy she *did* know—Mitch, holding what looked like a very old telephone. "Hey, Mrs. W!" he said.

And so, with no explanation forthcoming, she asked the obvious question.

"Caitlin, honey, why are you holding a baby?"

"Oh, this?" Caitlin said, as if noticing it for the first time. "It's not a baby." At which the baby smiled. "I mean, it *is* a baby. But it's for a school project."

"Yeah," said Zak. "For our Life Skills class. Everyone volunteers their infant siblings for a day."

"It was Principal Watt's idea," Caitlin added.

And although it sounded ill-advised, who was Mrs. Westfield to question the wisdom of a middle school administrator?

She let them in and the kids went straight to Caitlin's room and closed the door, to perform whatever experiments on the baby the project required.

Once they were in the room, Mitch set the old telephone on Caitlin's desk.

"How do you know it was Tesla on the other end?" he asked.

Caitlin shrugged. "He said so, and he sounded very Tesla-ish." She laid the baby on her bed.

"Better be careful," Zak said, "that baby has no diaper."

"What do you mean? Babies always have diapers."

"Not this one," said Zak. "That's just a blanket."

"Actually," said Mitch, "I don't think it's a blanket."

And he was right. The baby was wrapped in a blue polo shirt. The baby looked around and cooed obliviously.

"Oh. My. God," said Caitlin, a girl who generally despised people who said "oh my God." "Nick, is that you?"

The baby just coughed once and put his fist in his mouth, then turned his head. If he was Nick, he didn't seem to know it. He just knew his fist tasted good.

"Are you saying that thing made him regress into infancy?" asked Zak, his voice dripping with either wonder or sarcasm, it was hard to tell.

"Maybe . . ." said Caitlin. She suspected there was more to it than that, though she couldn't figure out what.

"But I told you," Mitch said, "I saw Nick running down a different tunnel."

"Well, whatever the prism did, there's got to be a way to reverse it," Caitlin said, checking to make sure it was still in her pocket. "Somehow . . ."

They looked at one another, unsure what to do, until Zak said, "Gee, if only we had a mysterious device that would let us talk to the man who invented it."

Caitlin scowled at him. "You think you're so smart."

Once again she picked up the receiver, put her finger in the single hole, and dialed.

Just as before, she reached a nasal-sounding operator, who connected her, only to be met with a busy signal.

"I'm sorry, your party is not available," the operator said, and hung up.

When one is shredded into seven different versions of oneself, there is really only one place to go for comfort-food consolation: Beef-O-Rama.

Since Nick was still, in most ways, Nick, the various versions of him all had the same idea. While the youngest was incapable of leaving Caitlin's room, and the oldest, for the life of him, couldn't remember where Beef-O-Rama was, the other five converged on the spot, not even knowing the others existed.

It wasn't as if they all felt like Nick at fourteen. To the older Nicks, being fourteen seemed like it was many years ago, and yet they had no memories between then and now—just a sense of amnesia clouding all the years of their adult lives.

The seven-year-old Nick could only remember dreaming of being a teenager, because for him it hadn't yet happened. The only one who felt fully at home in his own skin was the one-seventh of himself that actually *was* fourteen, and yet deep inside he felt an unpleasant thinning, as if he were made of little more than foam that could wash away in the rain.

At first they didn't recognize one another. They each took a seat at the counter, until all five of them were sitting side by side. It was only when they saw that they had all ordered the same thing—a chocolate malt and cheese fries—and looked around, that they figured something was up. Especially when they realized they were all wearing the same clothes.

"I'm scared," said the youngest Nick, his seven-year-old eyes beginning to tear up.

The hipster-looking Nick, age twenty-something, put his hand on little Nick's shoulder. "It's gonna be okay," he said.

The Nick in his thirties asked the waitress for a booth in the corner, and the five piled in to make sense of their fractured existence.

Very quickly it became evident that they needed to find a new way of identifying themselves. Never was the word *Nick-name* more appropriate.

Fourteen-year-old Nick remained just Nick, while the seven-year-old became Little Nicky. "My mommy calls me Nicky," he said. "But . . . I think something bad happened to her . . . didn't it?"

The others chose not to answer.

The hipster twenty-something with the goatee answered to BeatNick.

The thirty-something, who sported a full but well-trimmed dark beard, chose to call himself Nicholas.

And the opinionated Nick in his fifties, with thinning gray hair and horrifying bushy muttonchops, was dubbed Nickelback, because no one particularly liked him.

Recalling there were seven tunnels, they quickly deduced that two of them were missing and roughly estimated what their ages would be—a very old man, and a baby (whom they agreed to call Old St. Nick and SputNick respectively).

"We need to find them," said Nick.

"Maybe they'll find us," said Nicholas.

"Not likely, especially not the baby," said Nickelback.

Their conversation, as one might expect among the various factions of oneself, was heated and animated.

No other patrons were listening, as they were too concerned

with the protesters outside chanting against nutria meat. But had people been listening—this is what they would have heard:

NICKELBACK: As the most senior of us, I'll be in charge.

BEATNICK: Nice try, old man.

NICHOLAS: This ought to be a democracy. We all get an equal vote.

LITTLE NICKY: I'm too young to vote.

NICK: Listen, we need to let Caitlin and Mitch know what happened.

NICKELBACK: What we need to do is get back to the Accelerati before they tear the town apart looking for us!

NICK: Looking for *me*, you mean. They don't know about "us."

LITTLE NICKY: My shake's all melted, can I get another?

NICKELBACK: You need more sugar like a hole in the head.

BEATNICK: Listen, mutton-man, you are not his father. Go ahead, Nicky, order as many shakes as you want.

NICHOLAS: Can we please stay on point? We have a lot to discuss.

NICK: Like how we're all going to become one again.

NICKELBACK: If that's even possible.

LITTLE NICKY: But I don't want to be you. I don't want to be any of you.

NICK: We can't change who we're going to be. Just how we get there.

NICHOLAS: Well said.

NICKELBACK: No one's going to get anywhere if we don't reunite ourselves. I say we take it to the Accelerati. Edison will know what to do.

BEATNICK: Is that all you ever want to do? Feed the power back to the Man?

LITTLE NICKY: Can I get a sundae?

NICHOLAS: You just had a shake.

NICK: Okay, fine, whatever we decide to do, we need to let Mitch and Caitlin know what happened to me. I mean, us. I mean, me!

NICHOLAS: I think we're all in agreement there.

BEATNICK: Great. Now, who's going to pay the bill for all this food?

NICKELBACK: Didn't any of you geniuses think to bring a credit card?

Several minutes later, the five Nicks performed a monumental dine-and-dash, and headed for Caitlin Westfield's front door.

Upon hearing the doorbell, Mrs. Westfield opened the door to see a throng of old and young men on and around her welcome mat.

"Hello, Mrs. Westfield," Nick Slate said cheerfully, at the front of the throng. "This is my uncle, my cousin, my nephew, and my biological father. Can we talk to Caitlin?"

Mrs. Westfield was still trying to process the crowd on her front porch when Caitlin, with the baby in her arms, came down the stairs, followed by Mitch and Zak. She froze for a moment when she saw them, but quickly regained her poise and continued down the stairs.

When they spotted the baby, all five newcomers shouted, "SputNick!"

"SputNick's my . . . foster . . . baby . . . sibling," said Nick.

"Oh," said Mrs. Westfield. "So you're the baby donor."

"Sure," said Nick as Caitlin put the baby into his arms and it began to cry.

"Nick's whole family has traveled to Colorado Springs to

support him," Caitlin said, turning to her mom. "He lost his house, you know."

"Good to see you, Mrs. Westfield." Nick waved as he and all the men in his family turned to go. He glanced back at Caitlin, Mitch, and Zak. "You're coming with us, right?"

"Of course," Caitlin said.

"Wait," said Mrs. Westfield. "Where are you all going?"

"They invited us to join them at . . . a big family reunion," Caitlin said, and gave her mom a kiss on the cheek. "I'll be back by ten."

And they all went off down the street.

Mrs. Westfield watched them go. *Should I be concerned about this?* she wondered.

She wasn't convinced Nick was the best influence on Caitlin. After all, his house seemed to be the epicenter of an unexplained cosmic event. On the other hand, he was a solid young man, and even if he turned out to be the spawn of Satan, he was better than Theo.

24 THE ICEMAN SCREAMETH

It was an unnatural thing to be confronted by the many ages of yourself. Nick could see why the man who bought the prism at the garage sale had been so bitter. The young selves look in despair at the worn-out old men they'll become, and the old ones can only mourn the youth that they have lost.

Nick was determined not to fall into that trap. There was something of value in each of his selves. He would learn to appreciate them all.

They couldn't go back to Beef-O-Rama, because of the way they had left, and with the Accelerati no doubt on the lookout for Nick, they couldn't stay out in the open for long.

It was Mitch who came up with the perfect place to lie low. "Vince's house!"

But Nick couldn't say he looked forward to the prospect of hanging out there. Besides the enforced cheer, Vince's mother had so many little figurines and fragile things he felt like he'd be six bulls in a china shop. And nothing would be baby-proofed.

They found an unlocked window in back and let themselves in.

Vince lived far enough from Nick's house that it had been spared the worst of the electromagnetic pulse. Most of the appliances that had been plugged in at the time had burned out, but only half the lights were blown.

Mitch settled in with the antique phone. He kept dialing it, but continued to get a busy signal every time. Caitlin, who had rocked SputNick to sleep, gently set him on a sofa cushion she had set up as a makeshift crib.

"Our first order of business," Nickelback said, always intent on taking charge, "is to track down Old St. Nick."

Caitlin then turned to Zak, whose part in all of this Nick had yet to understand.

Zak looked up from the cards he was shuffling and glared at Caitlin. "I didn't sign up for any of this weirdness. I want to find the money so I can save my mom, then go home and forget any of this ever happened."

Nick watched as Caitlin reached out and gently took the deck away from him.

"Finding that seven hundred and fifty million dollars isn't all there is to it," she said. "The future of the world is at stake, and you're part of this now. You have to see it to the end along with the rest of us."

Zak looked away for a moment, casting his anger to the wall. Then he grabbed his laptop and flipped it open. "Fine. We know where we found the baby," he said. "If the rest of you tell me where you emerged, I can roughly estimate where Old St. Nick's tunnel led." Then he turned to Mitch, pointing. "And you! Hasn't it dawned on you yet that the reason you keep getting a busy signal is because you're calling Tesla at the exact same moment in time that Caitlin did? You can't get through because Caitlin's already talking to him! Figure out how to use those rings around the dial, and you'll be able to call back at a different time."

"Well, you're the numbers guy," Mitch countered. "You figure it out."

"Do I have to do everything around here?" said Zak, and he went over to study the phone while Mitch took up the laptop and got input from all the Nicks as to where they had surfaced.

The only area that didn't seem to be covered was downtown Colorado Springs.

"Maybe it was too much for him, he had a coronary, and croaked," suggested Mitch.

Various versions of Nick shot him a look. "Let's keep our thoughts more positive," said Nickelback, a sentiment that was reinforced by the artificially cheery house.

Little Nicky had already taken down some of the more interesting figurines and was setting them up as armies to battle one another.

Was I ever so easily amused? thought Nick. Well, if this was him, he must have been. He wondered how many figures Little Nicky would end up breaking, and if Vince's mother would notice if and when she got back from Scotland. *Of course she will*, he decided. She was the type to take a daily tally.

Nick went over to take them away, but Nicholas, having the same idea, got there first and removed them from Little Nicky's sticky hands. The child protested, but only for a moment.

"There must be a way to reverse the polarity or something," said BeatNick. He took the vacuum tube from its velvet sheath and held it up to get a clearer look at the prism inside.

"Careful," said Caitlin, "if it catches the light again, it could make seven more of you."

BeatNick quickly put it down, away from all sources of light. Nick wondered if it was exponential, and if he was caught in the fragmented beam again, would there be forty-nine of him?

"Whatever we do," said BeatNick, "we can't let the Accelerati have it."

"Are you out of your mind?" said Nickelback. "They're the only ones who can reverse-engineer the thing and put us back together. They've used us; it's time we used them for our own benefit."

Through the debate, Nick just listened. These, he knew, were all the voices in his own head. The pros and the cons, the fears and the hopes. They all had validity. Nickelback's approach was practical, BeatNick's was full of idealism, and Nicholas, always thoughtfully stroking his beard, was middle-of-the-road. Nick didn't know where that left him.

"Well, we're *not* giving it to the Accelerati," proclaimed Caitlin, "any more than we'd let them have Nick back. Right, Nick?"

Nick found he couldn't look at her, because his going back to the lab was not out of the question. He hadn't even told her about Edison—he hadn't told any of them. It was a story he didn't know how to begin.

"I can't go against them. They have Danny and my father," he said.

Caitlin, it seemed, had developed a great deal more insight into herself and others since he'd first met her. She took a step closer and looked at him more deeply than he thought he could bear. "It's more than that, isn't it? They've changed you."

Nick got angry at that. "They didn't 'change' me."

"Yeah, they did. I have those memories too," said BeatNick—the traitor! "Edison really did a number on us."

"Edison?" said Zak, looking up from the telephone. "*The* Edison?"

"Nick, you couldn't possibly mean Thomas Edison," said Caitlin. "He couldn't be alive . . . unless"—she gasped—"there's another battery!"

More than one of the Nicks groaned.

"Look," Nick said to Caitlin, "in order for us to be able to fight the Accelerati, life on Earth has to continue, right? Well, they're the only ones who are anywhere close to discharging that satellite."

Mitch slowly shook his head. "I can't believe it. Nick's been seduced by the dark side."

"It's not like that!" insisted Nick. "Nothing's as simple as you're trying to make it!"

No one spoke for a moment. Then a tinkling of glass came from the corner where Little Nicky had just broken a tiny crystal unicorn.

"Got it!" said Zak. He brought the phone over and plunked it down on the dining room table. "All the rings around the dial are kind of like a clock. The five outermost rings measure years, days, hours, minutes, then seconds. The next two, with letters, mark the old-fashioned exchanges, and the next five rings are for the actual phone number." He pointed at the three innermost rings. "And these here have never even been used—but Tesla must have figured out that phone numbers would eventually have ten digits, like they do today."

Then he clicked the second ring one notch clockwise. "So if I'm right, your next call will catch Tesla one day later than your first call."

He cranked the handle to generate a charge, lifted the receiver, and held it to Caitlin. But she looked to Nick.

"You should make this call," she said.

And no one, not even the other Nicks, disagreed.

Nick took the receiver from Zak and held it to his ear, then he put his finger in the single hole, dialed, and held his breath.

"Hold while I connect you to your party," said the operator on the other end.

He heard the phone ring once, then it was picked up before the second ring.

"Hallo?" said a Serbian-accented voice on the other end.

"Hello, Mr. Tesla?" said Nick, trying to sound like one of his older selves, and trying to keep his voice from quivering.

"Ya, this is Nikola Tesla."

"My name is Nick Slate and—"

"Do you call about the Columbian Exhibition? If not, you'll have to call back at another time. All other business must wait until after I power the exhibition."

"No, it's not about that," Nick told him. "Actually, I'm calling from the future. We need help with your Far Range Energy Emitter."

There was silence for a long moment. Then Tesla said, "You think you are being funny? I am a busy man! I do not have time for this kind of joke. Bother me again and I will call the police!" Then he hung up.

"So what did he say?" asked Mitch, expectantly. "Is he going to help us?"

Nick hung up the phone. "I didn't get that impression."

Having a phone line through time is pretty useless if you call its inventor years before he invented it.

The nearest any of them could figure, they had reached him in March of 1893, while he was creating the electrical system that would power the Columbian Exhibition—the epic World's Fair in Chicago. He was still a young man then, and most of his achievements were ahead of him. It was before the War of the Currents, years before he fulfilled his dream of building a hydro-electric power plant at Niagara Falls, and a full decade before Wardenclyffe Tower. No wonder he thought the call was a prank.

If they were going to get what they needed from him, they would have to catch him at the exact right moment in his life, which was going to be very difficult indeed. Moving the time forward even as little as five years connected them to an ice deliveryman named Boris, who was already annoyed at getting calls for Tesla.

"This is not his number anymore! I don't know his new one," Boris screamed at them, "and I don't care! Leave me alone!"

No amount of research could yield a newer phone number for Tesla. It had been lost to history.

Yet even as they wrestled with the problem, in the back of Nick's mind he was beginning to consider another use for that phone. One he wasn't willing to share, even with his six other selves, although he was certain several of them must have been thinking the same thing.

Since Zak needed a more powerful computer in order to continue chasing the stolen money, it was decided that he and Mitch would go to the University of Colorado, to access its mainframe.

"We'll go in the morning," Zak said.

Mitch invited Zak to have dinner and spend the night over at his house, considering the current crowd occupying Vince's.

"My mom won't mind," he said. "I'll tell her you're a really big eighth grader."

Zak reluctantly accepted. "It will be just one more in a long list of humiliations," he said.

"If we take that money," Nickelback pointed out after they had left, "we'll put the whole world in jeopardy. The Accelerati are the only ones who can finish the machine before the asteroid becomes lethal."

"Not necessarily," said Nicholas. "We could let them finish the machine, and *then* hobble them by taking away their money—"

"—and when they're on their knees," added BeatNick, "we crush them and take back what's ours."

"Easier said than done," said Nickelback.

. . .

SputNick woke up just after sunset, screaming as only babies can.

"He's hungry," Caitlin said.

"So am I," said all the Nicks in unison.

Nicholas volunteered to go out and get formula and fast food, as long as Caitlin provided the money, since she was the only one who had any.

"And I'll go looking for Old St. Nick downtown before it gets too late," Nickelback said.

"I'll go with you," BeatNick chimed in, and sauntered out after them.

Now it was just Nick, Caitlin, the baby, and Little Nicky, who was content to watch cartoons on the one TV that hadn't been fried by the EMP. It all felt awkwardly domestic.

Once Caitlin had calmed the baby down, she held him out to Nick. "You should hold him."

"He cries when I hold him."

"He's *you*," she pointed out. "It only makes sense that you hold him."

And so Nick sat down and let her put SputNick in his arms. To his amazement, the baby didn't cry. He just looked up at Nick with those deep blue eyes that were so familiar.

This is what my father saw, he thought, *when he used to hold me. . . . This is what my mother saw.* The pain of thinking of his mom made him hold the baby closer, and the baby relaxed in his embrace.

"It's okay, little guy," he said. "It's all going to be okay."

Then Little Nicky sat beside him too, leaning his head on Nick's shoulder. Nick put his free arm around the child and, for a moment, felt that they were both part of him again.

. . .

Nicholas returned shortly after dark with formula for SputNick and an industrial-size bucket of chicken with fixings for everyone else—although, predictably, all the Nicks fought over the same side dishes, leaving the macaroni salad and steamed vegetables (both of which Nick hated) untouched.

"You're all such children," Caitlin said, even as she also reached for the more preferred items.

Since SputNick seemed a little old for just formula, and since the blender had been spared by the EMP, Nick had the bright idea of making baby food out of the steamed veggies. Caitlin took it upon herself to supervise.

"I've done this for my cousin," she told him. "You have to add a little water and put it on puree."

"I know how to use a blender," he told her—but secretly added a little bit of water when she turned away.

"And don't overblend it—it should have a little bit of texture."

Whether it was due to Caitlin looking over his shoulder or his own carelessness, Nick turned on the blender prematurely and spewed partially processed vegetables all over the kitchen.

"You might want to put on the lid next time," said Caitlin, in a sarcastic tone that would have frustrated Nick had his mind not suddenly ricocheted elsewhere.

"There was no lid," he said.

Caitlin reached right beside him and held it up. "Hello? It's right here?"

"No," said Nick. "Not *this* blender. . . ."

He thought back to the blender sitting in Edison's lab—the copper one that was a part of Tesla's machine. When he'd taken inventory with Edison, he couldn't remember—but now he was certain that he had sold it without a lid. In fact, he recalled wondering what the buyer could possibly do with a lidless blender.

He told Caitlin about it as they cleaned up and made a new

batch of vegetable mush for the baby. She couldn't remember the blender at all, since it had sold before she'd even arrived at the garage sale.

"Well, if the lid wasn't in the attic, then maybe the machine doesn't need it," she reasoned.

Still, Nick felt that it was important somehow, though he couldn't put his finger on why.

By the time Nickelback returned from his search for the eldest Nick, all that remained of the meal were some picked-over wings and the unwanted macaroni salad, which he ate under protest, griping that the younger Nicks could have been a little more considerate.

"What happened to BeatNick?" Caitlin asked.

"The city's nightlife called to him," Nickelback said with a shrug. "He's over twenty-one, he can do what he wants."

"Any leads on Old St. Nick?" Nick asked.

Nickelback shook his head. "Not a one. And I didn't want to stay out there long—downtown gets sketchy after dark. All nature of things are for sale in dark corners. There was even a hobo who offered to sell me a talking coat."

BeatNick returned not long after that, having been refused admittance to any nightclubs, because he had no ID to prove his age and, like the rest of them, had no money even if he could have gotten in.

"It's not fair," he grumbled. With nothing but grease and sporks left of dinner, he found a Slim-N-Fit nastypack in a corner of the mostly empty pantry and nuked it. Clearly the biggest problem of being divided was going to be keeping everyone fed.

"I'll come back in the morning with a bunch of food from my house," Caitlin told them as she prepared to leave. "I'll tell my parents there's a food drive at school or something."

Nick walked her to the door. There was an awkward moment as she stood at the threshold.

"I'm glad you're back and that you're okay," she said. "Well, relatively okay." She leaned forward for an instant, as if she might give Nick a hug, but then looked around and stopped. If she hugged one, she'd have to hug them all, and that would just be weird.

"See you all tomorrow," she said, and closed the door behind her.

That left the Nicks alone—which made Nick's fourteen-year-old self anxious. All afternoon he had dreaded the thought of being alone with himself. He thought of the man who had bought the prism. He'd been broken and resigned. What must it be like, day after day, to see your life endlessly flashing before your eyes? A lifetime of your own bad choices. A crystal ball of diminished hope, and past regrets.

"It's not all bad," BeatNick pointed out, glancing over at Nicholas, who was burping SputNick. "Nicholas looks like he's got his act together, and Nickelback has an air of success about him, even if I don't agree with all his opinions."

Nick supposed that was true—but it was akin to the way people never like the way they look in pictures. When you reflect on yourself, sometimes all you can see are the imperfections.

"This house only has two bedrooms, plus Vince's room in the basement," Nickelback said, "which smells like Vince, but not like death. Believe it or not, there's a difference."

They all laughed at that, which was an odd moment, because it sounded fake, like an old-fashioned TV laugh track, starting and ending at the exact same moment. They all had the same sense of humor, after all—who could blame them for finding their own jokes funny?

Between the bedrooms and the basement and a variety of

sofas, everyone found a place for the night. Nick ended up on the couch in the den, which was itchy and rough, but he was exhausted enough to fall asleep quickly.

Nick snapped awake at sunrise. He didn't remember dreaming, and wondered if perhaps their dreams had to be shared and his 14.29 percent wasn't enough to recall.

He went to check on the others. The baby had slept through the night in the master bedroom beside Nicholas and was still asleep; Nickelback was snoring in the guest room; Little Nicky had tumbled off the living room love seat sometime during the night and now slept in a tangled blanket on the rug; and BeatNick was sprawled on Vince's bed in the basement, still far from consciousness.

Soon they would all be awake, the day would become hectic, and the weight of all the decisions and questions before him would fall upon them with a vengeance.

Did seeing Edison's side of things make Nick a traitor, or just practical?

Would rejoining Caitlin in a battle against the Accelerati be noble, or would it be foolhardy, now that the safety of the world—and of his father and brother—relied on his cooperation?

And if he did go back to Edison to save the world, could he really change the Accelerati from the inside out?

Each version of him had a different opinion—and he himself was torn between them all.

There was one thing, however, that he realized he could do. One decisive action he could take. And there was something he needed to find out. . . .

25 DON'T EVEN THINK ABOUT IT. . . .

Nick grabbed the bulky Teslaphone, took it into the bathroom, and locked the door. Perhaps Zak was the master of numbers and codes, but Nick was somewhat of a genius too—at least various tests and Thomas Edison thought he was. He took in the many rings around the dial, trying to decipher them.

Both times they had reached Tesla, the inventor had been there in his lab, which meant the time of day was set correctly. The next ring had no numbers, just notches. A few hundred of them. Maybe 365? thought Nick. His proof was one notch that appeared as a dotted line. No—*366!* That dotted line was February 29—leap year! This was the ring Zak had clicked one notch clockwise.

Nick turned the ring to February 29, then clicked it ten notches forward to the tenth of March. He moved to the outer-most ring—which was for years—and clicked it three notches clockwise. He had a pretty good idea that four notches would connect him with Boris the Iceman.

Then he put his finger in the single hole, and dialed it. As before, it connected him to an old-school operator, who then connected him to Tesla's lab. This time Tesla didn't pick up until the fifth ring.

"Ya, this is Tesla," he said.

Nick cleared his throat. "Mr. Tesla," he said, "in three days, there's going to be a fire. Your lab will burn down, and all of your work will be lost."

"What did you say?" Tesla sounded horrified—and furious. "Is this a threat? Who is this?" he demanded. "Who are you working for?"

Nick ignored the questions. He knew enough to expect this response. "Your lab will burn down," he repeated. "I know because I'm calling from the future, just as I told you when I called three years ago."

"This is preposterous!" Tesla raged. "I will find you hooligans and have you, and your employer, arrested!"

"You need to save your inventions, and save your papers. Get them all out now, before the fire," Nick told him.

"I will not be intimidated!" Tesla yelled, but Nick kept his cool.

"Oh—and on November eighth, a guy named Roentgen will prove those weird rays you discovered really exist. He'll call them X-rays. And maybe then you'll believe me."

With that, Nick hung up.

There was a computer in the den. When Nick left the bathroom with the Teslaphone, he got online to see if he had changed history. He had read all the articles, knew everything there was to know about Tesla. He'd quickly be able to tell if anything had changed because of the call.

To his dismay, he found that all the news reports remained exactly the same. Everything was lost in the fire. Nick hadn't changed a thing. He slammed his fist on the desk and pushed back from it, right into Nicholas, who'd been standing behind him.

"You called him, didn't you?"

"Maybe," said Nick.

Nicholas smiled. "No maybe about it. I know you too well.

In fact, when I woke up, I was going to warn him about the fire myself, but you beat me to it."

Nick shrugged. "It doesn't matter. It didn't change a thing."

"I guess Petula was right," Nicholas said. "Can't change what's already happened." Then he went off to fill a bottle for SputNick.

For a moment Nick was mystified, but then he remembered the box camera. A couple of months ago, Petula had raced into his house in a panic. She had taken a picture of the future and knew that someone would die in Nick's house at precisely that time, although she didn't know who it would be. Rather than try to stop it, she had attempted to get Nick out of the house, so that when it happened, it would happen to someone else. That someone had turned out to be Vince.

Nick had been furious with Petula at the time. As far as he was concerned, she had killed Vince by not stopping it, and now, thanks to her, Vince needed Tesla's wet-cell battery to stay alive.

But perhaps Petula's perspective had been correct after all. As much as Nick blamed her, and as much as he hated to admit it, maybe she had seen the big picture more clearly than he had.

What happens happens.

The only changes you can make are the ones that don't affect the known outcome. Fact: Someone would die in Nick's house. Fact: Telsa's lab would burn.

But on the other hand, what if Petula was wrong? What if you *could* alter an event in the past? Maybe even prevent it? What if all Nick needed to do was try harder? More than anything he wanted that to be true, because . . .

He looked at the Teslaphone, darkly considering it.

Then, from the doorway, BeatNick said, "Don't even think about it."

"I have no idea what you're talking about," Nick told him,

but they both knew it was a lie. Because when it came to certain things, all the Nicks were of a single mind.

With the city crawling with Accelerati, all of them hunting for Nick, he knew he had to lie low. The other Nicks had more freedom. No one was looking for them, because no one knew they existed.

Mitch and Zak stopped by on their way to the university's computer lab, and BeatNick offered to go with them, wanting to experience, if only briefly, the college life he felt he was missing.

Caitlin arrived with groceries, as she had promised, but left quickly. "Believe it or not, I have to go take my math final," she told Nick. "I guess life goes on even when we wish we could put it on hold."

Then Nickelback got up to leave, determined to find Old St. Nick. "I'm checking all the soup kitchens and hospitals," he said as he reflexively rubbed the small scar on his forehead that was now visible, thanks to his receding hairline. It was a mark they all had, from that first day in Colorado Springs, when Nick had been hit in the head by Tesla's toaster. Only the baby and Little Nicky were scar-free.

Now just four Nicks remained in the house.

"You all don't have to stay cooped up here," Nick said to the others, and suggested that Nicholas take SputNick and Little Nicky to the park—an idea that made Little Nicky jump up and down.

Nicholas looked at Nick a moment too long. "All right," he said. "We'll leave you alone for a good half hour," he said. "That should be long enough."

"Long enough for what?" Nick said, pretending that he had nothing in mind. But Nicholas knew. How could he not?

"Make it count," Nicholas said, and he left with SputNick and Little Nicky.

Nick stood in the middle of the living room for a whole five minutes before he could will himself to move. And when he did move it felt like the weight of the world was set firmly on his shoulders, past, present, and future. But mostly past.

He went to the Teslaphone that now sat in the den, waiting for him. Waiting for this inevitable moment. It felt like an enemy. It felt like a friend—not one or the other, but both at the same time.

Slowly, carefully, he set the dials to where they needed to be, this time changing the settings on every ring—including the rings that marked the phone number.

He took five slow breaths, like he was about to dive deep underwater. Then put his finger in the hole and dialed.

The call was picked up on the third ring.

"Hello?"

What motivates the world's greatest minds? While we'd like to believe it is something lofty, noble—like the pursuit of knowledge for knowledge's sake—more often than not, what those great thinkers truly want, deep down, are things that every human wants. Fame, perhaps, or to prove to schoolyard bullies throughout the ages that intellect is more important than might. Or maybe something as ugly as greed, or as beautiful as love.

And maybe, for some, it is that ever-unsatisfied desire to find something—or some*one*—irretrievably lost in the tumultuous waters of time.

"Hi, Mom," said Nick into a telephone receiver that had just reached nearly five months into the past.

"Nicky," she said, "it says your number is blocked—whose phone are you calling from?"

"A friend's," he said gently, even though he felt that his heart—in fact all of his internal organs—were about to dissolve.

"What is it? Is practice done early? Do you need me to pick you up?"

"No," he said. "No, nothing like that. But there's something . . . there's something I need to talk to you about."

"Are you all right?" she asked. "You don't sound like yourself."

"I'm fine," he insisted. "But . . . but—"

"I'm making a special dinner tonight!" she said, cutting him off. "It's a surprise."

Nick felt his eyes begin to fill with tears. "Eggplant Parmesan."

"How did you guess?"

Nick remembered this day. He remembered the meal. He remembered how hungry he'd been and how he had burned his mouth because he ate a big forkful when it was still too hot.

"Mom, listen to me—something's going to happen this weekend. Something bad."

"Honey, you're breaking up—what about this weekend?"

"I said, something's going to—"

"Hold on a sec." He heard her call to Danny, telling him to "get down from there," wherever "there" was, before he fell and broke his neck.

Then she was back on the phone with Nick. Listening. Ready to hear.

And Nick was silent.

"Honey, are you still there?"

Nick said nothing.

"Honey?"

"I'm here," he finally said.

"Are you getting a ride home, or do you need me to pick you up?"

"Pick me up," he told her. "Usual time."

"Okay," she said. "Let me get back to dinner, so it's ready on time."

"Mom?" Nick said.

"Yes?"

"Mom?" Nick said.

"What is it, honey?"

Nick could barely get it out. He felt his throat closing like a wormhole through time.

"I love you, Mom."

"Awww, Nicky," she said. "I love you too."

Now his voice was barely a whisper. "Bye," he said. And hung up.

He sat there, letting the tears flow, not even trying to wipe them away. He could have warned her about the fire, but just like Tesla, she wouldn't have believed him. He could have told her he was calling from the future. She would've believed that even less. There was nothing he could have said that would change the fact of what happened. He knew that now beyond a shadow of a doubt.

Because he remembered that day. Everything. He not only remembered coming home and burning his mouth on dinner, but also Mom mentioning his phone call. But, of course, he hadn't called her that day. She'd insisted that he had, and Nick had just shrugged it off, thinking his mom was just being weird, as moms can sometimes be. But now he knew the truth.

This was the call she'd been talking about. It had already happened, which meant that Petula, curse her, was right after all. What happens happens. You can't change it; you can only become a part of what has already been. Nick's phone call hadn't prevented the fire. It didn't save their house. It didn't save her. No matter what he said, it wouldn't have mattered. He could have screamed and screamed, and it wouldn't have changed a thing.

Yet he couldn't shake the feeling that there was something he wasn't seeing. Something he had missed.

There was somebody behind her.

It was all too much to think about. Too painful to consider. All he could do in the moment was mourn. He held himself tightly and rocked back and forth, his emotions rolling through grief, fury, self-pity, and more fury. Even though he was only one-seventh of himself, he felt the full emotions of all of his other selves, and he cried until finally he was spent. Then he wiped his eyes, stood up, and got on with the day, focusing his attention on the many things that needed to be done.

Now he knew what he had to do. He had no time for indecisiveness anymore.

When Nicholas came back with the younger versions of himself, he must have seen the redness in Nick's eyes.

"You okay?" he asked.

Nick nodded.

"It didn't work, huh?"

Nick shook his head.

Then Little Nicky said he was hungry, and they all had themselves some comfort food, which wasn't all that comforting, but at least it was something.

"I'm going back to Edison," Nick told Caitlin when she returned early that afternoon. "I'm taking him the prism. I'm going to put the machine together."

Caitlin folded her arms and stared at him. She didn't glare; she just stared. Like you might look at someone you thought you knew but realized you didn't. "There's nothing I can say that will change your mind?"

"No," Nick told her. "Until I go back, I'm putting everyone else in danger. And we have to discharge that asteroid. We can do it without the globe, like we did at my house last time. It'll be messy, but it will work. And as long as Edison doesn't have the globe, he can't make that machine do anything more."

"And if they find the globe?"

Nick took a deep breath. "If they find it, we'll deal with it then."

He thought Caitlin would fight with him. Maybe even grab the prism from him and run. But she didn't.

Instead she said, "Wait one hour."

"Why?"

"You're just going to have to trust me. But I promise I won't stop you from going."

Nick thought about it. Even though they were pulled in opposite directions now, he *did* trust her. Because if he didn't have that, he had nothing.

"Okay," he said. "One hour."

Caitlin left without another word.

Exactly one hour later, Nick said good-bye to Nicholas with a handshake, hugged Little Nicky, and gave SputNick a kiss on the cheek. "I'll see you when I see you," he said to his other selves, then strode out the front door to return to the Loyal Order of the Accelerati.

26 GRAVITY OF A GASEOUS GIANT

Even with only one-seventh of Nick gone, it seemed like a whole lot more was missing, because that was the seventh that Caitlin knew. Though she didn't want to admit it, the others made her uncomfortable. They all spoke to her as if they knew her, but she didn't know them. Not really. More than anything, they were like ghosts of Nick's future, and of his past. She tried to disguise how awkward she felt among them, but she didn't think she was doing a good job of it. She imagined they must be self-conscious around her too. Realizing that it must be an uneasy situation for everyone made it a little easier. They were all in the same boat. Unfortunately that boat seemed up the river, and Tesla hadn't left them a paddle.

Was Thomas Edison really still alive, as Nick had said? If so, she wondered what Edison had told him. How had the man managed to convince Nick that joining forces with him was for the best? How could Nick think that he could find any sort of fulfillment with the Accelerati, or change them from the inside? They'd been doing things pretty much the same way for over a hundred years. Did he really believe he could alter that? Or was he just telling himself that to make going back easier?

Whatever the reason, Caitlin realized that unless she did something quick, she and the others would be sidelined. Nick thought he was protecting them—and maybe he was, but they had begun this as a team, and as a team they had succeeded against a group that should have been able to crush them like flies. She had to believe that their whole was greater than the sum of their parts. Perhaps that was true of Nick too.

Edison was like a searing celestial body, and Nick was Icarus, his wings on the verge of flames. Although Caitlin was far from the pull of that particular sun, there were plenty of outlying threats. Then she remembered hearing how deep-space probes would use the intense gravity of the outer planets to slingshot into new trajectories.

That's when she got the idea. . . .

The maneuver would be tricky—the particular gaseous giant she had in mind was a dangerous one—but if it worked, it would put her on a much more effective path.

Wait one hour, she had told Nick. Then she quickly went home, found the tea bags she had taken from Zak's mother, and brewed herself a pot of Oolongevity.

Jorgenson was cleaning up after third lunch when Caitlin arrived.

It was torture enough to serve just a single round of meals to thankless human larvae, but it was a new definition of hell to have to serve three lunches in a row because the cafeteria was too small to fit everyone at once.

The other food workers wouldn't even come near him, let alone talk to him. That was, of course, by his design, but over time he found the isolation more unpleasant than he'd expected. It wasn't easy being the lone halogen lamp in a crate of energy-saving appliance bulbs.

And the cherry atop this cake wreck was the sight of Caitlin Westfield approaching.

"Lunch is over," Jorgenson snapped, removing the remains of some truly inedible lasagna from the warming tray.

"I'm not here for lunch," Caitlin told him. "I'm here to talk to you."

"There is no spectrum of time or space in which we will have anything to say to one another."

Her eyebrows lifted in an exaggerated raise. Was she about to mock him?

"Sounds like you're bitter. Maybe I can help you with that."

He guffawed at the very concept that she could help him in any way. Or that she would even want to after their previous encounters. *What is she playing at?* he wondered.

Jorgenson was no further along in his plot to extinguish Evangeline Planck than he'd been days earlier. He had even misplaced his sole accomplice, Theo, whom he had zipped into the lining of his coat. Unfortunately, the coat was nowhere to be found. Jorgenson had returned to the park as soon as he realized he'd left it there, but of course it was gone.

Was he actually in such a low place that he would accept charity from the enemy? On the other hand, she was certainly as anti-Planck as he was. Some people said that the enemy of one's enemy was one's friend, but Alan Jorgenson had never subscribed to that philosophy. As far as he was concerned, his enemy's enemy was his enemy squared. With that in mind, he listened to Caitlin with interest, and also intense suspicion.

"How could you possibly help me?" he asked. "And why?"

"I have information," she told him. "Information that might get you back on Mr. Edison's good side."

That got Jorgenson's attention. The fact that she knew about Edison meant she had spoken with Nick Slate, and he had told her about the Old Man—which would no doubt infuriate him. And it would all be blamed on Planck, because Nick had escaped on her watch! Why, things were already looking up!

"And what would you want in return for this information?" he asked. "Some proprietary Accelerati prototypes?" he suggested. "A dream catcher that can predict impending doom, perhaps—or a loom that can spin the hair from the ears of swine into silk?"

"Nothing like that," Caitlin, her manner measured and calm. "It would be an even exchange. Information for information."

Jorgenson looked around. There was no one left in the cafeteria or serving area. "You tell me yours first," he said. "And if I find it worthy, you may ask me a question. I will answer truthfully."

Jorgenson, of course, had no intention of doing any such thing. Truthfulness was not in his nature—especially when it came to friends of Nick Slate.

But then she produced a thermos. "We'll both answer truthfully," she said, grabbing two paper cups from the counter. She poured them each some tea with a refreshing and very familiar aroma.

"Oolongevity," he said, a little impressed—and a little frightened—by her resourcefulness.

"Two months ago you and I enjoyed a little tea party," she said simply. "I think it's time we did so again."

Jorgenson hesitated. She held out the cup, but he didn't take it. In addition to clarity of thought, and a slightly extended lifespan, the Accelerati-engineered tea had the unique side effect of causing the drinker to be absolutely honest. It was a wonderful interrogation tool. But both of them drinking it at once would be a dangerous game of chess. Last time that game had ended in an annoying stalemate. But might it play out in his favor this time?

"Tell me the nature of the information you plan to share," he said.

She didn't hesitate at all. "I can tell you where Nick is, and what he's planning to do," she said. "I'd tell you right now, but I doubt you'd believe me unless I had the tea to convince you it was true."

Jorgenson took the paper cup. "Very well, then."

They held up their cups in a toast.

"Bottoms up," Caitlin said.

They began to drink. The tea was warm but not hot, and they were able to down it in just a few gulps. The bell rang, and Caitlin didn't move.

"You'll be late for class," Jorgenson taunted.

"Finals week," she pointed out. "It's a half day." Which meant they had all the time they needed for the exchange of secrets.

In a few moments, Jorgenson's sense of well-being peaked, and when he remembered where he had misplaced his car keys—twenty years ago—he knew it was time.

"So," Jorgenson began, "you would betray Nick Slate?"

"No," Caitlin said, almost dreamily. "It won't make any difference to him if you know . . . but it'll make a big difference to you."

"And he knows you're here, telling me this?"

"I didn't say that," Caitlin said enigmatically.

"So where is Nick?" he asked. "What does he plan to do?"

Caitlin showed no sign of even trying to deceive him. "Nick is about to turn himself in," she said. "He's going back to Edison. He's going to try to finish the machine for him."

Jorgenson actually gasped.

"So if you call Edison first, you can take credit for it," she said. "You can tell him you're the one who convinced Nick to go back. It won't make you Grand Acceleratus again, but it might just get you out of the doghouse . . . or at least out of this lunchroom."

And Jorgenson knew she was right. If he got credit for Nick's return, this purgatory would end! No more dishing slop for the pubescent rabble of Colorado Springs. Perhaps he'd be allowed to return to the university. And wouldn't that just make Planck burn!

"Now my turn," Caitlin said. "I want to know what the Accelerati are up to. What are they going to do next?"

Jorgenson tried to tell her that he didn't know, but all that came out was a stutter. He wanted to tell her that they had no activities outside of Colorado Springs, but his mouth did nothing but drool. The tea was strong, and very effective. He could not answer with a lie. He had to tell the truth.

"They," he said, then cleared his throat. "We . . . have begun construction of the most important project we've ever attempted. The Accelerati have acquired land in Shoreham, New York," he told her. "We are rebuilding Wardenclyffe Tower."

Wardenclyffe Tower should have been the greatest accomplishment of Nikola Tesla's career. It should have been the fulfillment of his life's dream—to bring free, wireless energy to the world. *Free*, however, can be a very dangerous word. It not only strikes fear into the hearts of dictators and oppressive regimes, it sends stock prices plummeting and can make the very rich very poor, very quickly.

Tesla had no love of money; he felt it was beneath him. He'd wanted to share his gift with the world. Unfortunately, those who invested in his invention were only interested in gifts that could return large amounts of cash.

Back in 1901, a tower that could provide free energy to the world would also poke holes in the pockets of the world's richest men. If it worked, their fortunes would fall.

So, rather than allow Tesla to deliver on his promise, they tore the tower down and sold the parts for scrap. Electricity would continue to be expensive. Powerful businessmen would continue to get rich. And Edison's name became a part of almost every electric company in the nation, instead of Tesla's.

But the investors who killed Wardenclyffe Tower all those years ago were extremely shortsighted. Even Edison could see that. He understood that wireless energy delivered across the globe would transform life as we know it.

And it didn't have to be free at all. Not if it was completely managed by a single scientific entity that knew how to make a silk purse out of a sow's ear. A bigger, better Wardenclyffe Tower would allow Edison and the Accelerati to control the world's electricity from a central source.

Which meant that, in every way that mattered, they would control the world.

27 THE ENDS OF THE EARTH

Vince's inability to sleep made his Scottish captivity all the more unpleasant.

The fisherman and the woman whose house now rested at the bottom of the lake had taken the globe from him and locked him up in a back room somewhere. Not being accomplished criminals, they didn't know what else to do.

They couldn't release him, for fear he would tell the world about what they had. They couldn't kill him, because, after all, they were not murderers. Until they came up with a plan, the back room would have to suffice.

The fisherman knew how to tie knots. The rope wasn't hurting Vince's wrists, but it was definitely secure. Without help, he'd never be able to break free.

They came to check on Vince several times a day, bringing him food and allowing him potty breaks.

"That doohickey in your rucksack is a lot like the globe, in'it?" asked the fisherman on one of these visits. "Keeps ye alive, like some kind of electric soul."

Vince didn't like the sound of that. He liked to think that his soul was his own and the battery merely served as an ignition, keeping the pilot lit.

"My mother's just across the lake, you know," Vince told him, nodding toward the window that afforded him a view of Loch Ness. Police boats were visible in the distance, dragging the lake. "Looks like she's already started an investigation." *Although if they can't find a monster,* he wondered, *how do they expect to find a fourteen-year-old kid?* "It'll probably lead them right to your door," he said.

"Mebbe so, and mebbe we'll be elsewhere," said the fisherman, implying that they'd use the globe to travel to the ends of the earth.

The woman's curiosity was Vince's best hope.

"I'll wager that you know what the globe is, and where it came from," she said to him while bringing him breakfast on his third day of captivity.

"I might," he answered. "Untie me and we'll talk."

She didn't untie him, just spoon-fed him some beef stew that he knew would wreak havoc in his undead digestive system.

"I thought at first it was a bit of magic, or a military sort of thing," the woman said. "But now I'm thinking it's something else."

"Something else," confirmed Vince. "And more dangerous than you think."

The woman did not like the sound of that. "Dangerous how? It's not radioactive or anything, is it?"

"I don't know about that, but there are people out there who want it, and they'll kill to get it. You're lucky I found you first."

The woman scoffed at the idea, but Vince could tell she was worried.

"I can't see why you'd want it," he said. "You don't need it anymore."

"Of course we need it," she told him. "It brought me to Bertie. He's my soul mate, you know. We want to travel and see the world."

"Maybe *he* does," Vince chanced a guess. "But not you.

Coming here, finding him, that's what *you* wanted. It's what the globe did for you. And as far as you were concerned, you'd have been happy for it to stay at the bottom of the lake after that, right?"

"Never mind that," she said, not looking him in the eye. "It's not at the bottom of the lake, it's here. And we mean to use it."

He had baited the hook. She had taken it. And now he began to reel her in.

"I wonder how interested he'll still be in you, with all the women of the world at his fingertips."

"You hush up," said the woman, beginning to sound a little bit bitter. "I'll have none of that talk here."

"Most women in these parts just have to worry about their men going down to the pub. But for you that pub might be in Japan, with all those geisha girls."

The woman fixated on the thought and just stared at him, nonresponsive.

"Let me take the globe," Vince went on, "and you'll never have to worry about that."

"You're a wily one," she said.

Just then, Bertie came into the room. "I got our honeymoon all planned out," the fisherman said, fanning out some brochures in his hand. "A different place every day, mind you, now we don't have to worry ourselves about airfare. We'll start in Paris, then hop over to Venice. Then to the Pyramids, and the Great Wall of China." He smiled at her. "And then, my dear, we will have sushi in Tokyo."

The woman threw Vince a quick glance, so quick he almost didn't catch it. "Sounds wonderful, darling," she said. "But I'm happy just to stay here."

He scoffed at that. "Nothin' here but fish, fish, an' more fish."

"Exactly," said the woman. "You want sushi, we can have it right here."

He grunted and waved his hand, as if to ward off the very notion. "I don't understand ye, woman," he said. "We have the whole world at the click of a button. I, fer one, am not stayin' put."

He laid the brochures on the table. "You pick where you want to go, but we will be goin' somewhere." And he left her to ponder the colorful pictures of places she no longer had any desire to see.

Vince said nothing. Sometimes silence is the best way to make your point.

When the woman returned that evening to bring him dinner, the silence continued. She didn't even make eye contact with him.

She did, however, leave his bonds looser, and the door to the room unlocked.

Vince waited until long after the couple was asleep to make his move.

Wriggling his fingers back and forth in the rope, he finally broke free.

The house was dark; the only light the flicker of the aurora in the sky that was becoming a little more intense each night. He could hear the snores of the fisherman, and Vince imagined he could hear the steady breathing of the woman feigning sleep while listening for their captive to flee.

The globe, he discovered, was in a place of honor: the center of the dinner table, as if it were its own feast. She had not shown him how to use it, as he had hoped, but he was a quick study and knew he could figure it out.

Vince grabbed it. Even though the room was cold, the globe was warm to the touch. It seemed to vibrate with a deep, resonant pulse. Then he burst out the front door into a windy night.

Hefting his backpack onto one shoulder, being careful not to dislodge his electrodes at this crucial moment—because how stupid would it be to drop dead right outside the house?—he ran.

Just then, the fisherman appeared at the door behind him, wearing nothing but a nightshirt. "Halt, laddie! Or face the consequences!"

Vince chose to face the consequences—and since the man did not carry a shotgun in his nightshirt, the consequence was to be chased by a man wearing slippers.

Vince hurried down a slope, away from the main road; in front of him was a small dock and two skiffs with outboard motors. He hopped in one, cranked the motor, and unmoored himself from the dock just as the slipper-footed fisherman arrived.

"Give it back, or I'll make ye wish ye'd never been born!"

"I've already wished that," answered Vince. "You'll have to do better."

Vince aimed the rudder, punched the motor, and powered away from the dock.

Undeterred, the fisherman got in the other boat and pursued across the dark, windswept lake.

Vince had a healthy lead, but he had chosen the boat with the smaller motor, and the fisherman's boat was slowly but steadily gaining. Vince estimated it would overtake him in two more minutes. Then he realized he had a much more effective mode of transportation.

His eyes had just adjusted to the dim, and there was just

enough aurora light for him to make out the landmasses on the globe. Major cities were marked by what appeared to be tiny diamonds. Colorado Springs was so marked as well, perhaps because it had been such an important town to Tesla himself.

At the base of the globe was a sliding switch with a plus at one end and a minus at the other. The switch seemed to shrink and expand the globe's field. Vince set it to the middle. At the very top of the globe, right where the North Pole should have been, was a little red button. Vince had seen enough of Tesla's objects to know that if there was a thing on it that looked like a button, it was a button.

He took a very deep breath, held it, closed his eyes, and pushed the button. He disappeared, along with half a million gallons of water beneath him, and a single scale of some unidentified water creature.

The Colorado Springs Inland Quasi-Tsunami, as it came to be known, was just one more annoying, anomalous event marking the town's Dark Time.

People were surprised and yet not surprised; people were shocked, yet not really shocked at all. It was just one of those things, as everything in Colorado Springs lately had become just one of those things.

The deluge occurred at about 4:15 in the afternoon, which had been 11:15 at night in Scotland. As Loch Ness contains more water than all the lakes of England and Wales combined, the loss of half a million gallons from it was not even noticed.

The diameter of the spherical teleportation field had been set to thirty feet, and since Vince was in the middle of it, he appeared in his boat precisely fifteen feet in the air, with enough water to fill Shamu's tank beneath him. The water instantly flooded Acacia Park and the surrounding streets, washing small children away from Uncle Wilbur Fountain and creating serious traffic headaches.

Vince was unaware of most of this, however, because the boat had overturned in the deluge and dislodged his battery, leaving him facedown and dead in a pond that had previously been a parking lot.

An elderly man who had been wandering around the downtown area for over a day witnessed the occurrence.

He recognized the dead kid right away, even facedown.

While others around him struggled to comprehend, recover from, or flee the flash flood, the eighty-year-old man sloshed through the water, found the backpack, and knew what to do. He'd done it several times . . . but wasn't that many years ago? He couldn't be sure. He took the two wires extending from the backpack and connected them to the EKG electrodes behind the dead kid's ears.

The kid immediately opened his eyes.

"Where have you been, Vince?" the old man asked cheerfully. "Someplace wet, it looks like."

Vince stared at him. "Who are you?" he asked.

"It's me," the old man said with a wide grin. "Nick."

A horrified look came over Vince's face. "Nick? How long have I been dead?"

28 YOU WILL NOT ALWAYS BE NECESSARY

Right around the time Acacia Park was flooding, Nick returned to his ruined home. The Accelerati found him sitting on the couch in the timber-strewn mess that had once been his living room, reading a paperback of *The Lightning Thief.* The irony was lost on the Accelerati. They aimed their weapons, and called for the Grand Acceleratus.

Ms. Planck, looking very un-lunch-lady-like in her vanilla skirt suit, arrived several minutes later. By her side was Petula, her pigtailed Mini-Me.

"Explain yourself," Planck said.

"I don't need to explain myself to anyone but Edison," Nick told her.

Around them, the Accelerati cringed. No one talked to the Grand Acceleratus with such disrespect.

Nick waited to see what she would do, but he suspected she would have to swallow whatever he dished out. One perk of being Edison's pet was that Nick did not have to grovel before her.

"Where's the prism?" Her voice simmered with a pre-volcanic fury that Nick found very satisfying.

"All that time serving up lunch and advice, and you were just a spy," Nick said. "And to think I actually liked you."

"The prism," she said again.

Nick sighed and pulled it out from beneath him. "The things you find under old sofa cushions."

She tried to grab it, but he held it out of her reach and stood up.

"Get the jet ready to take me back to New Jersey," he told Ms. Planck, making it sound as much like a demand as he could. "I'll give it to Edison myself."

Ms. Planck nodded to her minions, and they left to make preparations. Nick looked to Petula, who appeared like one of those rubber toys you squeeze to make its eyes pop out. *I can't believe you spoke to her like that*, those bulging eyes said.

Ms. Planck took a step closer to Nick and spoke in a smooth, controlled voice, any lava forced way, way down beneath the surface. "You will not always be necessary," she said, and it chilled him. Jorgenson was fond of threats, but this was not a threat. It was a mere statement of fact.

Nick could only hope that Evangeline Planck became unnecessary before he did.

Petula's eyes were not, in fact, bulging in horror at Nick's treatment of Ms. Planck. That was her look of intense concentration. She was studying Nick, because there was something about him that was just . . . wrong. She couldn't place what it was. He sounded like Nick. He acted like Nick. He looked exactly the same as when he had vanished the day before . . . and yet . . .

Petula knew she had a sensitivity to ripples in the cosmos that others lacked. When she had plucked the cosmic-string harp, it had awakened something in her that she could not explain to this day. *You will compete the circuit* was the message the universe had imparted to her in that profound moment of transcendent connection. And yet it had been Nick who had completed the circuit, making the machine work.

Petula could only conclude that the universe was a liar, just like most people in it. But she still held out hope that a deeper meaning would reveal itself. Probably on her deathbed, because the universe was cruel that way.

Be that as it may, a fine-tuning of her personal cosmic antennae was a lingering aftereffect of having plucked the harp. Perhaps Nick looked and sounded all right, but to Petula, he didn't *feel* right. He was . . . diminished.

That was the only way she could think to describe it. She told no one, because she knew not even Ms. Planck would take her seriously. Instead she kept the feeling to herself, resolving to figure out exactly what had happened to him.

Mitch and Zak were the only ones whose efforts against the Accelerati bore fruit that day—although not at first.

BeatNick was of no use to them at all. Upon their arrival at Colorado State University, he wandered off to talk with some college girls who looked like Caitlin, but ten years older.

As for the school's mainframe, it was formidable but nowhere near as powerful as the one in Princeton's math department—yet that didn't deter Zak. "It's more about memory space than the speed of the processors," he told Mitch as he got down to business.

As Zak worked his digital magic, they heard the others in the computer lab start complaining about how slow their applications were running. Zak smiled. The users were falling victim to the random number algorithm, which he had set to take priority over everyone else's work.

"Tell me I'm not a genius," he said, gloating. "I dare you."

Yet, after three hours of circuit-searing computation, he still couldn't catch up with the money—he was always just behind the account number. "Nine-point-three seconds!" Zak lamented. "I can only find the account where the money was sitting nine-point-three seconds ago, and that's the closest I can get!"

"Bummer," said Mitch.

"It's like mass approaching the speed of light. . . ." Zak flexed his fingers above his keyboard and focused on the screen. "Like the closer we get, the more difficult it becomes, until it's just impossible to reach."

In spite of Zak's genius, it was Mitch who solved the problem. "Instead of trying to catch up with the money," he suggested, "why don't we just jump past it? Then we can be there waiting for it."

Zak just glared at him. "Great idea, Einstein. And how are we supposed to do that?"

But before Mitch could answer, his phone rang.

"Yeah?" said Mitch, taking the call. "Okay, I'm listening." He grabbed a pen from the table and scribbled a number on his palm. "Got it. Thanks." He hung up then showed his palm to Zak. "Try this number."

"Who was on the phone?" Zak asked.

Mitch just held his palm closer to Zak's face. "I said, try this number."

With no better ideas, Zak humored him. He had already hacked into the World Bank, so entering the digital account number was simple. He hit return and, in a fraction of a microsecond, everything changed.

When a slot machine hits the big bucks in Vegas, there are enough bells, whistles, and flashing lights to induce a seizure. Security is called in, the machine is temporarily shut down, and the Jumbotron in front of the casino projects a smiling middle-aged face, proclaiming BERTHA JOHNSON JUST WON $500,000—YOU COULD BE NEXT!

But in the world of digital banking, money moves with deathly silence and lightning speed.

To Zak's utter amazement, the account he had just accessed began to fill with virtual money that seemed to spill from the heavens. Or, more accurately, the Cloud. Approximately $750 million worth.

Zak stared at it, bewildered.

"Quick!" said Mitch. "Pull it out before it moves again! You've only got twenty seconds!"

Snapping out of his stupor, Zak opened the "trapdoor" account he had created and dumped the entire fortune into it—all except a single penny. When the twenty seconds were up, the Accelerati algorithm kicked in again to send that penny ricocheting away.

The rest of the money was now theirs, hiding in an account no one else could access. And there it would stay. They had stolen the Accelerati's stolen fortune.

Nine-point-three seconds later, Zak's algorithm spit out the number that Mitch had written on his hand. Then the screen froze, the server crashed, and around the computer room there was much weeping and gnashing of teeth.

Mitch grinned proudly, and Zak stared at him as if witnessing the Second Coming.

"Who was on the phone?" Zak asked again, almost afraid of the answer.

"Me," Mitch told him happily. "One hour in the future."

Unlike Zak, Mitch was not bound by linear logic. The moment he thought about jumping ahead of the money, he also thought, *Wouldn't it be funny if I called myself on the Teslaphone to give us the number?* No sooner had he thought that than the phone rang, so he wasn't surprised at all to hear his own voice on the other end giving him the number. All that remained now was getting back to Vince's house so he could place the call to himself in an hour.

"Tell me I'm not a genius," Mitch said. "I dare you."

But Zak was still too stunned to comment.

29 THE DREAD FINGER OF DOOM

Vince was not expecting to find squatters in his house. In fact, he'd thought he would have to break in, because he didn't have a key on him. Instead, no sooner had he and his elderly companion reached the welcome mat than the door opened, and he was faced with a man with a dark trim beard.

"Vince!" said the man with a surprised smile. Then, seeing the much older man, he added, "And you found Old St. Nick!"

"Old St. Nick!" said elder Nick. "I like it!"

Inside were several other people, many of whom appeared to belong to the same gene pool.

"Look," said a middle-aged man, "Vince has the globe!"

It required a lot to put Vince off his game. He took his own death and reanimation in stride; he'd even kept his cool while being held hostage in Scotland. But being accosted by a whole bunch of strangers who apparently knew him just tweaked him the wrong way.

"Who are you people and why are you in my house?"

A smiling kid whose front teeth hadn't entirely come in looked up at him and said, "We're Nick!"

"Oh," said Old St. Nick, getting it before Vince did. "So that's what the prism did."

"Yeah," said a twenty-something Nick dude with a goatee. "Welcome to the family, old man."

This was one curve that Vince didn't mind being behind. The moment was already spiking way too high on the TMI scale.

Vince scanned the room and saw that the only Nick who *wasn't* present was the fourteen-year-old one he knew. Mitch was there too, having just hung up a funny-looking old telephone; as well as a kid Vince didn't recognize.

"Are you gonna tell me you're Black Nick?" Vince asked, only half kidding.

"Nope, I'm Zak," the teen said, shaking his hand. "You look pretty good for an undead guy."

"Right," Vince said. "And now this undead guy is gonna go downstairs and listen to some Death Metal until I find my Happy Place."

Caitlin arrived about an hour later, and went down to the basement to talk to Vince. It had only been a couple of weeks since he'd last seen her, but it seemed like a whole lot longer. So much had changed.

"How was Scotland?" she asked.

"A weebee cloister-feebee," he told her, happy to leave her baffled by his response. "The globe is a teleportation device," he went on. "I should call my mother and tell her to cash in my return ticket—although she's probably still dragging the lake for my body," Vince said with a smirk of many mixed emotions. "This may finally break her of her cheeriness."

"You can call her yesterday, and cut her worrying short," Caitlin told him, and she seemed happy to leave him baffled in return. "All the objects from Nick's attic have been found," she continued. "The globe was the only one still missing, which means the Accelerati have everything except that . . . and your battery."

Vince swallowed a little bit nervously. "I intend to keep it that way."

Caitlin offered him a slim smile. "So do I," she told him. "Because yours isn't the only life that depends on it."

She explained to him that Nick had become divided, and how the one-seventh of him that they knew had returned to the Accelerati. "I really don't know what he's thinking anymore . . . he just doesn't seem . . . *right.*"

"Well," Vince said wryly, "he's not entirely himself."

Caitlin wasn't amused. She called the others downstairs, and they crowded into Vince's basement bedroom, which, mercifully, his mother had tidied before they left for Scotland.

Vince found the kaleidoscope of Nicks hard not to stare at. He wondered what the Seven Ages of Vince would be like, and decided that he was lucky he didn't have to find out. Mitch seemed pretty chummy with that Zak kid—which emphasized how alone Caitlin seemed to be—and not just because she was the only girl present. Vince knew all about being solitary, but it must have been a new experience for Caitlin.

"I found out what the Accelerati are planning," Caitlin told them. "They're rebuilding Wardenclyffe Tower."

The Nicks gasped in unison, then responded at random.

"As a base for the F.R.E.E.!"

"It'll be a hundred times stronger than the original."

"A thousand times!"

"Whoa!"

"It's all our fault! We never should have had that garage sale!"

On that, all the Nicks could agree. Even the baby, who gave what appeared to be a very serious burp.

"So are we going there?" asked Mitch, "Because if I miss another final, I'm screwed."

"Dude," said Vince, "you gotta consider the big picture."

Mitch sighed. "I know, I know, but sometimes the little picture is all in your face, y'know?"

"We have to be there," Caitlin told the Nicks. "Because if you're ever going to get put back together, that's where it'll have to happen—that's where the prism will be."

"So what's the plan?" Zak asked. "I mean, we've got the money—and I don't think the Accelerati have figured out they're broke yet. That gives us an advantage, right?"

Vince tried to wrap his mind around the $750 million. Then he realized you don't wrap your mind around it, you just dive into it and wallow.

"Yeah," said BeatNick. "We can use that money to take them down!"

Nickelback folded his arms. "And how are we supposed to do that?"

BeatNick shrugged. "I don't know. Maybe buy a mercenary army?"

Nickelback gave a bitter laugh. "Face it. You have no idea how to launch a large-scale offensive against the Accelerati."

"Oh, and you do?"

Nickelback sat up a little straighter. "I have more life experience."

Nicholas laughed at that, shifting the baby to his other shoulder. "No, you don't. None of us do. Our last memory was being split by the prism—then it's like we slept for twenty, or forty, or seventy years. None of us knows any more than we did at fourteen."

"Well, I know something," said Little Nicky. "I know that you all just talk, talk, talk and never get anything done."

That left all the other Nicks silent and chastised, because he was absolutely right.

"We do have an advantage," Vince pointed out. "You can be seven times more effective than just one Nick."

"Or cause seven times more problems," Zak grumbled.

"No," Caitlin said. "They're all Nick." Then she turned to the various ages of Nick Slate and said, "You'll get the job done. I have faith in you."

"Even me?" said Little Nicky.

She smiled at him. "Yes. Even you."

"Well, this is all wonderful and heartwarming and stuff," said Zak, "but my mom's life hangs in the balance, so do we have a plan or not? Because with or without a mercenary army, we might be leaving a whole lot of people a whole lot less alive." He turned to Vince. "No offense."

"None taken."

Caitlin took a deep breath. "I do have a plan," she said. And they all turned to her, eagerly awaiting her brilliant strategy.

Caitlin had been dreading this moment. Planning was not her strength. Her life strategies were like her artwork: she would smash something that was no longer useful, consider the pieces, and then rearrange them into a masterful pattern that she couldn't see before she'd done the smashing.

But then, isn't that what was required now? Everything—including Nick—had fallen apart. What she needed to do was move the pieces around and make something glorious out of them. She'd always been a little envious of the way Nick could see the pattern of the machine and put it together—but she didn't have to be envious, because she did the exact same thing, just in a different way. Perhaps that's what made them work so well together.

She looked around, thought about everything she knew, and began to conceive a new masterpiece. The only objects they had now, aside from Vince's battery, were the telephone and the globe—and that gave her an idea.

"Tell me," she posed to the group, "what do you get when you combine a telephone that talks through time, and a globe that teleports objects through space?"

Silence all around. Then Mitch raised his hand uncertainly. "A time machine?"

Caitlin pointed at him. "My thought exactly!"

Zak started giggling uncontrollably. "Okay, now I know you're just messing with me."

"The scary part," said Vince, "is that she's not."

"Congratulations," she told Vince and Zak. "The two of you have a new science project."

Zak just continued to giggle like a kid who'd been up too long past his bedtime.

Caitlin had no idea if it were possible, or how they'd even use it, but it would be a fine mash-up, and mash-ups were her specialty.

Then she turned to Little Nicky. "You—you're seven years old, which means you're really good at annoying people. It's your job to tick Mitch off so he starts blurting things that can help us."

"Cool!" said Little Nicky, and he got right to work.

Caitlin, hitting her stride, turned to BeatNick. "You're going to get on a plane to New York—Shoreham, Long Island, to be exact—and you're going to sweet talk your way onto the construction crew that's rebuilding Wardenclyffe Tower. You'll be our inside man. And if Nick's there, don't let him see you, just in case he really has been turned by Edison."

"Espionage," said BeatNick. "Awesome! When do I leave?"

She then assigned Nickelback to go to Princeton, to try to convince Nick's father that he had another son.

"The memory's got to be in there somewhere," Caitlin said. And Nickelback agreed, trying to hide the fact that he'd gotten a little teary-eyed at the thought of seeing his dad.

She turned to Nicholas next. "First thing in the morning, you're going to go to Atomic Lanes to bowl—and to keep an eye on the Accelerati's comings and goings."

"I'll report on anything I see," Nicholas told her. "You can count on me."

"Don't I figure into your plan?" asked the eldest of the Nicks.

Caitlin considered, then took SputNick away from Nicholas and put the baby in the elderly Nick's arms. "I'm going to need you to take care of SputNick and Little Nicky until it's time to bring you all together again. Do you think you can do that?"

"Of course I can," said Old St. Nick. "Just because I'm old doesn't mean I'm an idiot."

"And what about you?" Vince asked. "What are you going to do?"

Caitlin knew her answer. Usually the artist would stand back to gain perspective on her piece—but not this time. She was as much a part of the work as all the others.

"No one has the right to live forever," Caitlin said. "I'm going to pull Edison's plug."

The human body wasn't made to last all that long.

While every culture has legends of near-immortal beings, the oldest person who could ever present a verifiable birth date was a 122-year-old French woman. She was understandably cranky in those last few years. Even by French standards.

Currently, the world's oldest people are only in their hundred-teens, with Japan and the United States dominating the list. That hasn't stopped people from searching for ways to live forever, though—from microdieters who claim that their teeny-tiny meals add years to their lives (although it may just seem that way) to tech billionaires throwing millions of dollars at pharmaceutical companies, hoping that results in mice can be replicated in people.

As usual, humanity as a whole was far behind Tesla. Thanks to his battery, Edison had already lived longer than he could have dreamed possible, and would continue to do so.

Unless, of course, Caitlin succeeded in her plan.

As far as her current plans were concerned, her mash-ups were shaping up nicely. Until the canvas was torn away.

Caitlin never should have answered the door, but we all have a kind of Pavlovian response to a doorbell ring. And Nickelback had gone out to get them food, promising a veritable feast now that they had access to the Accelerati's money.

"Tonight we dine like kings," he said before he left. "Not a single spork or chicken wing."

Caitlin had assumed it was him when the doorbell rang. So the person standing there couldn't have shocked her more had he been wearing a Halloween mask.

"Dad!"

There was a rare look on his face—a stern sort of fury from which Caitlin had to avert her eyes.

"Get in the car," he said. "Now!"

"But, Dad—"

"I won't say it twice."

And when Caitlin didn't move, he stepped inside and looked around.

"Is this the company you're keeping?" he asked. "Who are all you people?"

"We're Nick!" said Old St. Nick, far too jovial for the moment.

Then Mr. Westfield zeroed in on Vince. "I know you! You're the troubled son of that woman who sold us our house."

"Guilty," said Vince.

"And you!" he said, pointing at Mitch. "Your father's in prison for life!"

Mitch only looked down.

"And these are the kinds of people you're spending your time with?"

Now Caitlin's mother was on the threshold, peeking inside nervously, like she was about to enter a pit of snakes. "Caitlin, what are you doing here?"

"Uh . . . homework?" She knew it was weak, but it was all she had.

"We had an eye-opening conversation with your principal," her father told her. "He said you've been missing school, and you've fallen in with a bad crowd. I can see now that it's true."

Nickelback stood up. "Let me explain—" he began.

But Caitlin's father cut him off in true lawyer fashion. "Say another word and I will bring you up on charges of harassment and verbal assault! From the moment my daughter met your grandson, or nephew, or whatever he is to you, her life has been nothing but a downward spiral."

"That's not true!" Caitlin said.

"Principal Watt told us everything, honey," her mother added. "How Nick threatened you. How he manipulated you. How he had his thugs attack poor Theo, who was only trying to help you."

"Those are lies! And what does Theo have to do with it?"

"This ends now!" her father said. Then he pointed his dread Finger of Doom at the others, who were rendered speechless by his rage. "And if I catch any of you within one hundred yards of my daughter ever again, I will shove so many lawsuits down your collective throats, you'll all need the Heimlich maneuver."

An instant later she was in the backseat of her father's Audi, being lectured about life choices and guilt by association, and being "grounded, young lady, until the end of time."

In one fell swoop all her plans had been torn asunder. And she realized that the Accelerati were nothing compared to parents.

ЗО GENIE OF THE COAT

The journey of Theo Blankenship was a curious thing, like a penny changing hands multiple times until it winds up back in the pocket of the person who originally tossed it into a fountain.

The vagrant who discovered the pink Madagascan spider-silk coat draped over a park bench found the jacket warm, and the conversation issuing from it—mostly about baseball—diverting.

His current station in life made his talking to the coat seem par for the course, so no one took notice of it. For a time, the man thought that Theo was a genie and refused to let him out of the lining until he granted the obligatory three wishes. When no wishes were forthcoming, the hobo lost interest and traded the coat for some good shoes at a thrift store.

Next Theo endured the ordeal of dry cleaning, which wasn't as unpleasant in two dimensions as it might have been in three, and was hung on a rack, awaiting purchase. By this time he had not just become resigned to his situation, he had come to embrace it. He was one with the coat. Peering out through a hole in the lining, he would heckle customers and spook small children. "Mommy, a haunted jacket!" they would say, and Theo would snicker.

Then he spied his very own principal perusing the thrift store. Principal Watt, a notorious tightwad, always bought his clothes used, and when he came close to the coat, Theo played the genie card, and to his own amazement, played it convincingly. Principal Watt fell for it, bought the coat, and Theo began a new life, well positioned to affect the power structure of Rocky Point Middle School.

"Pink is the new beige," Principal Watt told his staff when he wore the coat to school.

Theo had no intention of granting his principal any wishes, but he did convince him to call in Caitlin's parents and royally mess things up between her and Nick Slate—who, for some reason, Watt insisted did not officially exist.

Theo soon found Watt was not the most interesting company. The man liked to quote Shakespeare, talk back to the news, and complain to his wife about students who filled his life with sound and fury, signifying nothing.

For Theo, tomorrow, and tomorrow, and tomorrow would bring more of the same, and he was beginning to wish that the hobo hadn't given him up.

As for the principal, he was willing to give his talking coat the benefit of the doubt. Strange things were happening in the world. What might have seemed preposterous to him a few months earlier now fell much more firmly into the realm of possibility. "'There are more things in heaven and earth, Horatio, than are dreamt of in your philosophy,'" he mused.

"Darn right," Theo agreed. "And don't call me Horatio."

However, when the wishes were not granted, Watt began to suspect that perhaps the voice he heard was in his own mind and not within the lining of the coat. Or worse, the garment was a victim of demonic possession. As calling in an exorcist would be far too awkward, he decided his best course of action would be to burn the coat in ritualistic fashion, then find a support group.

Principal Watt lit a fire in his fireplace while his wife was off playing bridge, then he began to chant from chapter three of *Exorcism for Dummies*. And although Theo didn't know what three-dimensional fire would do to a two-dimensional kid, he suspected it would probably hurt. A lot.

"You don't want to do this," Theo begged as Principal Watt prepared to roast him alive.

To which Watt responded, "'Is that my soul that calls upon my name?'"

"No, it's me! Your genie! And you're ticking me off!"

Nevertheless, Principal Watt balled the coat up against Theo's muffled complaints. Theo waited for the flames to engulf him. But Principal Watt couldn't go through with it. He hurled the exorcism book into the flames instead, and fell to his knees.

Theo tried to comfort him with some Shakespeare of his own. "'Now is the winter of our discotheque,'" he said, but it just made Watt burst into tears.

And so, genie that he was, he chose to grant Principal Watt his wish.

"I will leave you alone forever," Theo told him, "if you bring me to Caitlin Westfield, and drape me around her shoulders."

This explains why, on the night that Caitlin was officially grounded until the end of time, Principal Watt showed up at the Westfields' front door.

"It is imperative that I give this to your daughter," he told Mrs. Westfield. Since he was her principal, and it did seem rather important to him, she called Caitlin out of her room, and he put the coat on her.

"What's this all about?" Caitlin asked.

Her mother just shrugged. "I don't think it's yours. It's too big on you."

"There now," Principal Watt said. "All is as it should be." Then he turned and ran into the night as if chased by a puma.

"Well, that was weird," said Caitlin, and she stomped back to her room.

And within the lining of the coat, the winter of Theo Blankenship's discontent was made glorious summer.

Caitlin threw off the coat the moment she got into her room. Only when she held it in her hands did she realize it was like no fabric she had ever touched, and she gasped. Was this the feel of Madagascan spider silk?

She hung it on her closet door and stared at it, trying to make sense of why Principal Watt would bring it to her.

Was he Accelerati? No, that couldn't be right. He was too small-minded to be evil-scientist material.

Another mystery I'm never going to solve, she thought.

She knew there was no way she could tell her parents everything that was going on, because there was no way they would ever believe her. She'd tried giving them the tip of the iceberg but had about as much success as the *Titanic.* "What happened here in Colorado Springs was no accident," she had told them. "I'm trying to make sure it doesn't happen again."

They'd just scoffed. "You're fourteen, Caitlin," her father reminded her. "Your only concern should be keeping your grades up, and what clothes to wear."

Could they really think she was so shallow? So two-dimensional?

She lay on her bed, pounding her pillow in frustration, when the voice behind her made her gasp.

"Caitlin," the voice said, "it's me. Don't be afraid."

"Who is it? Who's there?" She spun around, but the room was empty.

"It's me, Theo."

As if things weren't miserable enough, Theo was here? Where was he hiding?

"I know this is going to sound weird," Theo's voice said, "but I'm in the pink jacket."

Slowly she approached it. Was this some Accelerati trick? Was there a speaker in the pocket? She looked, but found nothing.

And then Theo spoke again, much closer this time. "I'm in the lining," he said. "This guy put me in his coat and then left it on a park bench. A guy named Jorgenson."

"Jorgenson?" said Caitlin. "Alan Jorgenson?"

"That's him," said Theo. "He's the new lunch dude at school, but he's really part of this secret society. And they've got this sweet hideout beneath Atomic Lanes."

"Just keep quiet," Caitlin told him, "and let me figure this out."

She turned the coat inside out and found a hidden zipper that ran the length of it. Slowly, reluctantly, she pulled the zipper down, and when she did, out crawled Theo.

He scooted across the floor and pulled himself up the door.

To call him "flat" didn't do it justice. He was thinner than onionskin, flatter than one of her posters. Caitlin might have screamed, might have run, but she had seen so many bizarre things since coming in contact with the Accelerati that her surprise registered only somewhere in the yellow zone.

"Who did this to you?" she asked.

"I don't know," Theo told her. "One minute I was shooting video of a tornado that was hurling out cats, and the next I was flat against a wall like this."

"And Principal Watt knew about this?"

Theo shook his two-dimensional head. "He just thought I was a possessed coat. But hey, now that I'm here, can I stay with you? I won't be a bother. I don't have to eat, and I don't take up any space at all."

But the idea of keeping Theo as a personal poster child just felt weird. And then something occurred to her. She might be locked up like a suburban Rapunzel right now, but Theo was not.

She was about to say something to him when the door opened. It was her father. He'd never been particularly suspicious of her, but now he eyed her with distrust and a little bit of pain—the pain of suddenly becoming an outsider in her life.

"I heard voices," he said. "Who were you talking to?"

"You took my phone," she said, "so I have no one to talk to but myself, do I?"

"You'll get your phone back," her father said, "when you start behaving responsibly again."

He looked around to confirm there was no one else in the room, then closed the door, never noticing that Theo was right there on the wall behind the door, as stealthy as could be.

"Theo," Caitlin whispered, "do you think you could find Jorgenson if you needed to?"

"I don't want to be within five miles of that guy."

"But you'd know how to find him?"

Theo shrugged. "I guess."

Caitlin took a deep breath. Could it be that the only person who might save her from this untimely grounding was Jorgenson? She'd already made a deal with him. She supposed that when you deal with the devil once, you're doomed to repeat the transaction.

"Theo, I need you to slip out of here and find him. Tell him . . ." Caitlin hesitated. What on earth could she say that would bring Jorgenson? "Tell him I have his coat and some more information, but he has to break me out to get it."

Theo frowned. "What's in it for me?" he asked.

"I'll find a way to make you three-dimensional again," Caitlin told him.

"That's what Jorgenson said. I don't believe you any more than I believed him." Then he sighed. "But I'll do it, Caitlin, on one condition. When I'm done, you let me stay here."

"But, Theo . . ."

"Please. I have nowhere else to go. I can hang out in your closet, or live under your bed."

"Ew," said Caitlin.

"Okay, then, maybe just the closet."

Caitlin hesitated, which was apparently close enough to an agreement for Theo, and he slipped out of her barely open window into the night.

Jorgenson was actually pleased to see Theo slide under his front door.

"But where's my coat?" he asked, because a spider-silk garment, regardless of its color, was very expensive and hard to come by.

"If you want it, you have to get it back from Caitlin."

Jorgenson bristled. "Caitlin Westfield has my coat?"

"Yeah," said Theo, "but I'm sure she'll give it back. It's way too big for her."

Later that evening, Jorgenson rang the Westfields' front bell, and when Mrs. Westfield came to the door, he smiled as warmly as a man like Alan Jorgenson could.

"Can I help you?" she asked.

"I've come for my coat," he told her as he pulled what appeared to be a gold pen from his shirt pocket. "Oh, look at that," he said, pointing over her shoulder.

And when she turned, he pressed a button on the pen and projected a spot of light against the far wall.

"Ohh," she said, "what is it?" Completely forgetting Jorgenson, she ran to try to catch the light on the wall.

Mr. Westfield, entering the room and seeing the glowing spot on the wall as well, dropped the sandwich he was eating and leaped for the light.

"What is that? Have you ever seen anything like it?" he asked.

"Where did it come from?" his wife asked.

For a few moments Jorgenson shined it around the room and watched them follow.

"There it goes!"

"Try to catch it!"

Theo came creeping around the doorjamb and watched the action, not knowing what to make of it. "They're like cats jumping at a laser pointer," he said.

"Precisely," said Jorgenson. "The BSO Projector is set at the exact wavelength to stimulate overwhelming curiosity in the human mind. They've already completely forgotten about me. Now take me to Caitlin."

He turned off the Bright Shiny Object Projector as Theo led him up the stairs.

"Wait, where did it go?" asked Mr. Westfield.

"I think behind the sofa," answered Mrs. Westfield.

"Well, what are you waiting for? Pull it away from the wall!"

Jorgenson found Caitlin pacing in her room. He grabbed his coat, which had been thrown over a chair.

"Thank goodness you're here," Caitlin said.

Jorgenson grinned from ear to ear. "What irony," he said, "that you need me to rescue you from your own home. Although I can't see why I would want to."

"Has Edison let you out of the doghouse yet?"

Reluctantly, Jorgenson admitted that the information she had given him had been useful. "Let's just say that part of my life is a rapidly fading memory." He gestured toward Theo, awkwardly attempting to sit in a beanbag chair. "Mr. Blankenship here tells me you have more intel for me. I may be able to spirit you away from your gilded cage, if I like what I hear."

"I want to surrender," Caitlin said. "Nick's one of you now, and I won't fight him. I want to be on the same side he is."

"What?" said Theo. He attempted to stride closer to her, but only managed to slide across the floor, which clearly did not have the impact he intended.

But Jorgenson was unimpressed. "What use could we possibly have for you? You're clearly not Accelerati material."

"If Edison wants Nick to do his best work, he'll do it if I'm there." Still Jorgenson wasn't convinced that she was worth the trouble. "And," Caitlin added, "personally bringing me to Edison would be another brownie point for you."

Jorgenson tapped his chin, considering. She seemed sincere, but she had already proven herself to be duplicitous. So, to be sure, he reached into his pocket, pulled out the woven circle of a dream catcher, and dangled it in front of her.

"What are you doing?" she asked.

"Testing you," he said simply. "The Doomcatcher picks up the slightest vibrations of an approaching chaos front and pulsates an alarm when doom is impending." However, the Doomcatcher was now motionless, which meant that Caitlin Westfield was currently not the Pandora he had suspected her to be.

"Very well," he said, putting the Doomcatcher back in his inside pocket. "But you will come as my prisoner and be treated as such."

"Fine," said Caitlin.

. . .

The Doomcatcher gave Caitlin pause. Did its silence mean she would fail in her attempt to pull Edison's plug? Or would doing so bring more order than chaos to the world?

There was no way to know. All she could do was move forward with her plan.

When she and Jorgenson stepped out of her room, her parents were already on their way up the stairs, the effects of the BSO Projector having worn off.

"Who in blazes are you?" yelled her father.

And so Jorgenson sighed, pulled out the projector again, and aimed it at the wall downstairs.

"Oooh, it's back!" shouted Caitlin's mother.

"Quick, catch it this time!" her father said, completely forgetting Jorgenson as they both ran downstairs.

Caitlin turned to Theo. "Theo, stay here. When they snap out of it, let them know that I'm okay, I just have something really important to do."

"But they'll freak out when they see me," Theo pointed out.

"Exactly," said Caitlin. "And maybe then they'll believe you."

Then she left with Jorgenson, got into his pearlescent SUV, and became a prisoner of the Accelerati.

31 A VERY CLOSE SHAVE

Even in her absence, the gears of Caitlin's plan continued to turn that night.

Little Nicky, as she had predicted, could be very, very annoying when he wanted to be. Between his poking and mimicking and I-know-you-are-but-what-am-I's, Mitch was about ready to pound him into the ground.

When Mitch was whipped up into an emotional meringue, all the others took turns posing questions.

"We can stop Thomas Edison by—" BeatNick prompted.

"—applying the brakes on his wheelchair," Mitch concluded.

"Evangeline Planck—" began Nickelback.

"—had a root canal on February twenty-second."

"The key to beating the Accelerati—" started Nicholas.

"—doesn't fit into any standard ignition."

"Mitch," said Vince, "you have to do better than that."

"It's not my fault," said Mitch. "What comes out, comes out. You have to start the right sentence."

"We can reunite—" Nicholas began.

"—with ghostly light," Mitch blurted.

BeatNick threw up his hands. "What's that supposed to mean?"

"I don't know," said Little Nicky, "but I don't like it."

All the answers that Mitch gave were either useless or too

enigmatic to help them. Eventually, he went home, and had dreams about being poked and prodded and teased.

Zak and Vince, meanwhile, were quick to discover that it's not easy to take two machines that defy known scientific principles and create a third one that's even more defiant.

"We can't take them apart," said Zak. "What if we can't put them back together?"

"Well, we can't join them if we don't take them apart first," Vince pointed out.

The furthest they got was to open the casings and peer in at circuits and wiring and tubes like two skittish members of a bomb squad, uncertain of which wires to cut.

They pulled an all-nighter, and by morning had mapped out schematics for both devices. The one promising lead they found was that each had precisely twelve internal wires that went absolutely nowhere, and they wondered whether or not those could be interconnected.

"Do you want to risk it?" Zak asked, bleary-eyed from lack of sleep.

Although Vince was usually up for a death-defying challenge, he had to admit that connecting those wires without a little more information sounded like a really, really bad idea.

"Who needs a time machine, anyway?" Zak said. "In movies, nine times out of ten, time travel doesn't end well."

The others had a full night's sleep. BeatNick was ready to leave for Shoreham, and Nickelback to Princeton, and Vince helped them fix their obvious travel problem.

"I know a guy who knows a guy who can make you fake IDs while-u-wait, as long as you have enough money. And we've got plenty of that now, don't we? Make up any names you want," Vince told them.

Vince gave them the address of the guy who the guy knew, which was on the way to the airport, called a cab, and they left.

As for Nicholas, he planned to stay long enough to have breakfast, because Atomic Lanes didn't open until ten a.m.

Had the bowling establishment opened earlier, things might have turned out very different.

Of all the Accelerati in Colorado Springs, Petula was the only one who noticed signs of activity at Vince LaRue's house. The other agents were far too absorbed with the Wardenclyffe project, or were sidelined by some hush-hush financial crisis that no one seemed to want to talk about.

It left her in the perfect position to see what was going on under everyone's noses. There were a bunch of people in Vince's house. A veritable family reunion, it seemed. And while many of the relatives resembled one another, none of them looked like Vince.

Ms. Planck had not given Petula much Accelerati technology to help her in her endeavors. She had the Temporal Bouncer—the same "birthday-suiting" weapon Nick had used when retrieving the prism. She had a Doomcatcher in her pocket that only seemed to vibrate when she went home—which made perfect sense to her, since her family always seemed like doom incarnate—and she had a temporal dilator to slow down time in case of emergency.

But she had none of the really good stuff.

Plus it was hard to be stealthy with one arm in a cast—but at least it was down to just a wrist cast now.

The voices from inside the house were muffled and muted, but she clearly heard the words *time machine*, which made her ears perk up.

She ducked down as two of the men, a twenty-something with a goatee and a middle-aged guy with muttonchops, left the house, bickering as they stepped into a taxi. They looked familiar, but she couldn't place their faces.

As soon as they were gone, she started the temporal dilator.

Now, moving between the seconds, she opened the window and climbed in. She had three minutes to do what she needed to do, while in the outside world only three seconds would pass. When time returned to its normal pace, everyone present was securely attached to chairs and other stationary objects with cable ties—which Petula always carried on her, because you never know when you might have to tie someone up.

The five victims were bewildered by their sudden predicament. Then the little kid zeroed in on her, and moaned. "Petula . . . why did it have to be Petula?"

Petula looked down at him. "Do I know you?"

He just glared at her. Why did that glare seem so familiar?

"Let us go, Petula!" said a thirty-something guy with a dark beard. He struggled futilely against his bonds. "Let us go, or I swear I'll—"

"How do you know me?" demanded Petula. She glanced at Vince, who just shrugged uselessly, then looked back at the bearded guy. "I don't know you—why do you know me?"

She held eye contact with him for a good long moment, and something occurred to her. She looked to the kid, then the man in his thirties, and then the old man, and truth came to her in a flash.

"You're all Nick!" she announced. "You made a time machine, went back in time, and became your own grandfather," she said. "Uh . . . and father."

"No, dummy," said the younger Nick. "It was the stupid prism! It broke us into seven parts."

"Nicky!" chided Nicholas.

Nicky looked down at the floor. "Sorry."

It all made sense to her now. It explained why Nick had only seemed partially there back at the ruins of his house. In a way, he had been.

The old man offered her a deal. "Don't do this, Petula," he said. "I'll go out with you! I mean, when I'm put back together and fourteen again, I'll go out with you." He gave her a smile with very few teeth in it.

"Ew," said Petula. "Ew, ew, ew, ew, EW!" And then she realized there were simply not enough *ew's* in the world.

Somewhere else in the house, a baby began to cry.

"If you're gonna keep us all tied up," said the black kid, "then you're gonna have to change SputNick's diaper."

Rather than being annoyed, she was intrigued. She found the baby in a makeshift crib in the master bedroom. Same dark blue eyes. This was also Nick. And he was helpless! It thrilled her to suddenly have Nick so completely at her mercy. She picked the baby up and it promptly gerbed all over her blouse.

"Yeah," she said, "you definitely are Nick."

But in the baby's eyes she saw none of the animosity, none of the baggage that their nonexistent relationship carried. The baby was truly an innocent, unaware of anything beyond eating, sleeping, and filling his diaper. This was the only Nick that didn't despise her! She changed his diaper, and put him down to sleep with a pacifier to joyfully suck on.

Then she called Ms. Planck.

Ms. Planck, in her office beneath the bowling alley, did not want to take Petula's call. All morning she had been dealing with issues that were only getting worse. It began with an irate call from the Old Man.

"Can you please explain why my gardener is at my door with a bounced check?" Edison asked. "In all my unnaturally long life, I have never had a check returned for insufficient funds."

"I'm sure it's a mistake," Planck had told him, a bit bewildered.

"Do we not have three-quarters of a billion dollars in an encrypted floating account? Or have you spent it all?"

The fact was, they had barely dipped into that money. The interest alone was enough to fund most of their operations. Of course the excavation of the Slate home and the building of the new Wardenclyffe Tower had put them pretty deep into debt—but they had more than enough money to pay off the loans. So why were they bouncing checks?

"I'll look into it," Planck told him. Then, not five minutes later, she received a call from the Accelerati cafeteria—apparently the caterer was withholding delivery due to issues with a payment that should have gone through the evening before. The Accelerati were worse than middle schoolers when it came to lunch. Once, when their cafeteria workers went on strike, some of the more militant members had threatened to roast the laboratory animals. It infuriated her that even now, when she was finally freed from being the world's most overqualified lunch lady, she still had to deal with food-service issues.

But the third punch was the worst. She had requested a printout of their latest financial figures. The accountant who entered her office was wearing a sherbet-green spider-silk suit, and his face seemed a bit green as well, as if he might pass out at any moment. He held out the piece of paper with a shaky hand.

"You're not going to like it," he said. He took a step backward once she had the page, as if it might blow up in her hands.

According to the printout, the full value of the Accelerati's cash holdings was one cent.

The look on her face must have been truly terrifying, because the accountant said, in the weakest of all possible voices, "Please don't kill me."

She narrowed her eyes even further. "Just get out," she said. The very idea that he would assume she would kill the messenger for bad news infuriated her. She made a mental note to submit him for genetic experimentation, as punishment for thinking her so evil.

Clearly this was just some banking glitch that could be easily corrected, but that didn't make it any less irritating. And it made Edison doubt her leadership. As powerful as she had become, all the Old Man need do was wave his hand and she'd be replaced just as quickly as Jorgenson had been.

That's when her secretary told her that Petula Grabowski-Jones was on the line.

"Tell her I'm busy."

"But she says it's an emergency."

Ms. Planck sighed. With Petula *everything* was an emergency—and the last thing she needed was more bad news. Had it been it a mistake inviting Petula into the Accelerati? She wondered if perhaps the girl might be another perfect candidate for the genetics lab.

"Petula, dear, how are you?"

"I found the globe!" she said. "I'm holding it in my hands as we speak."

Ms. Planck found herself standing up in excitement. "Where are you?"

"Vince LaRue's house. Come as soon as you can!" she said. "Oh, and one more thing. It looks like they were using it to build a time machine."

And in that one instant Petula went from being a problem to being Evangeline Planck's savior.

. . .

"Don't touch any of the buttons!" Vince shouted as Petula examined the globe.

"Not even this one?" Petula teased, moving her finger toward the button.

"Especially not that one!"

Petula laughed. She was familiar enough with Tesla's inventions by now to know that misuse of them could lead to pain or death. That job would be left to the research and development people who would attempt to reverse-engineer it.

She looked over at the odd telephone. "So is that the time machine?"

"Just because we were trying to make one doesn't mean we succeeded," said the black kid.

"Don't answer her, Zak," said brown-bearded Nick. "The less we give her, the better."

Funny, but the more Petula looked at the man Nick would become, the more she felt like she knew him. Nick grew up to be handsome, his eyes staying that same deep shade of blue. Of course, the facial hair made it hard to see much of anything.

Since she had nothing to do but wait until Ms. Planck arrived, she decided to entertain her curiosity. She went to the bathroom and found a razor. It was a lady's razor, but a blade was a blade.

She slathered him up with shaving cream and, ignoring his protests, began to shave him clean.

"What are you doing? I like my beard!"

"Shut up and stop moving or I might nick an artery."

When she was done, she took a step back to look at him. When the truth hit, it hit like a shock wave. She nearly fell over.

"No. Freaking. Way," said Vince, also seeing what Petula saw.

She had never known Vince to be surprised by anything.

"Well, I'll be a monkey's uncle," said the elderly Nick.

"I am not seeing this," said Zak. "Tell me I'm not seeing this."

Little Nicky just stared, and shook his head.

"What are you all talking about?" said the clean-shaven man.

"Why don't I show you?" said Petula. Then she pulled out her phone, snapped a picture, and held it out for him to see.

"Very funny," he said. "Why are you showing me a photo of Nikola Tesla?"

She could see in his eyes the moment that he caught on.

And in the other room, once more, the baby began to cry.

32 THE IDEA OF BEING PERMANENTLY DEAD

Throughout history, facial hair has been both the most convenient and the most convincing disguise. Even the still-evolving science of facial recognition has been thrown off track by the well-placed beard, mustache, and muttonchops—hiding firm jawlines, distinctive lips, and striking cheekbones.

Over the centuries, beards, mustaches, and elaborate sideburns have gone in and out of style. At various times, in various places, some societies prized facial hair as a symbol of strength and maturity. (Although nothing quite explains the nineteenth-century neck beard, a look embraced by both Horace Greeley and Henry David Thoreau.)

Nowadays, various forms of facial hair happened to be in fashion. So Nick Slate's older selves all had some form of it—and it had disguised the truth from everybody, including themselves.

Until now.

This changed everything.

Petula considered herself a loyal Acceleratus, but this trumped all loyalties. Now she understood that Nick's connection to the inventor went far beyond just finding the stuff in his attic.

She held the baby until he stopped crying, and paced, trying to think. Atomic Lanes was not all that far away, which meant that Ms. Planck would be there in minutes. Should Petula tell her about this? The moment she had that thought, the Doomcatcher in her pocket started to vibrate. But she didn't need that contraption to tell her it was a bad idea.

At this point, all Ms. Planck knew was that the globe was here. Who said she needed to know anything else?

Petula looked to her prisoners, then pulled out her birthday-suiter. "You're going to go away for twenty minutes," she told them. "When you come back, you'll find your clothes in the closet."

"Wait," said Zak. "What about our clothes?"

She didn't have time for further explanation. She quickly zapped Zak and the three Nicks. They vanished, but their clothes remained. Then she put the baby down on the sofa and zapped him too.

She gathered all their clothes, threw them into the closet as she had promised, and moved all the chairs into the kitchen so that when they reappeared they would no longer be bound to them. Of course, they would fall to the floor, as if the chairs had been kicked out from underneath them, but them's the breaks.

Vince watched all this, still a bit stunned by Petula's sudden change of heart. He was the only one left, and he wasn't sure why.

"Uh, I think you forgot me," he said.

"I didn't forget you," she told him.

Then he realized, and began to despair. "You're keeping me here so you can give my battery to the Accelerati, aren't you?"

She looked at him for a moment like she might be considering it, but then she said, "Once I give them the globe, your battery will be the only thing they need, and I do *not* want to be responsible for killing you again."

Then she grabbed the globe, stood next to him, and fiddled with the controls.

"No, wait!" he said.

Too late. She hit the green button.

They immediately found themselves on some rocky terrain, far, far away, with half of a coffee table and a circular piece of the floor.

Luckily the teleportation field hadn't been set any wider, or there would've been another house missing from the neighborhood.

Petula kicked Vince's chair over. He fell over backward, backpack and all. He thought the jolt might disconnect him, but it didn't.

Always prepared, she tossed him a Swiss Army knife, which landed on his chest. "Use this to cut the cable ties," she told him.

"You're just going to leave me here?"

"If you stay in Colorado Springs," Petula said, "they'll eventually find you and take the battery. But they won't find you here." Then she looked at the globe. "So I'm guessing the button with the exclamation point will take me back."

And although Vince did not like the idea of being stranded, he liked the idea of being permanently dead even less. "Yeah," he said. "But the second you get there, jump to the side. Otherwise you'll fall through a hole into the basement and break your other arm."

"Thanks for the tip," she told him. Then she hit the button and vanished.

It took a couple of minutes for Vince to cut himself free, and when he did, he stood up and examined his surroundings.

He was on a cliff above a rugged shoreline. He could hear heavy surf pounding the rocks below. It was chilly, but he no longer had sensitivity to cold. He couldn't be sure of where he was, but he had an idea.

Because around him were penguins. Lots and lots of penguins.

When Ms. Planck arrived, Petula was standing in the living room holding the globe crooked in her good arm.

There was a hole in the floor and part of the coffee table was missing.

"I kind of tried it out," Petula said. "It's a teleporter."

"We already suspected that," Ms. Planck told her as she took the globe away. "This confirms it." Then she looked around. "What about the time machine?"

"I believe they were trying to build one using the globe and that telephone thingy."

Ms. Planck instructed one of the other Accelerati to take the phone.

"Excellent work, Petula," she said. "I'm very proud of you. And Edison will be, as well."

Then they all left together in Planck's pearlescent Bentley.

Approximately eight minutes later, Mitch Murló arrived to find the front door of Vince's house ajar. Fearing the worst, he went inside.

"Hello?" he said. "Where is everybody?"

He checked the bedrooms, but nobody was there either.

When he returned to the living room, to his surprise he found Zak and several of the Nicks, as if they had just appeared out of nowhere.

"Oh, there you are," Mitch said. "Uh . . . how come you're all naked?"

33 HOW TASTY IS THY EEL

Lightning strikes were on the rise again. And commercial airline pilots were once more having to "fly by braille," which is what they'd come to call flying without the standard avionics telemetry.

People were already beginning to adapt to the static buildup in the atmosphere. After all, it had happened once before and the world had survived. So it was easy to assume that the world would come through again, with minimal casualties. The charge was a nuisance, certainly, but nothing more. In another week, folks assumed, the energy would discharge somewhere on the planet, frying electronics and blowing out light bulbs, as it had in Colorado Springs.

In fact, casinos in Las Vegas were already taking bets on which area would be struck. The odds-on favorite was Oslo, Norway, although no one could figure out why.

However, the bulk of humanity was missing some crucial information: none but a handful knew that the only reason the first lifesaving discharge had occurred was that Tesla's machine in Nick's attic had made it happen. Without it, the entire world would have been fried. Nothing but the cockroaches would have survived, and even that was questionable.

So the planet was blindly heading toward that same destiny

once more. And this time, it seemed, only the Accelerati could save it.

Luckily for life on Earth, saving the world was a better business proposition for the Accelerati than letting it be destroyed—because certainly, if more money were to be made from global extinction, the Accelerati would have been all over that instead.

Thomas Edison, Nick realized, was an extremely important ally to have when their goals were the same. The conflict would come exactly five minutes after the next discharge. That's when Edison's goal of serving the world would shift to making the world serve Edison.

Now that Nick was back in Edison's mansion, where everything was beset by Victorian order and peacefulness, it was easy for him to forget what was at stake. And as he lay on his bed, looking up at the intricate woodwork of the ceiling, he tried to remind himself why he was here.

To protect his family and friends from the wrath of the Accelerati, to make sure that the reconstructed machine would take the discharge, and to keep an eye on Edison. Nick had to find a way to either change the old man or, at the very least, distract him long enough to foil whatever plan he had for using the machine.

Nick's strategy wasn't fully formed. It was as incomplete as he was. And he didn't know if he'd ever be complete again.

There was a knock at the door, and Mrs. Higgenbotham came in holding a tuxedo. "Dinner is formal tonight, dear. By order of Mr. Edison. Guests will be joining us."

A short time earlier, Nick had seen lights go on and silhouettes appear in the windows of the carriage house, where Edison put up short-term visitors.

That's all Nick needed—an evening of stodgy bores. Who was Edison entertaining? Nick mused. The heads of other secret societies? Celebrities who had faked their own deaths?

"Who's coming?" he asked.

"Can't say as I know. He doesn't tell me these things. All I know is the table will be set for six." She hung the tuxedo in his closet. "The bow tie is a clip-on, love. I made it easy for you."

After Nick dressed, he couldn't help but admire himself in the mirror. Dressing up like this wasn't something he had ever enjoyed, but he'd never worn a tuxedo before either. He looked good. *Debonair*, his mother would have said.

History can't be changed.

He took a deep breath and tried to dispel the melancholy that came with memories of his mother. *Is this really so bad?* he thought, looking at his reflection again. *Dressing up in fancy clothes and being the heir to an electrical dynasty?*

To Nick, those thoughts were the scariest of all. That he might eventually want this more than he wanted to end it.

Caitlin paced in her room on the second floor of the carriage house, dressed in a gown that some silent-film star must have worn to the Oscars eighty years ago.

The indignation of having to wear such a thing was trumped only by the indignation of her room being next to Alan Jorgenson's, whom she could hear through the wall, in his shower, singing show tunes.

Jorgenson wanted to be the one to present her to Edison, but she was not about to allow that. She would meet Edison on her own, and if she had her way, she'd never even have to shake his hand.

Caitlin had already been responsible for one man's death: the jeweler Mr. Svedborg. Had she not cajoled him into telling them the truth about the Accelerati pin she had found, the man would still be alive. But she had never killed anyone intentionally.

On the other hand, could pulling Edison's plug really be considered murder? Can you kill a man who should have, by all laws of nature, died nearly a century ago? Disconnecting him from the battery would be righting a wrong.

With that in mind, while Jorgenson wailed on about the music of the night, Caitlin left the carriage house, crossed to the main house, and rang the bell.

The door was opened by a British housekeeper with a weird air about her that Caitlin couldn't put her finger on. The woman escorted her into the drawing room, where Caitlin suspected she might meet Colonel Mustard wielding a lead pipe. But no such luck.

Instead, an obscenely old man in an odd wheelchair contraption rolled in to greet her.

"Miss Westfield," creaked Edison, "a pleasure to make your acquaintance. I must say that Clara Bow's evening gown becomes you."

"Yeah, well, I hope I don't become *it*," Caitlin said.

The old man offered his hand and Caitlin hesitated, then shook it, trying to hide her disgust at the pasty, skeletal feel of his fingers. Behind him, attached to the back of the wheelchair, was a tall cylindrical object draped by a velvet cozy.

The battery, she thought. It was much larger than Vince's. From this angle, she couldn't see the wires, but she knew they had to be there.

"You're a bit early for dinner," Edison said. "But I'm glad you're here, so we can talk. We share something in common, you and I."

Caitlin couldn't imagine anything they had in common, so she had to ask, "What's that?"

His smile was a cross between that of the Grinch and the mummy of Ramses. "We both share an admiration for Nick Slate."

"Nick. Where is he?"

Edison waved the question away. "Oh, you'll see him at dinner. And won't he be surprised to see you!" He rolled his chair back a bit to take a good look at her. "I must admit that when Jorgenson told me you had surrendered to him, I was dubious. But here you are, and I'm grateful that you finally realize I am not your enemy."

Caitlin, nearly gagging on the very suggestion, cleared her throat. She took a step closer to him. "At first, I thought Nick was lying when he said you weren't all that bad. Then I thought he must have been brainwashed." She took another step closer.

"And what do you think now?" Edison asked.

Caitlin wasn't about to tell him what she really thought. "I think I need to get to know you and decide for myself," she said.

"Well," said Edison, "I may look a bit like the bogeyman, but you'll find that I am not. Just as Nick has learned."

She took one step closer. Now she could see the insulated wires running into the back of his tuxedo. She knew that if she was going to do this, she would have to do it quickly. Before he could call for the guards who were probably waiting everywhere in the house.

She would have to disconnect him and then smash the glass battery, to make sure he wouldn't be able to come back to life. She already had that covered—there was a fireplace poker only a few yards away, heavy enough, she figured, to break the glass.

"I understand you're an artist. I hope you might create something while you're here."

Yeah, thought Caitlin, *there are lots of things I could do with the smashed pieces of that battery.*

Edison turned his head and raised his hand to light a cigar—

Caitlin reached toward the wires to yank them—

Then a hand grabbed her wrist. Not an old bony one either, but a young, strong hand. Nick's.

"Caitlin!" he said. "I'm so glad you're here!"

He pulled her away from Edison, holding her wrist just tightly enough to make it clear that he knew exactly what she'd been about to do.

Like Edison, Nick was dressed in a tuxedo. He looked remarkably good, but it didn't change the fact that at this moment he was upsetting her plan.

"I see you've met Mr. Edison," Nick said, finally letting go.

"Yes," said Edison, turning to them with his cigar, puffing away. "Another girl claiming to be your girlfriend."

If Caitlin hadn't already been derailed, this would have flung her off the tracks entirely. "Another girl?" she asked Nick.

Nick shook his head. "Petula," he told her. "The true love of my life."

Caitlin laughed in spite of herself, her feelings more than mixed. She was still furious that Nick had stopped her, but she was thrilled to see him nonetheless, even as she was embarrassed to be caught wearing Clara Bow's evening gown and was somewhat disgusted by the way that Edison stared at them with an "ah, young love" sort of look in his eyes.

"So," said the old man, "she's who she claims to be."

"We'll see," said Nick, not quite glaring at her.

Before he could say anything more, Jorgenson arrived, his hair still wet and his shirt not fully tucked in. When his eyes lit on Caitlin, he seemed both livid and relieved.

"I thought we'd lost you," he said to her. Then he turned to Edison. "Al," he began magnanimously, "I'd like to present—"

"Don't bother," said Edison, waving him off. "We've met."

Just then, Mrs. Higgenbotham came in. "Our other guests have arrived. Would you like to join them in the dining room?"

History is full of painfully awkward meals.

Take, for instance, the first Thanksgiving, when the American Indians did all the work because the Pilgrims were still fairly useless in this new-to-them world. Contrary to popular belief, there was no turkey served. And how does one convincingly say to one's new American Indian friends, "My, how tasty is thy eel!"

And then there was the Donner Party. One could scarcely imagine more awkward dinner conversation.

Human being was not on the menu at the Edison mansion that night, but that particular combination of dinner guests made for a truly distasteful evening.

There were Jorgenson and Planck, who hated each other with every fiber of their beings. There were Nick and Caitlin, both of whom seemed to be suffering from indigestion before they even sat down. There was Z, who was clearly anxious upon seeing Caitlin and desperately wanted to ask about Zak, but was unable to in front of the others. And, of course, there was Edison himself, who seemed to take great pleasure in everyone else's discomfort.

"I am honored," Edison said, holding his wineglass toward Nick, "to be breaking bread with the next generation of Accelerati." Then, nodding toward Planck and Z, he added, "Along with my two highest-ranking officers. Oh, and you too, Alan," he tossed in dismissively.

Jorgenson maintained his poise. "The best thing you ever did for me was take me to task, Al," he said to Edison. "You broke me of my complacency. As evidenced by the fact that I've handed you Nick and his friend here. Both of whom, I might add, slipped through the hands of your new Grand Acceleratus."

Planck reached out to grab her glass, intentionally displaying her ring in Jorgenson's direction. "I've been busy with more important things than chasing small children," she said.

Through all of this, Mrs. Higgenbotham kept circling the room, slamming a swatter down on the table to catch a pesky fly. Unfortunately, she was not a mechanism of great speed, and so the insect evaded each and every swat.

"Let it be," Edison told her. "Just bring the meal."

As for the fly, it was more than happy to buzz in the dinner guests' ears, and partake of the meal as best as it could. It was resting on the lip of Edison's soup bowl, enjoying some cream of asparagus, when Edison said, "Nick has expressed a concern about one of the objects in the lab."

"The blender," Planck guessed, waving her spoon as she spoke, which was more than enough to attract the fly to it. "We've determined that it serves as a voltage regulator, and as such doesn't require a lid."

"And what if it does?" asked Nick.

"This could be a question worth pondering," Z admitted.

At that point, the fly narrowly escaped being sucked up Jorgenson's left nostril as he drew in an exasperated breath of air. "Why do any of you care what he thinks?" he said. "The boy knows nothing about the objects; he just sold them out of his garage."

"He knows a lot more than you," Caitlin said in his defense.

The fly became a joyful one-insect swarm when the main course arrived. Scandinavian squab cooked in its own juices. It took no interest in the verbal snipes delivered around the table—mostly by Jorgenson and Planck, who lived to antagonize one another.

"How's headquarters, Evangeline?" Jorgenson asked. "I hope you haven't replaced the Renoirs and Monets with sad clowns and dogs playing poker."

"I'd send some art to your workplace," Planck replied, "but I don't think they allow oil paintings in cafeteria kitchens."

"I'm no longer there—or haven't you heard? It took me less than a month to be promoted out of that position. How many years did it take you to get out of food service, Evangeline?"

And so it went until dessert: cherries jubilee and a dessert wine served in chilled glasses that fogged and smoked like dry ice when they were set on the table.

As for the fly, it had taken an interest in the dessert wine, because it had landed on the lip of the bottle and discovered that it was sweet—although now it was buzzing about a bit haphazardly.

For this reason, Mrs. Higgenbotham picked up her flyswatter again after the wine had been poured to everyone but Nick and Caitlin.

"Really?" said Caitlin. "Not even a little?"

"I'm not programmed to serve wine to minors, dearie," Mrs. Higgenbotham said as she pursued the drunken fly. "Except in religious ceremonies, of course. You'll have to get someone else to pour." But of course nobody did.

"Blandy's Madeira, and a 1995 vintage too!" said Jorgenson with uncharacteristic cheerfulness. "You must try our host's aged Madeira, Evangeline. Edison and I have shared many a glass."

"Not so many," grumbled Edison.

But before Ms. Planck could pick up her glass, Mrs. Higgenbotham, hell-bent on victory, slammed the swatter down, missing the fly, but knocking over and shattering Planck's goblet.

"Mrs. Higgenbotham, please!" complained Edison.

"Dear oh dear oh dear," Mrs. Higgenbotham lamented. "I'm all thumbs and axle grease. No matter—I'll fetch you a fresh glass."

The incident turned Jorgenson back into his unpleasant self. "That woman should be dismantled and sold for spare parts."

"Watch what you say, Al," said Edison. "You know I have a penchant for old machines."

Dinner concluded without further incident. Even the fly no longer troubled them, because it had taken a sip of the spilled wine and promptly died on the table from cyanide poisoning.

34 HEADS WILL ROLL

Jorgenson was absolutely infuriated. Not so much by the disrespect, but by the fact that Evangeline Planck was still alive. He had gone to great lengths to coat the inside of her glass with a poison that could mimic a massive heart attack.

The one variable in the plan he'd not foreseen was Mrs. Higgenbotham and her blasted flyswatter.

But Alan Jorgenson never had just one plan. There was always a backup.

Though he no longer had the same level of security access he'd had when he was Grand Acceleratus, he was, through some sleight of hand, able to nab a newly constructed pocket-size device, reverse-engineered from the antigravity machine. It shifted the center of gravity of any object it was aimed at, making said object unstable. When aimed at an individual, it could cause them to stumble—which might not be a big deal, unless, of course, that person was at the top of a staircase.

And so that evening, when most everyone had gone to their rooms, Jorgenson positioned himself in his carriage-house bedroom, which had a clear view of the upstairs hallway window in the main house.

The device, not unlike a radar gun, could project a gravitational beam, which the nerdier Accelerati were already calling a "tractor beam." While the aerospace applications of the device could be highly profitable, the only thing Jorgenson was currently interested in was tugging Evangeline Planck off the top step, so she might plunge ungracefully to the first floor and break her stinking, pathetic, power-usurping neck.

He waited in his room until he finally saw a female figure pass by the window, and he hit the button. Even from nearly thirty yards away, he could hear the scream and the satisfying cascade of thuds down the steep steps.

"Sic semper tyrannis," Jorgenson said. "So perish all tyrants."

Then he went to the main house to view his handiwork. When he entered, there were already servants fretting around the bottom of the stairs.

"What happened?" he asked with feigned innocence. "I heard a scream."

And when he looked, he could see that there was indeed a body lying sprawled at the foot of the staircase.

But it was not the body of Evangeline Planck.

"Oh my," said Mrs. Higgenbotham's head, several feet away from the rest of her body. "Isn't this embarassing?" Her neck was sparking, revealing torn wires and circuitry. One eyelid was blinking repeatedly, as if she was winking at Jorgenson. "Stairs can be such a nuisance."

Edison wheeled out of his downstairs suite, took one look at Mrs. Higgenbotham, and sighed. "Call the robotic engineers," he declared, and the servants went running.

Then he rolled back into his suite and closed the door.

Jorgenson trudged over to the carriage house and spent the evening stewing in his own juices.

At the same time Mrs. Higgenbotham suffered her unfortunate decapitation, Nick was taking Caitlin on a moonlit stroll of the grounds. Which might have been romantic, if they weren't so aggravated with each other.

"Why did you even come here?" Nick asked, breaking the tense silence. "You could have messed everything up!"

"*Me?* You're the one who stopped me from pulling his plug!" Caitlin angrily whispered. "Ending Edison would have ended all of our problems."

"No," Nick growled. "He's rebuilding Tesla's machine. It's the only thing that can keep the world from frying. Do you really think the Accelerati could pull it off without him? With Jorgenson and Ms. Planck fighting it out?" He stared at her another angry moment, then his face softened. "Besides, those wires you were going to pull were just the visible ones. He has backup wires hidden beneath the chair."

Caitlin opened her mouth to speak, but found she had nothing to say.

"Why do you think he was in there alone? Because he trusted you? No, it was because he *didn't* trust you. He did it to see if you would try to pull out his wires."

Caitlin crossed her arms. "Well, what do you want me to say?" she huffed.

"Maybe 'Thank you Nick, for saving my life'?"

But of course she didn't say anything. Nick kept walking. "Anyway," he said, "you're here now. Maybe you shouldn't be, but I'm happy to see you."

This gave Caitlin pause, and she realized that rebuilding trust would require effort on both of their parts. So she told him everything that had happened since he'd left Vince's house: that Vince had returned soaking wet with the globe, that Wardenclyffe Tower was being rebuilt, and that she had been grounded for life.

"Your other selves are all keeping busy," she told him.

"Doing what?" Nick asked her.

Caitlin shrugged. "Doing what you're trying to do: save the world. Of course, they can't settle on how to do it."

Nick shook his head. "Typical of me."

At last, something they could both agree on.

"But I don't get Ms. Planck's ring," Nick said.

Caitlin nodded. "I know, me neither, but it looks familiar."

"If we could get it away from her," Nick suggested, "we could find out just how important it is."

Caitlin grinned. "Being with the Accelerati has turned you evil, Nick Slate."

"Yeah," Nick said with a smile. "But in a good way."

And then he took her hand. Caitlin tried not to show how glad she was that he had. It meant that trust had been restored, and maybe a whole lot more.

When they returned to the house, Mrs. Higgenbotham was sitting in an upholstered chair with her head in a crystal punch bowl on the end table.

It came close to making Caitlin scream, but she managed to swallow it.

"Don't mind me," Mrs. Higgenbotham said. "I am quite indisposed at the moment. I 'ope you will understand if I don't bring the evening milk and cookies."

"Will it be hard to fix?" Nick asked.

"Not at all, dear," she told him. "Mr. Edison 'as 'is own private genius bar for this sort of thing. I'm just going to pretend this didn't 'appen."

"Good idea," Nick agreed.

The servants had all retired for the evening, and as Nick and Caitlin made their way through the quiet house, they found that they could hear, through the heating grate in the hallway floor, muffled voices coming from Edison's suite, so they both knelt to listen.

"We got it to work, Al," they heard Ms. Planck say.

"You sent a chimp," Edison replied. "That's not proof—"

"A one-way journey is better than no journey at all. And for the trip I need to make, I only have to go in one direction. As for the return, I have no problem taking the long way home."

Caitlin detected discontent in Edison's voice. He grumbled something, then said, "I still don't believe this . . . extreme measure . . . is necessary."

"The evidence speaks for itself," Planck told him.

Caitlin looked to Nick. "What are they talking about?" she whispered, but he shushed her.

"I do not approve," Edison said. "We need you here. Do I have to remind you that our entire cash reserve has been stolen, and without those funds our situation is dire?"

"Here's the beauty of it," Planck told him. "Once I do what I must have done, I'll find that money before it's even stolen. And when I get back, I can tell you exactly where it is."

Edison heaved a big sigh. "It's far too late, and I am far too annoyed, to deal with a time paradox, Evangeline."

Caitlin gasped. "The time machine!" she whispered. "They must have built it!"

Nick looked at her like she was crazy. "Time machine?"

"Zak and Vince were trying to make one out of the phone and the globe."

Nick gaped at her. "That sounds like a really, really bad idea."

"Wait. . . . If the Accelerati have the globe and the phone, then that must mean . . ." She couldn't even say it out loud. Had the others been captured by Planck at Vince's house? Had they ripped the battery away from Vince?

As if reading her mind, Nick shook his head. "If they had the battery, I would know—Edison wouldn't be able to shut up about it."

"But would Edison tell you if it also meant telling you that Vince was dead?"

Nick hesitated, considering it. In the end he said, "The battery is the last piece they need to complete the machine. Everyone would be buzzing about it, even if Edison clammed up. I don't believe they have it. Which means Vince and the others must have gotten away, somehow."

Caitlin wasn't convinced, but she chose to trust Nick's instincts.

The voices continued to waft through the grate as Planck and Edison bickered about the perils of using the time machine before it had been properly tested with lives that were more expendable, and Edison kept pointing out the flaws in Planck's plan, whatever that plan was. They heard Edison's wheelchair creak as if he had shifted back in it, then he heaved another world-weary sigh.

"If going into the past helps you find the stolen millions, you have my permission. But as for the other bit of nasty business, should you choose to do it, that's entirely on your head." Then he added, "Since it's already happened, I don't imagine I can stop you anyway."

Caitlin turned to Nick. "If Planck goes into the past, she can do anything. . . ."

Nick shook his head. "It's not like that—she can't do anything *new*. She can only become a part of what's already happened."

Now Caitlin was catching on. "And if it's already happened, then, like Edison said, we can't stop her anyway."

As far as Caitlin and Nick were concerned, Ms. Planck's taking a giant step backward in time would do nothing but get her out of their hair for a while. And that could only be a good thing. Right?

35 THAT MINTY-FRESH FEELING

Time paradoxes are a pain where the sun don't shine—such as black holes and neutron stars, where the laws of physics break down entirely. They're troublesome on Earth as well. Take, for instance, the vexing paradox that the Accelerati researchers had in building and testing the time machine.

They had yet to turn it on when a vortex appeared in the lab and a chimpanzee ambled out of it, then looked at them as if to say, *You got a problem with that?*

The researchers were deeply troubled and perplexed, until they realized this was the *exact* same chimpanzee they had been planning to use once the machine was ready for testing tomorrow. Now there were two of them.

This proved that they would be successful in sending the chimpanzee back a day in time. All that remained was to actually get the machine to function . . . which posed yet another question:

Now that they knew the chimpanzee had come back in time, what would happen if they decided *not* to send it through the time machine after all? Could they challenge reality and create their own time paradox?

They found this question much more exciting than actual time travel. So, once they got the machine working, they refused to send the chimp, and then they waited to see if such a decision would bring about the end of the universe.

While the researchers slept that night, the chimpanzee, extremely agitated by having to stare at himself in an adjacent cage, managed to undo his latch. He got out, banged randomly on the controls of the connected phone and globe, then stumbled into the vortex—thereby sending himself back a day in time, where he was forced to stare at himself again, but from the other cage.

The next morning, when the scientists discovered evidence that the chimp had used the machine, this proved to their satisfaction that it is impossible to prevent something we already know *must* have happened in the future.

This fact was not lost on Evangeline Planck. She understood the way these things worked—which is why she had held up an enlarged image of the end of the world for the future-predicting box camera two months earlier. In doing so she had prevented the world from actually having to come to an end in order for the camera to produce the photo.

There was now something she had to do in the past. She knew beyond a shadow of a doubt that she would go back in time and do it, because there was evidence of Accelerati involvement: specifically, one of their member pins had mysteriously turned up where none should have been. Ms. Planck understood that no matter how careful she was in carrying out this errand, she would lose her pin at the scene.

At the end of their conversation in Edison's suite—which Ms. Planck never would have guessed could have been overheard—the Old Man had finally relented.

"Since it's already happened, I don't imagine I can stop you anyway," he said. Then he held out his hand and waited. He didn't have to tell her what he was waiting for, because it was obvious to both of them. She pulled the ring off her finger and placed it in Edison's wrinkled palm.

"Hmm," Edison said. "Not as heavy as I thought it would be." Then he slipped it onto his own finger, barely able to get it over his knobby knuckle.

She was expecting him to accompany her to the lab, but he didn't budge from his spot. "If you do this, Evangeline," he warned her, "you do it alone. I will have no part of it."

"Agreed."

But as she turned to go, he stopped her, wringing his fingers, apparently trying to wrap his aging brain around the principles of the fourth dimension.

"If you were successful," he pointed out, "wouldn't you be back by now to tell us so? After taking the 'long way home,' as you put it, you would have walked in here days ago, like that chimp, to tell us of your success. Weeks ago, even. The fact that you haven't already come back concerns me."

Ms. Planck offered a shrug. "Perhaps I'll have better things to do in the past, and I'll make my presence known tomorrow." Actually, she was convinced that she would, in fact, have better things to do, and she went out the door without looking back.

The way Edison saw it, her absence meant that her mission in the past had failed. But Evangeline Planck had a completely different view of the matter. Since she knew about the stolen money, and she'd be going back to a time before it was stolen, she reasoned that *she* must have been the one who stole it. And at this very moment, her future self (after a short jump to the past), would now be living on her own private island somewhere, with $750 million at her fingertips.

What other possible explanation could there be?

Before stealing that money, though, she had to take a brief

side trip and do that one other thing—the thing Edison wanted no part of but also wasn't about to stop.

Alan Jorgenson was no longer in the loop, so he had no knowledge of the time machine in Edison's laboratory. However, when he observed from the carriage-house window that Planck was on her way toward the lab alone, he knew that if he was going to end her miserable existence, this would probably be his last chance.

Jorgenson crossed the grounds some distance behind her. Getting into the laboratory building was no problem, as he had borrowed Z's key card at dinner (he couldn't stand the fact that his own security clearance couldn't get him into so much as an Accelerati bathroom). He knew the key card would come in handy; he just hadn't realized how soon.

Silently, he followed Planck to a lab on the second floor.

He had brought with him a water pistol filled with a green hypobaric gel that would create a high-pressure zone around anything it coated, and thus would cause Evangeline Planck's head to implode. As anyone can tell you, imploding heads are far less messy than exploding ones.

But as it turned out, he would not need the deadly gel, because she was standing in front of what appeared to be a very convenient vortex of death. It annoyed him that the Accelerati had created a vortex of death in his absence, when he had struggled so hard and so long to create one himself.

She looked up at him with a start. "Alan, what are you doing here? And why are you holding a water gun? If I didn't know better, I'd think you were planning to shoot me with hypobaric gel." Then she smiled. "Luckily for me, I refilled all of Edison's hypobaric gel containers with mint jelly. So, unless you're planning to serve me some lamb, I'd lower your weapon."

Jorgenson tried to hide his irritation as he obeyed. "I merely thought we had an intruder." He gestured toward the pulsing vortex. "May I ask what that thing is?"

"It's called the Great Nexus of None of Your Business. Now please leave, before I have you forcibly removed. Preferably in pieces."

At that moment, Alan Jorgenson knew exactly what he had to do. He raised the water pistol again and squirted mint jelly into Planck's face.

She screamed and clawed at her eyes. "Yagh! The mint! It stings! It stings!"

She stumbled, and Jorgenson wasted no time. He strode toward her, grabbed her shoulders, and shoved her into the vortex. Oddly, she offered no resistance whatsoever.

The vortex disappeared and, just like that, Planck was gone.

Jorgenson wiped up the globs of incriminating jelly and left, satisfied that Planck was history . . .

. . . not knowing that, technically, she now was.

🗿 A TWO-TON ELECTROMAGNET SPINNING AROUND YOUR HEAD.

Forty-some-odd miles away, in Princeton, New Jersey, Wayne Slate carried his moaning son into the emergency room.

"Help us!" he shouted. "My son fell off his bike and hit his head!"

Although there were no contusions or abrasions visible on the boy, the way his eyes had rolled into his head suggested some kind of brain trauma. And what father would lie about such a thing?

They lectured Wayne about the importance of helmets, and prepped Danny for a CAT scan of the brain.

"No!" his father insisted. "He needs an MRI."

The attending nurse was used to panicked parents in the emergency room, and she tried, gently, to reason with him. "Sir, a CAT scan is standard procedure, and—"

"I couldn't care less about standard procedure!" Mr. Slate insisted. "I don't want my son exposed to radiation."

"I assure you," said the nurse, keeping her calm, "it's perfectly safe. The radiation levels of a CAT scan are well within accepted limits."

"No! I want him to have an MRI."

The nurse took a deep breath. "After the CAT scan, if further tests are indicated, I'm sure the doctor will call for an MRI."

Mr. Slate crossed his arms. "I know my rights! You can't force him to have a CAT scan against my will. My son is having an MRI."

The nurse took another deep breath then let it out, realizing this was just not an argument worth having.

"All right, but if your insurance doesn't cover it—"

"That's my problem," said Mr. Slate.

And she left to find a doctor to order the test.

MRI stands for Magnetic Resonance Imaging and is a common medical procedure that gives doctors a peek inside the human body through a combination of powerful magnetic fields and bursts of radio waves.

The MRI machine is also well known for its loud, irritating, and sometimes frightening thumping noises.

Less well known is the unit of measurement for the magnetic output of an MRI: magnetic fields are measured in "teslas."

The standard MRI's magnetic field equals 1.5 teslas. So the question was, how many teslas would it take to defeat an Accelerati mind-block?

Needless to say, Danny Slate had not been in an accident. Danny could never claim to be the world's best actor, but his father had given him great direction.

"Just behave like you do when you're trying to convince me you're too sick to go to school."

Danny's experience on the beach with the metal detector had been mind opening—but whatever memory the magnetic field had released was once again trapped the moment the metal detector moved away. What they needed was a magnetic field powerful enough not just to open the door of memory, but to rip it off its hinges.

All they had to go by were the words Danny had scrawled on a napkin: *I have a brother and his name is Nick.* That napkin would still have been hanging on their refrigerator had they not taken all the kitchen magnets and affixed them to their heads with duct tape a few days earlier, trying to create a large enough magnetic field.

Realizing that this was neither effective nor a particularly attractive fashion statement, Mr. Slate had come up with another plan.

"Your son doesn't have any metal stents or rods in his body, does he?" the MRI technician asked Mr. Slate as they prepped Danny. "Because the magnetic field this baby puts out is unbelievably strong."

"No, no, nothing metal," Mr. Slate assured him.

"Dad, I'm scared," Danny said, which was genuine. Being shoved headfirst into a giant steel donut is no one's idea of fun.

"Don't worry," said the technician cheerfully. "It doesn't hurt or anything. It's just a two-ton electromagnet spinning around your head."

Danny just whimpered.

"It is pretty loud, though," continued the technician, and he gave Danny plastic noise-canceling headphones, which played country music. This, to Danny, a boy raised on classic rock, was much more offensive than the noise of the machine.

The moment the MRI started, images and memories began to flood Danny's mind, as if some magnetically sealed door in his brain had flown open. Everything came back to him. Everything.

Nick's garage sale. Nick's room in the attic. Nick saving him on the baseball field from the asteroid Danny had pulled out of the sky. And finally, the memory of the attic rising above the rest of the house and being struck by lightning.

All the memories were there. They hadn't been erased, just suppressed—probably by that guy in the vanilla suit. Danny wished he could write it all down, but he was immobilized in the machine.

When the MRI was over and the conveyer spit him out, it was as if the Accelerati's spell had been broken. The intense magnetic field had wiped out his mind-block.

He still remembered.

As soon as they removed the straps from his forehead, he sat up and called out to his father, who was waiting just outside the room, "Dad, I remember! They have Nick! They took him. We have to save him!"

The technician looked at him, not quite sure what to make of this. And he was equally confused by the way they ran out, not just leaving the MRI suite, but fleeing from the hospital altogether.

Ten minutes later, they showed up at another hospital across town. This time it was Mr. Slate who was suffering from head trauma and desperately in need of an MRI.

37 CONVERGENCE AT WARDENCLYFFE

After business tycoon J. P. Morgan pulled the plug on Tesla's funding in 1903, Wardenclyffe Tower and the surrounding property were foreclosed on by Tesla's creditors. The tower was torn down, and Tesla's laboratory building remained vacant for years. Eventually it was sold, and for half a century, it was used for the production of photographic paper, until it was abandoned once again, and the entire property disappeared behind a thicket of brambles, like Sleeping Beauty's castle (if Sleeping Beauty's castle had been rat infested and covered with graffiti).

In 2013, Nikola Tesla's lab was saved from demolition by a nonprofit organization that planned to turn the property into a science museum dedicated to his memory—but that plan was derailed by the Accelerati, who purchased the land out from under them for their own undisclosed purposes.

People in the quaint neighborhood around the abandoned property generally ignored it. Few of the nearby residents knew that this was the very location where Tesla had made his greatest stand for a worldwide free-energy system—and failed.

When construction finally began on the site, it piqued local curiosity—especially as the girders rose higher and higher, quickly making the resurrected Wardenclyffe Tower the tallest structure in town.

Yet, for some reason, the local newspaper had never mentioned it.

The Accelerati didn't completely control the media, but they did manage to manipulate it. Much like acupuncture, they stuck pins in just the right people and in just the right places to either grant them more attention than they deserved or create a diversion when necessary.

So the new Wardenclyffe Tower became, for the town of Shoreham, New York, one of those things that people pay no attention to, because it doesn't concern them.

Within the gates, the activity went on 24/7. A truck arrived with carefully packed crates filled with objects that could have been sold as junk, and actually once were, but had now been gathered, studied, and shipped here to be reintegrated into the grandest machine humankind had ever known.

The first taste, Edison had decided, would indeed be free, just as Tesla had wanted. And once all the other utility companies had crumbled and the world was completely dependent on his source of power, he would demand high fees from every user, and they would have no choice but to pay them.

Thus was the way of the world, as Edison saw it. Business is business. "Free" is never really free. It is merely a means to a more lucrative end.

There were powerful forces converging on Wardenclyffe Tower. Fourteen, to be exact—although seven of them were the various versions of Nick. The first force to arrive was already perched atop the tower, high above Shoreham. BeatNick, who was sent to infiltrate the site and gather intelligence, had a small lead on everyone else. He was working under an assumed name, and now looked out over the Long Island Sound, wondering when the others would arrive.

In addition to the nearly completed tower on which he stood, there were several other, much smaller, connected structures elsewhere in town. He could only see a couple of them from the tower, but he knew there were seven. They were squat stone buildings, each no larger than a garden shed. They had been here for more than a hundred years, and as such were just part of the landscape. The community assumed they were old utility substations that either still did their jobs and thus could be ignored, or served no modern purpose whatsoever, and thus could be ignored even more. Now, however, the little buildings were being restored as a key part of the Wardenclyffe reconstruction project.

Their purpose was kept from the construction crews, and the crews didn't really care; they were just doing a job. BeatNick, however, knew exactly what they were, as he had recently been part of the welding team on building seven. They were the entrances to the seven tunnels that converged beneath Wardenclyffe Tower—just like the ones under his old house in Colorado Springs.

"Back to work, Farnsworth!" shouted the foreman when he saw BeatNick gazing out at the view. "You're not being paid to sightsee."

BeatNick lowered his protective visor and returned to welding the panels of the platform into place. His forged documents said he was a Certified Welding Engineer. And the Accelerati were, of course, Certified Geniuses . . . which meant that none of them had the hands-on construction experience to handle or manage the building of the tower. They therefore had to bid out the project as a regular construction job. To the local subcontractors, Nick's bogus skill set was in high demand.

On his first day, he'd been lucky just to avoid burning a hole in himself. It wasn't easy to mask his huge learning curve at a job he'd never been trained for—especially a dangerous one like welding. He quickly got the hang of it, though, and could soon pass for the real thing. He imagined that if he failed to reintegrate with his other selves, and if the world didn't end before the F.R.E.E. was finished, he could have a future in this trade.

Once the foreman had gone back down in the gantry elevator, BeatNick looked back toward the little stone structures masking the tunnel entrances. The rusted, moldy interiors of all the structures were being restored with stainless-steel walls and floodgates over the tunnel entrances.

But the floodgate covering tunnel seven, he secretly knew, had been so poorly welded that it would only take a tug to pull it open at the right moment, allowing him and the six other Nicks to gather beneath Wardenclyffe Tower where the seven tunnels met.

The second force to arrive at Wardenclyffe was Petula, who watched the final stages of the tower's construction as a full member of the Accelerati upper tier, in a brand-new shimmering spider-silk suit. A lavender one.

Before Ms. Planck's unexplained disappearance, she had promoted Petula as a reward for having located the globe. This had even fulfilled one of Petula's lifelong ambitions: to have minions.

"Bring me a cold beverage."

"Yes, Miss Grabowski-Jones."

"Go to the nearest five-star restaurant, and order me something that's not on the menu."

"Yes, Miss Grabowski-Jones."

"I'm bored. Amuse me."

"Yes, Miss Grabowski-Jones."

Her underlings were tireless in fulfilling her unreasonable requests. And she hated them for it. She missed the fury-inducing rush of not getting what she wanted.

But mostly she hated the fact that all of this, especially her life, would go away when Edison found out that she had sent Vince to Tierra del Fuego, at the southern tip of South America, rather than ripping him free from his battery and presenting the device to the Accelerati. But what else could she have done, now that she had a very fresh and unfortunate perspective on everything?

Nick Slate was Nikola Tesla.

Kinda sorta.

It was heady and dizzying to know something that not even Edison knew. And she still wasn't sure how she could use the information to her advantage. First she had to ascertain exactly what it meant. There were only four possibilities she could imagine:

1. Nick had been cloned from a random bit of Tesla's DNA.
2. Once Nick reintegrated, he would go back in time to become Nikola Tesla.
3. Nick was actually an android modeled after the inventor; or
4. This was all a dream and she'd wake up in her bedroom and be very, very annoyed.

Theory number one seemed unlikely, as Tesla had died with virtually no possessions and his remains were cremated, leaving absolutely no DNA from which to clone him. Theory number two was equally unlikely, because plenty of evidence existed, both photographic and written, to prove that Tesla was raised in Serbia. Since Nick didn't speak Serbian, it would be impossible for him to pass as the inventor, even if he'd wanted to.

Number three was also unlikely, because if he were a robot, like Mrs. Higgenbotham, he couldn't have been divided into seven ages of himself.

Which left number four, the dream, and that was just too depressing to think about.

It was all so maddening, it just made her want to send her minions on even more unreasonable excursions.

She looked up at the tower before her. The girders were already in place and the circular platform at its top almost completed. A caged elevator clinging to the central shaft would soon lift every piece of the F.R.E.E. to the platform, where it would be assembled. Every piece, that is, but the battery.

I complete the circuit, she thought, and she wondered if that meant she would have to go and retrieve Vince to make the thing work, in spite of everything.

It made her wish that this was a dream after all. But she knew she was not that lucky.

The next group of not-so-random forces traveled in a subset of six—a journey made possible by the combination of a daring e-mail and a staggering electronic wire transfer.

Most beloved greetings. I represent His Highness, Prince Zakia Thuku of West Zenobia.

His Royal Highness and a small collection of friends wish to fly from the Colorado Springs to the Long Island of New York. We therefore request to charter one of your private jets.

Toward this end, we have already wired sixty-thousand dollars ($60,000), which is twice your advertised price, into your business account. We expect the plane and crew to be ready by fifteen hundred hours today (3:00 PM in your odd American measurement of time) at your hangar facility at the Municipal Airport of the Colorado Springs, along with a variety of refreshments, a moderately sized lunch buffet, and a multitude of beautiful women.

With great and kindly thankfulness,

Murmitch Ló,
Royal Attaché of West Zenobia

"Hmm," said Zak. "Maybe take out the beautiful women part."

"Do I have to?" asked Mitch.

"Well, the rest of the stuff they can probably scrounge up by three. But a harem, aside from being degrading to women, would probably take at least until five, and we don't have that kind of time. Plus, we'd need a bigger plane."

The idea of having a bankroll of $750 million at his disposal was still a very new idea to Mitch Murló. What does one do with that kind of money? And although he knew it wasn't really his, it was his to wield. For the time being, at least.

At first, Zak had suggested they buy a couple of Rolls Royces and the six of them caravan to Shoreham—him, Zak, Nicholas, Old St. Nick, Little Nicky, and SputNick—riding in style.

"Nicholas could pull off the deal," Zak had pointed out. "He'll drive one of them, and I'll drive the other."

But Mitch realized an airplane charter could be done entirely online, and would get them there faster. Even if the people at AirPlay Jet Charters thought the e-mail was spam, once the transfer appeared in their bank account, no matter how questionable the e-mail sounded . . . well, money talks.

Mitch sent the e-mail, after removing the request for beautiful women. And by the time they arrived at Colorado Springs Municipal Airport, sure enough, AirPlay Jet Charters had refreshments and a sumptuous buffet waiting for them, along with a Learjet 40XR, complete with crew.

Zak totally owned the role of the prince. The African robe they had found at a costume shop downtown was a little over-the-top, but Zak was really working it. He carried himself with such royal aloofness that Mitch couldn't stop calling him "Your Highness" even after he no longer had to.

"I can't believe you guys pulled this off," Nicholas said as they arrived at the hangar.

Mitch avoided his gaze. It was just too bizarre, talking to a man who looked just like all the pictures of Tesla, and yet knowing he was one-seventh of his best friend.

Old St. Nick just couldn't stop giggling as he looked at the plane, and he filled his plate from the elaborate spread of food.

Little Nicky, however, turned his nose up at the various delicacies and wouldn't eat. At one point he tugged on Mitch's arm and pointed at Nicholas. "Does he freak you out as much as he freaks me out?"

"He's you," Mitch reminded him.

"Don't say that. It freaks me out even more."

Nicholas himself seemed to be in denial of his Tesla-ish appearance.

Mitch couldn't stop thinking about it, though. He hadn't yet figured out what it meant, but he had four theories:

1. They were all living in the Matrix, and he'd stumbled upon a glitch in the system.
2. Tesla was actually an alien, who'd left versions of himself throughout history.
3. Nick was the antimatter version of Tesla, which meant it was a good thing he and Tesla never met, because they would annihilate the universe; or

4. This was all a dream and he'd wake up in his bedroom and be very, very relieved.

Mitch knew that trying to puzzle it out was a path down which madness lay. So he tried to enjoy the buffet: the oysters that were slimy; the caviar that was salty; and the foie gras, which was just plain disgusting.

Then he, Zak, and the quartet of Nicks boarded the jet—which got as far as Nebraska before being grounded by magnetic issues related to the asteroid and the overwhelmingly powerful aurora.

"Our navigational system is all pell-mell," the captain told them. "We'll have to take short hops, avoiding the worst of the disturbances, or we could slam headfirst into a mountain."

None of them—not even the older Nicks—knew what pell-mell was, but they did grasp the concept of slamming into a mountain. It wasn't something you wanted to hear from your pilot.

All told, it took a full day to complete the journey. They made six roundabout stops on their way to Long Island. From Omaha they went to Milwaukee, then to Detroit, then Cincinnati, then Richmond, finally landing in New York—a path that, coincidentally, traced the stars in the Big Dipper.

While the jet was still diverting around the handle of Ursa Major, four more forces headed toward Wardenclyffe from Edison's mansion. Fourteen-year-old Nick (still blissfully unaware that his thirty-something clean-shaven self was the spitting image of Tesla) joined Edison, Caitlin, and Z in the old man's luxury jalopy, specially designed to fit his huge battery.

Just as the driver engaged the engine, Jorgenson appeared at the passenger window. "Good morning, all. I wasn't informed we were leaving this early," he said jovially, scanning the faces in the car. "Oh, is Evangeline not joining us?"

"She's indisposed," Edison said without expression. "Z here will be filling in as interim Grand Acceleratus."

Jorgenson did not seem pleased by this news. He opened the car door to enter before Edison stopped him.

"Sorry, Al," Edison said, "my battery takes up too much room to allow a fifth passenger." Then, to intentionally add insult to injury, he pulled out his wallet and handed him a few bills. "Here's bus fare."

Then he pulled the door closed on Jorgenson's astonished expression, and laughed heartily as they drove off.

"You're bad," Z said to Edison, who continued to chuckle.

"We take our guilty pleasures where we can find them, Z."

Nick and Caitlin said very little to each other on the way. Nick was a little terrified, and a little exhilarated, at the prospect of seeing Tesla's greatest achievement, Wardenclyffe Tower, rebuilt on the same spot where it had once stood.

According to the Accelerati's Doomsday Clock, they had about a day and a half until the electrical charge from the asteroid would reach lethal proportions again. Everything was in place—all that remained to be done was for Nick to assemble the machine.

Clearly the Accelerati had raided Vince's house after Caitlin had left, because they had the globe. Did they, as Caitlin suggested, have the battery too? And what did that mean for Vince? The Accelerati would have no reason to keep him attached to it. They would just take it and leave him dead in the water—or dead in the family room, as the case may be.

On the other hand, if they didn't have the battery, would Edison be willing to give up his own, and sacrifice himself to save the world? Nick sincerely doubted it.

The only certainty was that in less than two days the world would either be drastically changing, or drastically ending.

Thomas Alva Edison kept his thoughts to himself as they took the long ride to Shoreham, New York. The car wove down side streets all the way through New Jersey, because Edison, like most of humanity, detested the New Jersey Turnpike. It was, perhaps, the most hated road in creation, second only to the proverbial highway to hell. Edison much preferred roads that absorbed the character of a town to those that plowed over it, so a trip that should have taken just a couple of hours took most of a day, with stops for meals and afternoon tea. In spite of the Doomsday Clock, he was a man who refused to be rushed.

Besides, all the work that needed to be done was being done in his absence. The tower was being completed, the pieces of the F.R.E.E. were ready to be assembled, and he had teams scouring the globe for Vince LaRue and his blasted battery. They would find him too, because Edison always got what he wanted in the end. He knew no other way to see the world.

What filled his thoughts now was the absence of Evangeline Planck. If it were her sole intent to take a one-way trip into the not-too-distant past, she should already be back with little more than an extra gray hair or two. So why wasn't she?

Bus fare? The nerve!

Dr. Alan Jorgenson—the eleventh and perhaps the most dangerous force—refused to even entertain the concept of lowering himself to take a bus. Instead, he took a commuter train. Even so, he could barely abide riding with the rabble.

This turn of events had made it very clear that Edison had no intention of reinstating him as Grand Acceleratus. The honor was obviously going to Professor Zenobia Thuku, that glorified math teacher.

Jorgenson leaned back in his seat. As unpleasant as this ride was, he knew that he would arrive in Shoreham first, thanks to Edison's peculiar travel habits. For a man so far ahead of his time, he was still woefully trapped in a nineteenth-century mentality.

That would work to Jorgenson's advantage, as he would have several hours to assess the situation at the tower before Edison arrived. Then, if necessary, he could create a problem for which only he had the solution, thereby reinforcing how important he was to the Accelerati.

His thoughts returned to Professor Z, with whom he'd never been on a first-name basis, much less a first initial.

Would he have to do away with her as well?

The thought made him weary. So many people to crush and so little time.

Wayne and Danny were not planning to go to Shoreham at all. In fact, they planned to travel in the opposite direction: west from Princeton, not east. They were frantically packing bags for a trip back to Colorado Springs.

"We'll find him," Mr. Slate told Danny. "I promise you, we'll find him."

The plan was to go back to their house in Colorado Springs and start there. Someone must know what happened to Nick, and he vowed to leave no stone unturned in his search for the son they'd tried to make him forget.

Whoever "they" were.

But just as the two were about to leave, the doorbell rang.

Mr. Slate opened the door to reveal a middle-aged man with muttonchops. And although Wayne Slate couldn't place him, there was something very familiar about his face.

For a moment the man seemed almost teary-eyed, but he wiped it away. "Uh, Mr. Slate, my name is, well, never mind my name. I'm here to talk to you about your son."

Mr. Slate eyed him cautiously. "Which son?" he asked.

The man's eyes practically twinkled. "So you remember that you have two?"

Wayne wanted to grab the man by his muttonchops, but he didn't know whether he was friend or foe.

"Where's Nick?" he demanded.

"That question is far more complicated than you think. But if you want to help him, you have to come with me to Shoreham, New York."

And thus the final three were on their way.

All told, fourteen not-so-random forces, many with different desires, different objectives, and different manners of achieving them, were converging on an unsuspecting town on Long Island's north shore.

There was no question that something momentous would happen there. But whether anyone would be left alive to notice was the greatest unknown of all.

Meanwhile, at the very southern tip of South America, in Tierra del Fuego, as far as one might get from Shoreham, New York, Vince LaRue was the talk of the town.

In this case, the town was just a quaint fishing village of about forty people, but Vince did enjoy being a big fish in a small pond.

They called him *El Niño Electrico*, the "Electric Boy," thinking him some sort of robotic NASA experiment that had crash-landed in their icy midst. Vince didn't bother to correct them.

He was taken in by a family and given food and shelter. His two years of middle school Spanish had taught him about as much of the language as a dog might learn, but he was able to communicate by simple phrases and gestures. And when he mimed putting a phone to his ear, they were more than happy to give him one.

He dialed his mother's phone number, and she burst into tears upon hearing his voice. Apparently she was still in Scotland, scouring the lake for his remains, as he had predicted.

"I'm fine, Mom," he told her. "You're overreacting."

"Where are you?" she asked.

"I'm in Chile. Tierra del Fuego, to be exact."

"Chile?" she said incredulously. "What on earth are you doing *there*?"

And since he didn't want to go into the whole explanation, he merely said, "Having lunch."

He told her not to go home, as there was some trouble there, and that he would be in touch again soon. Then he hung up and went back to his bowl of mutton stew, which would terrorize his undead digestive system, but was too good to pass up.

This far south, the *Aurora Australis* was spectacular, and some of the locals had come to believe that the Electric Boy was somehow responsible. Of course others believed it was a sign of the end of the world. Actually, both factions were correct.

Without his battery to complete Tesla's machine, the world *would* end. It blew his mind to think that he, Vince LaRue, could bring about either the destruction or salvation of life on Earth. Not that life had ever done anything for him, but even so, the entire future relied on either his personal thumbs-up or thumbs-down. It was far too much responsibility for a poor undead kid like himself.

Something, he thought, *would have to be done about this.*

For the moment, though, he was content to eat his mutton stew.

38 A QUANTUM OF ACCELERATI

It was nearly dusk when Edison and his entourage arrived. Nick, who had dozed off during the long drive, opened his eyes as the car rolled up to the wrought-iron gate of the Wardenclyffe property and stopped, its engine idling.

A large sign was plastered on the gate: NOTICE OF DEFAULT AND SALE.

Apparently the property had been foreclosed upon and was going up for public auction. While Nick didn't say anything, Caitlin couldn't restrain herself.

"I think you're being evicted," she announced, and then added brightly, "Oh, I hope the Accelerati aren't having money problems. That kind of thing could put you completely out of business!"

Edison bristled. Nick could swear he heard the man's battery acid boiling with fury beneath its velvet sheath. "Let them try to throw me out," he said. Then he ordered his driver to rip down the foreclosure sign.

The car drove through the gate and deposited them in front of the large brick building that was once Tesla's Wardenclyffe laboratory. It had now been restored to its previous glory, full of gleaming brass and polished mahogany, as well as huge windows that gave it a clear view of the tower. This was the tower's command center.

With Z pushing Edison's chair, they entered and made their way to the control room, where Accelerati scientists and technicians stood around a long, elegantly curved desk. Some looked down at their instruments while others glanced up through the arched windows at the nearly complete tower.

"Z, why don't you familiarize yourself with operations," Edison suggested, waving a hand at the control desk. Then he pressed the button that engaged the wheelchair's motor. "I'll take it from here."

Already looking over the instruments on the desk, Z nodded.

Edison wheeled over to the base of the large windows, followed by Nick and Caitlin.

The tower was impressive, even by modern standards: a delicate latticework of silver-white metal soaring nearly two hundred feet into the air, topped by a copper platform.

"They've informed me that the structure is almost complete," Edison told them. "In the morning, we will begin loading the pieces of the F.R.E.E. into the elevator cage and bring them up to the platform." Then he smiled at Nick. "And you, young man, will assemble it, as you've promised."

"I'll assemble it," Nick told him, "but without the battery to prime it, the machine will never start."

Mentioning the battery was a calculated move. Nick hoped that Edison might give something away, but the old man's face was unreadable.

"Your only concern is assembling the parts that we have," Edison told him. "The battery is my affair."

Then Edison turned his wheelchair around and looked past Nick and Caitlin. "Well, well, look what the cat dragged in."

They turned around to see none other than Petula, seeming more Accelerati-ish than ever in her lavender spider-silk suit. It looked more natural on her than any clothing Nick had ever seen her wear.

"The cat didn't drag her, Mr. Edison," Nick said. "It's more likely that she dragged the cat. And probably by its tail."

Petula scowled at him, and the quantum of Accelerati accompanying her looked at one another nervously, as if she might take her anger out on them. They were clearly her entourage. The fact that Petula now had an entourage could not be a good thing for anyone—especially not its members, whose eyes all seemed to be screaming *Help me!* or *Save me!* or maybe even *Kill me!*

Edison had to go deal with Jorgenson, whose pants had been accidentally set on fire by one of the welders and who was now raising a ruckus.

"It wasn't Farnsworth's fault," the foreman insisted as they walked away. "That Jorgenson guy shouldn't have been on the platform in the first place."

Petula stayed to entertain Nick and Caitlin, although gloat seemed more like it. She dismissed her entourage and led Nick and Caitlin to a large, well-appointed work space. By now night was beginning to fall, and the tower, as impressive as it was during the day, took on an eerie glow as spotlights came on. Workers were laboring through the night to complete it by morning. And just in case there were any slackers, Doomsday Clocks were posted everywhere. Twenty-five hours and counting.

"Is this Edison's office?" Nick asked.

"No. It's mine," Petula said, sinking into a leather office chair. "Being a darling of the Accelerati does have its perks." She raised an eyebrow. "As you must know."

"I'm only here because I have to be," Nick said.

"Oh, right, to save the world," Petula said. "That's become your specialty, hasn't it?"

Caitlin stepped between them. "As much as we don't like you, Petula, we have to work together, so can we at least pretend to get along?"

Petula just stared at her for a moment, then said, "But I *am* working with you, you idiot." Then she leaned in closer, lowering her voice. "The other Nicks are fine. So is Vince. I hid him—and his battery—where they won't find him, which means that Edison will have no choice but to surrender his own battery when the time comes."

She couldn't have shocked Nick more if she had zapped him with the F.R.E.E. The very idea of Petula being helpful seemed a concept from some alternate universe. Both Nick and Caitlin were stunned into silence.

Then Petula looked at Nick strangely—as if seeing something in his face she hadn't noticed before. She opened her mouth to speak, then closed it. Whatever information she had, she wasn't telling. That seemed more like the Petula they knew.

"After everything you've done, why should we trust you?" Nick asked.

"After everything I've done?" She stood up and glared at Nick. He had to admit she had a good glare. If its power could be harnessed and weaponized, it would melt cities. "I tried to save your life the day that Vince first died. I led you into Accelerati headquarters to steal the harp, so you could keep the world from becoming toast. And now I just saved four-sevenths of your life again—along with putting Vince where no one will ever find him, which was extremely generous of me, because I find Vince entirely worthless, even undead. So don't you *dare* treat me as anything other than the wonderful human being that I am, or I will rip your heart out with my bare hands and squish it beneath the heel of my shoe!"

"Try it! I dare you!" said Caitlin.

And because it was Nick's heart they were talking about, he decided it was best not to antagonize Petula any further.

"Thank you, Petula," he said, to Caitlin's utter disbelief. "I appreciate all you've done, but—"

"—but if you really want to make a difference, then you'll help Nick reintegrate," Caitlin said.

Nick shook his head. "There'll be time for that later."

Now it was Caitlin's turn to get angry at him. "No, there won't, and you know it! Once that machine is put together, you'll never get that prism back, and you'll never be whole! Is that what you want?"

Of course it wasn't what Nick wanted, but how could he put himself before saving the world?

"The prism!" said Petula. "Now I get it—seven colors of light, seven diffracted Nicks!" She turned to Caitlin, as if Nick suddenly wasn't there. "I'll help you put our little Humpty-Dumpty back together again, on one condition."

"And what would that be?"

"I complete the circuit," Petula said.

Caitlin and Nick just stared at her. "What does that even mean?" Caitlin asked.

Petula hesitated. "I don't know yet. But when I do, you'll be the first to know." Then she added, "Maybe."

"Even if we do put me back together," Nick pointed out, "we still have a much bigger problem. Edison's pretty stuck on the idea of living forever. I don't think he'll give up his battery willingly."

Petula smiled and tilted her head so that her pigtails fell at an awkward angle. "Then I guess you'll just have to take it by force."

. . .

As the Accelerati's Doomsday Clock ticked down to the final twenty-four hours, the rest of the world labored under the popular misconception that another random discharge somewhere in the world would solve the problem. In the meantime, everyone could enjoy the wild auroras and ride out the increasingly nasty carpet shocks and occasional electrocutions.

That might have been true had the first discharge been a random one. But it hadn't. In actuality, a world-saving discharge could not occur without the F.R.E.E.

Which was now nothing more than a pile of antique parts.

The upper floor of the control center had been converted into a set of Victorian bedrooms for Edison and his guests.

"If the Accelerati need money, they can always rent this out as a bed-and-breakfast," Nick commented.

"It's the Accelerati," Caitlin pointed out. "It would be a *dread*-and-breakfast."

This drew a polite laugh from the underling who had been assigned to escort them to their quarters—apparently they were not trusted to be on the grounds alone. That meant they couldn't track down BeatNick and learn whatever intelligence he'd gathered as a welder.

They were locked in their rooms for the night, while outside the sounds of construction continued.

All building work ceased at midnight. Not because the tower was complete, but because word had reached the foreman that the Accelerati had written them a bad check for services rendered. His response was to tell the night shift to stop until they were paid.

It was Alan Jorgenson who saved the day in his own special way. He simply pulled out an Accelerati *devolver*, and with a single shot, turned the foreman into a bubbling mess of primordial ooze that would take millions of years to evolve back into intelligent life. The rest of the labor force took the hint and continued work on the tower.

Due to the delay, the tower was not finished until noon. Nick remained confined in his room all morning, then, around one o'clock, an Accelerati tech came to get him. Finally Nick was put to work doing what only he could do: turning a collection of garage-sale items into the F.R.E.E.

As Nick entered the largest room of the building, the parts lay spread out as a grid before him. A beady-eyed Acceleratus, holding a clipboard like a shield, told him all the things that he already knew about the objects.

"Be careful not to touch object number twelve, or depress the red button on object thirty-two," the man said, indicating the harp and the globe. "Object twenty-nine appears to be missing a lid," he said, pointing to the blender, as if it wasn't Nick who first noticed it. "But we believe it won't be crucial to your assembly process."

The Acceleratus was clearly insulted that he had to work for Nick, and not the other way around. "We thought you could assemble it in pieces, down here, and then we'll bring it up in the gantry elevator partially assembled."

Nick shook his head. "No. It has to be assembled all in one place. That's the only way it will hold together."

"Well, our studies show—"

"Your studies are wrong," Nick said flatly, and then directed him to organize a team to take the pieces up to the tower. Since the gantry elevator was so painfully slow, it took more than an hour to get everything to the top.

When they came for the telephone, Nick told them to leave it behind. "It's not part of the machine," he told the beady-eyed clipboard tech, who insisted that Nick was mistaken but didn't have the authority to do anything but sniff in disapproval and stride insultingly away.

Once the other objects were gone, the telephone sat alone in the center of the room, and seemed forlorn and purposeless—which troubled Nick, because Tesla never created anything without purpose.

39 THE SPACE BETWEEN US

In the grand scheme of things, Nick's reintegration was a minor issue. Each of the Nicks knew this. Still, the prospect of living separately and turning into a miserable spectrum of incomplete souls was horrifying.

The man who had purchased the prism at the garage sale had turned into his own personal dysfunctional family. Had disunification done that to his fractured selves? The way that the Nicks bickered when they were all together seemed to point to an unsettled shattering; a life of bitter disagreement, each age of himself resenting the others. But even worse than that was the gnawing sense of incompletion. A hunger in each of them to be more than he currently was. It's a feeling everyone experiences from time to time, but when you're only one-seventh of yourself, that feeling becomes unbearable. Although none of the Nicks spoke it aloud—and certainly would not confess it to each other—their longing to be of one mind and one body was overwhelming, and colored everything they did.

While fourteen-year-old Nick labored to assemble the F.R.E.E., he was distracted. Unfocused.

Even with the Accelerati lifting the heavier pieces into place, it took him hours. He finally finished around five p.m, drenched with sweat. Then he stepped back to admire his work. The device was now more complete than it had ever been—but the absence of the battery was glaring.

Nick now stood before it, trying to feel the sense of connectedness that had always been so comforting back home . . .

. . . but he couldn't. Something else was missing; it was more than just the battery.

The blender lid?

Maybe the lid was part of it, but he sensed it was more . . . much more than that. There was a fatal failure in the gear work—not the mechanical parts, but the human ones.

Nick had long known that this great device was more than metal and electronics. In order to work, it required an intricate human interaction, like a musical instrument—but one that had to be played by a vast number of people. Everyone had a part, every action was the turning of a complex, invisible gear.

And something was missing.

Now, as he stood there, instead of feeling a deep connection to each piece of the machine, and the world around him, he felt a screaming disconnect. It was almost like a silent accusation that he had failed to complete something essential. Was it because he himself was disunified, or was it something else— something he wasn't yet seeing?

He looked at the grand view of the town below, the landscape that would be singed beyond recognition if he didn't complete his task. Everyone was relying on him, but he only had one-seventh of his courage, one-seventh of his fortitude—and today, in this moment, it wasn't enough.

Near him Accelerati spoke, but he couldn't hear them anymore. All he heard was the horrible *need* of the world, and the sense that some crucial act remained undone.

At last he sat down beside the device, closed his eyes, covered his ears with his hands, and stayed like that, much to the chagrin of the Accelerati around him.

The other Nicks felt his anguish. It radiated out from the tower like bolts of invisible lightning. BeatNick was the closest, down at the base of the tower, being reprimanded for having "accidentally" set Jorgenson's pants on fire. When he felt the pain of his fourteen-year-old self, he resisted the urge to run away screaming.

Nickelback, who still hadn't revealed his true identity to Mr. Slate and Danny, began hyperventilating in his hotel room as he waited for word from BeatNick about their next move. Nickelback knew this panic attack was not a random thing, although he couldn't be sure what it meant.

And, in a limo coming from Long Island MacArthur Airport, Old St. Nick began to sob uncontrollably, as did Sputnik. Nicholas shuddered, and Little Nicky curled into a ball and began to suck his thumb like he was regressing to infancy.

"What's going on?" Zak asked the Nicks when he noticed their sudden change in demeanor. Nicholas was the only one able to articulate it.

"The space between us . . ." he said. "It hurts. . . ."

Meanwhile, on the platform atop the new Wardenclyffe Tower, the fraction of Nick that was still fourteen tried to get his overwhelming sense of incompletion under control. *Caitlin was right—I can't go on like this*, he thought. *I need to be whole.*

If only there was something that had the power to pull them together. . . .

And suddenly the proverbial light bulb went on over his head. Literally.

It had all begun with the turning of a light switch. The garage sale on that dark and gloomy day would have been a failure if they hadn't turned on that antique lamp in Nick's garage. Once they did, people began to come like moths to a porch light, even in the torrential rain.

Each of those people had needed something. They found something. They went home.

Tesla couldn't have known who those individuals were, or what their specific needs might be—but he was a man of vision. He saw the big picture, and he knew the gear work that was behind it. He didn't need to see the turning of those gears to know the result; just the knowledge that they *would* turn was enough. The idea of the electric motor had come to him in a vision—he knew it would work even before he actually built it. So it was with the F.R.E.E. Each component served its own unique function, and when combined, the whole was greater than the sum of its parts.

One of those parts was the old stage "ghost light" that had stood like a glowing electronic Q-tip in the center of Nick's garage that day, drawing people toward it, bonding them in ways they might never understand. Now the lamp stood at the center of the F.R.E.E. atop the platform of the new Wardenclyffe Tower.

It took a while for any of the Accelerati to notice that its bulb was missing after Nick had left.

When Nick told Caitlin what he had taken from the machine, she knew it was a dangerous move—but she also knew it was necessary. He had made himself scarce just in case his theft was noticed before he could return what he had taken—hopefully as his whole self once more. He left it to Caitlin to inform the others.

She finally tracked down BeatNick as he was being escorted off the grounds. Apparently he had just been fired.

"Did you really have to do it?" Caitlin asked him as they stood on the street.

"Is it my fault Jorgenson stepped too close to the welding torch?" he asked with a smirk. "And I did hurl a bucket of water at him right away—you'd think they'd give me points for saving him."

On the other side of the gate, which had just been shut, Caitlin saw her personal escort searching the grounds for her. She was a pleasant enough woman, for an Acceleratus, but far too trusting. Caitlin had told the woman she was going to the restroom, and then easily slipped away. Now Caitlin ducked out of sight with BeatNick before she could be spotted.

"If you're going to reunite," Caitlin said, glancing at the flaring night sky, "we're running out of time."

BeatNick assured her that he could get them into the underground tunnel system. "I've been in touch with the rest of me," he explained. "Tell the fourteen-year-old me that we'll rendezvous at the entrance to tunnel seven at seven thirty tonight. Of course, without a plan to get us all back together, I don't see what good that will do."

"Don't worry—Nick has a plan."

BeatNick took some offense. "I'm Nick too, you know."

Caitlin looked at him, catching his eyes, which were, of course, Nick's eyes. It was nice to know what Nick would look like in ten years or so.

She smiled at him. "I'm sure a twenty-five-year-old me would be very much in love with you."

BeatNick left, and Caitlin lingered by a tall hedge until the gate opened for an exiting construction crew, then slipped back in. She found her escort and complained about her faulty directions to the bathroom.

• • •

Several miles away, on another piece of property that also had a foreclosure sign slapped on the gate, Thomas Alva Edison oversaw a crucial phase of the operation.

He and his wheelchair rested in the center of a circular concrete platform just over one hundred feet in diameter. The platform consisted of a stabilized subgrade of hydraulic cement overlain by eighteen inches of lime cement and surfaced with fourteen inches of steel-reinforced compression-proof concrete. In other words, it was so sturdy, it could serve as the landing pad for an alien spacecraft. But it had a very different purpose.

Z came up behind Edison. "Are you sure this will work?" she asked.

He scoffed. "If there's one thing I know, it's electricity." Then he held up his hand and removed the shiny titanium ring from his finger. He gave it to Z and said, "You may do the honors."

In the very center of the huge platform was a copper disk that was hardwired directly to the electrical grid. It was no coincidence that the Long Island Power Authority was controlled and operated by Consolidated Edison Energy, Inc., better known as Con Ed.

Z placed the ring in the very center of the copper disk, on a spot engraved with a small *X*. Then she wheeled Edison off the concrete platform to a control booth shielded by several layers of Accelerati-designed blast-proof glass. Just in case.

Waiting for them there was an Accelerati courier with an urgent message. "The package has arrived," he told Edison.

Edison clapped once, which sounded like an ancient book full of brittle pages being slammed shut.

"Splendid," he said. "But first things first." He reached over to the control panel. It was very old-school, featuring a heavy switch that had to be thrown. He preferred it this way. Computer screens with virtual buttons and pull-down menus manipulated by pathetic little mouse-clicks stole all the joy from the act of completing a circuit. He put his hand on the switch's ivory handle.

"This," Edison said, "is why they call me the Wizard of Menlo Park." And he threw the switch. For a few moments all the lights on Long Island dimmed, and then the small ring in the center of the huge concrete platform began to expand.

40 THE NEW YORK NICKS

It was dusk, and the aurora was already flaring in the eastern sky when the one-seventh of Nick that was still fourteen, along with Caitlin and Petula, approached the entrance of tunnel seven. It was within a small stone structure at the edge of a parking lot behind an abandoned Toys "R" Us. The *s* had fallen from the crumbling sign, which now solemnly announced that "Toys 'R' U," because clearly toys were no longer them. At least not in Shoreham.

Petula was there because, in exchange for successfully sneaking them out of the gated and guarded Wardenclyffe facility, she had insisted on joining them.

Caitlin still didn't trust her. "If you're spying for the Accelerati, Petula, I swear—"

"If I were spying for the Accelerati, you would have been sent to their experimentation program hours ago."

And since that was likely to be true, Caitlin said no more.

Several of the Nicks were already there when they arrived. BeatNick was filling his face with junk food. "Hey," he said with a shrug, "this could be my last meal as a twenty-four-year-old for ten years."

Old St. Nick was there, jovial as ever, with Nicholas, who held SputNick, and Little Nicky, who clung nervously to the hem of Nicholas's shirt.

Mitch was also there, along with Zak, still dressed in his fake royal robe, long after he needed to wear it. While Zak was a bit royally standoffish, Mitch ran up to Nick and threw his arms around him in an awkward, and never-to-be-repeated, show of affection.

"They didn't kill you!" he said. "We were all worried."

"So what's the plan?" Zak asked.

Nick reached into his sack and produced the prism in its protective sleeve, along with the oversize ghost lamp bulb.

The Nicks all gasped in unison as they made the connection.

"Of course!" said BeatNick. "Why didn't I think of that?"

"You did," said Nick. "Kinda."

Nicholas, who'd been in the shadows, was caught in the beam of a flashlight. When Nick got a good look at his clean-shaven face, he nearly dropped the bulb and prism along with his jaw.

Nick Slate had had to endure many unusual and unsettling things in his fourteen years—most of them over the last few months. If, a year ago, someone had told him that he'd be standing at the entrance to a secret tunnel, behind Toys "R" U, gaping at a thirty-something version of himself who happened to look exactly like Nikola Tesla, not only would he not have believed it, but he would have called the police.

"It's not what you think," said Nicholas.

"I don't know what I think," said Nick.

"Oh," said Nicholas. "Neither do I, so I guess it's exactly what you think."

Mitch turned to Petula. "You mean you didn't tell him?"

Petula ignored him. She was not speaking to Mitch. She was furious at the fact that he had given Nick a hug but not her. She was, after all, Mitch's girlfriend. Or at least she had been before she'd betrayed them all to the Accelerati. But now she'd betrayed the Accelerati, and that should count for something. It made her so furious she realized that not speaking to Mitch was not enough. So she slapped him.

"Ow! What was that for?"

The fact that he didn't know earned him a second slap.

"Ow!"

She wound up for a third, but this time he caught her wrist as she swung. "One more time and I will cut off your braids and use them to play Pin-the-Tail-on-the-Petula."

She found the image somehow both disturbing and enticing.

"I'd like to see you try," she said. "No, really, I'd like to."

"Okay," said Mitch. "Another time, maybe."

Thus their stormy relationship entered a reluctant truce.

But Nick didn't allow himself to get distracted by them. "Why do I look like Nikola Tesla?" he asked, to anyone who might be able to shed light on the situation.

"Really?" said Petula. "You want to have this conversation now? Is it just you, or are all seven of you this stupid?"

That sent Old St. Nick into a laughing fit, which might have been contagious, if everyone else hadn't been so positively dour.

A headlight came swinging around the building, and at first they thought they'd been caught by the Accelerati—but it wasn't a pearlescent SUV, it was Wayne Slate's drab Subaru.

"My father and brother are a part of this?" Nick said.

Zak turned to Caitlin. "You mean you didn't tell him?"

"Well, I wasn't sure Nickelback would convince them to come."

But apparently he had—which meant Nick's father and brother must finally remember who he is! Whatever technological spell the Accelerati placed them under must have been broken!

Nickelback—the seventh and final fraction of Nick to arrive—was the first to step out of the car. "Did I miss anything?" he asked.

Zak shined his flashlight at Nicholas's clean-shaven face in response.

"Oh," said Nickelback. "Wasn't expecting that."

When Wayne Slate stepped out of the car, Nick handed Caitlin the bulb and the prism and ran to him. It would have been a wonderful, tender reunion, but Little Nicky stuck out his foot, tripped Nick, and then proceeded to hurl himself into his father's arms instead, nearly tackling him.

"Daddy! Daddy! Daddy!" Little Nicky wailed joyfully, and all the other Nicks converged on the man as well.

To say Mr. Slate was confused would be putting it mildly. "Nick?" he said, looking at the little boy in his arms, then turning to the fourteen-year-old version. "Nick?" he said again. Then he turned to the baby, who had just begun to coo in Nicholas's arms at the sight of him. "Nick?"

"You mean you didn't tell him?" Zak said to Nickelback.

"What, that I was one-seventh of his son?" said Nickelback. "How do you think that would have gone over?"

Danny, meanwhile, stayed by the car, watching the scene unfold in the headlights. He wisely decided that distance was his best option. Although he kind of liked the idea of having a larger family—particularly a younger brother, who might be even worse at baseball than him—it was tempered by the knowledge that this younger brother was actually his older brother, who was actually some old guy, who was actually an even older guy who, for some reason, couldn't stop laughing at Nikola Tesla, who was holding a baby.

In the future, whenever Danny would hear someone say, "I wouldn't touch that with a ten-foot pole," this was the moment that would always come to mind.

And he wasn't the only one.

With all the sudden revelations, it was, to say the least, a WTH moment of the highest possible order—and it might have continued as such a little longer, but a few hundred yards away, alarms began to blare at Wardenclyffe Tower as if it were the scene of a prison break. Suddenly the questions Nick still had seemed less important than the reason they had all gathered.

"Edison must know we're gone!" said Caitlin.

"And," added Nick, "that the F.R.E.E. is missing a few more pieces."

"We'd better get going," said Petula.

They stepped into the small stone utility structure and pulled open the poorly welded gate to reveal tunnel number seven, which led to the secret chamber directly beneath the tower.

"When we got divided," Nick said, "we each found ourselves at the end of the seven tunnels, so that's where we have to go."

"I'll stay here at the end of this tunnel," said Nicholas.

"And I'll guard the entrance," said Mr. Slate, "in case that Jorgenson guy shows up. I have a bone to pick with him."

Nicholas handed SputNick to Old St. Nick, and the baby was content to play with his bushy white beard.

"I'm scared," said Little Nicky, facing the tunnel.

"Don't be," said Danny, finally joining the throng. "If you've gotta wait at the end of a tunnel, I'll wait with you." Then he put up his fist for a knuckle bump, and Little Nicky obliged, visibly relieved.

"Thanks, Danny," Little Nicky said.

"No worries, bro," said Danny, thrilled to be, if only this once, the cool older brother.

Leaving Mr. Slate and Nicholas at the mouth of tunnel seven, the others hurried down the long passage.

At last they found themselves in the central chamber.

"This looks awfully familiar. . . ." said Zak.

He was right—it was just like the one beneath Nick's house, carved out of the bedrock, but here there were no cobwebs and the tunnel entrances had been reinforced with concrete and were clearly numbered one through seven. The shaft in the center that went up to the tower was narrower than the one beneath Nick's house—only about six inches wide. No light came through the shaft now, but it did bring down the sound of the alarms, which echoed in the chamber.

The room was lit with work lights in the ceiling, evenly spaced. Nick pointed to the fixture closest to the very center. "Mitch, I need you to unscrew that bulb."

Mitch climbed onto a four-foot-high metal cone to reach the light. Nick remembered there had been a metal cone in the chamber beneath his house too—but that one had rusted away to nothing, while this one was in perfect condition. Mitch considered the bright light bulb. "It'll be hot!"

So Nick pulled off his spider-silk hoodie—a special gift from Edison—and tossed it to him. "Use this."

Nick looked closer at the metal cone on which Mitch was precariously balancing. It was actually a pyramid with seven sides, each coated with a smooth reflective metal. Figuring out its purpose was as instinctive to him as putting together the device in the tower had been.

"Of course!" he said. "This chamber and the tunnels are for the energy overflow. When the prism is in the machine up above, it divides the energy surplus and directs it downward into this chamber, so it can shoot through the tunnels."

"I get it," said Zak. "Like the exhaust deflector trenches beneath a rocket launchpad."

"Wow—that's so cool!" said Little Nicky.

"Will you all stop geeking out?" Caitlin said. "We don't have time!"

But Nick's mind was already reeling out of control. "I see what Tesla was getting at!" he said, excitedly. "How it connects, how it all works—but there's still something wrong, something missing. . . ."

"I know," Caitlin said gently, doing her best to bring him back into the moment. "The battery. We'll deal with that after you've pulled yourself together."

"No," said Nick, "it's not that, it's something else. Something I have to do to complete the circuit."

Petula looked up when she heard that and furrowed her eyebrows as if insulted, but she said nothing.

With Nick distracted by Tesla's great mechanism, Caitlin took charge.

"Nickelback, tunnel one," she ordered. "BeatNick, tunnel two; Little Nicky, tunnel three . . ."

No one argued with her. They all knew what they had to do.

"Good-bye, everyone," BeatNick said wistfully.

"You'll be back," Nickelback pointed out. "And a lot sooner than I will, might I add."

Danny put his arm around Little Nicky and led him down tunnel three. "It'll be okay," Danny told him. "It'll probably be like going on a roller coaster. Or a particle accelerator."

Petula stepped forward. "I'll go down tunnel four with the baby."

"Actually, I was going to do that," said Caitlin.

Petula glared at her. "Selfish to the end!" she said. "Holding that baby is the *only* chance I'll *ever* get to hold Nick, because all the older versions of him hate me. And you want to rob me of that?" She turned to Old St. Nick. "Hand him over!"

The eldest Nick hesitated, but in the end gave the baby to Petula.

To everyone's surprise, SputNick did not cry in Petula's arms. Instead he just went from playing with St. Nick's beard to playing with Petula's braids.

"See?" said Petula, with surprising warmth. "*This* Nick actually likes me."

"Only because he doesn't know any better," said Caitlin.

Petula gave her a halfhearted sneer, then turned to Old St. Nick. "Out of my way; tunnel four is mine."

"Fine with me," said Old St. Nick with a shrug, and he ambled off down tunnel five. "Ah, to be fourteen again," he said with a laugh. "Can't wait to be rid of this arthritis."

"Just live long enough to make it to the end of that tunnel, old man," Zak said. Then he sighed. "Ah heck, I'd better make sure the geezer gets there," and he trotted after him.

With Nicholas already at the end of tunnel seven, only one version of himself remained.

"Nick, it's time," said Caitlin.

Finally Nick brought his thoughts back to the here and now. He handed Mitch the bulb from the old ghost light. "Screw this in," he told Mitch. "Carefully."

Mitch did, and the light in the chamber changed. It was as if all the other bulbs had been enveloped in a glowing embrace.

They all sensed it. The other six Nicks at the end of their respective tunnels felt themselves being called toward the center.

Caitlin was reminded of the moment she'd seen the reel-to-reel tape recorder at Nick's garage sale. She'd been inexplicably drawn to it . . . and was almost run over by a speeding car. Nick had saved her life that day. Now she found herself involuntarily reaching for the light.

Mitch, the closest to it, just stared right into it, still standing on the pyramid. "Oooh!" he said, like he was watching a particularly impressive fireworks display.

"Mitch, snap out of it," Nick said. "I still need your help."

Mitch shuddered and reluctantly came down from the pyramid. "What is it?"

"This," Nick said, opening the velvet pouch just enough to show Mitch the top of the prism, encased in its protective vacuum tube. "When the time comes, take this out of the bag and hold it up to the light."

Nick handed the bag to Mitch, who looked at it like he'd been handed a stick of dynamite.

"M-me? You want *me* to do it?"

Nick smiled. "Who else can I trust to do it right?"

Then Nick turned to Caitlin and took her hand. "Wanna take a walk with me down a cold, dark tunnel?"

"Any day of the week," Caitlin answered.

Nick calculated it would take about a minute and a half for them to make it to the end, so he told Mitch to count to one hundred. That would give them enough time.

Hand in hand, Caitlin and Nick's fourteen-year-old fragment hurried down tunnel number six, and Mitch began to count.

"One Mississippi . . . two Mississippi . . . three Mississippi . . ."

Edison arrived behind the old Toys "R" Us with an entourage of armed Accelerati at right about the time Mitch reached fifty-five Mississippi. Edison immediately recognized Wayne Slate, who was standing in front of the stone utility building. "Take care of him," he ordered his men. "I want him out of the way."

Wayne saw them approaching and gestured to Nicholas to stay out of sight inside the tunnel entrance. Wayne had had the forethought to prepare his own personal arsenal. Nothing as technologically advanced as Accelerati weaponry, of course, but it would do the job.

He picked up a stone, wound up, and threw it with the precision of a former major league baseball pitcher.

After he took the first Accelerati down, the others scattered and cowered behind a Dumpster. The old man, laboring out of an odd-looking vehicle in an oversize wheelchair, bellowed at them furiously for not standing their ground.

The Accelerati tried to fire on Wayne from their hiding places, but his aim was much better than theirs. He even disarmed one of them with a well-placed chunk of concrete.

Now the old man rolled across the parking lot toward him. Unlike the others, he had no fear of getting beaned by a rock.

And sure enough, Wayne found that he just couldn't throw stones at a decrepit old man in a wheelchair.

"Mr. Slate," said the old man angrily, "you're in my way." Then he pulled a device out from under his lap blanket and fired, hitting Wayne squarely in the chest.

Wayne Slate vanished. Only his clothes remained, falling to the ground in a heap.

"Must I do everything myself?" Edison chided.

His henchmen seemed reluctant to come out of hiding.

"He's gone, you cowards!" Edison yelled. "He won't be back for twenty minutes."

Edison rolled his way over weeds and maneuvered himself into the stone utility structure that marked the entrance to tunnel seven.

At the center of everything, Mitch nervously fidgeted with the velvet-covered prism, afraid that he'd forget how to count.

". . . eighty-eight Mississippi . . . eighty-nine Mississippi . . ."

• • •

At the end of tunnel one, Nickelback looked at his Rolex impatiently, then realized he didn't have a Rolex—but he was content in the knowledge that someday he would.

At the end of tunnel two, BeatNick pulled a Snickers bar out of his pocket and, unsure whether it would survive the rejoining with his six other selves, unwrapped it and stuffed it into his mouth.

At the end of tunnel three, Little Nicky and Danny perfected a secret handshake as they waited for Nicky to ride the roller coaster and/or particle accelerator.

At the end of tunnel four, things were so blissfully quiet one might think that Petula and SputNick weren't even there.

At the end of tunnel five, Old St. Nick gripped his chest and grimaced. "Whoa, Nellie!" he cried. "My ticker! I think this is the big one."

"No!" said Zak. "Don't you dare die on me, old man!"

Old St. Nick pointed and grinned. "Gotcha!"

At the end of tunnel six, Nick took a deep breath and realized he had to let go of Caitlin's hand. She had been stronger than him through all of this—and not just because he was one-seventh of himself. He would have to find a way to thank her when all this was over.

But for now, he just turned to her and said warmly, "See you in a minute."

". . . ninety-four Mississippi . . . ninety-five Mississippi . . ."

. . .

And at the end of tunnel seven, Thomas Edison peered into the darkness—and found himself looking into a face he thought he'd never see again.

"Nikola?" he said incredulously. "It can't be!"

Nicholas had the presence of mind to see this moment for exactly what it was: a golden opportunity. And so he used it, milking it for all it was worth.

"Tom . . ." he said in a ghostly voice that echoed satisfyingly in the tunnel. "Tom . . . what have you done?"

And Edison did something he hadn't managed to do in years. He rose from his chair, on shaky legs. "Nikola," he said, "I—I . . . I never meant to . . . I—I never wanted it to be like this. . . ."

"You can still make it right, my friend. . . ." Nicholas said in a fake accent. "You can still make it right. . . ."

Then, in the center of the chamber, Mitch reached one hundred Mississippi, tore the prism from the velvet bag, held it up into the light—and the ghostly vision of Nikola Tesla wailed, "Make it right. . . ." as he was drawn down the tunnel away from Edison, like a spirit pulled into the spectral nexus of eternity.

41 STRUJA

It wasn't exactly the spectral nexus of eternity. It wasn't like a roller coaster or particle accelerator either. It felt more like bouncing off a diving board and spinning in an uncontrolled flip that ends in a monumental belly flop.

Only with a whole bunch of other bodies hitting the water in the exact same spot at the exact same moment.

For an instant, Nick felt like he was in a shrinking box with multiple versions of himself, all jockeying for position. Then he couldn't tell which version of himself he was, and then he was all of them, and then he was just him, and the box was gone, and he was standing in front of Mitch, who was holding the prism in the air, grimacing and covering his eyes.

"Good job, Mitch!" Nick said. "You can put it away now."

Mitch slipped it back into the velvet sleeve and handed it to Nick. "It worked?"

"Looks like it," said Nick, and yet he still felt an empty space inside of him. It wasn't nearly as strong as it had been before, but it was still there.

Caitlin came running out of their tunnel, then Danny and Zak from theirs. Nick remembered being at the end of each tunnel with them. He remembered impatiently looking at a Rolex that didn't exist yet. And he remembered the look on Edison's face as he faced the ghost of Nikola Tesla.

"You're whole!" Caitlin said, and gave him a crushing hug. It made him remember what she'd said to BeatNick earlier that day. He had always been awkward with his affection when it came to Caitlin, but he drew a bit of confidence from his older self.

"This is from BeatNick," he said. "Something he would have saved for the twenty-four-year-old Caitlin, if he could."

And then he kissed her. This wasn't an ordinary kiss. It was the kind of kiss that changed lives, saved worlds, and became emblazoned in one's memory, becoming the yardstick by which every future kiss would be measured.

For a brief moment, Caitlin thought she must have been struck by some Accelerati weapon herself, because she could swear she was melting into a puddle of protoplasm on the floor. And when it was over she had no idea what to say, except "Did you just eat a Snickers?"

It was Zak who suddenly realized what should have been obvious to all of them. "Where's that annoying girl with the braids?"

They looked toward tunnel four, and that's when Nick knew. He had memories from every other Nick, but he had no memory of being held in Old St. Nick's arms, or playing with Petula's pigtails. He began reflexively patting himself down, as if he'd misplaced his wallet—but the answer wasn't in any of his pockets. It was at the end of tunnel four. SputNick was missing.

"PETULA!" he wailed, and took off down the tunnel.

Meanwhile, at the far end of tunnel seven, Edison, looking paler than usual, if that were even possible, wheeled out of the small stone structure, where his fairly useless entourage waited for instructions.

"Sir?" one of them asked. "Are you all right?"

Instead of answering, Edison considered the pile of clothes on the ground. "Return to the command center," he said. "Now."

"But what about—"

"Mr. Slate is the least of our concerns. Leave his clothes. Leave him be."

The others looked to one another in confusion and disbelief.

"But, sir—"

"You heard me."

Then he rolled back to his car, they loaded him in, and he ordered his driver to return him to the tower.

Tunnel four ended in a stone mausoleum. The name carved on the outside of the small moss-covered structure was STRUJA, which was a dead giveaway to anyone who spoke Serbian, because it was the Serbian word for "electric current."

The crypt was located in an old graveyard with dozens of similar marble structures. Twilight was fading, and the cemetery was filled with shadows as dark as open graves. Nick thought to call out to Petula, but he realized that if she was trying to evade him, this would only give away his position. So he stood quietly and listened . . . until he heard to his left the scraping of iron against stone, and the cooing of a baby. He ran down an aisle just in time to see Petula pulling the gate closed on another tomb.

The idea of Petula with a baby in a graveyard did not sit well with him. She could be up to any number of unpleasant things, none of which he cared to think about. Nick didn't know who he was more furious at—Petula, for yet another betrayal, or himself, for being stupid enough to trust her.

He reached the mausoleum he had seen Petula enter and he rattled the gate, but couldn't get it open. She had padlocked herself and SputNick inside.

"Petula—what do you think you're doing?"

"Completing the circuit," she told him, which made absolutely no sense, and sounded like any other obtuse, irritating thing that Petula might say.

SputNick saw Nick through the gate and began to cry, reaching out for him. Though the baby didn't understand what was happening, he wanted completion as much as Nick did.

That's when Nick saw what she had with her. The telephone and the globe. They were intricately wired together. Petula, holding the baby with one arm, made final adjustments on the jury-rigged device.

This was the time machine he and Caitlin had heard Edison and Ms. Planck talking about. Petula had reassembled it or, more likely, had blackmailed Accelerati scientists into reassembling it for her.

She finished her tinkering, stuck her index finger into the rotary dial of the phone, and turned it.

As it spun back into place, Nick saw something that a less intelligent person might call a swirling vortex of death. But he knew what it was. It was a passageway to another time.

"Petula! Stop!"

He began to kick at the gate with all his might. At last it gave, and he charged through.

That's when Petula finally put her black belt in theoretical jujitsu to good use. She thrust the heel of her palm into Nick's sternum, knocking the wind out of him. He fell to the floor of the mausoleum.

"It has to be done, Nick!"

Nick gasped for air, still unable to lift himself up. "Have you . . . lost . . . your mind?"

Petula cradled the baby and spoke with calm acceptance and resolve. "*I* complete the circuit. Not you, not anyone else. Me." She turned to the undulating tunnel of light before her. "When you think of me—and you'd better—remember how I hurled myself into the abyss for you. Maybe you'll hate me a little less."

Then, holding SputNick tight, she leaped into the portal.

It closed the moment she was gone, leaving Nick alone with the globe, the phone, and six-sevenths of himself.

The reality of what Petula had done was only beginning to infiltrate Nick's mind when half a dozen Accelerati appeared at the crypt's gate, weapons drawn.

"Don't move! Hands in the air."

"How can I put my hands in the air if I'm not allowed to move?"

While the Accelerati thugs pondered which of the two requests was the more urgent, one more member of the Accelerati stepped forward. The one person in the world Nick least wanted to see in any time period.

When Dr. Alan Jorgenson stepped into the mausoleum, the situation was crystal clear to him: Nick Slate, the sniveling traitor, had stolen the light bulb, the prism, and the globe in order to sabotage the F.R.E.E.

It looked like the boy was attempting to use the globe and the antiquated telephone to create that vortex of death into which Jorgenson had thrown Evangeline Planck. And while hurling Nick State into the same vortex was a cheery thought, there were more important things to do right now.

"Your abject selfishness and stupidity boggle the mind," Jorgenson seethed. "Rather than see the Accelerati triumph, you would allow the world to be destroyed. Who is the villain in this equation, Master Slate, you or me?"

"Let me explain," said Nick. "It's not what it looks like."

Jorgenson laughed at the boy's audacity. He'd been caught red-handed and still he was telling lies. "I suppose now you're going to tell me you were going to bring it all back."

"I was!" Nick said.

Jorgenson had had enough. He instructed the Accelerati to disconnect the globe from the phone and return it to the platform, along with the prism, which they pulled from Nick's pocket.

"You need me to put them back in!" Nick insisted.

"Actually, we don't," Jorgenson said, with a gloat he could not contain. "The scientists in attendance took photos and notes when you assembled the machine. They know exactly where to place these parts. The truth is, Nick, neither I nor Mr. Edison has any further use for you."

"Dr. Jorgenson, what about the telephone?" one of the others asked.

"Leave it," Jorgenson said. "It's not a part of the machine."

Then Jorgenson ordered the broken gate sealed with a molecular fuser with Nick still inside, where he'd have plenty of time to think about the consequences of his insolence.

"Wait!" Nick called, his hands gripping the iron gate with the gratifying semblance of a criminal behind bars. "You'll need Edison's battery to start the F.R.E.E. You'll have to make him give it up!"

"Actually, we won't be needing Edison's battery at all," Jorgenson said, immensely pleased with himself. "We've resolved that issue."

That made the boy's face blanch in a most satisfying way. "Resolved it? How?"

Jorgenson chose to say nothing more. Let him wonder.

"Resolved it HOW?"

But Jorgenson left Nick trapped and alone, except for the silent dead entombed around him.

42 OUR UNIQUE CONDITION

Vince stood in Edison's office looking through a large window at Wardenclyffe Tower. Night had fallen quite a while ago and the aurora was bright, but not as bright as it had been in Tierra del Fuego.

Sparks were beginning to arc across the sky now. Lightning without the benefit of clouds. A sign that things were coming to a head. It wouldn't be long before the charge reached the critical stage.

Vince hadn't expected to be alive to see this. He thought the Accelerati would have ripped him from his battery by now.

He was resigned to death. Actually, he had been resigned to it for years, long before the first time he had actually died. It was a lifestyle, after all.

Vince LaRue had not been captured. He had turned himself in.

His choice to surrender really wasn't difficult at all. The math alone was a compelling argument:

1. Give myself up, I die.
2. Stay hidden, I still die, and so does everyone else.

While Vince had no recollection of what it was like "on the other side," he did suspect there'd be a very special punishment awaiting someone selfish enough to kick everyone else's bucket along with his own.

The decision, therefore, was easy. The hard part had been making his surrender stick. He simply couldn't find the Accelerati.

True, they were searching the globe for him, but they were, after all, a secret organization that did not wish to be found, making surrender very inconvenient.

First he posted pictures of himself and details about the Chilean town that was harboring him on every social media site he belonged to. But since he had very few followers, nobody noticed or cared—except for his Spanish teacher, who told him to try the ceviche.

He called the Shoreham Police Department and attempted to get them to take a message to Wardenclyffe Tower concerning his whereabouts. But since it was not official police business, they felt no particular sense of urgency. They took his number and promised to get back to him, and then reconsidered when they realized it was an international number. In the end, he posted an ad on eBay for a battery that brings back the dead.

He got several lowball offers. Then the Accelerati finally noticed the ad, traced it back to the computer he had used, and stormed the sheep farm where he was staying with enough manpower to overthrow the Chilean government.

That was yesterday. Now, after eating a dinner fit for a vegan king in Edison's office, he awaited his first audience with the man himself.

When Edison rolled in, Vince was taken aback by his decrepit appearance, as well as the large, shrouded object on the back of his motorized wheelchair. The old man seemed humorless, distracted—as if he'd just seen a ghost.

"Vincent Bartholomew LaRue, I presume?"

"Just Vince," he told Edison. "Bartholomew was a parental brain fart for which they will never be forgiven."

Edison extended his hand for Vince to shake. Both of their hands felt cold, clammy, and not entirely alive.

"Thanks for the grub," Vince said, pointing to the spread set out before him. "It's pretty good for zombie food."

"Yes," said Edison. "My chef is well versed in preparing dishes for our unique dietary needs."

Edison took a plate for himself, but his hand shook so much that he dropped it and it shattered. "You'll have to excuse me," he said. "I just had a very disturbing experience and I'm still a bit shaken."

Vince got him a new plate and filled it for him, wondering if it was appropriate to serve dinner to your own executioner.

"You and I are unique in the world, Mr. LaRue," Edison said. "It's a pleasure to finally meet someone who shares the same condition."

"Undeath?"

Edison sighed. "I prefer to think of it as being 'electrically maintained.'"

Vince looked at the object on the back of Edison's wheelchair, wrapped in what looked like a homemade cozy for something that wasn't very cozy at all. And Edison caught him looking at it.

"If you wish to see it, be my guest," Edison said. "Indulge your curiosity."

Vince removed the cozy to reveal a cylinder that looked similar to his, except much taller and made of glass. The liquid inside had gone cloudy and brown, so dark that for the most part it hid the metallic cells within.

"It was, of course, an invention of Tesla's," Edison told him. "I acquired it in a wager. You see, Nikola created it as a tool for law enforcement. He believed that violent crime would become a thing of the past if a murder victim could be reanimated long enough to identify his killer. I bet Tesla that not only would the police refuse it, but also they would actively deny its existence. I won the bet."

Edison ate a spoonful of pureed carrots and ginger that looked like baby food but tasted much better. "Tesla's greatest flaw was an inability to understand human nature," the old man continued. "You see, the battery would have put homicide detectives out of work. In the end, solving crimes is less important to the world's criminal justice system than being *paid* to solve crimes."

Then Edison put down his plate and leaned toward Vince. "May I see yours?"

Vince stepped back protectively. Then he nodded. He carefully removed his backpack, making sure not to dislodge the electrodes from his neck. Then he pulled out the battery.

"Extraordinary," Edison said. "So mine was the prototype. I always suspected Nikola had built a more compact version."

Edison looked out at the tower, standing silhouetted against the sparking sky. "I assume that its inclusion in the F.R.E.E. is to give the machine a sort of spark of life." Then he turned back to Vince. "The world will never be ready for free energy," he insisted adamantly. "To be valued, it must have a price. That is the way of the world. Nikola labored under the false assumption that everyone was as altruistic as he. That everyone's goal was the enrichment of the world, rather than the enrichment of their own pockets. I, on the other hand, understand that those two things must go hand in hand."

Then he took on that unsettled gaze again. "He never forgave me for succeeding at his expense. So much water has passed under the bridge that I don't know how, after all these years, he can expect me to make things right."

A particularly large lightning bolt sizzled across the sky. Vince grimaced. "So . . . what happens now?"

Edison explained with neither remorse nor glee. He merely stated the facts. "The asteroid will soon pass overhead. As it does, we will have a ten-minute window in which to turn on the machine. The first discharge will be massive. A spectacle to behold, certainly. Then, once the machine is engaged and functioning, the asteroid will discharge on every orbit, several times a day."

"And my battery?"

"I'm afraid it must be there to start the process every time. Once you're disconnected, it will be, unfortunately, for good. And for the good of mankind."

Vince took a deep breath and slowly let it out. "How much time do I have?" he asked.

But Edison didn't have to answer, because the Doomsday Clock on the wall was at thirty-eight minutes and counting.

43 HAVE I CAUGHT YOU AT A BAD TIME?

Nick stewed with anguish in the mausoleum as the heat of day gave way to the damp chill of night.

It was all going to happen without him.

After everything he'd done—after all he'd put his friends and family through—Jorgenson had booted him beyond the sidelines. He wasn't even a spectator anymore, he was entirely out of the picture with no way back in. How cruel the universe was to instill in him a burning need—and an absolute certainty that he was at the core of the equation, the central human gear of Tesla's machine—only to be ripped out at the last moment and tossed aside. Or maybe it wasn't the universe at all. Maybe he had been deluding himself from the beginning. Perhaps Jorgenson was right, and Nick was just a sad, sorry kid with confidence issues who needed to be a part of something larger than himself.

Self-pity was not Nick's style, but sitting powerless in a mausoleum, a few hundred yards away from what was about to be the world's greatest source of power, made a person feel inadequate on every level. His friends had probably been captured. And what about Vince? Did they have his battery, as Jorgenson had seemed to suggest?

Nick got up and kicked the gate again and again, to vent his frustration as much as to break the gate down, but neither goal was achieved. He still felt miserable, and the fused iron held firm. He was truly trapped there until someone came to free him, or fry him.

He slid back down to the ground and put his head in his hands. Now it was just him, the deceased, and the blasted telephone.

Which began to ring.

The harsh sound filled the cold stone chamber and made him jump. In the silence before it rang again, he could still feel it shrieking in his ears like a fire alarm.

After the third ring he reached out, lifted the receiver from the cradle, and brought it to his ear.

"Hello?" he said.

Then he heard a familiar accented voice.

"Hello. This is Nikola Tesla. Have I caught you at a bad time?"

Typically, dead people don't make phone calls. Lines may go dead, and in a particularly awkward phone conversation there might be dead air, but dead people are not inclined to pick up the phone to chat with the living.

Clearly, then, Nikola Tesla was alive when he dialed the phone number assigned to the time-transmitting phone he must have just built. Most people receive a busy signal when they dial themselves. But then, most people can't program their phone to dial itself more than a hundred years in the future.

Nick just sat there on the mausoleum floor slack-jawed.

"Are you there?" Tesla asked. "Hello? I am returning your phone call. If you're there, please say something."

"I'm here," Nick said.

"Good, good!" Tesla said. "It works. I had my doubts, but

knowing you were able to reach me two years ago, well, it convinced me that I must have built a temporal sound transducer."

"Two years ago?"

"Yes," Tesla said, "but I imagine it may only be a matter of days, or weeks, for you. Or perhaps I've reached you before you made that call, in which case I'll hang up and try again."

"No, no, don't hang up!" Nick scooted closer to the phone, trying to untangle the curly wire connected to the receiver. What do you say to the man who sent you on a fool's errand during which you proved you were indeed a fool?

"I must admit, I was skeptical that this telephone could be built," Tesla said cheerfully, "but while I was in Germany defending my patent on the electric turbine, I had an interesting conversation with a young patent clerk. Arnstein or Ernstein—something like that. Odd fellow, but he had interesting ideas about the relationship between time and space."

He seemed content to simply chat. But Nick was in no mood. If Tesla had called to help him, he wasn't doing a very good job. "The Accelerati have your machine," Nick announced. "Edison took it, and I'm trapped. What should I do?"

"Edison?" Tesla said incredulously. "Edison is alive in your time? That's extraordinary! How is this possible?"

Nick found himself getting increasingly frustrated at the inventor. "Your battery—but that's not important right now—"

"Hmm," said Tesla. "A battery that sustains life. What an intriguing notion."

"Didn't you hear me? He's putting together your machine! The Far Range Energy Emitter."

"My what?"

Nick began to stammer. "Your . . . your life's work—your greatest invention—free wireless energy to the world—"

"What a grand concept!" Tesla said.

Was the man toying with him? If he was trying to be funny, Nick was not amused. "You have to tell me what to do," Nick pleaded. "You and me . . . we're connected. You're the one who set this in motion, so you have to know—how do I get us out of this? How do I make things right?" He held his breath and waited for the genius to give him the answer.

And Tesla said, "I have no idea."

The fact that Nikola Tesla didn't have the answers was horrifying to Nick. After all, the inventor had designed the mechanical and human gear work churning toward this climactic moment. If he was behind it all, how could he not know what was supposed to happen next? And then Nick realized . . .

Tesla hadn't done it yet.

The man was calling from a time before he had even conceived of the F.R.E.E. and all the individual inventions within it. His life's work was yet to begin. That realization left Nick speechless, caught in a mental feedback loop. Was *he* the one who inspired the F.R.E.E., through this phone call? Was all of this ultimately Nick's own fault?

"I'm sure whatever trouble you're in, you'll work it out," Tesla said reassuringly. "You sound like a clever boy."

Considering his current situation, Nick didn't feel very clever at the moment. In fact, he was feeling so dense he was beginning to doubt the existence of his own brain.

"Even though I've never met you," said Tesla, "I feel an uncanny kinship, as you said. A connection. Perhaps even . . . a completion."

And then, finally, Nick connected two thoughts.

"I complete the circuit," Petula had said. And then she had jumped with the baby into the time vortex to escape. But maybe escape hadn't been her plan. . . .

"I must get back to my labors now," the inventor said. "I wish to thank you for helping me."

"Helping *you*?"

"Yes—thanks to you, when you warned me that my lab would burn down, I moved my designs and prototypes, and saved them."

Nick gasped, and got to his feet. "You did? But . . ." This meant that Nick had changed the past . . . or had he? The newspapers still reported that Tesla had lost everything in the fire. Unless . . .

"You hid everything!" Nick said. "You hid your inventions and no one ever knew!"

"Yes, it seemed the most sensible thing to do. One can't change the past, after all, only one's perspective on it. According to history, all my work was destroyed in the fire. Only you and I know the truth of it."

Nick's head was swimming, and he found himself spiraling back up from the hopeless depths he'd been drowning in just a few moments earlier. Possibilities were dividing and mutating in his mind. In spite of his current helpless situation, a plan was beginning to form that made him feel anything but helpless. It fell into place so completely it took his breath away. Perspective. That was the key to everything! Even that missing blender lid!

Tesla sighed. "I'm beginning to think that perhaps I will eventually need to hide all of my work to keep it from getting into the wrong hands," he mused. "I'm considering a move to Colorado Springs. Lots of space for grand experimentation! Perhaps there I shall find a suitable repository for my most sensitive inventions."

Nick grinned. "Sounds like a good idea."

"I must be going," Tesla said. "I have lectures to give, turbines to approve, and, apparently, an electrifying future. Godspeed to you, young man. And good day!"

Then the inventor hung up, breaking a circuit that had spanned more than a hundred years.

Without even realizing it, Tesla had told Nick everything he needed to know. The tumblers had rolled in his head, and the impossible combination had finally clicked into place, with a mathematical precision Zak would be proud of.

"I know what I have to do!" Nick shouted, and hearing the words come out his mouth made him laugh, because they were absolutely true. The answer was shining before him like a flare in the night sky.

"Glad to hear it," said Caitlin from the other side of the mausoleum gate. "But what you have to do right now is move back, so we can blow up this gate without blowing you up with it."

⁴⁴ THE RING OF POWER

Caitlin, along with Mitch and Danny, owed her life to Zak. Or at least to the fact that his mother was the Grand Acceleratus.

No sooner had Nick taken off after Petula than the Accelerati burst into the chamber from three other tunnels, a swarm of pastel suits with a frightening array of deadly and disfiguring weapons.

Caitlin had always been a "never surrender" kind of girl, but the Accelerati had proven to be trigger-happy in the past. She did not want to end up flat like poor Theo, or have her vital organs pureed inside of her.

So she put up her hands, and Mitch and Danny followed her lead.

Only Zak refused to yield—perhaps because he saw something Caitlin didn't. His mother was leading the charge.

"Hold your fire!" shouted Z. She reached out and knocked the arm of a particularly determined associate, whose weapon melted a hole in the wall instead of any of their heads. "Edison needs them alive!"

Caitlin didn't believe that for a minute.

Z went up to Zak and said sternly, "If you know what's good for you, you'll get on your knees with your hands behind your head." It took Caitlin a second, then she got it. Z was pretending she didn't know him.

Zak stared at his mom and slowly obeyed. The other kids did the same.

An Acceleratus tried to unscrew the light bulb, and burned his fingers in the process—proving once more the curious disconnect between genius and common sense.

Z turned to Caitlin. "Where is Nick? And the other items he took?"

"Not here," Caitlin said, as unhelpful as she could be. "Obviously."

"This is no time for games," Z chided. "We have to discharge that asteroid. If you do not tell me where he went—"

"—he'll be caught by Jorgenson anyway," Mitch blurted.

Mitch covered his mouth, but it was too late. Z had already heard him, and she didn't seem surprised. Either she had been made aware of Mitch's strange, prophetic bursts, or she guessed the truth of it.

"Jorgenson was sent to the mouth of tunnel four," she said with a nod.

"Should I take a team to assist?" asked one of her subordinates.

"No," Z said. "He can handle it himself." She tried to order her retinue of Accelerati back to the surface, but they refused to leave her alone down there, so she allowed two to stay.

"Regardless of what you think you are doing," she told the kids, "we are running out of time."

And then the equation changed again.

"Hey," said one of the remaining Accelerati, "isn't this one your son?"

"I was afraid of this." Z sighed as she pulled a small device from her purse and fired at her two associates.

A translucent spherical force field immediately surrounded the two men. Caitlin could see them pounding the surface inside, to no avail. Even their shouts were muffled. When they moved at the same time, the ball rolled, giving the impression they were in a human hamster ball.

Z couldn't help but smile at Caitlin's surprised expression. "A little something we reverse-engineered from your force-field flour sifter. But it only lasts a minute or two, so we have to be quick."

Unable to escape from the ball, the two Accelerati agents rolled down one of the other tunnels, where it promptly got stuck.

Z's phone rang and she answered. Caitlin could hear Jorgenson confirming that the globe and prism had been recovered.

"What about the boy?" Z asked.

"Nick Slate is no longer a factor," Jorgenson said.

Caitlin did not like the way that sounded.

Z clicked off and looked down the tunnel where the two men were trying to rock the stuck sphere back and forth. "I have had quite enough of this organization," she said. Then she reached behind her ear, removed the Accelerati earring, and dropped it to the ground. "I should have done that years ago." Then she looked lovingly at Zak. "But I was afraid of what they would do to you."

"I can take care of myself, Mom," Zak told her.

"I see that now," she said, and gave him a hug.

"Hey," said Danny, "are we going to save my brother or just stand here?"

And the five of them hurried down tunnel four to see what had become of Nick.

It was Caitlin who spotted the mausoleum with a fused gate.

When she heard Nick shout about knowing what to do, she had no idea what he was talking about. She was just thrilled that Jorgenson had left him alive.

"Nick! Stay as far back as you can," Caitlin instructed him, seeing the weapon that Z had pulled out. In fact, this one seemed much too large to fit in the purse. It wasn't the hamster-ball generator that Z now aimed at the gate. It was the same type of weapon that had melted a hole in the wall earlier.

Nick moved to the farthest corner, Z fired, and the iron melted into white-hot liquid and the stone around the entrance became dripping magma.

"Whoa," said Danny. "Can I try?"

Z gave him a withering look and put the weapon back in her purse.

"You okay, Nick?" called Caitlin.

"Yeah, I think so," he called back, then he jumped over the pools of molten steel and magma, carrying, of all things, the Teslaphone.

"What are you doing with that?" Caitlin asked.

"And where's Petula?" asked Mitch.

"Gone," Nick said.

Before he could explain, the air was filled with the deafening chop of approaching helicopters—four of them, carrying a massive circular object.

"Is that . . . a flying saucer?" Danny asked.

"Great," said Mitch. "Aliens. Just what we need."

"Wait, I've seen that before!" Caitlin said.

Nick nodded. "So have I. . . ."

A quartet of Sikorsky Skycrane heavy-lift construction helicopters hauled their massive payload over the treetops of Shoreham. Citizens came out of their homes to marvel as it passed overhead, all asking the same question: *What* is *that thing?*

It was, in fact, a ten-foot-high titanium alloy ring, one hundred feet in diameter; a band of highly conductive metal designed to safely absorb a discharge of celestial energy that would otherwise electrocute the planet.

The "ring of power" had been downsized in a giant Accelerati shrinking machine to make its transport from Colorado Springs more manageable. Evangeline Planck and Edison had each worn it for a time. But now that the ring had been restored to its original size, it required the world's most muscular helicopters to airlift it to Wardenclyffe Tower. Once there, it would be dropped around the tower like a Titan's ring toss. The operation, however, could not be done in a cavalier or casual manner. It had to be precise. If a cable slipped, or the positioning was slightly off, the result would be disastrous. The ring might not land around the base, but instead tumble and wipe out the entire tower.

It also had to be done quickly—not because of winds, or the neighbors, or even the countdown of the Doomsday Clock. The time limit was due to the fact that the Accelerati were quite literally running on fumes, as they no longer had enough money to fill the helicopters' gas tanks.

Unfortunately, as with so many organizations, the right hand was only faintly aware, and somewhat resentful, of whatever the left hand was doing. The ring could not be lowered into place until the rest of the machine was ready, because once it was down, it would block all entry or exit from the tower. No one had expected Nick Slate to run off with several key items. And no one told the helicopter pilots. Thus, they arrived too soon, and had to hover above the tower as their gas tanks ticked toward empty.

As he watched the giant ring hang in the air, Edison chided himself for trusting Nick—and for placing his entire organization in the hands of Dr. Zenobia Thuku, who he had just learned had betrayed him.

He rolled from the control building to the tower with Jorgenson, Vince right beside him.

"Don't you dare try to escape," Jorgenson threatened the boy.

"Dude, I chose to be here," Vince reminded him. "Why would I bolt now?"

"Fear of death's dark embrace, perhaps?"

"Been there, done that," Vince said. "Bring it on."

In the tower, the globe, bulb, and prism had just been installed, and the team of Accelerati engineers were riding down in the cramped gantry elevator. Up above, the helicopters held their position, but Edison didn't know how much longer that would last. Now at the base of the tower, Edison turned to Vince.

"I'm sorry, son, but we're out of time."

"Wait," said Vince. "I have some last words." Having apparently prepared for this, he pulled a page of the finest parchment paper from his pocket, cleared his throat, and began to read with dramatic import. "I, Vince La Rue—"

"Good enough," said Edison, then he nodded to Jorgenson, who ripped the wires out from behind Vince's ears. Vince fell to the ground in a heap, his eyes open, his heart still, and his words left unsaid. The page, torn from his hand by the breeze, fluttered away.

And in Edison's mind, he heard once again the ghost of Tesla say, *"Make things right. . . ."* Surely taking Vince LaRue's battery was not making things right, but what choice did Edison have? *Sorry, Nikola,* he said silently to himself, *but I have to do what I have to do.*

The elevator arrived, and the team of engineers got out of Edison's way as he trundled inside. "Give me the battery," he said to Jorgenson.

"It's too dangerous—you should watch from the control room," said Jorgenson. He pointed to one of the engineers. "You! Take the battery up and connect it."

"No," insisted Edison. "*I* will complete the circuit."

He realized, however, that he did need a take-charge sort of person to run things on the ground, at least until he returned. Even if it was a take-charge person he did not particularly care for.

Jorgenson had successfully retrieved the prism and the globe, capturing the double-crossing Nick in the process. Yes, he had returned with a head swollen full of told-ya-so attitude, but he had every right; Jorgenson had been correct about the boy, and Edison had been wrong. A reward was called for.

"Al," Edison said, "I hereby reinstate you as Grand Acceleratus."

Jorgenson nodded, as if he had expected it all along. "I'll need a new suit."

"Later. Right now I'm leaving the ground operation in your hands."

Then, with the battery in his lap, Edison closed the elevator grate and rose to the top of the tower.

45 A CLOCKWORK LEMON

The great clocks of Europe are complex mechanisms, composed of massive wheels, pulleys and pendulums, gears, cogs, and springs, all hidden within stone towers. With a mystical regularity that must have seemed like magic to medieval minds, the bells toll a precise number of times to mark the hours, and the truly elaborate clocks send out a collection of figures to dance around a platform while mechanized music plays.

Yet those who marvel at such feats of old-world engineering rarely think of the *human* part of the mechanism: the men who mined the iron for the gears, the workers who hoisted them into place, the masons who laid the stones, and the artists who painted the dancing figures.

Only a rare few can truly see the larger picture of a complex machine. Nick Slate was one of the few.

Once he understood how the pieces fit together, all that remained was to move them into place. Those pieces, however, didn't always want to move. Nick knew that without the human element in place, even the greatest machine can be a lemon.

Nick hurried from the graveyard toward Wardenclyffe Tower, gripping the clumsy phone as he ran. Caitlin, right beside him, demanded to know what he was up to.

She did deserve an explanation. "I know where the missing

blender lid is," he told her. "It's more important than I thought, and I have to get it!"

"It's at the tower?"

"Not exactly. . . ."

"So why are we running toward the tower?"

Nick didn't slow his pace. How could he explain to her that it wasn't just knowing where the piece was, but *why* it was there? The *why* was far more important than the where.

It was then that Caitlin began to connect some of the critical dots.

"You're going after the globe!" she said. "Are you telling me the blender lid is hidden in the past?"

"It's not hidden," Nick told her. "It's exactly where it's supposed to be: in my attic!"

Nick pulled slightly ahead, and Caitlin put on speed to keep up with him. The others were too far behind to hear, which was fine with Nick.

"No, it was never there!" insisted Caitlin. "You said it yourself: you sold that blender without a lid!"

"Which means that someone took it before I moved into that house!"

"But why?"

To that, Nick could only smile. "Exactly!"

The tower was only a few blocks away now. Nick knew timing was crucial, and that any number of monkey wrenches could be hurled into the works. The first monkey wrench was his father, who would go to the ends of the earth to keep Nick safe, and thus prevent him from doing the highly dangerous thing he needed to do.

Nick had Nicholas's memory of Edison birthday-suiting his father—so he knew Wayne would show up in just a few minutes.

Nick slowed down enough to allow his brother to catch up. "Danny, I need your help," he said as they continued to run.

Danny had been waiting for this—hoping for it even. Although he didn't understand the big picture the way Nick did, he did sense that there was a big picture to see. And it was a thrill to be a part of it.

"There's something I need you to do," Nick told him, "but you can't ask any questions. You just have to do it."

"Okay," Danny said.

"In about five minutes, Dad is going to reappear in the parking lot behind the old Toys "R" Us."

"Uh . . . okay."

"When he shows up, give him back his clothes, which are there waiting for him."

Danny had to run that through his head twice. "He . . . won't have any clothes?"

"Long story," said Nick. "Once he's dressed, you can't let him go anywhere. Pretend you sprained your ankle. Fall to the ground, scream a lot—and scream even louder if he tries to pick you up. Don't let him move you, and don't let him leave you."

"I can do that," Danny said, then frowned. "Why am I doing that?"

And his brother said, "No questions, remember?" Which is exactly what Danny had suspected Nick would say.

"How long do I have to keep Dad there?"

"Until either the sky stops sparking," Nick told him, "or the world ends."

"Oh. Okay." Danny decided that his brother was right. Best not to ask questions about these sorts of things. Not even to himself. So he hurried off, trusting Nick's judgment.

Meanwhile, Z, who had made the mistake of wearing heels today, was struggling to keep pace with Nick and the others.

She did not regret throwing away everything to save her son and his friends—but why in the name of all things reasonable would the Slate boy head back to the tower? Stumbling on her Prada stilettos, she finally pulled alongside him and grabbed his arm hard enough to almost make him drop the phone.

"You must stop!" she insisted. "Jorgenson will vaporize you on sight. I will not let you go back there!"

To Nick, Dr. Zenobia Thuku was monkey wrench number two. She had a whole host of weapons in that bottomless purse of hers. He knew she wouldn't hurt him, but she could certainly find a way to remove him from the situation. She could mesmerize him with the Accelerati laser pointer, for instance, and make him abandon everything to chase its seductive beam.

Nick pulled himself out of her grasp. "You have to trust me."

"Trust you?" Z said. "I hardly even know you."

Which is why, thought Nick, *you won't be expecting what I'm about to do.* He plucked the purse out of her arms and tossed it to Caitlin. "Run!" he shouted to her.

She obeyed, holding the handbag that seemed far too small for all the objects inside. She didn't have to be asked to trust Nick. Even when he made a horrendous mistake, it always seemed to take them to where they needed to go—even if they hadn't realized it at the time. Which meant that his mistakes were not mistakes at all—even when it seemed like he was racing them toward certain doom.

But Caitlin also knew that without her clearheaded thinking, it might actually become certain doom. Their gears were now forever meshed, their fates intertwined.

"Use Z's key card to open the gate!" Nick called after her, so she began to fish through the seemingly bottomless purse as she ran.

Dr. Thuku chased Caitlin, yelling, "Stay out of my purse!"

along with a warning that Caitlin could inadvertently blow her head off, or worse. Z broke a heel in the pursuit but still managed to keep going in a rapid limp.

"You realize that if my mom catches her, she's toast," Zak yelled to Nick from several paces behind. "There is no force in nature worse than my mother when she's mad."

But the sparks flying from the asteroid hundreds of miles above their heads proved Zak wrong. There were far more dangerous forces in nature.

"Nick!" called Mitch, between his huffing and puffing. "Will you at least tell us your plan?"

"No time!" he shouted as they rounded a corner. He could see the tower up ahead, lit by spotlights, drawing the attention of the entire neighborhood. Four helicopters hung above the tower, suspending the giant ring. He picked up his pace, pushing past the crowd, who were not sure whether to feel awed or horrified by the sky and the tower.

Up ahead, Caitlin, still fumbling through Z's purse, reached the gate and simultaneously found the key card. As all Accelerati eyes were on the tower—and on Edison slowly rising in the elevator, nearing the top—no one saw her swipe the card and open the gate.

Z arrived an instant later and grabbed her purse from Caitlin. It turned over, and seemed to vomit its contents of weapons, cosmetics, and breath mints onto the ground in a pile that was much larger than the bag.

Z groaned and knelt down to gather it all up—giving Nick and the others time to push through the gate and onto the tower grounds.

They hadn't been seen yet, but there were scores of Accelerati between them and the tower.

"Zak," Nick said, "I need a distraction."

Zak had never seen the machine in action, and had no real reason to trust Nick—but he was riding a thrilling wave of adrenaline that had begun the moment Caitlin, Mitch, and Nick had come into his life. He knew something had changed in him, because he didn't feel the urge to shuffle his deck of cards anymore. Up until now, he had lived his life with mathematical precision. This free fall of randomness was like skydiving, and as long as the ground remained out of sight, he had no intention of deploying his parachute.

"I'm on it!" Zak said, pulling out his laptop.

Dr. Alan Jorgenson was pleased with the current state of affairs. He was in charge again! In spite of his pink suit, and the fact that part of the left pant leg had been burned away, he took the reins of the operation as if he'd never been forced to surrender them.

"Clear the area around the tower!" he commanded from his position behind the booming microphone of the control center. "Make sure the helicopters hold their positions, and await my orders."

It was finally Dr. Alan Jorgenson's chance to shine, and he was determined to outshine Edison himself. Henceforth, he would be known as the man who tamed the raging beast that was Celestial Object Felicity Bonk.

He was poised for long-overdue greatness when he, and every single Accelerati in the control center, received an urgent text message.

In unison, they all looked at their phones.

The message had no sender's name or number attached, and it consisted of just a single word:

DISTRACTION

And by the time Jorgenson turned back to the window, a gaggle of kids was halfway to the tower . . . led by none other than Nick Slate.

How was this possible? Jorgenson immediately regretted not having disposed of the miserable boy when he'd had the chance. The thought of leaving him sealed in a mausoleum to ponder the torturous depths of his failure had been much more appealing at the time, but here was the consequence. The boy was as slippery as a graphite-lubricated swine.

"Draw your weapons!" Jorgenson ordered. "Shoot to vaporize."

"Just Slate?" one of his underlings asked.

"No, all of them."

The Accelerati around him poured out the door toward the tower, and various blasts, beams, and pulses began to fly from a whole variety of Accelerati weapons. The agents, however, were not very accurate in their aim. This was due to several factors.

1. The strobing of strange lightning in the sky was even more distracting than Zak's text.
2. They were scientists, not soldiers, and were not well trained in the use of their own weapons.
3. Many of them didn't really want to kill a bunch of kids.
4. It was now widely known that the Accelerati were broke, so faith in their reappointed leader was at an all-time low; and
5. None of them much liked Jorgenson anyway.

The result was a *Star Wars* sort of weapons battle. In other words, lots of intimidating guns were fired, yet, somehow, no one actually got hit.

Only Dr. Zenobia Thuku's aim was true—but the kids were not her targets. Having gathered the contents of her dimensionally elastic purse, she pulled out her temporal bouncer and fired at her colleagues, birthday-suiting at least a dozen Accelerati.

Soon she had drawn the fire of most of her remaining coworkers.

Zak, seeing that his mother's life was in danger, joined her in the battle. He reached into her purse and pulled out the first weapon he could get his hand on—which turned out to be the force-field generator. Soon there were hordes of Accelerati rolling around in human hamster balls, which their own weapons could not penetrate.

"We make a good team," Zak told his Mom.

"We will have a long talk about all of this later, Zakia," she replied. Zak suspected he might need to put himself in his own protective hamster ball for that conversation.

When Jorgenson saw that the Accelerati were failing to vaporize Nick and his cohorts, he left the control center to do it himself.

Three kids were heading to the tower, and Jorgenson realized that if he ran, he might be able to cut them off before they got there. But as Jorgenson neared the tower, he slipped on Vince's last will and testament, which was still blowing around the property, and he fell just before catching up with Nick, Caitlin, and Mitch.

Jorgenson picked himself up, muddied but unhurt, and resumed the chase—but now the kids had the advantage.

He increased his pace until he was just a few strides behind Mitch, the slowest of the bunch. . . .

Nick kept his eye on the prize: the tower.

Edison had just reached the platform at the top. "Hurry," he shouted to Caitlin and Mitch behind him, who didn't need to be told.

Meanwhile, high above their heads, a drama was unfolding

as the quartet of hovering helicopters burned through their final cc's of fuel. With little choice, the first pilot to reach the danger level announced he was releasing his cable.

If only one cable were released, the ring would begin to swing, taking out the tower and dragging the three other helicopters down with it, so they had no choice but to release all the cables at the same time.

Mitch Murló had just hit his stride, nearly catching up with Caitlin and Nick, when the cables were released, and he was caught entirely by surprise when a wall of shiny metal appeared directly in front of him with a deep *clang* that shook the ground enough to wake the dead back in the graveyard.

Mitch slammed into the metallic wall at full speed and bounced back. He would have been knocked to the ground, but instead he bumped into Jorgenson, a few steps behind, who broke his fall.

As Mitch rubbed his bruised nose, he realized what had happened. Nick and Caitlin, along with Edison, were now within the circumference of the ring. Everyone else was outside.

Jorgenson realized this as well. In the heat of the moment, he had been thinking very two-dimensionally. Not Theo Blankenship two-dimensionally, but 2-D enough to have forgotten all about the forty-ton ring above their heads. He was now beyond fury. "Who," he demanded, "ordered the release of the ring?"

He looked up to see the four helicopters hurrying away in the dangerously sparking sky. The ring's polished metal walls were too high to climb. Whatever Slate was planning to do, Jorgenson could no longer stop him.

He turned to Mitch, grabbed him, and pushed him up against the metal, unable to restrain his anger. "When this is over, you will suffer," Jorgenson snarled. "I will make you and your friends feel the full force of my wrath."

Mitch saw the fury in his eyes, and knew Jorgenson might well strangle him on the spot. But in this moment, Mitch suddenly saw an opportunity. Still in Jorgenson's grip, he ignored the man and appealed to the other Accelerati around them, many of whom were still hamster-balled.

"Is this the kind of leader you want?" he said to them. "Someone who would make children suffer?"

Jorgenson got even angrier. "Shut up or—"

"Or you'll what?" Mitch said. "Go on, tell them exactly what you'll do. I'm sure everyone wants to hear."

Mitch was calm. He wasn't blurting. Perhaps he didn't have to finish anyone else's sentences anymore, only his own.

It was Jorgenson who was now caught in a mental stutter, knowing that whatever he said would make things worse.

"What has he done for any of you but make your lives miserable?" Mitch continued. "You're geniuses—the best in your fields, just like my father—and you're going to let him order you around like slaves? How long until each of you takes the fall, like my dad did?"

Jorgenson pushed Mitch away. He didn't have time for this. He looked at his watch, which was synchronized to the Doomsday Clock. The asteroid was about to move into range. Once it did, they'd have ten minutes to start the machine.

"Get a ladder!" he ordered his underlings as their hamster bubbles popped. But apparently they didn't see themselves as underlings anymore, because no one moved.

"Did you hear me?" he demanded. "I said, get a ladder."

They didn't even dignify him with an answer.

"Oh, and by the way," Mitch said quietly to Jorgenson. "*I'm* the one who stole all your money."

That's what made Jorgenson snap. He pulled out his devolver and aimed it at Mitch. He was fully prepared and willing to turn the boy into a puddle of bubbling goo, but one of the other Accelerati grabbed his arm, bent it painfully backward, forced Jorgenson to his knees, and then ripped the weapon out of his hands.

By now most of the force-field bubbles had popped, but no one was firing at Z or Zak anymore, so those two lowered their weapons as well.

"We're falling back to the command center so we don't get electrocuted," the man said coolly as the rest of the Accelerati hurried away. "But by all means, Jorgenson, stay right here. In fact, we'd all prefer it." And the Acceleratus, now loyal to Z once more, hurried off with her, Zak, and Mitch, leaving Jorgenson there alone.

Inside the ring, Caitlin was the first to realize that Mitch was no longer behind them, and that they had been cut off from the rest of the world.

"Nick, we lost Mitch. . . ."

But Nick's attention was caught by something else. A figure lying limp just beside the elevator. Vince. Without his battery. As dead as dead can be.

"Oh no. . . ." said Caitlin.

Nick took a deep breath. "We can't think about it now. We've got to get to the top of the tower," he said, pushing the button to call the elevator.

"But we can't just leave him here."

"We won't," said Nick. "We'll come back and do . . . whatever we have to do, but right now we have to get up there. Vince would understand."

Around them an air-raid siren began to blare. "The asteroid is in range!" came the announcement from the control center, "The asteroid is in range!" And a ten-minute countdown began.

46 CREATING REALITY

Nick shifted the telephone that was clearly weighing him down and looked up at the caged elevator gradually rattling down toward them. "It's too slow! Come on."

He led Caitlin to a ladder that ran up the back of the elevator scaffold, then he took a deep breath and began to climb with one hand, while precariously carrying the telephone in the other.

Caitlin had pieced together a good portion of Nick's plan, but she was still baffled by some key elements.

"How do you know someone took the blender lid from the attic?" she asked as she climbed behind him. "How can you be sure?"

And Nick said, "Because I must have been the one who took it!"

That left Caitlin reeling in a vertigo that had nothing to do with the height of the climb.

"It could be missing for a hundred reasons," Nick said. "But if I go back, I can lock in a single reason. I can create the reality in which I'm the one who took it!"

"You can't create a reality!" Caitlin reminded him. "You can only become a part of what already happened!"

"Precisely," said Nick. "And I'm going to make sure *this* is what happened!"

The logic was as circular as a Tilt-A-Whirl, but Caitlin had to admit that despite her reservations, it made sense. Still the big question remained.

"Why would you do that?" she asked. "Why would you force yourself to go back in time?"

"I was sending myself a message," Nick told her. "When I take it, I must know something important. Something I know then, that I don't know now."

And finally it fell into place for Caitlin as well. She knew exactly where—and when—he was going. If Nick was right, it would, indeed, change everything.

But if he was wrong . . .

Edison set the battery in place. Now all that remained was to connect its terminals to the posts on the washboard. Once the machine was engaged, he would ride the elevator down. He could only hope that thanks to his own battery, he'd be impervious to the electricity surging around him—indeed he would be its master, wielding the power like Zeus himself with lightning bolt in hand.

But before he could complete the circuit, Nick and Caitlin appeared out of nowhere. Edison was a man who planned for every contingency, but he had not seen this coming.

"What in blazes are you doing here?" he roared. "I thought Jorgenson had you locked away!"

Up above, the sparks from the asteroid—which was almost overhead now—were becoming longer. Spidery fingers of electricity shot forth from the celestial hunk of copper, longing to be grounded. There were five minutes left before the machine had to be turned on.

"Quick," Nick said to the girl, completely ignoring Edison, "open the dryer and pull out the globe."

The boy was going to dismantle the machine? Now? Was he mad?

Nick was anything but mad. He was, however, single-minded. Edison thought Nick had betrayed him. That Nick was working against him. But it didn't matter what Edison thought anymore—Nick was a man with a mission.

While Nick fumbled with the old telephone, Caitlin opened the door to the "dryer," and Edison wheeled forward.

"NO!" yelled Edison. "I won't let you!"

He rose from his chair for the second time that day, grabbed Caitlin, and pulled her away from the machine.

So Nick used his trump card. It was a little underhanded, but desperate times called for desperate measures.

"You saw Tesla's ghost, didn't you?"

That made Edison freeze. "How do you know that?"

"He wants you to make things right. How are you going to do that, Mr. Edison?"

For a moment, Edison was lost in the question. It gave Caitlin the time she needed to break out of his grip. He reached for her again, but she dodged one way and pulled the other, bumping into the machine, hard. The F.R.E.E.'s many parts rattled, and the sky itself seemed to react with its loud, strobing complaint.

Then, as he grappled, trying to keep her from getting the globe, Edison brushed his hand across the cosmic-string harp. That seemed to stun him.

"Wh . . . what was that?" Edison said, staring at the harp in astonishment.

He let go of Caitlin and deflated back into his chair.

But before he could say another word, the toaster, which had been teetering during the scuffle, fell from the machine, hit Edison squarely in the head, and knocked him unconscious.

The toaster bounced once on the platform, and then tumbled

off before either Nick or Caitlin could catch it. They could only watch it plummet two hundred feet to the ground below, and land in the soft, muddy earth with a thud.

Without the toaster, the F.R.E.E. was useless—and there was no time to go all the way down to retrieve it.

"I'll get it on my way back," said Nick.

"From where?" Caitlin asked.

"You mean from *when*."

That might have been easy for Nick to comprehend—after all, he had had plenty of time to think about his trip to the past—but Caitlin was still struggling to stretch her mind into four dimensions. She grabbed the globe and placed it down next to the telephone, watching closely as Nick's hands moved at lightning speed, pulling out wires from both devices, creating the temporary connections.

"As soon as I'm gone," he said, "you have to disconnect the two devices and put the globe back where it belongs."

Caitlin nodded, hoping she could remember which wires went where.

Once the two devices were joined, Nick turned the many rings of the phone to the combination he needed. Then he dialed it and pressed the button on the globe.

A swirling spherical vortex appeared before them, terrifying in its depth; an intertwining of light and darkness impossible to fathom. It hovered about two feet off the edge of the platform, whistling as it sucked in wind.

"What if you're wrong?" Caitlin had to ask as she peered into the abyss, which she felt might, indeed, have been peering into her. "What if you go back, but never make it to the attic? What if the missing part's not there . . . because it's just not there? And jumping into that . . . that thing . . . kills you?"

Nick stared into the vortex, hesitating.

Down below, Caitlin saw someone use a grappling hook to climb over the ring. The figure dropped to the ground, then sprinted toward the tower. If Nick was going into the past, he had to do it now.

"Go," said Caitlin. "Do what you have to do!" It was too late for doubts. This was a very literal leap of faith, and Caitlin found that in spite of those doubts, she had faith in Nick's decisions. Even the crazy ones.

Nick gave her his best smile, and she knew this could very well be the last time she ever saw it, but she forced herself to give her best smile back.

"See you soon," he said. And with that, Nick leaped off the platform and into the unchangeable past.

47 HAWKING'S HALLWAY

Most theoretical physicists, from Gödel to Feynman to Hawking, admit that under very specific circumstances time travel should, theoretically, be possible. Even Einstein, enraged by the very idea of matter moving through time, ultimately relented in 1935, when he and Nathan Rosen came up with what is now called the Einstein-Rosen Bridge, better known as a space-time wormhole.

According to Stephen Hawking—who explained astrophysics to nongeniuses better than anyone—time travel involves a whole lot of things, like virtual particles, and virtual antiparticles, and saddle-shaped space—not that one would sit upon it and ride through time on a faster-than-light cosmic horse—but that space must bend like the sides of a saddle to allow for time travel at all.

Space-time does not bend for just anyone. But it did for Nikola Tesla.

Technically speaking, by jumping into the vortex, Nick ceased to be made of matter, and instead became a sentient sack of antiparticles, which have not only been shown to exist, but have proven to be capable of moving backward in time.

It wasn't painful, but it was extremely disorienting—even more so than being divided into seven parts and reunited again.

He was a shapeless mass of consciousness moving at an impossible speed through four-dimensional space.

It didn't resemble a wormhole at all. It was more like a hallway. He could sense doors on every side, all leading to places that either didn't exist, or wouldn't exist, or flatly refused to exist unless they were gently coaxed into being by some great hand of creation that may or may not itself exist, depending on who you talk to. There was an infinite number of doors, and Nick moved past them too quickly to open any. They pulled at the edges of his curiosity, but he knew that his destination was not beyond the doors around him, but was the door directly in front of him, which now opened.

Then he had the uncanny sensation of a hand being placed firmly on his back and pushing him forward, as if the space-time hallway wanted to be rid of him. It was rude, but perhaps less unpleasant than a cosmic kick in the rear. *"And stay out!"* he could almost hear space-time say before the portal disappeared, leaving him sprawled on the grass in the middle of a lightning storm, his antiparticle self restored to flesh and bone.

The flashes of lightning made him think for a moment that he had failed, that he was still at Wardenclyffe—but no, because now the night air had an oppressive Floridian humidity that he remembered well.

Had there been a lightning storm the night it happened? He couldn't remember.

The storm was passing. The ground was wet, but the rain had already moved on. He wondered if his passage through time had brought the storm.

Where was he? A lawn. In a neighborhood he didn't know. It was difficult to pinpoint a specific location when setting the globe. All he knew was that he was somewhere in or near

Tampa. The dials on the phone, however, were much more precise. He had arrived exactly thirty minutes before the event that had shattered his life. It was half an hour before the fire.

He ran until he got to the nearest main street. There was a supermarket, a tire store, and a Wendy's, all closed at two a.m. He saw the street sign: W. HILLSBOROUGH AVE. It was miles from where he lived. He was close, but not close enough! He kept running, but he knew he'd never get there in time, no matter how fast he ran. If only he could drive, but he had no car, or license. He needed a bus, but there were none running at this hour. He thought about waving down one of the few passing cars, but at this time of night and in this part of town, he realized it was not a good idea.

He had to find a reliable means of transportation, so he turned down a residential side street, searching until he spotted a bicycle lying in a side yard. That would do it!

He pedaled for all he was worth, and twenty minutes later—at right about the time the fire would have started—he turned onto his street and saw, five houses down, a home that in his time no longer existed, where a family slept peacefully with no inkling of the terror that was only moments away.

Dropping the bike on his lawn, he hurried around to the back door and found the rock under which his parents always kept the spare key. He could already smell smoke. The fire had started somewhere in the house, but he could see no flames through the windows yet.

He couldn't warn them, and he couldn't let them see him. They would awake in their own time, and no matter how much he wanted to, he couldn't interfere. Not yet. He would have to wait in the shadows.

Quietly he turned the key in the lock, pushed open the door, and there standing in his kitchen, looking as astonished as him, was none other than Ms. Evangeline Planck.

Evangeline Planck had left two days before Nick, but she'd arrived at the house only moments earlier.

The space-time wormhole had treated her less pleasantly than it had Nick, with a lot more hair pulling and slapping upside the head. And her nocturnal trip across town had been no walk in the park either, even when she had walked through the park. She'd been forced to debone a suspicious man by using an Accelerati decalcifier, and although she'd missed the lightning storm that accompanied her own arrival, she'd been caught in the downpour of a second short storm, which, this being Florida, she had assumed was natural. She idly mused about her past self, who was at that very moment still undercover as a lunch lady in Colorado Springs, having not yet met Nick Slate. Oh, if she could see herself now!

The front door of the Slate home hadn't given her any trouble; she entered using an Accelerati universal key, one of their most popular devices.

Then she'd made her way to the kitchen, at the back of the house, unconcerned about waking the family, because she already knew that she would be successful in her lethal mission. This was one of the many advantages of knowing the future.

She'd reached into her pocket and pulled out an Accelerati night-lighter. It looked like an ordinary night-light, but once plugged in, it would send a surge through the wires and start an electrical fire in the walls. She had bent down and plugged the device into an outlet.

It took effect much more quickly than she'd expected. She had smelled the burning insulation within seconds, and smoke began pouring from gaps between the wall and the floorboard. When a flame poked through an air vent, she'd known it was time to go.

She had raced to the kitchen door—which opened abruptly, and there stood Nick Slate, staring at her.

Her first thought was that this was the Nick Slate of the past, perhaps sneaking back home after hours. But then she recalled the second short, unexpected storm. It hadn't been a natural one after all—it had marked the arrival of another traveler.

"This was never an accident!" Nick said. "It was *you!*"

"I am not having this conversation!" She pulled out her decalcifier, realizing that she could debone him here, leave him as a shapeless blob to roast in the fire, and never have to deal with Nick Slate again.

But before she could pull the trigger, an air vent exploded overhead, and the entire kitchen seemed to burst into flames at once. The night-lighter had done its job quickly and efficiently; the fire hadn't started in a single place—every room had burst into flames simultaneously. There were shouts from upstairs.

And even though Evangeline knew that Nick was standing somewhere between her and the door, she couldn't see him anymore, only flames and billowing black smoke. She'd just have to deal with him later.

She made a dash for the door, but clipped the side of the kitchen table and lost her footing. She fell to the ground, her Accelerati pin falling from her lapel. Here, close to the ground, the air was clearer, and she could see the back door. She scrambled toward it, but someone grabbed her. No, not someone—some*thing.*

When she looked back, she saw that her right pant leg had gotten snagged on a doorstop poking out of the baseboard behind the kitchen door. She tugged, but the spider silk was strong and durable—one of its best qualities. It wouldn't tear. Now she could hear the family upstairs shouting instructions to one another. Finally she pulled herself free—just as the ceiling above her caved in.

Nick didn't have time to deal with Ms. Planck any more than she had time to deal with him. They both had missions here. It was clear that she had started the fire. But that didn't change anything. Except his perspective on it.

The fire was happening. His house would burn down. There was no question of that.

But there'd been someone behind his mother that night.

As the kitchen filled with flames and smoke, Nick dove through the doorway to the living room, dropping to the floor for clearer air. He coughed and tried shallow breathing. Déjà vu threatened to overwhelm him just as surely as the flames. He heard his mother scream something. He heard his father desperately calling for Nick and Danny. He heard them all bounding down the stairs. His father led the way, making sure the path was clear of burning debris. His mother brought up the rear.

"Keep going, Nick!" his mom said. "Don't stop!"

Those were the last words he'd ever heard her say. Nick pushed himself up from the floor. He could see them now. He could see her! His eyes hurt, his lungs hurt, but there she was, only a few feet away. He saw his past self glance back at his mom, as if to confirm she was right behind him in the billowing smoke.

He remembered doing that. And even as he took an involuntary step deeper into the shadows and billowing smoke to avoid being seen, Nick knew he *had* been seen, barely, by his past self—but his past self didn't know what he was seeing

Then an explosion blew the front door off its hinges. Nick saw his younger self, certain beyond measure that his mother was right behind him, jump through the opening.

Then, from this new perspective, Nick saw a burning beam drop toward the doorway, and time seemed to slow down.

Nick hurled himself forward and grabbed his mom's arm. She yelled as he held her back and the heavy, flaming timber narrowly missed her.

His mother turned then and saw him. The terror in her eyes blended with confusion.

"Nick? But—how—"

"This way," he said, gently pulling his mother away from the inferno. "We can't get to the front door; we have to go out the back."

She looked through the doorway then, and he did too, just in time to see Wayne Slate come racing back toward the house to save his wife, but the porch roof came crashing down before he got there, and the living room windows exploded.

His mother grabbed Nick and held him close to shield him from the worst of it. He could feel his shoes melting.

"The back door!" Nick told her. "Hurry!" This time he didn't let her bring up the rear. He made sure that she went first.

Everything in the kitchen was on fire: the table, the walls, the cabinets. He could see that part of the ceiling had caved in—and there, wedged beneath the fallen timbers, was Ms. Planck.

"Nick! Help me!" she begged. "Please help me!"

And he tried. In spite of everything, he tried.

He turned to his mom, pointed at the kitchen door, and shouted, "Go!"

Then he went to Ms. Planck. He grabbed her arm and pulled, but it was no use. The flames grew stronger, louder in his ears.

He felt seconds away from bursting into flames himself—but how could he just let her die there?

That's when his mother made the choice for him, grabbing him and pulling him out the door.

He looked back just as they cleared the doorframe. That was his final image of Evangeline Planck, lunch lady, Grand Acceleratus: with desperation and fear in her eyes as the rest of the ceiling came down upon her. And in that moment, Nick realized something.

A body had been found in the house, and still would be—but it had always belonged to Ms. Planck, not his mother. Everyone, even the coroner, would assume it was Mrs. Slate.

Perspective now proved otherwise.

Outside in the backyard, both Nick and his mom gasped and coughed, filling their lungs with good air, forcing out the bad. She started to go around the side of the house to get to the front yard, but the fire made that way impassable.

"We have to get to your father and Danny," she said. "They must think we're still in the house."

Nick realized there was nothing he could say at that moment that would stop her, so he led her to a thin spot in their back-yard hedge. "This way," he told her. "It's how I go when I want to sneak out without being seen."

"Nicky!" she said, a little bit chiding, and a little bit surprised, but said no more. They pushed through the hedge into their neighbor's yard, then went around the side of that house. By now, all the neighbors had come out to gawk. The wail of approaching fire engines grew louder. Wayne was out on the front lawn screaming, his eyes cast heavenward, as if the world was ending—and for him, in this moment, it was.

And there was Nick himself, half a year younger, in his

pajamas, holding his little brother, and rocking him back and forth. A neighbor woman brought blankets to wrap around both of them and moved the two boys out of the way when the firefighters arrived, too late to save anything that mattered.

Nick's mother wanted to rush out, but he held her back. She looked at the other Nick, then she looked at him. She shook her head as if she'd lost the power of speech.

So Nick did the only thing he could. He told her the truth.

"I came back from the future to save you," he told her. "But Dad and Danny, and the younger me, can't know. They have to think you died in the fire. For now."

"I can't do that!" she said, but she didn't move.

She was light-years away from understanding any of it, but that was all right. Every moment she didn't run out there and show herself was a moment closer to the past that Nick remembered.

"Mom, look at me," he said. "Really look at me. For me, it's been nearly half a year since this happened. And, until this moment, I never knew you were alive."

Now she was the one who was crying. And even though Nick felt like bursting into tears as well, he kept his emotions in check. Tonight he needed to be the strong one.

"This is all the past to me, and we can't change the past, no matter how hard we try," Nick told her, as calmly as he could. "Danny and Dad will be fine. And you'll see them again too. I promise. But not yet."

But she wasn't ready to believe him, and she couldn't take her eyes off his father and brother and younger self.

"You want to go to them, I know. And I won't try to stop you. But that's the thing—I don't have to. You won't be able to make it over there. Something else will stop you. . . ."

And just then the chimney of the burning house came crashing down, blocking access between the two backyards. Nick remembered the chimney falling, but of course never saw his Mom or himself in the shadows behind it, even though they were there. To Nick the past was like a movie now. Even with a new perspective, nothing would change in the second viewing.

"See, it's no use," he said. "And it's probably not a good idea to keep trying. I get the feeling that the space-time continuum has an attitude. You don't want to mess with it."

They watched for a minute more. The fire trucks arrived and began to futilely douse the house. Danny and the other Nick were checked by paramedics.

"Six months?" his mom asked.

"Closer to five."

"And they'll be fine?"

"Trust me."

His mom put a hand on Nick's shoulder and with her other reached up and ran her fingers through his hair. "I do trust you," she said with a hint of pride. "We'll do it your way."

Nick nodded. "The entire roof is going to collapse in about a minute," he told her. "We don't want to be here for that."

And his mother said, "No. No, we don't."

Then she looked at him, and in spite of everything, offered him a faint smile. "So where do we go?"

"Here and there, I guess," he told her. "But first there's something I have to get in Colorado Springs."

48 CITY OF LIGHT

Go," said Caitlin as she and Nick stood before the wormhole at the top of the tower. "Do what you have to do!"

"See you soon," he said. And with that, Nick leaped off the platform, and into the unchangeable past.

The wormhole collapsed as soon as Nick jumped into it— and immediately Caitlin disconnected the globe from the phone and got to work reconnecting the globe's wires as they had been before Nick had rerouted them. She only hoped she remembered the sequence correctly. When she was done, she snapped the halves of the globe back together and inserted it into the drum of the dryer. Beside her, Edison began to regain consciousness, mumbling incoherently about destiny, his light bulb, and his secret love for Mrs. Higgenbotham.

Down below, a figure grabbed the toaster from the ground and started climbing the tower ladder. Caitlin assumed it was an Acceleratus, maybe even Jorgenson himself. It was only when he neared the top that she recognized who it was. She was confused for the briefest instant.

"Hey," Nick said as he reached the platform, a little out of breath. "Long time no see."

"Speak for yourself," Caitlin said. "I just saw you a minute ago." Except, she noted, his hair was now about two inches longer. "You need a haircut," she told him.

"First thing tomorrow," he agreed. He placed the toaster back in position, then reached into his coat pocket and pulled out what appeared to be the lid of a blender.

"You got it!"

"Oh, yeah!" he said with the widest of smiles. He put it over the copper blender, where it fit perfectly. "It's the machine's timer!" he told Caitlin. "Once we engage the F.R.E.E., it will give us just enough time to get away."

And then, behind them, Edison said, "Turn around slowly. No sudden moves."

Caitlin and Nick turned to see him, fully conscious now and holding a small pistol aimed at Nick's chest. And his hand wasn't the least bit shaky.

"Time is short," Edison said. "We've nearly missed the window. So you will do exactly as I say."

Far below, another figure, this one in a damaged pink suit, clambered over the top of the metal ring.

When Jorgenson had been abandoned by the other Accelerati, he couldn't care less. Let them leave him for the "safety" of the command center. Cowards! Traitors! They would learn soon enough how long that safety lasted!

Instead, he circled the giant metal ring, searching for a gap near the ground, hoping it had landed on a boulder or spanned a crevice, leaving enough room for him to wriggle underneath.

On his second time around he heard a metallic clang. He hurried around the ring, and on the far side found a knotted rope dangling from a grappling hook. Someone else had just gone over!

He grabbed the rope and climbed up the sleek metal wall, then he dropped on the other side and hit the ground hard, which knocked the wind out of him. He got up and ran toward the tower, limping slightly.

He could see the dead boy, Vincent, his body sprawled beside the elevator. Not Jorgenson's problem. The boy should have died right the first time.

The elevator door stood open, as if it had been waiting just for him. Finally something was going right! He ran into the elevator cage, pulled the door closed after him, and pressed the button for the top.

With a rattle, the cage began to slowly climb.

Thomas Alva Edison had seen empires rise and crumble. He'd witnessed more wars than he could count, and experienced not only the industrial age, but the age of invention, the digital age, and the age of humanity lying on the couch complaining about how slow their Internet connection is.

It had been his intention not only to witness the worldwide transmission of wireless energy, but also to be its master. To possess its very source. To be the conduit of humanity's endless flow of electrons, powering a brilliant future.

But that was before he had brushed the strings of the cosmic harp. The vibration had been music to his soul—but not just any music. It was, simply put, the closing chord. As if his life, for nearly a hundred years, had been straining to hold the penultimate note of a powerful symphony and now the final note was at last being played, with a thundering of brass and a fiery explosion of strings. The harp had indeed spoken to him. And its message was: *"You're done."*

There was no questioning the truth of it, and it had doused his malignant ambition as completely as water on a burning candle. Only now did he realize what a burden that ambition had been. How light he felt without it! How free!

With that in mind, he knew exactly what needed to be done.

"Remove the battery from Tesla's machine," he said to Caitlin.

"What?"

"You heard me! Remove it! Now!"

The girl did as she was told. And once the battery was in her arms, he turned to Nick and lowered the weapon. There was no need for it anymore. "Now then, you, Master Slate, shall disconnect me from my battery—both the visible wires, and the backup ones beneath the chair. Then you shall use my battery to power Tesla's machine. In this way, I shall make things right."

Nick looked at him, stupefied, while up above the sparking asteroid began to move out of range.

"Did you not hear me?" Edison said. "Our window of opportunity closes in two minutes. Do you want to be responsible for electrocuting the world? Now do as I say!"

"Yes, sir."

Nick knelt down and disconnected the backup wires first. Now the only thing holding Edison to life were the wires that went from under his collar into the large battery on the chair behind him.

Edison looked to Caitlin, and offered her a smile. His smile used to be a warm thing when he was a younger man, but for many years now, it had been a leering jack-o'-lantern grin, suitable for frightening children away at Halloween, but nothing more. Ah well, it would all be remedied in a moment or two. "Take that battery back to your erstwhile friend, and reanimate him. But warn him to take care not to exceed his normal lifespan. Living this long . . . it *does* things to a person."

"Yes, Mr. Edison." Caitlin said. "It's been . . . an honor knowing you."

"I'm sure that it has. But now I must return my borrowed time to the bank. Master Slate, I'm ready."

Edison took a deep breath, relishing the electric smell of

ozone in the air, then fixed his eyes on the asteroid above, and Nick disconnected his battery.

Edison's borrowed time was apparently returned to the bank with much interest. The moment Nick disconnected him, he didn't just die, it was as if he crumbled from within. As life left him, his head lolled to the side, and his shoulders slumped. His worn body took on the semblance of a mummy. He didn't look horrible, though. He looked at peace. He looked satisfied. And he would forever be where he wanted to be: at the center of power.

"Give the timer a quarter turn, counterclockwise," Nick told Caitlin. "That will give us one minute. We can't risk any longer or the asteroid will be out of range." She set the timer and it began to tick. Then Nick connected the wires of Edison's large battery to the posts of the washboard, amazed that by moving only a few objects, he was able to open up a space in the F.R.E.E. that perfectly accommodated Edison's battery.

"Okay, let's go!"

They climbed down the ladder as quickly as they could, and on their way down, passed Jorgenson, who was in the elevator cage, slowly making his way up.

"Bad idea, Dr. Jorgenson," Nick shouted as they went in opposite directions.

"What have you done with Edison?" Jorgenson demanded, rattling the cage; but he was trapped in it as it rose. "Bring that battery back this instant!"

Jorgenson continued to bluster and make empty threats as the elevator ascended. He pulled out a weapon and fired, but Caitlin and Nick were already too far down the ladder and he didn't have a good angle to hit anything but the tower itself or the ground. His spleen-venting wail of frustration was worthy of the greatest of supervillains.

In the command center, everyone had watched Nick and Caitlin climb the tower. Everyone had also seen Nick race through the gate with a grappling hook and climb the ring while they could also still see him at the top of the tower.

Under normal circumstances this would have caused everyone to question their sanity, but as these were not normal circumstances, no one batted an eye. After all, there had recently been seven Nicks; two were hardly worth mentioning.

There was, however, some panic in the control room—the asteroid was about to move out of range, and the F.R.E.E. had not yet been turned on. In fact, it seemed to be falling apart, as evidenced by the toaster that had plunged to the ground.

All eyes and hope were on the second Nick as he climbed toward the platform, clutching the toaster under his arm like a football.

"That kid better know what he's doing," one of the Accelerati grumbled.

"That kid knows exactly what he's doing," said Z.

When Nick and Caitlin started down the ladder, Mitch leaped into action.

"No!" shouted Z. "Don't go out there, you're—"

And Mitch blurted, "—about to become a human kite." He had no idea what his blurt meant, but he knew he was about to find out.

Nick and Caitlin reached the base of the tower with fifteen seconds to spare, and there at the foot of the ladder lay Vince, just as Edison had left him.

"Give me the battery!" Nick said.

"He can carry it himself," said Caitlin. She put the battery in Vince's hands, and reconnected the wires to the electrodes behind his ears.

There was no lag time. Vince opened his eyes, fully awake, and said, "Wha'd I miss?"

Caitlin just smiled. "Ask me later."

They hurried from the tower, only to be met by the ten-foot-high curved wall of the ring.

"Well, that wasn't there before I died," said Vince.

"Stay low," Nick said. And that's when the machine powered on.

At first there was a low humming. Then a rhythmic clanking, plus a sound like the dragging of chains, along with a powerful vibration that made their bones ache. They felt more vibrations through the tower, and the ground, and the air itself. Then the sky seemed to explode, and they knew, without a doubt, that the asteroid had begun to release its charge into the machine.

Nick knew what was coming next and was the first to feel it: a queasiness in the pit of his stomach as the weight machine countered the force of gravity. He felt his hair standing on end, and watched as Caitlin's poofed out and rose, its ends stretching skyward.

"Lower!" Nick told them. "Hug the ground."

They all stretched out, their bellies to the dirt; but with nothing to grab on to, Nick felt himself beginning to weigh less and less. If they went entirely weightless. there'd be nothing they could do. . . . Then the massive ring began to rise, also caught in the antigravity field.

Nick only hoped that by keeping low, near the widening gap between the ring and the ground, they'd be close to the edge of the antigravity field and not be drawn up by it.

"Go!" he shouted.

Caitlin scrambled under the ring and Mitch was already there, waiting for them, a rope tied around his waist and Nick's grappling hook attached to a nearby tree. Mitch grabbed Caitlin and pulled her the rest of the way. Nick was right behind her, but Vince, who couldn't quite scramble because he had to carry the battery, was being lifted away.

Just before he rose too high, Nick reached up, grabbed Vince's ankle, and began to rise with him; so Mitch grabbed Nick, and in a moment all three had left the ground. Down below, Caitlin reeled in the rope, like one might reel in a kite caught in cross-winds, until she had pulled them out of the antigravity field. The three then hit the ground, suddenly feeling very heavy.

"We've got to get back to the control center," Mitch said, untying the rope from his waist. "We'll be safe there. I hope!"

But as they hurried from the tower, Nick couldn't help but look back. The ring had risen to the top of the tower and was encircling the F.R.E.E., which was now hovering above the platform and absorbing a massive bolt of continuous lightning from the asteroid.

With every component in place, the F.R.E.E. did what it was designed to do. The battery had primed the device, setting the weight machine pumping and powering up the other parts. The clothes dryer came online and shrank the globe to a singularity. The ghost lamp, encased in the dome of the hair dryer, became the ultimate lightning rod and drew down the asteroid's energy. That lightning bolt, which came in as a chaotic discharge, was then focused by the other parts of the machine and shot out in a well-ordered beam into the ring, which now hung around the machine at the same level. The overload was divided by the prism and sent straight down through the small grate into the chamber far below, where it was dispersed harmlessly through the seven tunnels.

And then something even more remarkable happened.

As before, every light began to glow, every appliance began to turn on—but unlike the first time, they did not explode or burn out. The power supply was steady and controlled. It began in Shoreham, but spread outward, town by town, until the sphere of power reached Manhattan. As bright as New York City is at night, it became nearly blinding as every single bulb within the city illuminated, turning the island of Manhattan into a true city of light.

Although he didn't want it, Jorgenson had the best view of the machine. A true front-row seat.

He was already weightless when the elevator cage opened automatically. He kept pushing the down button, but he floated out of the elevator before it could return to ground level, and he rose weightlessly toward the F.R.E.E., which now hovered above his head. He could not even hear his own wail above the deafening sound of surging electricity.

He hoped for a quick and painless death. But the moment the discharge from the asteroid ended, something unexpected happened.

The entire machine, and the ring around it, disappeared. It all just vanished, and Jorgenson, just beyond the edge of the teleportation field, fell to the empty platform with a thud and a pained groan.

His ears were still ringing in the silence. But he was alive! He'd been sure that hellion Nick Slate and the forces of the universe had conspired to kill him, now that they'd ruined him, but here he was. And without Edison in his way, he could do as he pleased. He would purge those who were disloyal to him. He would punish all those in need of punishment. He stood up, ready to face this glorious electrified day. . . .

Then, without any warning whatsoever, he too vanished.

In the control room, the Accelerati, no longer under the iron fist of a Grand Acceleratus or the influence of Edison, were not interested in ending Nick's or anyone else's life anymore. It seemed, for the moment, that everyone's goals had aligned, which left them on the same side. They all cheered as the F.R.E.E. lit up everything for nearly a hundred miles in every direction, and fell into stunned shock when the machine disappeared. Yet even after it was gone, the electrical charge hadn't faded.

"What happened?" everyone was asking. "What went wrong?" they wondered, just as Jorgensen, atop the tower, vanished as well.

Nick spoke up. "I don't think anything went wrong," he said. "I don't think it's supposed to stay in the same place for long."

"Right!" said Zak, the first to catch on. "Or else why would it have a teleporter built into its central design?" Then he sat at a computer console and began typing away. A map of the world appeared on the screen. "Com satellites are constantly monitoring energy around the globe, and I just hacked the data," he said. "This is a live shot of the planet's energy output."

The map clearly showed an extremely bright circle around the New York area, centered in Shoreham, but as they watched, a second spot began to develop—this one near Shanghai.

"The F.R.E.E.'s in China?" asked Caitlin. They watched the bright circle expand there for a few more seconds.

"No, look," said one of the Accelerati, peering over their shoulders. Another spot showed up in Iceland. Then another one in West Africa, and then another in South America. Around them the Accelerati leaped into action, settling behind different computer screens to study each of the regions more closely.

It was Z who figured it out. "It's random!" she said. "It's jumping to a new location every twenty seconds! It must be using a random number algorithm to set its coordinates!"

Nick smiled. "It's distributing power around the world."

"But what about Jorgenson?" Caitlin asked.

"That teleportation field was supercharged enough to have a wake," Z said. "He must have been caught in it and pulled in, the way a sinking ship sucks down everything around it."

"Oh no!" said Mitch, turning to Zak. "Remember when we tried to crack your mom's algorithm, and catch up with it? The closest we could ever get was—"

This time it was Zak who finished Mitch's sentence. "—nine-point-three seconds!" Now Jorgenson was caught in the F.R.E.E.'s teleportation wake, and he would never catch up with it. He would forever be nine-point-three seconds behind it.

"Well, Nick," said Caitlin, "it looks like Jorgenson won't be around to bother you anymore."

But when she turned to Nick, he was gone, having vanished as completely as Jorgenson.

49 THE LONG WAY HOME

Nick's disappearance was not the effect of a latent teleportation echo. It was caused by his own two feet.

The others could marvel at the F.R.E.E., and theorize about its journey, but Nick's connection to the machine was broken. His mission—his obsession—to complete it had turned off the moment the machine had turned on. It no longer needed him, but more significantly, he no longer needed it. There were far more important things to do now. At least as far as his life was concerned.

He found his father and Danny in the street, making their way toward Wardenclyffe's main gate. Danny was limping and moaning, still pretending that he had sprained his ankle.

"Nick!" His father ran to Nick when he saw him, and gave him a heartfelt hug. "What happened? Are you okay? Where's everyone else?"

"Everyone's fine," Nick said. Then took a deep breath. "Actually, better than fine."

Neither his father nor his brother knew what was coming. He was bursting to tell them—but wanted to break the news properly. The return of Natalie Slate to the world was a gift, and it should be presented as one. Fortunately, Nick had had several months to properly wrap it.

. . .

Evangeline Planck hadn't been able to take "the long way home," as she had put it. But Nick had. He'd had a whole five months to spend with his mom, and to consider his eventual return to Wardenclyffe Tower.

The first order of business was to go to Colorado Springs, break into the dusty old Victorian before his family moved in, and dig through the "junk" in the attic until he found the blender lid. After everything else he'd been through, retrieving the lid was remarkably easy. As he left the attic, he reflexively moved the toaster to a less precarious position, then laughed at himself, and put it right back where he found it.

As time travel turns hindsight into foresight, Nick knew that they wouldn't be spotted or found, even if they stayed in Colorado Springs, but to do so would taunt the space-time continuum, and that was probably not a good idea.

So they avoided all places that were familiar and took an extended vacation, traveling the country, just mother and son. The next stop on their journey was Las Vegas.

As it turns out, knowledge of the future, even if it isn't all that specific, is enough to make one financially stable. Nick didn't know anything about which stocks to invest in—but he did know which team won the Super Bowl, and which games the Tampa Bay Rays won early in baseball season. After a few well-placed bets, they had enough money to live comfortably for the next few months.

They were perhaps the only two people on the planet who were unfazed when it was announced that Celestial Object Felicity Bonk was on a collision course with Earth. They were not at all surprised when, about a month later, Colorado Springs was fried by a massive electrical discharge.

And when Nick returned to Shoreham, New York, he was

ready to pick up exactly where he had left off. After spending all that time in the past, it felt strange to not know what would happen next—but exhilarating as well. And the first thing he bought when he arrived in town was a grappling hook.

Now, nearly half a year older than he had been ten minutes ago, he stood with his father and brother just outside the gate of the Wardenclyffe complex, and dangled a key on a key chain.

"We've been living here in Shoreham for more than a month now," he said, casually. "Down this street, then turn right at the light. Fourth house on the left."

His father looked at him dubiously. "More than a month? But didn't you just get here?"

"Yes and no," Nick answered. "There's someone waiting for both of you there. She wanted to come, but I convinced her it was best if she waited."

Danny looked to his brother, his expression a little scared, and a little excited. "Dad, look at the key chain. . . ."

So he did. It was the type of photo key chain you can get made at any pharmacy. This one had a picture of Nick's mom on it. She was standing in front of the aurora, which had not been visible this far south until *after* the house fire.

His father's breath became unsteady.

"Nick . . . you couldn't possibly be suggesting . . ."

"I'm not suggesting anything," Nick said, and closed his father's hand around the keys.

That's when Caitlin came out through the gate. "You could have told someone you were leaving! Everyone's looking for you. Z and Zak thought you got caught in another teleportation wake or something." Then, seeing Nick's father, she added, "I'm glad you survived your birthday-suiting, Mr. Slate."

He didn't respond. He was still looking at the key in his hand.

"The address is Forty-two George Avenue," Nick told his father and Danny. "Can't miss it—it's the only blue house on the block."

Mr. Slate finally looked up, nodded at Caitlin, and then turned to head down the street. Danny lingered for a moment. "Do you remember the secret handshake I taught the part of you that was younger than me?"

"You mean this one?" Nick reached out his hand, and gave Danny the secret handshake—but apparently that wasn't enough for Danny, because without any warning he launched himself at Nick and hugged him with such force it almost took them both down.

When Danny let go, he backed away, embarrassed. "That's just in case they make me forget you again," he said. Then he ran off to catch up with his father.

"What was that all about?" Caitlin asked Nick.

Nick smiled. "Family stuff," he said. "Speaking of which, you should call your parents. Tell them you helped save the world, and you'll be home soon."

"Don't you mean helped save the world *again*?"

Nick laughed. "Let's hope this was the last time."

50 MEANWHILE, IN 1856

On July 10, 1856, Petula Grabowski-Jones pounded on the door of a small white house in Smiljan, a Croatian village in the Austrian empire. Her arrival in Smiljan brought an electrical storm far greater than the one generated by Nick's jaunt through time, because going back more than a hundred and fifty years was far more troubling to the space-time continuum than a mere five months.

Finally a stern man in a black robe opened the door and spoke to her in Serbian—a language she did not understand. Fortunately, she had her iPhone with her, and because she knew a wireless signal was a thing of the distant future, she had downloaded a handy Serbian translation app before she left.

The man at the door was Milutin Tesla, a Serbian Orthodox priest, who assumed that this girl was a member of his parish, seeking shelter from the storm. Why else would she be running around in the rain holding a wailing baby?

Even before he invited her in, however, she barged her way past him. Then she glanced at what seemed to be a rectangular mirror in her hand and spoke in an accent he could not place.

"Donosim ti ovo dijete oluje," she said. "I bring you this child of the storm. You will raise him as your own. And I will be his nanny. And you shall pay me well. And you may not refuse. Is that clear?"

By now the man's wife had come out, with their two young daughters and son in tow.

"Who is she?" asked one of the girls.

"Look how she's dressed," said the boy. "I think there's something wrong with her."

Mr. Tesla had to agree. Clearly the young woman was troubled. Her goulash was missing the meat, as they say. As a man of God, it was his sacred task to care for the feebleminded. This poor girl was certainly not equipped for motherhood.

By now the electrical storm outside had begun to fade. Mrs. Tesla took the baby from the strange girl's arms, bounced him a bit, and he stopped crying.

She looked to her husband. Just a month earlier she had lost a child at birth. She was still mourning that loss—but now this baby boy in her arms filled the empty space, as if it was meant to be. Who were they to refuse such a gift of providence?

"What is his name?" she asked the girl, who didn't seem to understand the question, poor thing. She just kept glancing at that little mirror—perhaps a nervous tick.

Meanwhile, Petula's frustration at future technology was at an all-time high. Of all the times for her translation app to get things wrong. It had translated the woman's question as *"How is the owl?"* which couldn't possibly be right. Well, thought Petula, it doesn't really matter, does it? She knew what came next, because it had always come next. They would take the baby. They would name the baby after the woman's father. Petula would be there to make sure that he grew up to be the genius he was destined to be—and this "Nick" would actually like her. Now Petula had something her entire life had lacked: a purpose. It was strange to think that this was all preordained somehow, and yet could not have happened without Petula's intervention.

Maybe that's what destiny is: free will and fate working hand in hand.

Mrs. Tesla knew none of this, of course. How could she? All she knew was that she felt an immediate attachment to the child.

"We'll call him Nikola," she said. "After my father."

Petula watched, understanding only the name. Then she looked to her iPhone once more, not to translate, but to review her extensive list of demands. But apparently iPhone batteries don't handle time travel well. The screen went dark, with the little swirly-do of death. Thus ended technology. At least for a while.

So she glared at them, crossed her arms, and said, "The name's PETula like spatula, not PeTULa like Petunia. Got it?"

They all just looked to one another and back to her with profound sympathy. Petula sighed, realizing that the past was going to be almost as annoying as the future.

51 A NEW SHADE OF NORMAL

Nothing stays wondrous forever. It's human nature to grow accustomed to that which becomes normal, even if it's a new shade of normal.

When people across the globe learned of the strange teleporting machine that absorbed the asteroid's charge and distributed the energy, they were amazed. For about two weeks. Then it became ordinary. Harmless discharges occurred daily, which meant they were no longer news, but just another part of life.

There was, however, the occasional F.R.E.E. appearance eyewitness who claimed that, shortly after the machine moved on, a man in a tattered pink suit appeared and then vanished as well, like a ghost.

"He plucked the sandwich right outta my hand, gobbled it down without so much as a howdy-do, then disappeared," said one farmer in Iowa. Of course, no one believed him.

Eventually the two-dimensional boy being studied at Princeton University was treated as unremarkable too. It had played on the news for a couple of days as a human-interest story. Conversations around the family television went something like this:

"Two-dimensional people. Is that a thing now?"

"It must be a thing, the news says so."

"Go figure. What's for dinner?"

Theo Blankenship was disappointed that his flatness had only warranted him a few talk-show appearances, but it wasn't surprising. After all, television itself is a two-dimensional medium, so watching Theo wasn't very engaging, and listening to him talk about it was even less so.

At Princeton, however, Dr. Zenobia Thuku and her research department continued to take an interest in him. Rumor had it that NASA had plans for him too, since two-dimensional space travel would be very cost-effective, but no one had asked Theo to be an astronaut just yet.

The world was also entirely uninterested in the stolen $750 million dollars. Mitch Murló had tried to do the right thing by contacting the country's biggest banks and offering to return the money. He was quickly shunted up the ladder to the muckety-mucks at the very top until he found himself in a boardroom of the Global Bank, with very serious executives in very serious suits. He didn't even know there was such a thing as the Global Bank, and suspected it was a secret society not entirely unlike the Accelerati, but probably far older.

As is often the case, the decision makers had made their decision before Mitch even walked into the room.

"It would be much too troublesome—and frankly, embarrassing to the banking community—to restore one penny to every bank account in existence," one of the suits said. With a wink and a whisper, he told Mitch to just quietly keep the money.

"What am I going to do with seven hundred and fifty million dollars?" Mitch asked.

"Whatever you like," said the man. "That's what I do with mine." His colleagues nodded in agreement.

Mitch was soon approached by entrepreneurs who were developing huge energy-storage farms, banks of batteries capable of recharging from the F.R.E.E., so they could then distribute the energy worldwide for "a nominal fee." They wanted him to invest in their schemes—but Mitch chose instead to steer his donations toward nonprofit organizations that didn't trick people into paying for free energy. It's what Tesla would have wanted.

On a warm day in July—about a month after the F.R.E.E. kicked into action—Nick Slate met with Caitlin, Mitch, and Zak at Beef-O-Rama.

Vince was supposed to join them, but he was late. Late as in "tardy," Nick hoped, not late as in "dead."

"I'm telling you, it's crazy down there," Zak said. He was an intern on a special scientific team sent to survey the Accelerati's old headquarters beneath Atomic Lanes. "Famous artwork that's been missing for hundreds of years, technology that's twisted every which way."

"We know," said Caitlin. "We've been there."

It felt odd for Nick to be with his friends and not have to talk in hushed tones, or look over his shoulder in fear of sinister scientists in pastel suits—but the Accelerati were gone. They didn't just disband, they had enacted their emergency self-destruct protocol: each member had had their memories of the Accelerati erased. So, aside from the occasional flash created by their encounters with airport and beach metal detectors, the scientists were clueless about their prior involvement. Only Z had retained her memory, so that she could facilitate the dismantling of their various secret lairs.

"You guys haven't told me what you think of the new and improved Beef-O-Rama," Mitch said, gesturing around him to the remodeled restaurant. "The grease is gone, but not forgotten."

"The waiters are still rude," Caitlin said after their server plopped a bucket of fries on the table with all the precision of an airdrop.

"Of course," said Nick. "It's part of the charm!"

Nick grabbed some french fries from the basket and stuck them in his mouth. Crisp on the outside, soft in the middle, just the way he liked them. He was glad Mitch had rescued Beef-O-Rama from bankruptcy. Once Mitch owned a controlling interest, the first thing he did was name a burger after himself. The Murló Monster consisted of a half-pound beef patty, mushrooms, onions, jalepeños, and double cheddar. It was already the most popular item on the menu.

"Where do you suppose Vince is?" Caitlin asked. "Do you think his mom is torturing him with a new collection of cute fuzzy things?"

"Maybe he's out checking the range of his new connection," suggested Mitch, taking a bite of his massive burger. Life for Vince was a little bit easier now that Nick had built a Bluetooth connection for his battery. Supposedly the range was fifty feet, but Vince was the kind of kid who constantly tested his limits. "That wireless hookup was a stroke of genius."

"Yeah," said Zak. "You out-Tesla'd Tesla!"

Nick grinned at that, but he was filled with mixed emotions. Deep down he knew he had Tesla's innate genius, but he also knew that he'd never have the man's all-consuming drive. What must it have been like to go through life as one-seventh of himself? Perhaps it hadn't just been a hindrance, but also the source of Tesla's endless passion—a burning need to achieve completion in any way possible.

As Mitch took another bite from his dripping burger, Caitlin shook her head at him in mock (or real) disgust.

"You could feed a small nation on that burger, Mitch," she said.

To which he responded, "Actually, I've already arranged to feed a small nation, so leave my burger out of it!"

Mitch went on to talk about how his father's case had been reopened. "If the appeal goes through, he could be out of prison by the end of the month—and since the banks would rather pretend the money doesn't exist, they won't testify against him. That gives him a good chance!"

"But, Mitch," Nick said gently, "didn't the Shut Up 'N Listen say your father would never be paroled?"

Mitch gave Nick a wide, ketchup-rimmed smile. "It said he wouldn't be *paroled*, but it never said he couldn't have his verdict overthrown. Those are two different things."

Nick had to admit he was right.

Mitch went on. "I figured if you could rescue your mom in the past without getting body-slammed by the universe, then I could rescue my dad in the present."

Caitlin listened to all of this, but her attention was on Nick. It still amazed her that he had grown five months older in what, in her timeline, was a matter of seconds. With more self-assurance and an easy confidence that wasn't there before, even with one-seventh missing, he seemed a more complete version of himself. No longer an assemblage of found objects.

As for her own assemblages, the "garb-art" her art teacher had scorned had earned her admission to the Colorado Springs Academy of the Arts on a full scholarship. She showed her acceptance letter to the others. It was a little bittersweet, because she and Nick would be at different high schools, but that just meant she would savor their after-school time together even more.

"So how's your new place?" Caitlin asked him. "Is there an attic?"

"Nope," Nick said. "It's flat-roofed, without so much as a lightning rod, and not a single secret tunnel that I'm aware of."

"Hmm," said Zak. "That's disappointing."

In a way, Nick agreed. On the other hand, he had nothing to complain about at home these days.

"My dad and Danny are still getting used to my mom being back," he told them. "My dad keeps calling it a miracle, but it's not—I mean, you can't come back from the dead if you were never actually dead to begin with."

"Vince was dead," Mitch pointed out. "Does that make him a miracle?"

"I guess so," Nick said. "A miracle of science."

"Oh, hey, that reminds me," said Zak. "There's something I want to show you. It's not exactly the dead rising, but it's just as freaky." He pulled out his laptop and went to a Wikipedia entry about a Serbian woman named Milica Ninkovic.

Nick scanned through it. "A women's rights activist in the 1880s?"

According to the article, Milica Ninkovic was a journalist who'd founded the most important women's rights organization in the Balkan Peninsula.

"What about her?" asked Caitlin.

Instead of answering, Zak scrolled down to an old-fashioned tintype picture of a woman in a buttoned dress. She had a stern face, as if she was about to start yelling at someone. And her hair was pulled into two perfectly parted braids.

"Petula?" said Nick.

"No way!" said Mitch, looking excited and horrified at the same time—which was his usual response to Petula.

"I didn't know her very well," said Zak. "But it sure looks like her to me!"

There was definitely a strong resemblance. The article went

on to say that she once had the honor of meeting Thomas Edison—and proceeded to slap him. If that wasn't proof, nothing was.

A sudden buzzing and crackling from outside gently rattled the ceiling of the restaurant. This was followed by a waft or two of ozone. Everyone knew this meant that somewhere in the northern hemisphere the satellite was discharging energy to the F.R.E.E., which would then distribute it randomly over the planet—and rebuild the earth's ozone layer as an added benefit.

Mitch finished his burger, and Nick took some fries from the basket, dipped them in ketchup, and offered them to Caitlin, who accepted them with a smile.

Then the silence began to get awkward—which, after all they'd been through, was unusual. They had begun as unlikely allies and had become the closest of friends. But now their lives had returned to normal. And "normal" had never factored into their relationships.

"Well," said Nick, "Vince better get here soon, 'cause I gotta get home. I promised my mom I'd mow the lawn."

"They need me beneath the bowling alley," said Zak.

"I've got to get some art supplies," said Caitlin.

"I'm buying an island," said Mitch.

Nick couldn't deny that there was a sense that something was ending. Dissolving. They would always be friends, but never again would they be the crucial elements of something much larger than themselves. . . .

Then the door of Beef-O-Rama swung open, and Vince stormed in. Was it Nick's imagination, or was he glowing green? Vince didn't waste time on small talk. He slammed something on the table in front of them—a rusty cube covered with gears and dials—and said two words:

"Enrico Fermi."

Nick, Caitlin, Mitch, and Zak leaned closer to study the odd contraption. It hummed and buzzed, looking like a puzzle box that begged to be opened. Then Nick turned to Vince with a smile he couldn't contain, and said:

"I'm listening."

ACKNOWLEDGMENTS

No two writers can produce a three-volume fantasy-action-comedy-adventure story on their own, and there are many people who deserve our thanks.

First, our team at Disney Hyperion, led by our brilliant editor, Stephanie Lurie; and everyone who helped with publicity, book tours, and conference appearances, including Jamie Baker, Dina Sherman, Mary Ann Zissimos, Heather Crowley, and Elena Blanco. We also owe a great deal to our amazing agent, Andrea Brown, and our incredible foreign rights agent, Taryn Fagerness.

A heartfelt thanks to director Jonathan Judge, who saw the cinematic potential of these books, and to DisneyXD for seeing it too!

We knew our story would only work if it were grounded firmly in reality. We looked to countless books and articles, particularly the recent biographies *Tesla: Inventor of the Electrical Age* by W. Bernard Carlson and *Edison and the Rise of Innovation* by Leonard DeGraaf. We were privileged to hear a discussion between the two biographers, courtesy of an invitation from Jacques Lamarre, Director of Communications and Special Programs at the Mark Twain House and Museum.

We would also like to thank Jane Alcorn, President of the Tesla Science Center, who invited us to tour the site of Wardenclyffe Tower and Tesla's laboratory in Shoreham, New York, which will open in the future as a science museum dedicated to Nikola Tesla.

A grateful shout-out to all the teachers, students, booksellers, and fans who supported the book tours, and a special thanks to our families, who continued to put up with us long after our minds were filled to distraction with character arcs and teslanoid objects.

And finally, we'd like to thank two geniuses: Stephen Hawking, whose book *A Brief History of Time* has filled both of us with awe for years; and, of course, Nikola Tesla himself, whose vision and tireless persistence will always be a source of inspiration.